3 9082 10282 1959

P9-DDL-900

DEAD
WRONG

J. A. JANCE

DEAD WRONG

WILLIAM MORROW
An Imprint of HarperCollins*Publishers*

DEAD WRONG. Copyright © 2006 by J. A. Jance. All rights reserved. Printed in the United States of America. No part of this book may be used or reproduced in any manner whatsoever without written permission except in the case of brief quotations embodied in critical articles and reviews. For information address HarperCollins Publishers, 10 East 53rd Street, New York, NY 10022.

HarperCollins books may be purchased for educational, business, or sales promotional use. For information please write: Special Markets Department, HarperCollins Publishers, 10 East 53rd Street, New York, NY 10022.

FIRST EDITION

Designed by Jeffrey Pennington

Printed on acid-free paper

Library of Congress Cataloging-in-Publication Data

Jance, Judith A.
    Dead wrong / J.A. Jance.—1st ed.
        p. cm
    ISBN-13: 978-0-06-054090-6
    ISBN-10: 0-06-054090-7 (alk. paper)
        1. Brady, Joanna (Fictitious character)—Fiction. 2. Cochise County (Ariz.)—Fiction. 3. Policewomen—Fiction. 4. Sheriffs—Fiction. 5. Arizona—Fiction. I. Title.

PS3560.A44D43 2006
813'.54—dc22   2005052236

06 07 08 09 10 WBC/RRD 10 9 8 7 6 5 4 3 2 1

To Jane Decker and
Ann and Roger Burgess, animal lovers all

PROLOGUE

A sharp rap next to his ear awakened Bradley Evans out of a troubled sleep and plunged him headlong into the worst hangover of his life. Or maybe it was a pre-hangover. Even before he managed to open his eyes, the world began spinning. He felt sick. He was so parched his tongue and lips seemed ready to splinter into pieces. Every bone in his body ached, and he was cold as hell.

The second sharp rap was accompanied by an authoritative voice. "Unlock the door, son. Then place both hands on your head and step out of the truck."

Bradley groaned. *Step out of the truck?* he wondered. *What truck? What the hell am I doing in a truck?*

"I'm warning you," the voice said again. "Unlock the door, hands on your head, and step out of the vehicle!"

Less than six months out of the army, Bradley was still accustomed to following orders from someone in authority, so he did his best to comply, but when he finally managed to open his eyes all he saw was blood—clots of blood everywhere: on the windshield, the dashboard, the rearview mirror. And on him, too—smeared on his hands, shirt, pants, and shoes. Somehow he managed to unlock the door, but he was incapable of stepping out of the vehicle on his own. Instead, he leaned out of the truck and retched onto the pavement, splashing bright yellow bile that still reeked of beer onto the deputy's highly shined pair of boots.

Suspended over the mess, Bradley tried to grasp what had happened. He remembered going to the bar and playing a couple of games of pool, but that was it. After he'd been given a DWI a year ago, he had promised Lisa that if he ever again had too much to drink, he'd call her to come get him, no matter what. Obviously he hadn't done that last night. Instead, he had wrecked his truck and now this huge cop was about to haul his ass off to jail. When Lisa found out, she'd kill him—or leave him.

Finally, he tried to straighten up. "Anybody else hurt?" he managed.

"You tell me," the cop returned. "Are you finished? Come on out now. Stand up. Hands behind your back."

Off in the distance, Bradley heard the siren of a second arriving cop car, but he had no intention of giving even this lone officer any trouble. He stumbled to his feet and then stood weaving unsteadily while the cop snapped a pair of metal cuffs onto his wrists. When he was able to look back at his old GMC, he was astonished to see that the pickup showed no visible damage.

Must be on the other side, he thought. *Maybe I veered off the road and sideswiped a telephone pole or a fence post.*

The problem with that line of thinking was that he didn't seem to be hurt, certainly not injured enough to explain that awful amount of blood.

"Who was with you?" the cop was asking. "Who else was in the vehicle?"

"I don't know," Bradley mumbled. "I don't remember. I thought I was alone."

He looked at the cop for reassurance. He was a balding, middle-aged, slightly portly man in a spotless stiffly starched khaki uniform and with a very large pistol strapped to a holster on his hip. The name tag over his shirt pocket identified him as Deputy Lathrop—Deputy D. H. Lathrop.

"I'd have to say you're mistaken about that," Deputy Lathrop returned with what Bradley recognized as a trace of an East Texas drawl. "And whoever was with you is hurt real bad or else he's dead."

Leaving Bradley standing alone, cuffed, and struggling to maintain his balance, the deputy returned to the pickup. Reaching in through the open driver's-side door, he brought something out. When he held it up, Bradley could only stare in stricken silence. It was Lisa's purse, the fringed dark leather one he had bought from a booth at the Cochise County Fair. He had given it to her on the spot even though her birthday was still weeks away.

"What's this?" Lathrop asked.

For a moment Bradley was too stunned to reply. *What's Lisa's purse doing here?* he wondered. *She wasn't with me at the bar, or was she?*

The deputy reached into the purse and pulled out a wallet— Lisa's wallet. As he opened it, Bradley dissolved into tears, muttering, "Oh, God, what's happened? What have I done?"

CHAPTER 1

Ken Galloway sauntered up to the lectern and wrenched the neck of the microphone to its full height. Then, smiling, he gazed out at the "Candidate's Night" audience assembled in the spacious meeting room of the Sierra Vista Public Library.

"First off," he said with an engaging grin, "let me say that I'm in favor of motherhood and apple pie. After all, if it weren't for my mother, where would I be?"

The anticipated ripple of polite laughter drifted through the crowd. This was Ken's favorite way of opening his stump speeches. It always served him well in getting things off to a good start. Beginning with a familiar joke was a way of putting his whole political agenda front and center.

Seated off to Ken Galloway's right, Sheriff Joanna Brady steeled herself for what she knew would come next. She folded her hands in her lap, plastered a faint and entirely fake smile on her face, and willed her ears not to turn red. This far into the campaign she should have been used to her opponent's constant references to what he described as her "delicate condition." Joanna should have been accustomed to it, but she wasn't. The subject still rankled her every time Ken Jr. brought it up. She resented his constantly drawing attention to her growing belly and casually discussing her pregnancy again and again as though she were nothing more than an obliging live-action mannequin in some high school sex-ed classroom.

"The point is," Ken continued, "when my brothers and I were little, our mother stayed home and took care of us."

Yes, Joanna thought, *because your father took off and left Lillyan Galloway penniless. She ended up living on welfare and raising her kids on Aid to Dependent Children.* But Ken Galloway never mentioned that part of his wonderfully idealized family history, and neither did Joanna.

"Call me old-fashioned," Ken went on, "but I think there's a lot to be said for mothers being at home with their kids. Cochise County is a big place. There have been times in the last four years when Sheriff Brady hasn't been as responsive to her duties as she might have been due to the very real conflict of having a child at home. How much more difficult will it be for her to attend to law enforcement needs when she has two children to contend with, including a newborn baby?"

In the back of the room a woman, applauding furiously, rose to her feet. "That's right, Ken! Way to go!" Eleanor Lathrop Winfield shouted. "You tell her."

Joanna's mother's enthusiastic outburst was enough to propel Joanna out of her dream. She awakened panting and sweating, but the dream stayed with her for several long minutes. Although those were likely Eleanor's true feelings, to Joanna's personal knowledge her mother had never made any such statement—at least not in public—not during the campaign or after it.

The election itself was now a full three months in the past. Joanna had managed to eke out a narrow 587-vote victory, so she should have been over the campaign nightmares, but she wasn't. Night after night, in some variation of that same dream, she was perpetually running for office, and night after night her mother's continuing disapproval was always with her.

She reached out, longing to cuddle up to Butch's comforting presence, but he wasn't there. He had left early the previous afternoon for El Paso and a weekend mystery conference, where he would be on what his editor called the "limbo" panel—made up of first-time writers whose books were sold but not yet published. Butch's first novel, *Serve and Protect,* wasn't due out until September, but his editor, Carole Ann Hudson, had engineered his being placed on a panel at the conference so he could "start getting his name out there."

"I'm not going to go running off to El Paso for three days when the baby's due in less than a week," Butch had declared.

"Due dates aren't exactly chiseled in granite," Joanna had responded. "Look at Jenny. She was ten days late, and I was in labor for the better part of eight hours before she was born. Think about it. El Paso is only five hours away, especially the way you drive. If I called you right away, you'd be here in plenty of time. Besides, Carole Ann must have gone to a lot of trouble to make this happen, including having bound galleys available. You need to be there."

But now, with the nightmare still lingering and her back hurting like crazy, Joanna wished she hadn't insisted Butch go. What she would have liked more than anything right then was one of his special back rubs. And although massages helped, Joanna was tired of having a sore back. Tired of not being able to sleep on her stomach. Tired as hell of being pregnant. And, as if to add its own two cents' worth, the baby stirred suddenly inside her and began hammering away at her ribs.

"All right, all right," she grumbled. "Since we're both wide awake, I could just as well get up."

Pulling on a wool robe that no longer connected around her middle, Joanna waddled out into the kitchen and started heating water. The bouts of morning sickness that had plagued the beginning of her pregnancy no longer existed, but her aversion to the taste of coffee lingered. Tea, not coffee, was now her drink of choice.

Joanna stood at the back door while Lady, the loving Australian shepherd she had rescued the previous summer, went outside to investigate the news of the day. In the crisp chill of early morning, Joanna savored the gentle warmth of the heated floor on her bare feet. Radiant heat in the floor was one of the things Butch had built into their rammed-earth house. At the time he suggested it, Joanna had thought it a peculiar thing to be worrying about heating a house in the Arizona desert. In the past few months, though, when her feet had been swollen after a long day at work, it had been wonderful to kick off her shoes and walk barefoot on the warmed floor. The dogs seemed to like radiant heat every bit as much as she did.

Once her tea was ready, Joanna repaired to her cozy home office, opened her briefcase, and removed her laptop. In the months before and after the election, she and Butch, along with her chief deputy, Frank Montoya, had strategized on how best to handle the complications of juggling being both sheriff and a new mother—the very question Ken Galloway had harped on throughout the campaign.

Under departmental guidelines, Joanna could have taken up to six weeks of paid maternity leave, but that didn't seem like a reasonable way to run her department. Barring some kind of unforeseen complication, she had settled on the idea of taking only two weeks of maternity leave. Beyond that, she'd do as much of her paperwork from home as possible. In a world of telecommuting, that wasn't such an outlandish idea. Between them, Butch and Frank had installed a high-speed Internet connection at High Lonesome Ranch and created a teleconferencing network that would allow Joanna to participate in morning briefings without her having to be at the Cochise County Justice Center in person.

"As long as you cooperate," she said, patting the lump of her belly where the as-yet-unnamed baby was still kicking away. Months earlier she had brought home the ultrasound report her doctor had given her that would have revealed whether the baby was a boy or a girl.

Butch had taken the envelope from her fingers and stuck it on the fridge with a heavy-duty magnet. "I'm an old-fashioned kind of guy," he told her. "When we unwrap the baby will be time enough to know what it is." And there the unopened envelope remained to this day—much to Joanna's mother's dismay and despite her many remonstrances to the contrary.

For the next hour or so, Joanna answered e-mail. Yes, she would be honored to be the commencement speaker for Bisbee High School's graduation. No, she would be unable to participate in the Girl Scout Cookie-Selling Kickoff Breakfast in two weeks. No, she would not be able to speak to the Kiwanis Key Club meeting on March first. Yes, she would come to the May 2 Career Day assembly at St. David High School. Baby or no baby, Joanna could see that her calendar was already filling up for the months ahead, even without a reelection campaign to worry about.

The next e-mail was an announcement that the annual sher-iffs' convention would be held in June. What about that? Some of her fellow lady sheriffs (there were now approximately thirty of them nationwide) would be having their first-ever meeting of the newly formed LSA (Lady Sheriffs Association) at the convention. Joanna was eager to meet some of the women who did the same job and faced the same struggles she did. In fact, she now corre-sponded regularly with someone she had never met in person— the female sheriff of a tiny department in San Juan County, Colorado. Much as she wanted to be in attendance, Joanna knew that a final decision on that needed to be discussed with Butch. She saved that e-mail as new.

At six, as Joanna began scanning on-line news articles and with the sun just coming up, Lucky, a gangly black Lab pup, trot-ted into Joanna's office, proudly carrying one of Jenny's socks. At sixty-plus pounds and less than a year old, Lucky's oversize paws indicated that he still had some growing to do. The dog had been born deaf, but he was smart, and Jenny's patient training was paying big dividends. When Joanna signaled for him to sit and to drop the sock, he immediately complied. After checking to see that the sock was still in one piece, Joanna rewarded the dog with one of the dog treats she kept in her top drawer.

"Mom," Jenny said from the doorway. "Since Butch isn't here, can I fix a pot of coffee?"

"May I," Joanna corrected. "And no. You're too young for coffee."

"Butch lets me have coffee," Jenny countered.

"He does?"

"Sometimes."

There was a lot that went on between Jenny and Butch that Joanna wasn't necessarily consulted on or even knew about.

Blond and blue-eyed, Jenny was a willowy teenager who was already a good two inches taller than her mother. She was a responsible kid who got good grades and did more than her fair share of chores around the ranch.

"All right," Joanna relented. "Go ahead."

As Jenny left for the kitchen, their third dog, an improbably ugly half pit bull/half golden retriever named Tigger, joined the others and padded along after her. Just then the phone rang. "I didn't know you let Jenny have coffee in the morning," she told Butch once she knew who it was.

"It won't kill her," he returned. "I started drinking coffee when I was eight. It didn't stunt my growth. Well, on second thought, maybe it did. Maybe I'd be a few inches taller if I hadn't started drinking java so early, but still. One cup isn't going to hurt her. Besides, wouldn't you rather have her drinking it at home with us instead of hanging out with her friends at the local Starbucks?"

"There is no local Starbucks," Joanna pointed out.

"Oh, that's right," Butch said. "I forgot."

Joanna couldn't help laughing. "So how's the conference?" she asked.

"Weird. Turns out Hawthorn put a bound galley of *Serve and Protect* in the goody bags they hand out to each of the conference attendees. I had dinner with Carole Ann last night. According to her, handing out bound galleys like that is good. It shows the publisher is putting some horses behind this book—and that's not all that common for a first-time author."

"It's a good book," Joanna said. "But what makes the conference weird?"

"For one thing, it means that people see my name badge and then they want me to sign their books, so I'm already signing autographs even though my book isn't actually published yet. One of my fellow newbies—a lady named Christina Hanson—is on the same panel I am. Her book is due out in June. At the pre-conference cocktail party she made it abundantly clear that she's more than a little annoyed that I have bound galleys here and she doesn't. I'm worried that later on today when we do the panel, the sparks will fly."

"Are you saying even mystery writing is political?" Joanna asked.

Butch laughed. "Evidently. Now, how are you?"

"Woke up early with my usual backache. And the baby's a busy little bee today. I've been doing paperwork, but it's about time to shower and go in to work."

"You don't have to work until the last minute," Butch said.

"I *want* to work," Joanna said. "If I stayed home, I'd sit around and worry. Besides, Marianne and I are supposed to have lunch at Daisy's today. If I don't go to work, I won't have an excuse to go out to lunch."

Marianne Maculyea, the Reverend Marianne Maculyea, had been Joanna's best friend since junior high. She was also the pastor of Tombstone Canyon United Methodist Church, where Joanna and Butch were members.

"Wish I could join you," Butch said. "I don't think lunch here will be that much fun."

Joanna's call-waiting buzzed in her ear. Caller ID told her it was Dispatch. "Got to go," Joanna said. "I've got another call. Have fun. I love you."

"Good morning, Sheriff Brady," Tica Romero said. "I hope it's not too early to call."

"It's not," Joanna said. "I've been up working for a while. What's going on?"

"We've got a homicide," Tica responded. "Halfway between Bisbee Junction and Paul's Spur."

Joanna's initial election to office had been in the immediate aftermath of her first husband's murder. Andy had been running for sheriff at the time, and Joanna's subsequent election had been regarded more as a gesture of community sympathy than anything else. Once in office, however, she had been determined to function as a real sheriff rather than sheriff in name only. Through the years she had done her best to show up on the scene of every homicide that happened within her jurisdiction. Now was no time to stop.

"How long ago did it happen?" she asked.

"A border patrol officer called it in just a few minutes ago," Tica answered. "Detectives Carbajal and Carpenter are already on their way. So's Dave Hollicker."

Dave was Joanna's senior crime scene investigator. Jaime Carbajal and Ernie Carpenter, sometimes known as the Double Cs, comprised Joanna's single team of homicide detectives. All three officers were tremendously overworked. Joanna had planned on adding another CSI, and she had wanted to promote two patrol unit deputies to detectives, so Ernie and Jaime could have worked with the new guys while they learned the ropes. Unfortunately the War on Terror had intervened. So many of Joanna's experienced deputies had been called up for National Guard duty that she couldn't afford to deplete the patrol roster further. Her homicide investigation team was overworked, and overworked it would remain.

Joanna glanced at her watch. If she showered and went to the scene with her hair still wet, she could probably be there within half an hour. "An illegal?" she asked.

It was a reasonable assumption. Border Road was called that because it ran for miles right along the sagging remains of a barbed-wire fence that constituted the official dividing line between the United States and Mexico. The unimpeded flood of illegal crossers pouring over that line posed a constant drain on Joanna's officers and her budget.

"The Border Patrol guy says it's not," Tica replied. "The victim is wrapped in a tarp, but from what the officer could see, he's male, balding, and with light-colored hair and fair skin."

"Which means he's probably some poor Anglo dummy who ended up in the wrong place at the wrong time. A coyote probably got him."

Joanna's coyote reference had nothing to do with the four-legged fur-bearing kind. In the parlance of Southwest law enforcement officers, coyotes were smugglers who trafficked in bringing illegal entrants across the border from Mexico into the United States. Often operating in stolen vehicles and with zero concern for the welfare of their human cargo, human coyotes had become a particularly dangerous category of criminal. Speeding vehicles, wrecking and spilling their hapless passengers, were almost everyday occurrences.

On one occasion, fifty-eight men had been crammed in the back of an eighteen-wheeler when the truck hauling them had broken down. The driver had abandoned the locked vehicle on the side of the road at high noon on a hot August afternoon. When someone finally pried open the locked cargo door, all but one of the men were dead, and he had perished on his way to the hospital.

"That would be my first guess," Tica agreed.

"All right," Joanna said. "It's going to take a little time for me to get there. I'm not dressed, but tell the Double Cs I'll show up as soon as I can."

"Show up where?" Jenny asked from the doorway.

She came into Joanna's office fully dressed and sipping coffee from one of the white oversize diner-style mugs Butch preferred. Jenny was drinking a whole lot more coffee than Joanna had originally envisioned, but she let it go.

"At a crime scene," Joanna said as she shut down her computer and began stowing it into her briefcase.

"Oh," Jenny said. "I was hoping you'd give me a ride to school. The bus takes so long, and it's so boring!"

As far as Joanna was concerned, when it came to teenagers, boring was the best of all possible worlds. "Can't, sweetie," she replied. "It's in the wrong direction. I can give you a ride to the bus stop, but that's about it."

"I can hardly wait until I'm old enough to get my driver's license," Jenny said. "It's just a little over a year and a half before I'll be old enough to get my learner's permit."

This wasn't a fact Joanna enjoyed pondering. She wasn't ready for her daughter to be old enough to learn to drive a car. One of the biggest concerns with the idea of Jenny's turning fifteen had to do with its being a mere two years away from seventeen, which is how old Joanna had been when she herself got pregnant with Jenny—pregnant and unmarried.

"Did you feed the dogs?" she asked.

Jenny gave her mother an exasperated look. "I fed the dogs and Kiddo and the cattle and chickens, too," she said. Kiddo was Jenny's sorrel gelding. "I told Butch I'd take care of all that while he was gone so you wouldn't have to."

"Thank you," Joanna said. If Jenny was old enough to do all that without having to be asked, maybe having that mugful of coffee wasn't out of line after all.

"I have to hit the shower," she said. "Can you be ready to go in fifteen?"

"I guess," Jenny said. When she left her mother's office this time, Tigger and Lucky followed. Lady stayed where she was.

Joanna made short work of her shower and makeup, then crammed herself into her uniform. When she had first purchased the two maternity uniforms, the tops had seemed hilariously big. The first time she put one on she had felt like she was dressing in a clown suit. Now, though, it fit snugly over her bulging middle. *Is this damn thing going to hold up until my delivery date?* she wondered. *Or am I going to end up popping the buttons?*

Twenty minutes later, Joanna dropped Jenny off at the end of High Lonesome Road. Then, munching a peanut butter sandwich, she headed for Paul's Spur, where she turned off the highway and made her way to the dirt track called Border Road. Ten minutes after that she arrived at the end of a long line of parked police vehicles. As she exited her Crown Victoria, she caught sight of a pair of hopeful vultures circling lazily in the air above. Up ahead Dr. George Winfield, Cochise County's medical examiner and Joanna's stepfather, was unloading his crime scene satchel from his van.

"Ugly critters, aren't they," he observed, following Joanna's glance.

She nodded. "They are that," she agreed.

"So how's my favorite mother-to-be?" George added as he dragged an unwieldy folded gurney onto the ground. His pleasant, upbeat manner never failed to surprise Joanna, especially since he spent so much time with her mother—a woman who was, in Joanna's estimation, one of the most difficult people on earth.

"Back hurts," Joanna replied. "And I'm not getting much sleep."

"The back part will get better soon," George observed, "but lack of sleep is going to get a whole lot worse before it gets better."

"Thanks," Joanna said. "That's exactly what I needed to hear this morning."

Ernie Carpenter had evidently spotted their arrival. He came marching purposefully down the long line of vehicles parked on the shoulder of the narrow road. Ernie was a stout bear of a man. His broad face included a line of thick black eyebrows that seemed to meet in the middle whenever he frowned.

"What have we got?" Joanna asked.

"Not much," Ernie grumbled. Effortlessly he picked up George's gurney and carried it as easily as if it were a kiddie tricycle. "This is a dumping scene, not a crime scene. Most likely the body's been here for a matter of hours. Looks to me like somebody dropped him out of the back of a vehicle—a minivan or a truck—and then rolled him over the edge of the berm of rocks that runs along the side of the road."

"In other words, no usable tire tracks or footprints."

"You've got it," Ernie agreed. "Border Patrol is up and down this road all night long, so any tracks that had been left would have been obliterated long ago. The body's wrapped in a brown canvas painter's tarp. It blended in with the rocks well enough overnight that no one actually spotted it until after the sun came up this morning. Dave has been scouring the area, but there's nothing to see. No cigarette butts, no soda cans, no garbage, nothing."

"Any sign of what killed him?" George asked.

"Like I said, he's all wrapped up in that tarp. We can see the top of his head and that's about it. Some blood seems to have leaked through the tarp. I'm guessing he's either been shot or stabbed, one or the other. We were waiting for Doc Winfield to get here before we did anything more."

George stopped walking long enough to remove a thermometer from his kit and check the air temperature. A chill brisk wind was blowing down off the Mule Mountains. "If this isn't the crime scene, then whatever we find inside that tarp is all we're going to have to go on. I'll remove enough of the tarp to check the body temp, but with the wind blowing like this it could easily blow away hair or fiber evidence without us even noticing. Let's unwrap him at the morgue, inside and out of the wind."

"You've got it, Doc," Ernie said. "All we needed was for you to give the word."

Joanna followed the two men as far as the scene itself. The dirt in the roadway showed signs that something heavy had been dropped out of a vehicle and then rolled as far as the edge of the road, where it had been heaved over the rocky bulldozed shoulder. The body had been placed far enough away from any passing traffic so as to be out of sight, but not so far that whoever had put it there would have risked leaving behind detectable traces of hair or fiber evidence.

One of the officers had surrounded the scene with a hopeful border of bright yellow crime scene tape. Inside the tape Joanna spotted the body, rocks, and a few tufts of brittle, closely cropped yellow grass. Outside the tape, a desolate landscape of scrubby mesquite trees stretched for miles in all directions. The thorn-studded, winter-bare branches might well have trapped some critical hair or fiber evidence. Unfortunately, the nearest of the spindly trees stood well outside the taped crime scene boundary.

Joanna stood on the edge of the roadway huddled in the

warmth of her long leather coat, while Dave and Jamie helped George wrestle the corpse into a body bag and onto the gurney. It may have been winter and cold as hell, but as they moved the body, a swarm of flies buzzed skyward while the stench of rotting flesh wafted in Joanna's direction.

Watching the process, she was struck by the total lack of dignity. She was glad none of the unidentified victim's relatives were present to see him hefted around like a hunk of unwieldy trash. He had been dumped out along the road with no more ceremony than someone would use when discarding a cigarette butt or an empty beer can.

And that very lack of dignity—the awfulness of it—was exactly why Joanna Brady, Ernie, Jaime, and Dave were all here. Redressing what had been done to this poor unknown man was what they did. It was their job to avenge man's inhumanity to man with justice. It was why Joanna had worked her heart out running for office and why taking a six-week maternity leave was far longer than she wanted to stay away from work.

With the cold wind blowing through her still-damp hair, she realized she had changed. Being sheriff was no longer an empty title she had wanted to achieve. Somehow it had become what she was. Finding out who the victim was and why he was now dead and encased in a body bag was what she had been summoned to do with her life. The good guy/bad guy game she had once discussed with her father had somehow seeped into her blood. Or maybe, as with D. H. Lathrop, the compulsion to be a cop had been there all along.

Oh my God! she thought with a start. *I really am turning into my father!*

"Are you all right?" George asked, bringing her out of her reverie.

"I'm fine," she said at once.

"You looked a little funny there."

"No, really. I'm fine."

"Nothing much is on my agenda for today," George continued, "so I'll try to get this autopsy out of the way first thing. Ernie Carpenter and Jaime Carbajal drew straws. Ernie lost, so he's coming along for the ride. What about you?"

Joanna thought about that peanut butter sandwich she'd gobbled down in the car and about what might happen to it if she ventured into George's stainless-steel-studded room to observe an autopsy in progress.

"Since Ernie's going," she said, "I think I'll take a pass."

George Winfield gave her a fond grin. "Good girl," he agreed. "I thought you might."

CHAPTER 2

oanna stayed at the scene long enough to listen as Jaime
Carbajal interviewed Wally Rutterman, the Border Patrol
officer who had discovered the body. Then she watched for a
while as Dave Hollicker did a painstaking inch-by-inch survey of the dump site. Neither effort revealed anything worth-
while. On the drive back to the department, Joanna found herself
chilled from the inside out in a way that boosting the output of
the Crown Victoria's heater did nothing to alleviate.

She radioed into the office on the way. "Any missing-persons
reports come in this morning?" she asked.

"None so far," Tica Romero answered.

"You'll let me know if there is one?"

"Yes, ma'am," Tica said.

When Joanna arrived at her reserved parking place, she was
surprised to see that the one next door—Chief Deputy Frank
Montoya's—was empty. After a moment's reflection, she remembered it was Friday morning. That meant Frank was probably

busy standing in for her at the weekly board of supervisors meeting.

Better him than me.

Entering the building through her private back entrance, she dropped her briefcase off on her desk and then poked her head out into the reception area outside her office. "How are things?" she asked.

Kristin Gregovich, Joanna's secretary/receptionist, was busy sorting through a newly arrived basket of mail.

"Not so hot," Kristin said. "Shaundra's teething. She didn't get any sleep last night, which means I didn't either."

"I'm in the same boat," Joanna said. "Not getting any sleep, that is. Let's hope my baby isn't teething."

Kristin laughed. "They say that parents of new babies lose bunches of IQ points. It's no wonder. They never get any sleep. How'd it go down by Paul's Spur?"

"Unidentified homicide victim," Joanna replied. "Ernie's on his way to observe the autopsy. Everybody else is working the problem. In the meantime, how much of that mail is for me?"

The daunting amount of paper that flowed across her desk each day made Joanna wonder how any trees remained standing anywhere. She wasn't surprised when Kristin picked up the largest of the several stacks and handed it over. As she headed into her office, mail in hand, it occurred to Joanna that it might not have been such a bad idea to tag along to Doc Winfield's office and observe that autopsy after all.

She paused just inside her office door. "Any calls?" she asked.

"Just Reverend Maculyea calling to remind you about today's lunch. And speaking of lunch," Kristin added, "there's an errand I need to run at noon today at the same time you'll be out. I know you don't like to leave the office unattended, so I already asked if one of the clerks from the public office could come over and cover for me. I hope you don't mind."

"I'm sure it's fine," Joanna said.

Once at her desk, she forced herself to put this latest homicide case out of her head and buried herself in dealing with the stack of correspondence. Her years of running an insurance office had given her superb typing skills, so she wrote, printed, and answered as much of the mail as possible without using Kristin's help for anything other than printing the envelopes. By the time Joanna headed out for her lunch date at eleven-thirty, Kristin was already gone.

Pulling into the parking lot at Daisy's Café, Joanna was surprised to see several familiar cars there as well as Marianne's antique VW bug. Joanna's mother's blue Buick was parked next to the VW and her former in-laws' Camry was parked next to that. She recognized Angie Hacker's husband's Hummer as well. It was only when she saw Kristin's little red Geo tucked in behind the Hummer and the pink and blue balloon bouquets on either side of the door that Joanna finally tumbled to what was going on. This wasn't just her usual weekday lunch with Marianne. It was a baby shower.

Grinning from ear to ear, Junior Dowdle, Daisy and Moe Maxwell's adopted developmentally disabled son, greeted Joanna at the door. "It's a party," he said, pointing at Joanna's belly. "A party for your baby. We've got flowers and cake and everything."

And "everything" was exactly what they had. Half of the restaurant had been cordoned off with strips of pink and blue crepe paper to accommodate the party. Much to Joanna's surprise, Jenny was seated at the makeshift flower-festooned head table.

"Aren't you supposed to be in school?" Joanna asked. "Who sprung you?"

"Grandma," Jenny said, nodding in Eva Lou's direction. Taking that as a signal, Joanna's former mother-in-law came over and gave her a hug.

"It's a big occasion," Eva Lou Brady declared. "I didn't think she should miss it. And I wouldn't miss it, either, not for the world."

Andrew Roy Brady, Joanna's first husband, had been gunned down years earlier. Nevertheless, his parents, Jim Bob and Eva Lou, continued to be unfailingly supportive and loving to their former daughter-in-law. Joanna didn't have the slightest doubt that they would treat this new grandchild, Butch and Joanna's baby, with the same love and attention that they had always lavished on Andy and Joanna's Jenny.

"Thank you," Joanna whispered, fighting back tears of gratitude.

Eleanor stepped in the moment Eva Lou moved away. "Don't make a spectacle of yourself," she warned. "It's only a baby shower, for Pete's sake. No reason to burst into tears."

Joanna's mother's reaction was in such stark contrast to Eva Lou's that it helped Joanna pull herself back together. "Right," she said, wiping her eyes. "No reason at all."

During lunch, Joanna sat between Marianne Maculyea and Angie Hacker. Eleanor still managed to look disapproving whenever Angie was around, but Joanna's and Marianne's unflinching acceptance of Angie had made it easy for most of Bisbee to forget about the woman's less-than-stellar past. The fact that she had once made her living as a prostitute had faded into the background. She was now recognized as the prime reason one of Bisbee's favorite watering holes, Brewery Gulch's famed Blue Moon Saloon and Lounge, remained open for business.

Marianne couldn't help gloating. "So we really did surprise you?"

"You certainly did," Joanna agreed. "Nobody breathed a word."

The whole thing was great fun and about as diametrically opposed to the grim way Joanna's day had started as humanly possible. When she finally returned to the Cochise County Justice Center, it was mid-afternoon and much later than she had anticipated. She drove there with the backseat of her Crown Victoria loaded down with a collection of baby gear—most of it in suitably impartial shades of pastel green and yellow. Eleanor's gifts, however, were all unabashedly blue—clearly announcing her preference for a boy. It surprised Joanna more than a little to realize that for some reason her mother was openly lobbying for a grandson.

Kristin was already back at her desk by the time Joanna got there. "Hope you didn't mind my little fib about what I was doing at lunch," she said.

Joanna's initial dealings with Kristin had been difficult. Over time, however, they had become much more cordial. "No," Joanna said. "I didn't mind it at all. It was a fun shower, and I'm glad you were there."

Chief Deputy Montoya emerged from his office and joined the conversation. "Did you pick up a lot of good loot?" he asked.

"You mean you knew about the shower, too?"

"Of course I did," he said. "The only person who didn't was you. So how was it?"

"The party was great," Joanna said. "How about the board of supervisors meeting?"

"Dull," Frank said. "Thank God for small favors. We weren't

in the hot seat for a change. Today's meeting mostly concerned sanitary landfill issues, so we lucked out."

"I'll say," Joanna agreed. "Time for the briefing?"

Frank nodded. "Coming right up. Ernie just got back from that autopsy. We can have the Double Cs sit in on the briefing as well."

When Joanna entered the conference room a few minutes later, Frank and the two detectives were already there. Ernie, sitting with his arms crossed, looked more somber than usual.

"Do we have a cause of death?" Joanna asked.

Ernie nodded. "Blunt-force trauma to the head from a single blow. But the cause of death isn't what makes this such an interesting case, Sheriff Brady. I've been in Homicide a long time, and I've never seen anything like it."

"Like what?" Joanna asked.

"All ten of the guy's fingers have been whacked off," Ernie said, letting his breath out slowly. "All ten of 'em! And not with a knife, either. Whoever did it probably used kitchen shears or maybe garden pruning shears of some kind. The only good thing about it is at least the guy was dead when they did that part."

Ernie's chilling words washed across Joanna like a bucket of icy water. It was a mind-bending shock to move from the carefree atmosphere of the baby shower to a recitation of murder and mayhem in the space of less than an hour. For a moment the room was totally silent. Gathering herself, Joanna was the first to speak.

"What actually killed him, then, and when?"

"The doc says he'd been dead for a good twenty-four hours and maybe more before he was found, and that he was killed somewhere else and brought to the dump site much later. There are some signs of defensive wounds—bruising and that kind of thing—that would indicate some kind of struggle."

"Any trace evidence from the perpetrator?"

"Doc Winthrop collected some hair and fiber from the body. I brought that and the bloody tarp back here to the lab. Dave is starting to go over it now—looking for prints, blood smears, and so forth. The bloodstains we saw on the tarp were due to leakage from the wounds to his fingers."

"Any ID found on the body?" Joanna asked.

"None at all," Ernie said. "Doc estimates John Doe to be in his mid- to late fifties. Lots of dental work, done on the cheap, that would help identify him if we end up having to use dental records. Other than that, the only distinguishing mark is a tattoo—a homegrown, do-it-yourself job—that says 'One day at a time.'"

"What does removal of the fingers tell us?" Joanna asked.

"My guess would be that the victim's prints must be in the system somewhere," Jaime offered. "The killer is betting that if we don't have fingerprints, we won't be able to identify him."

Joanna considered that suggestion. "So it's possible we're talking about a guy who has been in jail at least once at some time in the past, and he's also been involved in AA."

"Doesn't narrow the field much," Frank said. "Lots of ex-cons have issues with drugs and alcohol. The big problem with Alcoholics Anonymous is just that—they're anonymous. We're not going to get any help from them in making our ID."

"But that's exactly what we have to do—figure out who he is," Joanna said. "Until we take that first step, there's no way to trace his movements leading up to the homicide. Have we checked out missing-persons reports?"

"Yes, ma'am," Jaime Carbajal replied. "Already done. I've got MP info from Arizona, New Mexico, California, and Nevada. So far there's nothing that's even close."

"What are the chances," Joanna asked, "that we're dealing with someone who was locked up for a long time? Maybe he decided to make trouble for someone—maybe someone who helped put him away—as soon as he got out. Let's check and see if we have any recent parolees who have suddenly dropped off their probation officers' radar."

"Don't expect me to work overtime on this one," Ernie grumbled sourly.

Joanna studied her detective. Ernie had a tendency to be grumpy on occasion, but throughout the briefing his attitude had been one notch under surly.

"What do you mean, Detective Carpenter?" she asked. "Do you have a problem with this case?"

"Damn right I've got a problem with it!" Ernie growled. "We've got no crime scene. No suspects. So with nothing to go on, why the hell should we be out busting our balls to find out who knocked off some drunken ex-con?"

"I believe it's called equal protection," Joanna said evenly. "Just because someone's been in prison doesn't give someone else the right to murder them. Somebody killed this man and mutilated his body. It's up to us to find out who did it and why."

Recrossing his arms, Ernie shut his mouth and subsided into his chair. Joanna turned her attention to Jaime Carbajal. "Do you have any ideas?"

"Not right off. In addition to the missing-persons reports we should also keep an eye out for reports on any abandoned vehicles. The victim sure as hell didn't drive himself out to Border Road. If he left his car somewhere or if someone else abandoned it for him, chances are it's parked somewhere it doesn't belong. Eventually someone will get tired of seeing it, pick up a phone, and report it."

"It's a thought," Joanna said, "but it could take days for some-one to turn it in, especially with the weekend coming up."

Jaime shrugged. "Best I could do," he said.

Joanna turned to Frank. "Any bright ideas from you?"

"Nothing so far," he said.

"Well, then," Joanna said. "You guys do what you can," she said to Ernie and Jaime. "And let me know right away if anything turns up."

Once the door had closed behind the detectives, Joanna turned to Frank. "What got into Ernie? I don't ever remember seeing him act quite like that."

"He did seem out of sorts," Frank conceded. "I know he's taken a couple of sick days in the last couple of weeks, but I don't know anything more about it than that. I'll see if I can find out what gives."

Joanna and Frank then returned to the usual day-to-day busi-ness of administering the 120-person department. Because of a billing snafu, Mainstay Foods, the jail's major food vendor, was refusing to make further deliveries until the problem was solved. There were scheduling questions, sick leave and vacation issues, and all the difficulties that went along with trying to cover too many shifts and too many jobs without enough personnel to go around.

"I'm almost as tired of being shorthanded as I am of being pregnant," Joanna observed at last as Frank closed his notebook.

Her chief deputy laughed. "You've got me there," he said. "I wouldn't have a clue what being pregnant feels like, but I know all about being constantly shorthanded. It's hell."

When the briefing was over, Joanna returned to her office to find that a whole new stack of mail had been added onto the top of the one she had managed to whittle down during the morning. By five in the afternoon she had pretty well finished. She was loading up her briefcase to go home when Ted Chapman, the executive director of the Cochise County Jail Ministry, tapped on the doorjamb next to her open office door.

"Got a minute?" he asked.

Ted Chapman was a very nice guy, and Joanna genuinely liked him. His work with jail inmates went far beyond merely ministering to their souls. Single-handedly Ted had introduced and helped maintain ongoing literacy and GED programs inside the Cochise County Jail that made it possible for inmates to finish out their jail terms better educated than when they went in. As far as Joanna was concerned, however, Ted Chapman had one major failing—at times he could be incredibly long-winded. One of Ted's so-called minutes could expand to fill up all available time, and since Joanna was chronically short on time, it was difficult for her to rein in her impatience.

Not only that, with Butch out of town, Joanna was only too conscious that Jenny was at home alone. At fourteen, Jenny was certainly old enough to spend time on her own. Still, with chores to do and animals to feed . . .

"Come on in," Joanna said. "What's up?"

"It's about one of my guys," Ted said.

Knowing that a problem with one of Ted's "guys" could run the gamut from something as serious as an inmate's mother being on her deathbed to something as simple as a jail-yard feud over possession of the basketball, Joanna closed her briefcase and settled in for the duration. "Which one?" she asked.

"Oh, nobody here," Ted said quickly. "Not one of the inmates. I'm sure it's not anyone you know. Brad's actually an associate of mine."

"Brad?" Joanna asked.

Ted nodded. "Brad Evans," he said. "Got sent up twenty-five to life in the late seventies for murdering his wife. I first met him when he got shipped down to Douglas to work on the dorms for the new Arizona State Prison Complex they were building down there. Over the years, he got saved and got himself squared away. Took complete responsibility for what happened to his wife. Never gave anybody any trouble. While he was still locked up, he started working toward his jail ministry certification. Once he got out, he asked to work in the Papago Unit down there. Considering his former problems with booze, we thought it would be a good fit. Or at least I thought it would be a good fit. Now I'm not so sure."

Since Douglas was only thirty miles away from her office, Joanna knew a good deal about the prison complex located there. One of the three units, the Papago, was sometimes referred to as the Arizona State Prison Complex's dry-out wing. In the mid-eighties the ASPC had decided to separate inmates with DUI offenses from other incarcerated felons. With that in mind, prison officials had negotiated the purchase of a failed Douglas-area motel that now housed over three hundred male prisoners in a space designed for no more than two hundred and fifty.

Four-plus years of being in charge of a jail had taught Joanna a whole lot more than she wanted to know about people involved on the wrong side of incarceration. In her experience, having an ex-con working with and counseling current inmates seemed like a bad idea. And although Ted's programs did tend to produce good results, there were times when Joanna thought his ideas hopelessly naive. It didn't surprise her to hear that one of

Ted's protégés had pulled some kind of boner, one that would likely reflect badly on a man who consistently put himself out on a limb for the prisoners he served.

"Poor Ted," Joanna sympathized. "So now you're discovering what I learned a long time ago—no good deed goes unpunished. What did he do?"

"He just took off," Ted answered. "Everything was going fine, right up until yesterday, when he didn't show up for his counseling sessions. When he didn't turn up again today, his supervisor called him at home and got no answer. When somebody finally called me and let me know what was going on, I drove straight to his apartment down in Douglas to see if he was all right. He didn't answer my knock. There were two unopened newspapers in the driveway, mail in the mailbox, and no car. Given Brad's history with booze, I'm guessing he's had a relapse and is back on the sauce. I was hoping maybe you could help me find him before things get any worse than they already are."

Suddenly Joanna's impatience with Ted Chapman melted away. She was no longer nearly so anxious for him to get to the point so she could head home. Ted's "guy" happened to be just what her department was looking for—a released, long-term prison inmate with a history of alcohol abuse who had suddenly gone AWOL. Was it possible this Brad guy would turn out to be her department's Border Road John Doe? Unfortunately, both the Double Cs had already left for the day.

"What's his name again?" Joanna asked, pulling out a piece of paper and picking up a pen.

"I call him Brad," Ted replied. "But his real name is Bradley—Bradley Evans."

"How old is he?" she asked.

Ted shrugged. "I don't know for sure. Fifty-something, I suppose."

"And what does he look like?"

"Reddish-blond hair," Ted answered. "Balding. A little pudgy around the middle."

"Any tattoos?" Joanna asked.

"I wouldn't know about that," Ted returned. "Why?"

Without answering, Joanna picked up the phone and speed-dialed George Winfield's office number. "Are you still there?" she asked when the medical examiner answered.

"Not really," he returned. "At least I'm not supposed to be. I'm actually standing with my keys in hand and one foot out the door."

"Put down the keys and wait for me," Joanna told him. "I can be there in a few minutes."

"Why? What's the big hurry?"

"I have someone here in my office. I think he can shed light on this morning's case."

"You'd better hurry, then," George said. "It's Friday, and your mother is expecting guests for dinner. If you make me late again, Ellie will have my ears."

"Don't worry," Joanna said. "This won't take long." When she put down the phone, Ted Chapman was staring at her. "What's going on?" he asked.

"I'm not sure, Ted," Joanna said slowly, "but I'm afraid I may have some bad news for you. Early this morning a Border Patrol officer found an unidentified homicide victim out along Border Road. It sounds to me as though there's a lot of similarity between him and your Mr. Evans. Reddish-blond hair. Fifty-something. Homemade tattoo on his upper left arm that says 'One day at a time.' "

"You want me to see if I can identify him?" Ted asked.

Joanna nodded. "Yes, if you don't mind. Identifying the victim would be a big help to our investigation. Without knowing who he is, we're pretty much dead in the water."

It took Ted a moment to come to grips with what Joanna had said. Finally he nodded. "Of course," he said, getting to his feet. "I'll be glad to."

Ted sat quietly in the passenger seat of Joanna's Crown Victoria as she drove the several miles from the Cochise County Justice Center, through town to Old Bisbee, and then up the winding curves of Tombstone Canyon to the failed low-cost mortuary George Winfield had converted into a state-of-the-art morgue.

On the way Joanna considered calling Ernie and Jaime at home to let them know what was up. In the end she decided against it. If Ted did manage to make a positive ID, there would be plenty of time to send out for reinforcements.

George was waiting in the doorway and looking pointedly at his watch when Joanna pulled in and parked under the covered portico.

"This is Ted Chapman," Joanna announced once she and Ted were both out of the car. "He's head of our jail ministry. One of his colleagues from the Arizona State Prison Complex down in Douglas has gone missing. I'm thinking perhaps . . ."

"Of course," George said gravely, taking Ted Chapman by the arm. "Right this way."

George led them into a velvet-lined room that, in the building's mortuary days, had been a private family viewing room. As part of the county morgue it now served a grimmer but similar purpose. Joanna stood at Ted's side while George went into the next room, retrieved the body, and then opened the curtain.

When he removed the sheet to reveal the dead man's face, Ted swayed as though his knees were about to give way beneath him. Taking him by the elbow, Joanna eased him onto a nearby chair.

"It is him," Ted whispered hoarsely. "It's Brad."

She turned back to signal George to shut the curtain, but he had already done so. She gave Ted a few minutes to regain his composure. "Thank you, Ted. Does Mr. Evans have any next of kin?"

"Probably," Ted said. "But I have no idea who they are or how to contact them."

"My detectives are going to need to talk to you as soon as possible," Joanna told him. "Now that we have an ID, they'll be able to start making progress on the case. If I call them back in, would you mind talking to them?"

"Tonight?"

Unlike Joanna, Ted Chapman wasn't a cop. He didn't grasp the urgency of getting on the killer's trail while it was still warm.

"Yes," Joanna said. "Tonight. Right now."

"All right," Ted said. "But I'll need to call my wife and let her know what's going on."

While Ted used his cell phone to explain the situation to Ginny Chapman, Joanna used hers to call Jenny.

"When will you be home?" Jenny asked. "What's for dinner?"

"You're probably on your own for dinner," Joanna returned. "Something's come up here at work. I may have to stay late."

"With Butch gone, I thought we'd get to have a girls' night, just the two of us, the way things used to be." Jenny sounded genuinely disappointed.

"I thought so, too, sweetie," Joanna said. "I'm sorry."

"No, you're not," Jenny replied hotly. "You're not sorry at all."

With that, she hung up, leaving her mother listening to the empty hum of the phone line.

CHAPTER 3

On her way back to the Justice Center, Joanna called the Double Cs about interviewing Ted Chapman. Ernie wasn't home and didn't answer his cell. "You caught me in the middle of dinner," Jaime said. "I'll be there in a few."

"Any idea where Ernie is?" Joanna asked.

"Tucson," Jaime answered. "He told me before we left work that he and Rose were going there for a meeting of some kind."

"For someone who claims to hate driving back and forth to Tucson, it seems like he's been doing that a lot lately."

"Yes, it does," Jaime agreed, but he didn't say anything more than that, and Joanna didn't press it.

Joanna could see that Ted was shaken by what had happened to his friend, but he was eager to be of assistance in whatever way possible. While they waited for Jaime to show up for the interview, Ted called one of the jail ministry administrators.

"Hey, Rich," he said. "Ted Chapman here. Sorry to call you at home like this, but I have some bad news about one of your guys—Brad Evans. He's been killed—murdered."

Joanna waited during a long pause while the unexpected news was assimilated.

"It happened along Border Road," Ted continued. "Someone found the body early this morning. I just identified it, but the sheriff's department is trying to locate next of kin, and I was wondering . . . Sure, sure. If you wouldn't mind, that would be great. What's the phone number here?"

Joanna reeled it off.

"All right," Ted said into the phone. "Call this number when you have the information. If I'm not here, ask for Sheriff Brady."

Having put that in process, Joanna and Ted went into the conference room to await Jaime Carbajal's arrival. The young detective came bearing gifts—a grocery-bag care package that included paper plates and plastic silverware as well as several bean-and-green-chili burritos wrapped in tinfoil and still warm to the touch.

"You didn't eat, did you, boss?" Jaime asked.

"Not since lunch," Joanna answered.

"That's what Delcia thought," he said with a grin. "She claims pregnant women need to keep up their strength. How about you, Ted? Hungry?"

"Not really," he said, but once Joanna's first burrito was unwrapped he succumbed and had one anyway. Joanna plowed gratefully into hers. Until she took that first bite, she had been unaware of how close she had been to running on empty.

As Jaime sat down at the table, Joanna pushed him the piece of paper on which she had jotted down Bradley Evans's name as well as the address of his apartment in Douglas.

"I'm so sorry to hear about the loss of your friend, Ted," Jaime ventured. "What can you tell us about him?"

Ted Chapman took a deep breath. "I've known Brad for a long time," he said. "Before I broke away to start the Cochise Jail Ministry, I spent years working for the Arizona State Prison Ministry. Ginny's parents were from Douglas, and she wanted to live closer to them, so when there was an opening in Douglas, I transferred down here from Florence. Brad was already there when I arrived.

"Most convicts are con artists one way or the other. They're like politicians. They'll say anything to suck you into believing that their version of things is the gospel. Brad wasn't like that. He was always a straight shooter, but tough enough that no one messed with him."

Jaime looked up from taking notes. "What was he in for?"

"Second-degree murder," Ted answered. "He got twenty-five-to-life for killing his wife back in the late seventies. It happened out in Sierra Vista, or maybe it was just near there, I don't remember which."

"I've asked Maggie from Records to get us the file," Joanna said.

"I don't remember his wife's name, but she was pregnant at the time of her death," Ted continued. "He was drunk and evidently functioning in a blackout when it happened. I don't believe her body was ever found."

"They got a conviction with no body?" Jamie asked. "That's pretty unusual."

Ted nodded. "There was enough blood found in Brad's vehicle and on his body to make a pretty good case that she was dead. And with her pregnant, I guess feelings were running pretty high. Even without a body, the county attorney was prepared to go for murder one. Instead, Brad copped a plea to second degree. Like I told Sheriff Brady here, he accepted full responsibility for his actions. Based on good behavior, he probably should have been turned loose a long time before they finally let him go, but every time he came up for parole, his former mother-in-law was there at the hearing to speak in opposition."

"How long ago did Evans get out?"

"Three or so years ago. When I first met him, I would have to say he was what they call a dry drunk—an alcoholic who wasn't actively drinking but who hadn't done anything about working on the underlying issues. I helped him get into the program. You know anything about the twelve steps?"

Joanna and Jaime both shook their heads.

"There are twelve steps to recovery. One of them involves making amends to all the people you may have harmed. Once Brad got into the program, he wrote a letter to his former mother-in-law, asking her forgiveness, but nothing changed her mind about him. She was at the last meeting before the parole board set him loose, and she was still adamantly opposed to their letting him out. Still, once he was on the outside, Brad stayed with AA, and he's one of the ones who really worked his program. He was serious about it. That's why I thought he'd be so good working with the guys in the Papago Unit as a kind of peer counselor. And he was."

"You have no idea where Brad's former mother-in-law lives now?"

"No," Ted answered.

"Do you have any idea about Brad's friends or associates?"

"Not really. I'm guessing the people he was closest to will be the ones he was working with at the prison, maybe some of the guards, but they wouldn't know him nearly as well as the inmates he was counseling."

Jaime nodded. "We'll get down there tomorrow and talk to them. It's a start. Can you think of anything else?"

Ted shook his head. "Pride's a terrible thing," he said bleakly.

"Why do you say that?" Joanna asked.

"Because when Brad went missing, I was convinced he had fallen off the wagon. I was terribly disappointed in him, mainly because I thought it would reflect badly on me. The first thing that went through my head when I saw him uptown in the morgue was that at least he wasn't drunk. It makes me ashamed to think that idea even crossed my mind. What kind of person would think that way?"

"Lots of them, Ted," Joanna said. "Give yourself a break." She turned to Jaime. "Can you think of anything else we need to ask?"

"When was he last seen at work?" Jaime asked.

"Tuesday. He had Wednesdays off."

"All right, then," Jaime said. "That's about it."

"I can go, then?" Ted asked.

"Sure," Joanna said with a smile. "Go home to Ginny. I'm sure she's worried about you. If we need anything else, we know how to get hold of you."

Jaime waited until Ted Chapman had left the room. "So you win the prize, boss," he said. "John Doe turns out to be an ex-con with alcohol problems. I believe you called that one right on the money."

"But we still don't know who killed him," Joanna returned.

There was a light knock on the conference-room door. Maggie Mendoza came in carrying a computer printout. "This is what the Department of Corrections has on Mr. Evans," she said.

Joanna took the file. She hadn't planned to look at it in any detail. Her intention was to glance at it briefly and then pass it over to Jaime so he could study it, but then a familiar name leaped off one of the pages: D. H. Lathrop! When Brad Evans was first picked up in October of 1978, Joanna's own father had been the arresting officer.

Joanna felt a sudden shiver of recognition. It was as though her father had reached out from beyond the grave and tapped her on the shoulder. She hurried to the conference-room door and called after Maggie, who was on her way back to her desk.

"Wait a minute." She turned back to Jaime. "What's the wife's name?"

Jaime picked up the papers and scanned through them. "Lisa Marie Evans."

"Where are the homicide records from 1978?"

"In storage up in the old courthouse," Maggie said. "Why?"

"I need one," Joanna said. "Lisa Marie Evans. Murdered in October of 1978."

"Do you need it tonight?" Maggie asked. "If you do . . ."

Joanna glanced at her watch. The hour hand was edging toward eight. She didn't blame Maggie for not wanting to make a nighttime visit to the creaky old courthouse uptown, but it had to be done.

"We really do need it tonight," Joanna said.

"All right," Maggie agreed. "I'll go get it, but it may take time. Those files aren't in the best of order."

When Maggie left the conference room, so did Joanna. The pressure the baby was putting on her bladder was more than she could withstand. When she returned from the rest room, Jaime was finishing a call.

"Thanks," he said. "Thanks so much."

"Who was that?" Joanna asked.

"Rich Higgins," Jaime answered. "The guy Ted Chapman called. Rich is human resources director for Arizona State Prison System Jail Ministries."

"So we have a next of kin?"

"Her name's Anna Marie Crystal with a Sierra Vista address. She's listed in Brad's employment records as 'mother-in-law.' She's also the beneficiary of his group life insurance. It's not very much—a ten-thousand-dollar death benefit, but still . . ."

"Did Brad Evans remarry?" Joanna asked.

"If he did, Ted never mentioned it," Jaime replied.

"We should probably check this out," Joanna said. "Twenty-plus years ago Brad Evans went to prison for murdering his wife, but he still lists his dead wife's mother as his beneficiary? That strikes me as very strange."

"Do you want me to go talk to her tonight?" Jaime asked. "Since Ted already identified the body, we don't need her for that, but . . ."

Joanna looked at the computer printout. Even across the table she could make out her father's name, Deputy D. H. Lathrop. It was eight o'clock, and Sierra Vista was thirty miles away, but even if it meant getting home at midnight, Joanna wanted to be there when Jaime spoke to Anna Marie Crystal.

She picked up the phone and dialed home. "Hullo," Jenny said.

"How are you?" Joanna asked.

"Okay, I guess," Jenny mumbled unconvincingly.

"Is everything all right?"

"I suppose."

"What did you have for dinner?"

"Noodle soup."

"As you know, there's been a homicide, Jenny," Joanna told her. "We've just found an important lead, but it means I need to go to Sierra Vista. Will you be all right?"

"I guess. I'm watching TV, but there's nothing good on."

"The doors are locked?"

Jenny sighed. "Yes, Mother."

Joanna knew that being called "Mother" was never a good sign, but still . . .

"It's part of a case your grandfather investigated years ago," Joanna continued. "I really need to be there." *Want* was more like it, but that's not what she said.

"Go ahead," Jenny told her. "I'll be fine."

"You're sure?"

"Mother!"

"Good night," Joanna said. "I'll see you in the morning."

"Your car or mine?" Jaime asked as Joanna put down the phone.

"Yours," Joanna said. "I'm just along for the ride."

They had crossed the Divide in the Mule Mountains and had turned off Highway 80 toward Sierra Vista when Joanna's cell phone rang.

"I tried the house," Butch said. "Jenny told me you were still working."

"It's a homicide," Joanna said. "Jaime and I are on our way to do the next-of-kin notification."

"Didn't Dr. Lee say you were supposed to take it easy these last couple of weeks?" Butch demanded.

"I am taking it easy," Joanna returned. "Jaime's doing the driving."

"And you're wearing your seat belt the right way?" he asked.

"Yes," she said, a little annoyed by his fussing. "How was the panel?"

"Okay," he said.

"You don't sound very enthusiastic."

"I'm wondering how much good this kind of thing does, when what I really want is to be home. I always thought writers were like hermits. This seems more like being a politician out on the stump, having to meet and greet. Carole Ann tells me I need to get used to it."

Having just survived a bruising election campaign, Joanna knew exactly how it felt to be on the stump. She, for one, was glad to be off it.

"Jenny said this was one of your father's old cases," Butch said. "One of those cold-case-file deals?"

"Not really," Joanna answered. "The homicide victim whose body was found this morning turns out to be someone my father arrested and sent to prison for murder in 1978. When we requested the record, there was my father's name on the report. It was strange seeing his name like that, like there was some kind of weird connection between us. I don't know how to explain it."

"Jenny didn't sound too thrilled to be left on her own," Butch said. "I would have thought she'd be ecstatic. She's always saying we baby her too much."

"I think it's called attention deficit," Joanna said.

"Probably pretty typical," Butch said. "You've got a lot on your plate, Joey. No wonder Jenny feels neglected at times. Occasionally, so do I. We both want your undivided attention, and there's only so much of you to go around."

Joanna bit back the urge to apologize. She was, after all, simply doing her job, and a new baby was going to make it worse.

"Anyway," Butch added, "don't stay out too late. You'll wear yourself out. How was the shower?"

"You knew about the shower, too?" Joanna asked. It seemed that everyone had known about it.

"Who do you think sent the note to school so Eva Lou could spring Jenny?"

"The shower was great," Joanna said. "Lots of goodies. Come to think of it, they're still in the car."

"Don't worry about unpacking them," Butch said. "Let Jenny do it. Or wait until I get home on Sunday."

"Butch," Joanna cautioned, "I may be pregnant, but I'm not an invalid."

"And I don't want you to be, either."

"Have fun," Joanna said.

"I will," Butch returned. "Don't work too hard."

Joanna closed her phone. "He's worried about you?" Jaime asked.

"I guess."

"I remember how it was when Delcia was pregnant with Pepe," Jaime said. "I kept worrying and worrying. Delcia was fine the whole time. I was a wreck."

Joanna laughed. "Sounds familiar," she said.

They were quiet for a few minutes before Jaime asked, "Is this what you always wanted?"

"Having a baby?" Joanna asked.

"No. Being a cop," Jaime said with a laugh. "Because of your dad, I mean."

"I was proud of him," Joanna returned, after a moment's thought. "I thought what he did was important, and I thought he treated people fairly. And I was proud of Andy, too, but I never really thought about being a cop myself, not until after Andy's funeral when someone suggested that I run in his stead. So I guess you could say I stumbled into it. Now, though, I can't imagine doing anything else."

Jaime nodded. "Me, either," he said.

Anna Marie Crystal's house was a modest bungalow on Short Street, a block-long fragment of street a single block off Fry Boulevard, Sierra Vista's main drag. It was a small clapboard affair with a screened-in front porch. Tucked in behind a collection of strip malls, the house resembled some of the older houses from up in Old Bisbee. It was easy for Joanna to assume that it predated the reopening of Fort Huachuca in the early fifties. The yard, surrounded by a four-foot chain-link fence, looked clean and well tended in the glow of the security lights from the loading docks of the businesses across the street.

With Jaime walking just behind her, Joanna opened the gate and made her way up to the porch, where a single yellow light illuminated an old-fashioned buzzer-style bell. As soon as she punched it, a small dog began barking furiously inside the house.

"Fritz," a woman's voice ordered from behind the front door. "Quiet now. Come here!" And then a moment later, "Who is it?"

"We're police officers," Joanna responded. "I'm Sheriff Brady. Detective Carbajal is with me. May we come in?"

Several locks clicked before the inside door opened cautiously to reveal a gray-haired woman clutching what appeared to be a tiny silky terrier mix in one arm. A high-volume television set blared somewhere in the background.

"Police?" she asked, peering out at them. "What's wrong? Has something happened—a robbery or something? With all the people coming and going from that 7-Eleven on the corner, you just never can tell."

"Are you Mrs. Crystal?"

The woman nodded.

"It's not a robbery," Joanna assured her. "But we do need to speak to you."

After unhooking the screen door, Anna Marie took Joanna's proffered ID wallet and carried it back inside the house. She put the dog on the floor and then studied Joanna's ID in the illumination from an overhead light. Meanwhile the dog raced back to the screen door and resumed barking. Joanna held the screen door shut to keep the dog from bursting outside.

"Fritz," the woman ordered. "Stop that right now. Come here."

Fritz, of course, paid no attention. Finally the woman returned to the porch, scooped the dog back into her arms. "He doesn't mind very well," she said. "Wait right here while I lock him in the kitchen."

Returning from incarcerating the animal, Anna Marie Crystal held the door open. "Sorry about that," she said. "He's a little spoiled. Come in."

Joanna and Jaime entered a room that reeked of years of uninterrupted cigarette smoking. The massive green glass ashtray on the coffee table was full, but not to the point of overflowing. There were doilies everywhere—beaded ones on the coffee table and on the end tables and crocheted ones on the backs of the couch and chairs. A bookshelf against one wall was lined with what looked like a complete collection of Reader's Digest Condensed Books.

Anna Marie was a tall, scrawny woman with an ill-fitting set of dentures. She motioned the two officers onto an old-fashioned sectional that was far too big for the size of the room, then hurried across the room, where she used a knob to switch off the blaring television set. "Now then, Sheriff Brady," she said determinedly, "tell me. What's this all about?"

Jaime looked questioningly at Joanna. Nodding, she took the

lead. "Detective Jaime Carbajal is one of my homicide detectives," she said. "I'm afraid we may have some bad news for you."

"Homicide?" Anna Marie repeated, her gaunt face paling. "You mean someone's been murdered?"

"Yes," Joanna said. "The body was found early this morning on Border Road between Paul's Spur and Bisbee Junction. The victim has been identified as Bradley Evans, your former son-in-law."

The skin of Anna Marie's face tightened into a grimace, revealing a glimpse of the angular skull beneath her wrinkled flesh. For a moment she said nothing. "So he's dead then?" she asked at last. "That no-good son of a bitch is finally dead?"

"Yes," Joanna said.

"What happened?"

"He was stabbed to death."

"Good!" Anna Marie exclaimed bitterly, taking a seat in a wingback chair across from them. "It's about damned time! Bradley Evans murdered my daughter. Why on earth would you think hearing he's dead would be bad news for me? It's what I've been praying for every day of my life since 1978. Twenty-five years to life! He murdered Lisa and her baby and all he got was twenty-five years! How the judge could give him that and then look at himself in the mirror I can't imagine!"

With her hands shaking, Anna Marie shook a cigarette out of a packet of Camels on the coffee table, lit it, and then pulled the ashtray within easy reach.

"So you weren't close?" Joanna asked.

Anna Marie blew an indignant plume of smoke into the air. "Close!" she exclaimed. "Don't even think such a thing! Of course we weren't close."

"But he listed you as his next of kin."

"Well, I'm not. I'm no kin of his at all."

"He also named you as the beneficiary of his group life insurance policy. It's a small death benefit, but—"

"Just because he put my name down on a piece of paper doesn't mean I have to take the money!" Anna Marie declared. "Blood money is what I call it. He probably thought that by leaving me something I'd forgive him for what he did, but I won't. Not ever. No matter what. I hope he rots in hell."

It wasn't at all the kind of next-of-kin notification Joanna had expected. Instead of a grieving relative, she was faced with this daunting old woman whose whole body bristled with righteous indignation.

"So he hasn't been in touch with you since his release?" Joanna asked.

"Absolutely not. He wouldn't dare. If he'd shown up here, I would have shot him myself. I have a gun, you know. An old thirty-aught-six. My husband used to hunt. I kept the gun after he died. I know how to use it, and believe me, if Bradley Evans had turned up anywhere within range, I would have plugged him full of lead. They'd have had to drag him off my porch in one of those zip-up body bags."

Listening to the old woman rant, Joanna had no doubt that she meant every word. Anna Marie Crystal's fury with her daughter's killer was still white hot more than two decades after Lisa Marie Evans's death.

"Tell me about your daughter," Joanna said.

Anna Marie blew another cloud of smoke. Her face softened. "She was such a sweet, sweet girl," she said. "She met Bradley over at the bar that used to be right there by the main gate. You remember the one."

"The Military Inn?" Joanna offered.

Anna Marie nodded. "Right. That's the one. It wasn't a good

49

place for her to hang out. I told her that, too, but she wasn't about to listen. She was twenty-one and working for the dry cleaner's just up the street. She liked going there after work to relax. It was a place where she and her friends could meet guys, and they did."

"Did she and Bradley Evans meet there?"

"Yes. He was still in the army then. They got married only a couple of months after they met. Another bad idea. I told her she didn't know enough about him. He was from somewhere else— Oklahoma or Texas maybe. Didn't seem to have any family to speak of. That's always a bad sign. Either the family's bad or the one who's on the outs is bad. It's all the same. One way or the other it spells trouble, but Lisa thought Brad—as she called him—was the greatest thing since sliced bread. Nothing her father or I said could convince her otherwise."

"So they got married?"

"Eloped," Anna Marie said. "Ran off to Vegas and got married in one of those awful wedding chapels. I couldn't believe it. Neither could my husband. He was crushed. He'd always planned on walking his little Lisa down the aisle. It broke his heart when she died. He never got over it."

"You said Bradley was still in the army when he and Lisa met?" Joanna asked.

Anna Marie nodded. "Barely. He was about to get out. After he did, he managed to land some kind of job with the phone company. It was a good thing, too. A couple of months later, Lisa turned up pregnant. With him working for the phone company, at least she would have had maternity benefits. She didn't have any benefits at all from the dry cleaner's, even though she had worked there since her junior year in high school."

"What happened?"

"You mean why did he kill her?" Anna Marie asked.

Joanna nodded.

"I have no idea. I thought Brad was a bit of a rounder. For sure he drank way too much, but he always seemed to behave around Lisa, and I thought he loved her."

"Was there someone else involved?" Joanna asked.

"You mean like did Lisa have someone on the side? No way. She loved Bradley to distraction. I can't say the same about him. I suppose Bradley could have had a girlfriend. I've wondered about that over the years, but I don't know for sure."

"They seemed happy together?"

"As happy as newlyweds are when they're young and not making enough money. But Lisa was excited about being pregnant. She was never very interested in school. She did all right in high school, but she wasn't the least bit interested in going off to college. She told me once that all she wanted to do was meet a nice man, get married, and raise lots of babies."

"Did Bradley want the baby?"

"Who knows? I sure as hell didn't ask him," Anna Marie put in. "I mean, in those days, with the pill and all, if people got pregnant and it was after they got married, you assumed it was because they wanted to, but Bradley was a real good-time boy. On Saturdays, when he was off work and Lisa was at the dry cleaner's, he'd go hang out at the bar and play pool until it was time for them to go home. He had a company car during the week, so they only had the one car—his pickup truck—on the weekends. So he'd take her to work and then he'd come back and pick her up when she got off in the afternoon.

"The last time I talked to her was that Saturday morning, the day she was killed. Lisa loved fried chicken, especially my fried chicken. I called her at work to see if she and Brad wanted to come over for a chicken dinner on Sunday. Fried chicken and pecan pie—Lisa's two all-time favorites. She said she'd talk to Brad and let me know. I never heard her voice again. Sunday morning, about nine o'clock, a deputy sheriff showed up. He told me that they'd found Brad drunk out of his gourd somewhere up by Bisbee. He told me that they hadn't found a body, but there was enough evidence of foul play that they were afraid something had happened to Lisa. And they never did find her. Brad went to prison without ever letting on what he had done to Lisa and her baby. Claimed he was drunk and didn't remember."

Joanna heard the words and wondered if that "deputy sheriff" had been her father.

"They never did find her," Anna Marie repeated, grinding out the stub of her cigarette and looking off into the distance somewhere over Joanna's and Jaime's shoulders. "I always thought it would have been better if they had. If we could have found Lisa and the baby and buried them, maybe that would have made things better. 'Closure' is what they call it. These last few years, TV has been full of pictures of that awful Scott Peterson and that Hacker guy from Salt Lake, but at least those poor families found their daughters' bodies. At least they had something to bury. Two months after Brad went to prison, my husband, Kenny, drove his pickup truck out to the San Pedro, parked alongside the river, drank a bottle of bourbon, and then put a bullet through his head. Left a note. Said that with Lisa gone, he just couldn't see any point in going on. I didn't blame him, either. I would have done the same thing, if I'd had guts enough. The cops even kept Kenny's gun. Said they needed it for evidence."

There was a plaintive whimper from behind the kitchen door, followed by a persistent scratching. Without another word, Anna Marie got up and rescued Fritz from his prison. When the old woman returned, she collapsed into her chair as deflated as if she'd been a balloon suddenly devoid of air. She seemed utterly exhausted.

Quickly Joanna rose to her feet. "We'll be going then, Mrs. Crystal. I can see this has been very hard on you."

"Thank you for letting me talk about Lisa," Anna Marie said. "Most of my friends don't have the patience for it. Talking helps me remember her. Otherwise she'd be forgotten completely."

On an impulse, Joanna reached into her pocket and pulled out a business card. "Lisa must have been a wonderful daughter," she said. "Anytime you want to talk about her, feel free to give me a call."

Anna Marie studied the card for a moment and then looked at Joanna. There were tears in her eyes. "Thank you," she said.

As Joanna stepped off the porch and into the crisp, clear night air, she breathed in deeply, cleansing the cigarette smoke from her lungs.

Twenty-seven years earlier her father had probably come to this very house to make a next-of-kin notification. Despite the long slow passage of time since then, the grief that had filled the little clapboard house remained as palpable and overwhelming as it must have been that fateful Sunday morning in 1978. Through all the intervening years, none of the hurt had disappeared. It was still trapped inside the house right along with Anna Marie Crystal's collection of decades-old cigarette smoke.

CHAPTER 4

"Whoa," Jaime said, once they were back in his Tahoe. "I didn't see that one coming."

The conversation with Anna Marie Crystal had struck Joanna as a fairly normal next-of-kin notification. "Which one is that?" she asked.

"You heard what the woman said—that if Bradley Evans had shown up on her doorstep she would have plugged him full of lead herself. She's an old lady, all right, but it still sounds like possible motive to me. Having a gun and knowing how to use it can do a lot to equalize differences in age and sex."

"She said plug, not stab," Joanna corrected. "There's a big difference."

"Still," Jaime objected. "According to Ernie, Doc Winfield theorized that our perpetrator could very well be a female."

Joanna wasn't convinced. "I don't see it that way," she said. "Even after all these years, Anna Marie Crystal is still heartbroken over her daughter's loss—and why wouldn't she be? She lost her daughter, her grandchild, and her husband all within a matter of months, but to her it must have seemed like it happened in one fell swoop. Given those circumstances, I think I would have hated Bradley Evans's guts, too, but the woman doesn't strike me as a killer. Still, it won't hurt to check her out," Joanna conceded. "Let's see what if any kind of an alibi she had for when Bradley Evans was murdered."

"Good," Jaime said. "I'm glad you agree, because that's exactly what I intend to do."

They were still in Sierra Vista when Joanna's phone rang. "It's Maggie," the Records clerk said. She sounded annoyed and out of breath. "I'm still up here at the courthouse pawing through boxes. This place is a mess. I'm sure the file must be here somewhere, but I don't know where. It's like the movers just jammed things in wherever there was room with absolutely no rhyme or reason. I know you wanted it by tonight, but I'm due to get off at eleven . . ."

"It's fine, Maggie," Joanna said at once. "Who's working graveyard?"

"I think it's Cindy Hall. The problem is, there's only one clerk on that shift. If she comes up here to take over where I leave off, there won't be anyone in Records to support the guys in the cars."

"Never mind," Joanna said. "You've done the best you can, Maggie. It'll have to wait until morning."

When they got back to the Justice Center, it was after eleven. Joanna didn't even bother stepping inside the office to retrieve her briefcase. Instead, she transferred directly to her Crown Victoria and headed for High Lonesome Ranch. With all the dogs closeted inside the house with Jenny, it was unnaturally quiet when she drove up the road to the U-shaped ranch house with its two separate wings and parked in her designated garage at the end of the far wing. When she let herself into the family room, however, Lady was at the door waiting to greet her.

After kicking off her shoes and giving her grateful toes a relaxing wiggle, Joanna did a barefoot inspection of the house. Jenny was asleep in her room with the television set booming away and with both Tigger and Lucky curled up on the bed with her, one dog per side. In the kitchen Joanna found a collection of dirty dishes, along with evidence both of the noodle soup Jenny had eaten for dinner as well as the microwave popcorn she had snacked on later. There were two popcorn bags in the trash. One was empty. The other, clearly overcooked, was full of black cinders. Why the bag hadn't set the microwave on fire was nothing short of a miracle. Out in the laundry room Joanna found that the dogs had been well taken care of. The water dishes were full of water. The food dishes were empty. In other words, everything was fine.

For a moment, Joanna considered making herself a late-night cup of cocoa, but then she changed her mind. She was too tired. What she needed was rest instead of a late-night snack. She went into the bedroom, undressed, and tumbled into bed.

The phone awakened her at 6:07 A.M. "Sheriff Brady?" a hesitant voice said. "Sorry if I'm calling too early."

It took Joanna a moment to sort out who was calling. Finally she recognized her caller's voice. Jeannine Phillips was one of Joanna's two Animal Control officers. A year earlier, during a series of budgetary cuts, Animal Control had been added to Joanna's area of responsibility. At first she'd been told it was only a temporary measure, but so far nothing had changed.

"What is it, Jeannine?" Joanna asked groggily.

"I woke you up, didn't I?" Jeannine apologized.

"It doesn't matter. What is it?"

"I found another one."

Joanna didn't need to ask another what. She knew. Three times in the last month, people had reported finding the badly mauled bodies of dead dogs—all of them pit bulls—along roads in the far northeast corner of the county. At first, Joanna's Animal Control officers had thought they had tangled with something wild—a coyote or a mountain lion or even one of the far rarer jaguars which had, of late, strayed into southern Arizona from the wilds of northern Mexico. When the third dead animal was found, a microchip dog ID had traced it back to Tucson, where it had once belonged to the nephew of a known drug dealer, a man who had twice before been arrested for running a dog-fighting ring. It seemed likely that a similar operation was now up and running somewhere in Cochise County.

"Where?" Joanna asked.

"San Simon," Jeannine said. "On I-10 behind the port of entry. A long-haul truck driver parked his rig and went to take a leak. Found the dog in a trash can, except this one isn't dead," Jeannine said. "He was chewed all to hell and bloody all over, but he was still breathing. I was going to put him out of his misery. But when I started to lift him out of the garbage can, he tried to lick my hand, and I just couldn't do it. Then I thought, If he's made it this far, what if we could pull him through? Maybe we could use him as evidence when we finally nail these bastards."

Joanna heard the break in Jeannine Phillips's voice as she spoke—the hurt, along with an underlying streak of steely determination. "Where is he now?" Joanna asked.

"In my truck."

"Do you really think he can make it?"

"I don't know," Jeannine said. "Like I said, he's torn up pretty bad, but . . ."

"Take him to Dr. Ross," Joanna said after a moment. "Have her call me and let me know whether or not she thinks she can save him and how much it's going to cost."

"Yes, ma'am," Jeannine Phillips said. "I'm on my way."

With Lady on her heels, Joanna went to the kitchen to start water for tea. Then she called Frank Montoya. "What's going on and why so early?" Frank asked. "Are you on your way to the hospital?"

"Not yet," she said. "But I have an assignment for you. I just got off the phone with Jeannine Phillips. She thinks we've got a dogfight ring operating somewhere around Bowie or San Simon. I want a bunch of enforcement up there this weekend. I want you to pull deputies from Patrol—however many we can spare—and have them look for any kind of suspicious activity."

"What happened?" Frank asked. "Did she find another dead dog?"

"No," Joanna answered. "She found a live one for a change—if Dr. Ross can work some of her magic, that is. Jeannine is taking him to the vet's office even as we speak."

"Who's paying?" As chief deputy, one of Frank's areas of responsibility and expertise was keeping the lid on budgetary considerations.

"The department is paying," Joanna said. "The dog is evidence, Frank. Once we arrest the guy, seeing a live dog will make a much bigger impression with a judge or jury than seeing pictures of dead ones."

"But that could end up costing a fortune," Frank objected.

"I told Jeannine to have Dr. Ross check with me before she begins any course of treatment."

"With the budget the way it is, you can't afford to be soft in the head about every stray dog that happens to wander into harm's way."

"We'll find a way to pay for it, Frank," Joanna said, cutting him off in mid-objection. "Now did you hear from Jaime after our trip to Sierra Vista last night?"

"He called me after he got home."

"So you know what we came up with last night?"

"That you identified the John Doe?" Frank returned. "Yes, I heard the whole story. I told him I'd send someone up to the old courthouse first thing this morning to see if they can find Bradley Evans's missing file. And Jaime said he and Ernie would head out to Sierra Vista to see if the dead guy's ex-mother-in-law has an alibi for the time in question. What about you? Are you coming into the office?"

"For a little while," Joanna answered. "Jenny's Girl Scout troop is scheduled to do a car wash up at the traffic circle. Once I drop her off for that, I thought I'd stop by the office and stay until she's ready to come back home. I just want to be sure everything is in good order before . . ."

Frank chuckled. "Did anyone ever tell you that you're a control freak?"

"No," Joanna returned. "I'm sure no one has ever mentioned any such thing."

"Consider yourself told, then," Frank said. "And remember, you heard it here first."

Once Joanna got off the phone, she started a load of laundry and then hustled around making a breakfast that she hoped would help put her back in Jenny's good graces. And it worked. Jenny and the two dogs emerged from her room as soon as the first whiff of pancakes made it to her bedroom door.

"What's for breakfast?" Jenny asked, pausing in the kitchen door. "I'm starving."

"Paper-thin pancakes," Joanna told her. "Cooked just the way you like them."

By the time breakfast was over, Joanna had more or less worked her way off the "bad" list. When they got to the traffic circle, Joanna stayed long enough to have the girls wash her Crown Victoria.

"You have your cell?" Joanna asked. Having her own cell phone was the one thing Jenny had wanted for Christmas. Butch, over Joanna's objections of its being extravagant, had seen to it that she got one.

"Yes, Mom," she said. "I have it right here."

Joanna was relieved to hear that she had been promoted back to "Mom" status from an all-time low of "Mother."

"Call me at the office when you're finished," Joanna said. "I'll come get you. Maybe we can have our girls' night out and eat some Mexican food."

Joanna stopped by Dr. Ross's on the way to her office since the veterinary clinic was between the traffic circle and the Justice Center. Jeannine Phillips's truck was still in the parking lot when Joanna arrived.

Jeannine was sitting in the waiting room thumbing her way through a worn magazine when Joanna entered. "Where's the patient?" she asked.

Jeannine Phillips was a tough customer who looked as though she could have been comfortable working as a bouncer in a bar. But when Joanna asked the question, she looked down at her feet and blushed to the roots of her hair. "In surgery," she said.

"In surgery!" Joanna repeated. "I thought I told you to have Dr. Ross call me before she did anything."

"I'm sorry, Sheriff Brady," Jeannine muttered. "There wasn't time. I was afraid we were going to lose him. Besides, I told Dr. Ross that if the department wouldn't pay, I would."

Well, Joanna thought, taking a nearby seat. *At least I'm not the only softheaded one around here.* "So what's the prognosis?" she asked after a pause.

Jeannine shrugged. "She said we'd know more after she got him stitched back up. She's been working on him for over an hour now."

For some time the only sound was the small click of an oversize electric clock that hung on the wall behind the reception desk. Jeannine was the one who broke the silence. "I think I know who's behind the fights," she said quietly.

"Who?"

"The O'Dwyers."

Joanna's heart sank. If Cochise County had a natural, home-grown pair of troublemakers, the O'Dwyer brothers, Clarence and Billy, were it. Grandsons of one of Arizona's pioneer families, they had taken over their parents' ancestral home. The vast Roostercomb Ranch, established before statehood, had once stretched from Arizona's San Simon Valley across the northern Peloncillo Mountains and on into New Mexico.

Years of drought and a series of disastrous business decisions had caused the family to sell off huge tracts of land. Several years earlier, the death of their elderly mother had thrown her cantankerous sons into a pitched battle with the Internal Revenue Service over estate taxes. By the time the feds had collected what was due, the sons were left with a much smaller ranch and a permanent antipathy toward anyone in law enforcement. Their run-in with government officials had also left them with a fondness for high-powered firearms.

"How do you know that?" Joanna asked.

"I've been keeping an eye on them," Jeannine said.

"On your own?" Joanna asked.

Jeannine nodded.

The thought of one of Joanna's unarmed Animal Control officers facing down a pair of gun-toting conspiracy nuts wasn't something she wanted to contemplate. And she didn't want the actions of her ACO inadvertently to provoke a Cochise County version of Waco's Branch Davidian shoot-out.

"Leave them alone," she said.

"But, Sheriff . . ." Jeannine began. "If we ignore them, we're just letting them get away with it."

"No buts," Joanna snapped. "I'm ordering you to stay away from them, Jeannine, and I mean that's a direct order. Billy and Clarence O'Dwyer are dangerous men. The two of them would make mincemeat out of you."

"What are we supposed to do? Turn our backs? Let them keep on doing what they're doing?"

"What you *think* they're doing," Joanna corrected. "Look, Jeannine. I understand how you feel. Don't forget, I'm every bit as much of an animal lover as you are, but the sheriff's department is a law enforcement agency. What you suspect the O'Dwyers of doing is very much against the law, but in order to catch them at it, we have to have more than unsubstantiated suspicions. We have to put a team of people on this and conduct a real investigation. Not only that, we're going to have to follow the rule of law while we do it. We have to have probable cause, properly drawn search warrants, and all those other things—the crossed *t*'s and dotted *i*'s—that will stand up in court. Believe me, when we do go in there, we'll do it with officers who are armed and trained to handle those guys, not with one officer acting on her own. Understand?"

Jeannine Phillips nodded glumly. "Yes, ma'am," she said.

A swinging door on the far side of the lobby opened, and Dr. Millicent Ross strode into the room. She was a heavyset woman with gray hair pulled into a knot at the back of her neck. Her brusque exterior belied a life lived with unstinting kindness.

"It's still touch and go, Jeannine," she said. "But I think that tough little guy of yours may make it."

Jeannine's previously grim countenance brightened. "Really?" she asked.

"Really," Dr. Ross answered. "The damage looked far worse than it was. I've stitched him back up. He'd lost a lot of blood, though, and he was very dehydrated, so I'm keeping him sedated and on an IV. If you hadn't brought him in right when you did, though, it would have been an entirely different story. He'd have been a goner."

Jeannine scrambled to her feet. "I'll be going then. Thanks, Mil. Thanks a lot." At the door she stopped and turned back. "I'll come back later to check on him."

Once the ACO had left the waiting room, Joanna turned to Millicent Ross. "Jeannine told you the background on this?"

"The dogfight issue?" the vet asked. "Yes, she told me. And to that end, I took a number of photos to document the extent of the dog's injuries. You'll have those to use in court. If he lives, there'll be plenty of scars, too."

"About the charges then," Joanna said, opening her wallet and removing a business card. "Since we're hoping to use the dog as evidence, you should bill the sheriff's department. Send it to my attention and I'll see that it's taken care of."

"That won't be necessary," Millicent Ross said. "It's already been handled."

"Surely Jeannine didn't agree to pay for the treatment. With what she makes, she couldn't possibly afford—"

"There won't be any charges, Sheriff Brady," Dr. Ross said firmly. "This is a situation where I'm donating my services."

Joanna was taken aback. "Are you sure?"

Dr. Ross smiled. "Absolutely," she said.

"What about a microchip?" Joanna asked as an afterthought. "Did you find one so we'll be able to locate the owner?"

"No such luck," Dr. Ross replied. "And no tag, either. What a surprise."

Joanna was still scratching her head about Dr. Ross's not charging for her services when she arrived at her office in the Justice Center Complex. It may have been Saturday morning, but Frank Montoya's Crown Victoria was already in the parking lot.

"You work too hard," she said, poking her head into his office. "You need to get a life."

He grinned back at her. "Look who's talking," he returned.

"I have some good news. There won't be a big vet bill for that injured dog after all."

"What happened?" Frank asked. "Did the poor thing croak?"

"No. Dr. Ross decided to donate her services."

"Amazing," Frank said. "What caused that?"

"Who knows? But don't look a gift-horse doctor in the mouth. Just be grateful for small blessings. So what's going on around here?"

Frank gestured toward a cardboard banker's storage box sitting on the small conference table in one corner of this office. "That just turned up," he said.

"Lisa Marie Evans?" Joanna asked.

Frank nodded. "Not much to it," he added.

"Do you mind?" Joanna asked.

"Be my guest."

She went over to the box, removed the lid, and peered inside. The evidence log was the first thing that came to her attention. Leafing through it, she immediately recognized her father's distinctive scrawl. The written word had never been D. H. Lathrop's friend. He had often told people that, as a grade school kid in East Texas, he'd never once been given a passing grade in penmanship. Written missives from him had come in an oddball style that was comprised haphazardly of both cursive and printed letters.

It had been startling enough for Joanna to see her father's name appear on the printed documents that the Records clerk had retrieved. Now, holding the evidence log in her hand, it was touching and thrilling to be holding a notebook filled with pages over which her father himself had labored. In that moment she felt an incredible closeness to D. H. Lathrop, a closeness that took her breath away. She vividly remembered seeing him seated at the kitchen table with his shoulders hunched in concentration, painstakingly putting pen to paper. Maybe he had been working on this very document. Not wanting to sever that slender thread of spiritual connection with her long-dead father, Joanna held on to the book for a long time, studying what he had written. Finally, with a sigh, she put the notebook aside and turned once more to the box.

The casebook came next. In 1978 her father had been a deputy in the sheriff's department, so none of his handiwork appeared in the casebook. The information there had been compiled by the detectives on the case. Joanna recognized their names if not their individual handwriting. Some of them had been the very people whose lack of integrity had propelled D. H. Lathrop into running for office himself.

When she put the casebook down and returned to the box, she found only one additional item—a woman's purse. It was an old-fashioned pocket-style leather affair with fringe on the bottom and an overlapping flap closure. Parts of the outside were still soft and pliable while others were stiff, stained dark with a substance that Joanna suspected to be dried blood. Lots of dried blood! No wonder that, even without ever finding Lisa Marie's body, investigators had concluded that she was dead.

Sitting down at the table, Joanna upended the purse and let the contents fall into the cover of the banker's box. Old coins, time-faded and unreadable receipts, paper clips, a compact, outdated lipstick containers, and several cheap ballpoint pens tumbled out. So did a wallet. What surprised Joanna was what was missing. There was absolutely no trace of black fingerprint powder on either the purse or its contents.

"If this was the only evidence they had, why wasn't it in an evidence bag?" she asked. "And how come nobody ever dusted any of this stuff for prints?"

"I thought that was strange myself," Frank agreed, getting up from his desk and coming over to where Joanna was seated. "I suppose that, since they closed the case when Bradley Evans confessed to the crime, they must have had enough evidence on him without having to mess around with the purse. If you want to, I suppose we could see if Casey Ledford could lift prints off it now, but I'm not sure it would work."

"In other words, there's not much point," Joanna said. With that, she opened the wallet. Inside, the cheap plastic sleeves were brittle and yellowed with age. Thumbing through to the driver's license, Joanna studied the smiling visage of a sweet-faced young woman identified as Lisa Marie Crystal. She had gone to her death without ever having gotten around to changing her last name on her driver's license. The photo was one of someone who seemed confident and supremely happy and who had no idea that her life would be snuffed out within months of having that picture taken. In addition to the license, there were several other photos.

The first of those was a professionally shot pose of Lisa Marie and Bradley Evans, a picture that might well have been used for a wedding announcement in a local newspaper. One was clearly a high school photo of Lisa Marie, while another showed a crew-cut Bradley Evans proudly posing in his army dress uniform. Then there was one of a somewhat older couple. After examining it, Joanna recognized Anna Marie Crystal and the man who must have been her husband, Lisa Marie's father, Ken. There was so much loss and hurt in that small collection of photos that Joanna was glad to turn away from them.

In the back of the wallet she found twenty-three dollars, and in the snap-closing change compartment, she found another dollar's worth of change.

"Whatever the motive for Lisa Marie's murder," Joanna said, "robbery wasn't it."

Thoughtfully she picked up all the items and returned them to the box, lingering for a long moment over the evidence log before she put that away as well.

"You'll make sure Ernie and Jaime see all this?"

"You bet."

"Speaking of which," Joanna said, "have you talked to either one of them so far this morning?"

"They called in and said they were working," Frank replied. "Something about getting a search warrant so they can go through Bradley Evans's apartment down in Douglas."

"What about San Simon?" Joanna asked.

"I've got three cars scheduled to go there late this afternoon to hang out and sort of get the lay of the land."

"Good," Joanna said. "Tell them to pay special attention to Roostercomb Ranch."

Frank had been revising the schedule sheet. Now he put down his pen and studied Joanna's face. "Don't tell me. The O'Dwyers?"

"Yup," Joanna said. "At least that's what Jeannine Phillips thinks."

"We can't afford to have an armed confrontation with those guys."

"Don't I know it," Joanna agreed. "But at least it gives us an idea of where to start looking. Tell whoever's going there to keep an eye out but to be very, very discreet. None of my officers is to set foot inside their gate. We're talking surveillance only."

"Got it," Frank said.

His phone rang just then, and Frank reached to answer it. "Sure," he said after a moment. "She's right here. Hold on." Frank covered the mouth and turned to Joanna. "It's Lisa Howard out at the front desk. She says your husband is on the line. Do you want to take the call here or in your office?"

"My office," Joanna said, and hurried off to answer it.

Butch's greeting was something less than cordial. "What are you doing at work? I thought you promised to take it easy this weekend."

"I am taking it easy," she countered. "I came here to wait for Jenny to finish up with her Girl Scout car wash. It was easier and closer to just wait around here at the office than it was to spend the whole day running back and forth between town and home."

"Oh," Butch said, sounding somewhat mollified. "I forgot all about the car wash. So you're not working."

"Not really," Joanna said. "And how's the conference?"

"I've met a bunch of interesting people," he said. "And I've gone to several panels. Even though they all write murder mysteries, the authors seem to have all different kinds of ideas about how to do that job. And the woman I told you about yesterday, the one who was so upset because I had review copies of my book here and she didn't?"

"What was her name again?" Joanna asked.

"Christina Hanson. It turns out she's a pretty decent person after all. We had breakfast together this morning. It's like we're all in the freshman class of the writing business."

"So you're having a good time?"

"Yes, and I'm very glad to be here," Butch answered. "Thanks for encouraging me to come. Sometimes, when I'm working away all by myself, I feel like some kind of freak. The good thing about being here at the conference is that I'm finding out there are a whole lot of other freaks just like me, and they are going to like my book. Now tell me about you. How are you feeling?"

"Pregnant," Joanna replied. "Nine and a half months' worth, in fact, even though that's not quite true. So I'm a little grumpy, but it's nothing dropping twenty pounds or so of ballast won't help."

"Do you want me to come home tonight?" Butch asked. "There are a couple of panels I wanted to see tomorrow, but if you'd rather I came home . . ."

"No, Butch," she said. "You signed up for the conference and I want you to stay for the whole thing."

"Maybe you and Jenny should stay in town tonight—maybe with Eva Lou and Jim Bob. Or maybe they could come stay with you. I worry about you being out at the ranch all by yourself."

"I'm not all by myself," Joanna said. "As you just pointed out, Jenny's there, too. If the baby decides to come early, she's more than capable of summoning help. Besides, how could I come to town? Do you think Jenny and I could just show up on Jim Bob and Eva Lou's doorstep with three dogs in tow and say 'Take us in'?"

"No," Butch said. "I don't suppose you could."

"I'm a big girl," Joanna said. "In more ways than one. And I'm fully capable of handling whatever comes up."

"Right," Butch said. "And I didn't mean that you weren't."

But it is what you said, Joanna thought.

They talked a while longer, but Joanna was still slightly steamed when she got off the phone. After the call she stayed in her office for the next two hours, using the unexpected quiet time to read a few of the most recent issues of law enforcement magazines and journals that tended to stack up on her bookshelf without her ever having time enough to glance at them. At three o'clock her cell phone rang.

"I'm ready to go home," Jenny announced.

"How was it?"

"Great," Jenny said. "We made almost two hundred dollars, over twice as much as we made last year."

It was nearing four when they turned off High Lonesome Road and onto the rough dirt track that led to the house. As usual, the three dogs came out to the road to greet them and race them into the yard. The only problem was, when Joanna arrived at the house, someone else was already there. A huge Itasca motor home towing a Geo Tracker with Illinois plates was parked in the driveway, blocking access to Joanna's garage.

The door opened and Joanna's mother-in-law, Margaret Dixon, bounded down the steps, waving enthusiastically.

"Oh, no!" Jenny managed.

Joanna rolled down her window. "Those god-awful dogs of yours wouldn't let us out, but now that you're here, I'm sure it's all right. They won't bite, will they?"

"No," Joanna said. "They won't. What are you doing here?"

"What do you think?" Margaret returned. "You don't think Donald and I would miss the arrival of our very first grandchild, do you? I mean, better late than never."

"Did Butch know you were coming?" Joanna asked.

"Of course not. It's a surprise."

It's a surprise, all right, Joanna thought.

"Where is he, by the way?" Margaret Dixon continued. "Him being a house husband and all, I thought for sure he'd be here."

"He's in El Paso at a conference," Joanna said stiffly.

And I'll be damned if I'll call him and ask him to come home early!

CHAPTER 5

Dealing with Margaret and Donald Dixon made for a very long evening. Don Dixon wasn't all that bad. Margaret, though, was something else.

Prior to meeting Butch's mother, Joanna had often wondered why Butch found her own pill of a mother, Eleanor, so easy to tolerate. Unlike Joanna, Butch was always able to shrug off Eleanor's sometimes mean-spirited comments and biting criticism with an air of bemused indifference. It turned out he had been inoculated by a lifetime's worth of dealing with his own mother, who made Eleanor's pointed comments seem like nuanced suggestions made by a career diplomat.

In other words, Margaret Leona Dixon was a ring-tailed bitch. Her sole purpose in life seemed to be cutting everyone else down to size, starting with but not limited to the shortcomings of her own son. Butch's geographical cure to his mother's perpetually negative attitude had been to migrate from Chicago to Arizona, and he had done so without looking back. He hadn't seen his parents in years when they had unexpectedly shown up in the days prior to Joanna and Butch's wedding.

Now they were back. Without Butch there to run interference, they were back in spades. The RV park down by the country club was already filled to the brim with migrating snowbirds, so the Dixons' immense motor home was now parked next to Butch's garage, with a long orange extension cord providing power. Joanna's heart sank at the possibility that they were settling in for the duration.

For that Saturday evening, the Dixons' sole saving grace was that they both liked Mexican food. Chico's Taco Stand, south of Bisbee's Don Luis neighborhood, wasn't long on atmosphere. Its recycled fifties vintage red vinyl booths and serve-yourself counter-based food service didn't measure up to Margaret's high-end expectations, but the food was unarguably good. Even good food, however, wasn't enough to lessen the venom in Margaret's running commentary.

"With the baby due in the next few days," she said, toying with her paper plate loaded with peppery carne asada, "I simply can't imagine why Butch would run off to El Paso like this. It makes no sense. It's inexcusable."

"His publisher wanted him to go," Joanna said patiently. "And so did I. It's an honor to be invited to appear on a conference panel before your book is even released."

"Honor or not, it's irresponsible for him to leave you alone like this, especially in your condition. Besides, I don't see why it's such a big deal," Margaret replied. "His book is only a mystery, isn't it? After all, it's not as though it's a real book."

"It is too a real book," Jenny objected. "I've seen the cover and everything."

"Well, of course it would have a cover," Margaret conceded.

"All books have covers. But I belong to two book clubs—one in Chicago in the summer and one in Hot Springs, Arkansas, in the winter, and we don't read mysteries. Ever. They're just too . . . too . . ."

Fun? Joanna thought.

"Too light," Margaret finished at last. "Not enough literary merit. I'm sure you know what I mean."

"Yes," Joanna agreed with a pained smile on her face. "I know just what you mean."

"But of course," Margaret added, "if you're going to make money, I suppose you have to write the kind of thing that appeals to the unwashed masses." Then, without the slightest pause, she turned her full attention on Jenny. "So you're in what now, sixth grade?"

"Eighth," Jenny answered.

"And are you still as horse-crazy as you used to be, or have you outgrown that nonsense? Being a tomboy is usually just a stage, you know. Most girls, unless they're odd or lesbians or something, do outgrow it sooner or later."

Not waiting for Jenny to reply, Joanna charged to her daughter's defense. "Jenny's a fine young horsewoman, an exceptional horsewoman! She's already participated in several rodeos. As a matter of fact, we're already looking into the possibility of her applying for a rodeo scholarship. Several universities offer them."

It was Margaret's turn to look pained. "A rodeo scholarship for girls?" she asked. "I've never heard of such a thing. Only schools out here in the Wild West would do that. None of the schools in Chicago gives out rodeo scholarships."

At that juncture, Joanna's cell phone rang and the caller ID told her Jaime Carbajal was on the phone. Reluctant as she was to leave Jenny to face down Margaret Dixon on her own, Joanna excused herself and went outside to take the call.

"What have you got?" she asked.

"A big fat nothing," Jaime returned. "You're probably right about her, Sheriff Brady. Anna Marie doesn't look like our doer. We did some checking with her neighbors. None of them has a bad word to say about her. She doesn't get out much—still has her own car but needs someone to drive it for her. No one matching Bradley Evans's description has been seen on or even near Short Street. We know now that our victim drove a red Ford F-100 pickup truck, an old beater with a camper shell on it that he bought from Junque for Jesus. No one admitted to seeing a vehicle like that anywhere near Short Street, either. And, like Ted Chapman told us, it wasn't left at Evans's apartment in Douglas, either."

It was gratifying for Joanna to hear that her initial impression of Anna Marie Crystal seemed to have been validated by her investigators. Learning to trust that kind of gut instinct was an integral part of being a good detective. And in tight situations, well-honed gut instinct was sometimes the only thing that made the difference between life and death.

"You've issued an APB on the vehicle?" she asked.

"Yes, ma'am."

"And you've been through Evans's place?"

"Yes," Jaime replied. "That's where we spent most of the day. Evans's landlady was real coy about not letting anyone into his place without our having a valid search warrant in hand."

"And?"

"Believe me," Jaime returned, "it's not a crime scene. Nothing out of place. No sign of a struggle. The place was locked when we arrived and it was clean as a whistle. Dishes were all washed and put away. Dirty clothes were in a hamper. Everything else was either hung up or folded. A well-thumbed Bible was in the middle of the kitchen table. It reminded me of a room in a monastery."

"Did he have a computer?" Joanna asked.

"Nope. Evans was evidently a low-tech kind of guy. Just to cover the bases, I've made arrangements for Casey Ledford to come down here tomorrow and dust for prints, but I'm guessing the only prints we're going to find will belong to Bradley Evans himself."

"Did he have a girlfriend?" Joanna asked.

"We checked with the neighbors and the landlady on that. If he did have a girl pal, he was mighty cagey about it because nobody mentioned seeing a woman coming or going. And there's nothing in the apartment that indicates that a woman has ever even visited the place—the bed in the bedroom is definitely a single."

"Anything else?" Joanna asked when Jaime's voice trailed away.

"That's about it."

"It sounds like both you and Ernie have put in a long day," Joanna said. "Go home. We'll take another look at things in the morning."

"Okay," Jaime said.

Joanna ended the call and was putting her phone away when it rang again. "Joey?" Butch asked. His voice was alive with excitement. "I'm so glad I caught you. You'll never guess what's happened."

"What?"

"Carole Ann entered the manuscript for *Serve and Protect* into a contest for new writers, and I won. It's called a New Voice

Award and it comes with a check for ten thousand dollars. Can you believe it? Some well-heeled charitable foundation from back east hands out five of them a year, and they're planning on giving me mine tonight at the banquet. Carole Ann knew about it in advance, but it was supposed to be a surprise. A few minutes ago, at the cocktail party, I told her I had decided to skip the banquet and come home. That's when she told me. Is this exciting or what?"

"It is exciting, all right," Joanna agreed, trying unsuccessfully to match her enthusiasm with his. "Amazing and wonderful!"

Through the long, sometimes stormy months of Joanna's pregnancy, Butch Dixon had become extremely adept at deciphering his wife's hormone-driven mood swings.

"What's wrong?" he asked now. "You sound funny. Are you all right? Is the baby coming?"

"The baby is not coming," Joanna said. "It's still too soon. It's just that . . ."

"It's just that what?"

"Your parents came instead."

There was a long pause before Butch exclaimed, "You're kidding!"

"No, I'm not. They were waiting at the house when Jenny and I came home from the car wash this afternoon. We're having dinner at Chico's. Your parents are inside with Jenny. I'm out here in the parking lot. The RV park down in Naco is full, so they've parked their motor home at our place." She paused before adding, "Did you know they were coming?"

"I had no idea whatsoever!" Butch sounded genuinely exasperated. "I mean, I told them when we thought the baby was due, but I never expected they'd show up like this. If you want me to, I'll come straight home and send them packing."

"No. That's not necessary. We'll get through it somehow."

"But, Joanna . . ."

"As your mother said, it's her first grandchild." Joanna was careful not to add the "better late than never part," to say nothing about Margaret's snide "real book" comment. "And they must be terribly proud for them to have driven all this way," she added.

"With them under hand and foot, we'll go nuts," Butch said bleakly.

"No, we won't," Joanna returned determinedly. "We'll be fine."

"But I should come home tonight," Butch said. "As soon as they give me the award—"

"No, you stay right where you are and enjoy it," Joanna told him. "I'm sorry I won't be there to see it. Be sure to have Carole Ann take lots of pictures."

"Are you positive?"

"Like I told you earlier, I'm a big girl, and I'm the sheriff, too. If I can handle crooks or a live-ammo shoot-out, I should be able to handle your mother."

"A shoot-out might be less dangerous," Butch said.

Joanna laughed. "I'd better go back inside and rescue Jenny. I've been gone a long time, and she probably needs it. But have fun, Butch. You've earned it."

Returning to their booth, Joanna discovered that Jenny was gamely carrying on, regaling the Dixons with stories about Lucky and the trials and tribulations of training a deaf dog.

"I can't imagine why anyone would want to keep a dog like that," Margaret said. "If it were up to me, I'd have put the poor thing down. When animals are damaged like that, it's not fair to keep them alive."

Jenny may not have inherited her mother's red hair, but

Joanna's hot temper was very much in evidence in the scathing look Jenny leveled at her newest grandmother.

"He's not damaged, and he's not a poor thing, either," Jenny objected hotly. "Lucky's a happy dog, and he's also very smart. He can do all the things the other dogs do, but we use hand signals with him instead of words."

Don, realizing that his wife had spoken out of turn, tried to smooth things over. "Are there trainers who specialize in working with deaf dogs?" he asked. "Did you have to send Lucky someplace special?"

"I'm training him at home," Jenny declared. Sitting with her arms crossed, it was clear she wasn't at all pacified. "Butch and I found a whole lot of information on the Internet and in some books, too. It just takes patience."

And a little common sense, Joanna thought.

"Butch just called," she said. On her way into the restaurant she had decided to let Butch give his parents the news about his unexpected award. Now, though, needing an icebreaker, she changed her mind and told them herself. "He's receiving a new writer's prize tonight, based on the quality of his manuscript for *Serve and Protect.* A prize and a check for ten thousand dollars. That's why his editor was so adamant about him going to El Paso. She knew the award would be announced at the banquet tonight, and she wanted him there to receive it."

"Great!" Don Dixon boomed. "That's terrific news. Butch must be ecstatic."

Margaret's enthusiasm was notable for its absence. "Ten thousand dollars for a murder mystery?" she asked. "Imagine that!"

Her comment left Joanna grateful that Butch hadn't been the one broaching the subject after all. Jenny, on the other hand, bounded out of the booth and began clearing the table.

"She's a great little helper, isn't she," Margaret said. Fortunately, she didn't see the silent roll of the eyes Jenny gave her mother on her way to the trash containers by the door.

"Yes," Joanna agreed. "She certainly is."

Back at High Lonesome Ranch, Jenny was quick to take Tigger and Lucky and retreat to her own bedroom, leaving Joanna to deal with the unexpected company as best she could. Margaret was full of unsolicited advice. On childbirth? Natural with no unnecessary anesthetics. Child rearing? Definitely in the corner of "Spare the rod; spoil the child." Working mothers? A bad idea. Where did Joanna think this whole new generation of juvenile delinquents came from? Or ill-behaved household pets? Letting them have the run of the whole house was another bad idea—downright unsanitary and dangerous. How about all the children who ended up being mauled by family pets? Everything in Margaret's litany of modern evils was laid at the door of working mothers. For Joanna it was all amazingly familiar. At times she wondered if Eleanor Lathrop Winfield and Margaret Dixon hadn't been created with the DNA equivalent of a rubber stamp.

It was a relief when, at eight-thirty, the telephone rang. More than half hoping it was something that would necessitate her driving to a crime scene, Joanna lumbered her unbalanced center of gravity off the couch and went to answer.

"Sheriff Brady?" Ernie Carpenter asked.

"Yes."

"You weren't asleep or anything, were you?"

I wish, Joanna thought. "No," she said. "Not at all. What's up?"

"I know it's late," Ernie said, "but I was wondering if I could stop by for a while to talk to you."

For the first time since Joanna had known him, Ernie Carpenter sounded oddly ill at ease and uncertain.

"If you'd like me to meet you at the department . . ." she began.

"No," he said. "This is personal. If you don't mind, I'd really rather stop by the house. I'm in town, so it'll be a few minutes before I get there, but it won't take long."

"Sure," Joanna said. "That'll be fine."

She went back to the couch and found both Margaret and Don Dixon looking at her expectantly. Ernie had explicitly arranged to meet with Joanna away from the department. Obviously whatever he had to say he wanted said in private and without Butch's parents hanging on his every word.

"It's one of my detectives," she explained. "He's coming by to brief me on the developments in one of our homicide cases."

Fortunately Don Dixon took the hint. "Come on, Margaret," he said, taking his wife's hand and helping her to her feet. "We'd better turn in then. If Joanna has work to do, we certainly don't want to be in the way."

"You're sure you'll be warm enough out there?" Joanna asked. She had invited Margaret and Don to stay in the guest room and had been more than slightly relieved when they had turned her down.

"Oh, heavens, yes," Margaret replied. "The RV is just as cozy as it can be."

"Good night, then," Joanna said. "Sleep well."

Lady, who had made herself scarce with a strange man in the house, emerged from the bedroom and stayed next to Joanna on the couch. As soon as Ernie Carpenter turned up at the front door, Lady bailed again.

"Come in," Joanna said, ushering Ernie into the living room. "Can I get you something?"

"I'm not working at the moment," he said. "You wouldn't happen to have a beer, would you?"

Joanna went out into the kitchen and returned with Butch's last bottle of Michelob Ultra. "What's up, Ernie?" she asked, handing it to him. "You look upset. Is something the matter? Is it Rose?"

Ernie took a long sip of beer. "No," he said, lowering the bottle. "It's me."

"What about you?"

"It's not something that's easy to talk about," he answered. "I mean, you being a woman and all . . ."

"Ernie," she urged. "Tell me."

He took another sip of beer. "You may have noticed I've missed some shifts lately."

"Yes," she said. "Frank and I had noticed."

"Well," Ernie said, "it's because I've been seeing a doctor—up in Tucson. Rosie told me I needed to tell you about it, so you'd know what's been going on."

"What is going on?"

He sighed. "When I went in for my annual physical, Dr. Lee said my PSA was way out of whack. He sent me to a specialist in Tucson."

"PSA?" Joanna asked, feeling stupid.

"Prostate-specific antigen," Ernie explained. "It means I've got prostate cancer."

For a moment, Joanna could think of nothing to say. Finally she said, "Ernie, I'm so sorry."

He nodded. "Me, too. Believe me. I got the news a couple of weeks ago. For a while I just couldn't process it. Couldn't think how it was possible for me to have cancer. I've always been healthy as a horse. And then, just like that, you're sitting there in the doctor's office, he says the magic words and wham-o, all of a sudden you're a cancer patient. It's like falling off a cliff."

Joanna thought about finding Andy lying wounded along High Lonesome Road. Yes, it had felt just like that. One minute she had been mad as hell at him for being late for their tenth-anniversary dinner, and the next minute she was crouched in the dirt, praying for help, and applying pressure to his gunshot wound in hopes of keeping Andy from bleeding to death. It had been exactly like falling off a cliff.

"What's the prognosis?" she asked.

Ernie shrugged. "You know how doctors are. They think they caught it early and all that happy baloney, but who knows? Since nobody ever had me do a PSA test before, they're not really sure how long it's been around."

"What about treatment?" she asked.

"That's the thing. We've been trying to find out what all the options are. Surgery, radiation, whatever. Rosie and I have been meeting with people—doctors and patients both—trying to fig-ure out what's the best thing to do. Supposedly I'm a good candi-date for seeds . . ."

"Seeds?"

"Radiation seeds. Then there's some hotshot new treatment called cryo-something, where they freeze things, but my oncolo-gist says that's still out there in the experimental stages. He thinks if the tumor has spread at all, the radioactive seeding is probably the best course of treatment. So that's the way we're going to go—with the seeds. I'll probably end up being some glow-in-the-dark freak. Maybe my dick will end up qualifying as an alternate light source."

Dark humor at crime scenes was part of how homicide cops coped. Joanna recognized his glow-in-the-dark comment as part and parcel of that—a grim attempt to lighten the mood. But she made no attempt to reply in kind.

"How long does the seed treatment take?" she asked.

"They say it's not that big a deal. Supposedly it's a minor procedure. If there aren't any complications, I'll most likely be back at work after just a couple of days. My recovery would be a lot longer if we opted for the surgery."

"Whatever course of treatment you choose," Joanna said, "it has to be the one that's right for you. Don't choose one over another because of how much time you'll need off."

"Thanks, boss," he said.

"And thank you for telling me," Joanna said, meaning it. "Have you told anyone else?"

Ernie shook his head. "Haven't," he said. "Not even Jaime, and I should have. And I need to tell Frank—or you can—because he should know. But beyond that I'd like to keep a low profile because I don't want to make a big thing of it. People are funny. As soon as they hear somebody's got cancer, they sort of write 'em off. I'm not ready to be written off. Still, whatever happens, I don't want to leave you shorthanded."

"Don't worry, Ernie," she said. "We'll manage. The important thing is for you to do whatever you need to do in order to get better. How's Rose?"

Ernie Carpenter used the back of one meaty paw to swipe at something in the corner of his eye. "She's a brick," he said, his voice breaking. "I mean, she's always been there for me, but now—" He broke off, shaking his head, and took another sip of the beer.

"Anyway," he continued after a short pause, "all this sort of got my attention. Made me realize that I'm not gonna live forever. Last night Rose and I went to a meeting in Tucson. It's a support group for people who've had prostate cancer. That's why I wasn't home when you called about going to Sierra Vista. So today I got to thinking. What happens if I don't make it? What happens if the seeds don't work? Jaime and I have been working all right together. We're a good team, but considering what all's been happening around here lately, you're going to need another couple of detectives. Have you thought about that?"

"Some," Joanna said. "Why? Do you have a suggestion?"

Expecting him to tick off a couple of the male deputies, Joanna was surprised by his answer. "Debbie," Ernie replied with conviction. "Debra Howell. I know she's fairly new and all that. She's also a single mom, which would make the extra hours tough at times, but I think she'd be able to figure out a way to make it work. You of all people would know everything there is about that juggling routine, but Debbie's got a good head on her shoulders, and she's a real team player. That's what this business takes—a team effort."

"She'd have to pass the exam," Joanna said.

"That won't be a problem," Ernie said. "She's been studying. I've actually been giving her some coaching on the side."

Joanna laughed. "After all the grief you and Richard Voland gave me when I first showed up, now you're tutoring a female deputy to help prepare her for the detective exam?"

The smallest hint of a smile tweaked the turned-down corners of Ernie Carpenter's mouth. "Well," he said, "after all, you turned out all right, didn't you?"

"You think she can pass?"

"Absolutely. And not just barely, either. She'll ace the damned thing."

"When are you planning on going in for treatment?" Joanna asked.

"As soon as they can get me scheduled, probably sometime late next week."

"And you're thinking we should bring Debbie in on a provisional basis to help out with what we have going right now?"

Ernie nodded.

"Anyone else you think we should look at?" Joanna asked.

"My next choice would have been Dave Hollicker, but you already tapped him for crime scene investigation, so he's on the team anyway. Beyond Debbie, though, with so many of the experienced deputies off in the reserves, pickings around the department are a little thin."

Joanna and Frank Montoya had arrived at much the same conclusion—that pickings were slim. And she had discounted approaching Debbie Howell about the possibility of becoming a detective for exactly the reason Ernie had mentioned—the fact that she was a single mother. Joanna hoped Ernie was too involved in his own difficulties to notice the flush of embarrassment that flooded her face.

"I'll take it under advisement," Joanna said. "But don't say anything to Debbie about it until after Frank and I have a chance to discuss it."

"Right," Ernie said. "I won't breathe a word."

He stood up. "I'd better be going," he said. "It's getting late. I've taken up enough of your time."

At the door, Joanna reached up and gave Ernie a hug. With the baby in the middle, it was an awkward, lumpy gesture, but Ernie seemed to appreciate it.

"Good luck," she whispered.

There was another meaty paw swipe to the eyes. "Thanks, boss," he murmured. "Appreciate it."

After he left, Joanna dimmed the lights and returned to the couch. She sat there for a long time with one hand resting on her extended belly. It was night and almost bedtime, so naturally the little person in her womb was wide awake and raising hell. With Ernie gone, Lady once again emerged from the bedroom and cuddled up into a gray-and-white ball on the couch beside her.

"Did you know you're unsanitary?" Joanna asked, absently stroking the Australian shepherd's long soft coat. In answer Lady rolled her blue eyes in Joanna's direction, thumped her cropped tail, and sighed contentedly.

Half an hour or so later, Joanna got up and waddled off to bed. She was sound asleep when Lucky and Tigger began barking furiously. Getting up, Joanna staggered out of bed in time to see Butch's Subaru drive into the yard and come to a stop next to his parents' RV. Joanna hurried to the door to meet him as he came into the house.

"Congratulations, you big nut," she said, kissing him hello. "Welcome home, but I thought I told you to stay where you were. What time is it?"

"Three," he said. "Three forty-five, to be exact."

"What time did you leave El Paso?" she asked.

"Better you should never know," he said. "I'm taking the Fifth. Suffice it to say, though, there wasn't very much traffic and zero enforcement. I left the banquet as soon as I could. I wasn't about to leave you alone and in my mother's clutches any longer than necessary. How are things?"

"Fine," she said. "Come on. Let's go to bed. You must be beat."

"I am," he agreed. "And I'm very glad to be home."

Once in bed, Joanna curled up next to Butch. Comforted by her husband's radiating warmth, she was soon sound asleep and slept better than she had in months.

On Sunday, Margaret and Don declined to go to church. After fixing them breakfast, Joanna, Jenny, and Butch were more than happy to leave their guests on their own for a couple of hours. That morning, Butch had put out one of their home-grown, freezer-wrapped beef roasts to thaw. After church they stopped by Safeway to pick up fresh vegetables and salad makings. Then they called George and Eleanor Winfield along with Jim Bob and Eva Lou Brady and arranged for an impromptu late-afternoon dinner party. Joanna hadn't intended to be doing non-stop entertaining the last weekend before the baby's official due date, but there didn't seem to be any choice. Besides, there was always the dim hope that adding more people to the mix might help dilute Margaret's ever-toxic presence.

Butch was putting the finishing touches on a roast beef dinner when Frank Montoya called. Briefly Joanna brought him up-to-date on Ernie's revelations. "You want me to talk to Debbie about the prospect of her becoming a detective?" Frank asked.

"No," Joanna said. "Ask her to see us when she comes on shift tomorrow. We can talk to her together. Anything else going on?"

"Not much," Frank told her. "I had three deputies patrolling that northeast sector last night. Nothing at all turned up in San Simon. As far as anyone could tell, there was no unusual traffic coming and going from Roostercomb Ranch. The whole area was dead as can be. With that in mind, I'm thinking we should probably drop the increased surveillance. After all, Patrol is stretched so thin . . ."

"No," Joanna said. "Leave it as is again tonight. Maybe Sunday is when the O'Dwyers do their thing."

"Maybe," Frank agreed grudgingly. "But I doubt it. I can't help wondering if Jeannine has her facts straight."

"Let's give it another day," Joanna said. "And pray the rest of the county doesn't go haywire in the meantime. That's not too much to ask, is it?"

"We'll see," Frank said ominously. "We'll know more about that come tomorrow, when the reports are in and it's time for the morning briefing."

CHAPTER 6

On her way out the door on Monday morning, Joanna was surprised to find a stack of boxes sitting against the wall of her garage. The stack created a barrier that made it impossible for Jenny to climb into the passenger's seat of the Crown Victoria without having to go all the way around the back of the vehicle.

"What's all this?" Joanna asked Butch, who had just come in from feeding the animals.

"I have no idea," he replied. "George dropped them off yesterday afternoon when he and your mother came to dinner. According to him, they're getting ready for a big churchwide garage sale. Eleanor sent over some boxes of things she thought you should have."

"Great," Joanna muttered. "How like her. That way she doesn't have to get rid of it and we do."

"Want me to attempt a first sort?" Butch asked.

"Good morning," Margaret Dixon called.

The rammed-earth house Butch had designed and helped build consisted of two wings, each with its own separate garage. Margaret, who had entered through Butch's garage, had wandered through the whole house before finding them.

"Anybody home?" she asked. "I sure hope there's coffee. I could have made it out in the RV, but I decided to come inside instead. Have you already eaten?"

Joanna nodded. "Jenny and I have," she said. "I'm on my way to work. I promised to drop her off at school on the way."

Grumbling under his breath, Butch walked Joanna to her car. "I wish I was going to work," he said.

Joanna smiled sympathetically. "Don't bother doing any sorting," she said, giving Butch a good-bye peck on the cheek. "I think you're going to have your hands full as it is."

"So do I," he agreed.

"Some people are a real pain," Jenny said, settling into the corner of the Crown Victoria.

"Margaret Dixon isn't a very happy person," Joanna said.

"But why does she think we should have put Lucky to sleep?"

Joanna sighed. "I have no idea," she said.

"How long are they gonna stay?"

"Probably until the baby is born," Joanna said.

"Well, could you please hurry up and have it then?" Jenny demanded. "I want them to take their RV and go home."

"Believe me," Joanna assured her. "I'll do my best."

At the morning briefing, Frank Montoya wasn't any happier than Jenny had been, but his ill humor had nothing to do with an irksome stepgrandmother.

"Last night was the wrong time to have three cars in San Simon, especially since our people didn't spot anything out of line," he grumbled. "In the meantime, Border Patrol came up with at least a hundred and fifty UDAs who were all on foot and making a run for it east of Douglas. They called us for backup. Unfortunately, we didn't have anybody to send."

Joanna shook her head. The unending stream of undocumented aliens spilling across the international border was one of Arizona's—and especially Cochise County's—most intractable law enforcement problems. Each year at least half a million UDAs were being apprehended just in the Border Patrol's Tucson sector. Of that number, at least 25,000 a month were picked up after crossing into the United States along Cochise County's eighty-mile-long border with Mexico. Border Patrol employment numbers were way up, but there were never enough officers to stem the tide.

"How many did they catch?"

"Most," Frank said. "But there's no way to know how many got away."

"With those kinds of numbers, an additional three deputies probably wouldn't have made much difference," Joanna said.

"It would have helped," Frank replied.

But Joanna could see her chief deputy had a point. "It stands to reason that the O'Dwyers would be operating on weekends rather than during the week," she said.

"So I can pull the extra patrols for tonight?"

"Yes," Joanna said. "We'll revisit this later in the week. Now, what about the Bradley Evans homicide? Have we made any progress on that?"

Frank shuffled through the briefing papers. "Not much. Casey Ledford is down in Douglas."

"Dusting Evans's apartment?" Joanna asked.

Frank nodded.

"Still no sign of the vehicle?"

"Nope," Frank answered. "If I was the perpetrator, I'd probably take it up to Tucson and leave it parked in plain sight somewhere where no one is going to pay any attention."

"You've alerted Tucson PD to be on the lookout?" Joanna asked.

"You bet."

There was a knock on the conference-room door, and Deputy Debra Howell entered the room. "Sarge told me you wanted to see me?" she asked.

"That's right," Joanna said. "Have a seat."

"Is something wrong?" Debbie asked.

"Nothing at all," Joanna assured her. "But we're thinking about making some changes. I understand you've been studying for the detective exam?"

"Yes," Debbie said. "I have."

"Chief Deputy Montoya and I were wondering if you'd like to spend some time working as a detective for the next week or two with the understanding that the promotion is provisional until such time as you take and pass the exam?"

Debbie Howell flushed with apparent pleasure. "That would be great," she said. "But how come? What's going on?"

Joanna had hoped that Ernie might have mentioned his medical situation to his protégée, but clearly that wasn't the case. Since he hadn't confided in Debbie, Joanna didn't tell her, either.

"It won't come as any surprise that we're chronically shorthanded, and we need to add some depth to our investigation team. We're dealing with an unsolved homicide at a time when one of our homicide guys may be having to take some time off. You're the one we want to tap—if you're interested, that is. But homicide investigators don't punch time clocks the same way deputies do, Debbie," Joanna warned. "They work long hours and can be called out anytime, day or night. Will that be a problem?"

"Because of Bennie, you mean?" Debbie asked.

Benjamin was Debbie's five-year-old son. Joanna nodded, and Debbie grinned.

"If you'd asked me that question two weeks ago, it would have been a big problem," she admitted. "But last week my sister's jerk of a husband decided he didn't want to be married anymore. He took off and left Katy and the two kids high and dry. Rather than staying in Phoenix and paying rent she couldn't afford, Katy decided to come back home to Bisbee. She and the kids are staying with me right now until the dust settles and until she can find a job. In other words, working late won't be a problem as long as Bennie's aunt and cousins are here. When do you want me to start?"

"Today," Joanna said. "You'll be working plainclothes, so you'd better go home and change. Then track down Jaime and Ernie so they can bring you up to speed."

Joanna and Frank went on with their meeting. The last of the briefing papers was a single-page report from Animal Control. Eighteen dogs, twenty-one cats, and an eight-foot-long python were currently in the Cochise County Pound.

"A python?" Joanna repeated. "Where did that come from?"

"Sunrise Apartments in Sierra Vista," Frank replied. "A cleaning crew went into a recently vacated apartment and found the snake hiding in a closet. Sierra Vista Animal Control refused to have anything to do with it. They called us, so Jeannine Phillips and Manny Ruiz went out and collected it."

"Great," Joanna said. "So now we're stuck with a python?"

"For the time being," Frank said. "They're trying to locate the former owner. They're also trying to find someplace that will take him in."

"I know about Greyhound Rescue and Golden Retriever Rescue," Joanna said. "There's even that wiener-dog rescue up in Phoenix, but I've never heard of Python Rescue, have you?"

"Actually, I have," Frank said. "I was checking on the Internet just before I came in here. There are several python rescues listed. The problem is, there are more pythons looking to be rescued than there are people willing to take them in, so I'm guessing we could be stuck with this guy for a very long time."

"What do pythons eat?" Joanna asked.

"Mice, I think," Frank answered. "Live mice."

Joanna groaned. "Great. That's just what I wanted to hear."

After another tap on the conference-room door, Kristin Gregovich entered the room. "What's up?" Joanna asked.

"Sergeant Winston Brown from Huachuca City PD is on the line," Kristin said. She picked up the conference-room phone and handed it to Joanna. "They think they've found our missing pickup truck."

"This is Sheriff Brady," Joanna said. "You think you've found Bradley Evans's missing vehicle? How and where?"

"Where is right on Huachuca City's main drag," Winnie Brown told her. "The last couple of years we've been making a concerted effort to get rid of all our local eyesores. Periodically we go around and ticket all the 'For Sale by Owner' cars that are left on vacant lots inside the city limits. We had your APB for a red F-100. Since this one was gray—primer gray—nobody really gave it a second thought. But the bed of the truck is red, and when our officer ran the plates, they belonged to a '96 VW Passat. That's when we knew we had a problem. We tried calling the number listed on the For Sale sign on the dash. It's not a valid number. No surprises there."

"Where is it again?" Joanna asked.

"Corner of Highway 90 and Pershing," he said.

"Has anyone been inside it?"

"It's locked," Winnie Brown told her. "If you want me to, I'm sure someone could get inside . . ."

"No," Joanna said quickly. "It may be a crime scene. No one is to handle it inside or out. Understand?"

"Gotcha," Winnie Brown said.

"As soon as I can make arrangements," Joanna continued, "I'll dispatch a tow truck to retrieve it."

"Okay," Brown responded. "I'll tell the officers on the scene that the sheriff is sending someone to pick it up."

Joanna looked at Frank, who was already in motion, gathering his papers and heading for the door. "I'll make arrangements for the tow," he said. "I'll also track down Jaime and Ernie and let them know. Maybe Debbie can meet up with them out in Huachuca City and hit the ground running."

With a crew of perfectly competent people collecting the homicide victim's vehicle, there was no need for Joanna to go traipsing off to Huachuca City to bird-dog the process. Instead, she went into her office, where she found the morning's mail stacked high on her desk. Just looking at it made her sigh. According to the latest figures from the FBI, national violent crime figures were down. Paperwork, on the other hand, seemed to be way, way up.

Twenty minutes later, when her phone rang, a truculent Jeannine Phillips was on the phone. "Well?" she said. "What did they find?"

"In San Simon?" Joanna asked. "Nothing. We had three cars

stationed in and around there both Saturday and Sunday nights. There wasn't a sign of trouble or suspicious activities. Unfortunately, with everything else that's going on, we're just not going to be able to maintain that level of surveillance."

"So that's it, then?" Jeannine responded curtly. "We're just going to give the O'Dwyers a pass and let things go until the next dead dog shows up?"

"The next one?" Joanna said. "Did the one at the vet's office die, then?"

"No," Jeannine replied. "No, thanks to Mil—to Dr. Ross, he's going to pull through."

"And how about Monty Python?" Joanna joked.

"He's all right, too," Jeannine said. "Manny and I had to rig up special accommodations for him. We lined the inside of one of the kennels with Plexiglas and then hooked up lights so the damned thing wouldn't be too cold. Since the owner went off and left both the snake and no forwarding address, I'm working on locating a snake rescue organization of some kind."

So's Frank Montoya, Joanna thought.

"The problem is, they're mostly out of state. I'm concerned about transportation issues."

"Keep looking," Joanna advised.

All in all, it was a quiet day at the Cochise County Justice Center. Food deliveries had resumed and everything in the jail seemed to be running smoothly for a change. At noon she met Butch and his parents at Daisy's Café for lunch. Margaret's attitude toward Junior Dowdle was not unlike her attitude toward Lucky. Maybe he didn't need to be put out of his misery, but people had no business letting him out in public like that. Didn't they know that seeing him might upset some of their customers?

Toying with her food, Joanna wondered how the Dixons would react if this grandchild of theirs—the rowdy baby on the verge of entering the world—turned out to be less than perfect. Nothing in Joanna's medical chart had indicated anything of the kind, but still . . . What if she ended up with a baby who suffered from some kind of birth defect? Would Margaret and Don Dixon reject the child and think that it should be put out of its misery?

"What's wrong?" Butch asked as he walked Joanna to her car after lunch. "You look upset."

"It's nothing," she said.

"I know my mother's a handful," he said. "The way she talked about Junior! I wanted to wring her neck. Try not to let her get you down."

"I won't if you won't," Joanna returned.

"That's a lot harder," Butch said.

Joanna arrived back at the department in time to see Bradley Evans's freshly primer-coated pickup truck deposited inside the garage at the near end of the impound yard. When Casey Ledford, Cochise County's latent fingerprint expert, emerged from her lab to begin dusting the outside of the truck, Joanna walked over to join her. First she looked in through the window and was disappointed to see nothing out of line. They might have found Bradley Evans's truck, but the interior of that was no more a crime scene than his apartment had been.

"You've already collected prints from down in Douglas?" Joanna asked.

Casey nodded. "And it was just like Ernie and Jaime predicted it would be. I found lots of the victim's prints and a few that belong to his landlady. If there's been anyone else in Mr. Evans's apartment at some time in the distant past, it's long enough ago that they left no trace or else they wore gloves."

"What's the program here?" Joanna inquired.

"I talked it over with the Double Cs," Casey said. "The game plan is for me to go over the outside first, but I don't think that's going to be particularly helpful."

"Why not?"

"The truck has been sitting on that vacant lot for a number of days. Some of the prints may belong to whoever came by and looked at the truck thinking they might want to buy it. It could take a very long time, if it's even possible, to eliminate the ones that aren't connected to the crime. Once I finish on the outside, Dave Hollicker will pop the lock. Then he and I will go through the interior together, dusting for prints and collecting whatever trace evidence there is to be found."

"With any luck there should be some," Joanna said. "I'm pretty certain that the last person who drove this vehicle wasn't Bradley Evans."

Back in her office, Joanna tried to focus on the paperwork littering her desk, but she couldn't shake the feeling of malaise that had crept over her during lunch. Finally, late in the afternoon, she called her best friend and pastor, the Reverend Marianne Maculyea.

"Are you okay?" Marianne asked. "You sound a little down."

Joanna and Marianne's friendship went all the way back to seventh grade. There was very little they didn't know about each other's lives.

"Prenatal blues, I guess," Joanna admitted.

"That's to be expected," Marianne said. "I was a complete fruitcake the week before Jeffy was born. I almost drove Jeff crazy. What's going on?"

"Jeffy was perfect," Joanna said. "He is perfect. But what if he hadn't been?"

Marianne took a deep breath. "Has Dr. Lee said there might be a problem? Did something show up in an ultrasound?"

"No. It's not that. It's just that . . ."

"It's just what?"

"Butch's parents are here," Joanna said.

"You mentioned that yesterday at church," Marianne said. "And it explains a lot. Margaret Dixon won't win any Ms. Congeniality awards. What's she up to now?"

"She told Jenny that Lucky should have been put out of his misery, and at lunch, you should have seen her with Junior. What if the baby's born with some serious problem?"

Marianne Maculyea had more than a little experience in that regard. After years of trying to conceive, she and her husband, Jeff Daniels, had adopted twin baby girls from China—Esther Elaine and Ruth Rachel. Ruth was now a lively first grader, but Esther had been born with a congenital heart defect and had died within days of receiving a heart transplant.

"You cope," Marianne said simply. "You do the best you can, and you cope. You ignore the people who choose not to be in your corner, including your bitchy mother-in-law."

Her outspoken comment made Joanna laugh. "But you have no strong opinions about Margaret Dixon."

"Some people *require* strong opinions," Marianne returned. "When do you see Dr. Lee again?"

"Tomorrow," Joanna said. "That's my last scheduled prenatal exam."

"He's the one you should talk to about this," Marianne advised. "Not me, not Butch, and certainly not Margaret Dixon."

"Will do," Joanna said. She hung up the phone feeling infinitely better.

Late in the afternoon Joanna went back out to the impound lot, where both Casey Ledford and Dave Hollicker were still hard at work. "Finding anything?" she asked.

"Look at this," Dave said. He held up an evidence bag. Peering through it, Joanna was able to see a single thread.

"What is it?" she asked.

"I found it hung up on the tailgate latch," Dave said. "I won't know until I do my analysis, but I'm guessing it'll be from the tarp I already have in the lab, the one Bradley Evans's body was wrapped in. I noticed there was a tear in it when I did my preliminary exam. But the big thing is the Luminol."

"You got a hit?"

"You bet," Dave said. "Take a look at this." He switched off the overhead light. Peering under the camper shell, Joanna saw several thin lines of bright blue in the bed of the truck.

"Someone made a real effort to clean up the mess, but they didn't do a good enough job in the cracks where the sections join together. Without more tests, I can't say for sure that what we found in those cracks is blood, or if it's human blood or even if it's Bradley Evans's blood. We'll find that out later."

"But you're saying that the back of the truck might actually turn out to be the crime scene?" Joanna asked.

"It's possible," Dave replied. "Or maybe not. It all depends. I didn't find any visible spatter patterns, but it's conceivable the killer managed to wash them away. I think it's likely that the truck was only used for transporting the body."

"Did you find anything else?" Joanna asked.

Dave grinned. "As a matter of fact, we did," he boasted.

"Look at this." He produced another evidence bag. Inside Joanna saw a small yellow-and-black disposable camera with a coating of black fingerprint powder clinging to it.

"This was wedged in under the passenger's side of the seat. There are twenty-four shots per camera. Only sixteen of them have been exposed. Casey lifted plenty of prints. Her preliminary determination is that the prints on the camera belong to the victim."

"Which may mean Bradley Evans is the only person who used it," Joanna theorized.

Dave nodded. "And he stuffed it under the seat in hopes of making sure no one saw either the camera or what it was he was taking pictures of. I talked to Jaime a little while ago. He's still out in Huachuca City trying to find out exactly when the pickup showed up on the lot and who may have put it there. The Double Cs are sending Debbie Howell here to pick up the camera. She's going to take it to that One Hour Photo Shop out in Sierra Vista."

Obviously Debbie Howell was spending her first day in Homicide as Jaime and Ernie's gofer-in-chief.

"Good," Joanna said. "The sooner we see what's on those photos, the better."

Wanting to spell Butch, Joanna left work early that afternoon. When she got home, though, the house was quiet. Butch was seated at the kitchen table with his laptop open in front of him while tantalizing cooking aromas wafted around him.

"Where is everybody?" Joanna asked, kissing the smooth top of his bald head.

"Jenny and the dogs are hiding out in her room, and I don't blame them a bit," Butch said. "If I thought I could get away with it, I'd be there, too. As for my parents? They're out in the RV watching Fox News."

"In the RV?" Joanna asked. "Why not in the living room?"

"Because Dad likes watching on his flat-screen TV and he prefers using his own clicker."

"But what kind of reception do they get?"

"Didn't you notice the satellite TV antenna up on top of their rig? I went out earlier today and watched Dad locate the satellite. And don't think I'm not grateful. It gave me a couple of hours of peace and quiet. God knows I was ready for some of that. Believe it or not, I even managed to get some work done. I couldn't very well work in front of them. Somehow I never picked up on how much my mother despises mysteries. Did you know that about her?"

"She may have mentioned something to that effect," Joanna answered diplomatically. "But that's one person's opinion. Obviously the people who handed over that check have other ideas, and so do I. Now what's for dinner? I'm starved."

Butch patted her bulging belly affectionately. "You're always starved these days," he said. "We're having two of my father's favorites—roasted Cornish game hen and baked acorn squash with a side of coleslaw."

"Do you need any help?"

"No," Butch said, turning back to his computer. "Everything's under control. We'll eat about six-thirty."

"In that case, I think I'll go into the office for a little while. I need to work on my thank-you notes from the baby shower. Did you see all the great stuff we got?"

"It's great stuff, all right," Butch agreed, "but about your office—"

Butch's warning came too late. Joanna was already standing in the middle of the room and staring at the mound of boxes—the same boxes that had been impeding traffic in the garage earlier that morning, which were now piled in front of her built-in bookcases. The blockade made it all but impossible for her to reach the chair behind her desk.

"What are these doing here?" she demanded.

"In case you haven't noticed, my mother is an incredible busybody," Butch said. "When I was growing up, she was forever going through my stuff. I finally started leaving things I didn't want her to see at a friend's house. This morning she was all over me, wondering what was in the boxes. When I told her where the boxes came from, she was hot to trot to go through them. I told her I was sure you'd rather do that yourself. When she insisted that someone in your condition shouldn't be lifting heavy boxes, I finally moved them in here to keep them out of her reach. I put today's mail in here, too, for the same reason."

"You think she'd go through that?" Joanna asked.

"I wouldn't put it past her," Butch replied. "The good thing about your office is that we can always lock the door if need be. Come to think of it, I'll probably lock my computer in here, too, when I'm not using it."

"Poor baby," Joanna said and meant it.

For the next hour Joanna sat at the desk in her now-crowded home office and dutifully wrote thank-you notes exactly as Eleanor would have wanted her daughter to do. It was funny, in a way, to think that both she and Butch had survived being raised by very similar and extremely autocratic mothers. It went a long way to explaining why the two of them got along so well.

Dinner turned out to be more of the same, with Margaret monopolizing every avenue of conversation. Knowing that

Butch had been stuck with his mother all day, Joanna did her best to run interference for him. She was cheerful. She asked focused questions. And she kept Margaret rambling away. With Margaret's having downed a predinner cocktail or two, that wasn't difficult. It wasn't until dessert when Margaret finally managed to get under Joanna's skin.

"I guess I didn't realize your father used to be a sheriff," Margaret said with a smile. "I'm sure Butch must have told me, but it didn't sink in. Is that why you wanted to be involved in law enforcement?"

Joanna wasn't sure where Margaret was going. Joanna had grown accustomed to these kinds of unwelcome questions out on the campaign trail, but she didn't expect them to crop up at her own dining-room table.

"I didn't really want it," Joanna answered warily. "It simply happened."

"Are you saying you were elected to office by accident?" Margaret asked incredulously. "How is that possible? I was under the impression that election campaigns are a lot more complicated than that."

Joanna remembered how, in the painful aftermath of Andy's funeral, she had been asked to run for office in his stead. She had agreed—not because her father had been sheriff once or because Andy had wanted to be, but because it was something she actually wanted to do.

"I wasn't elected to an office," she said. "I was elected to do a job, and it's a job I do willingly every single day."

She would have said more, but the phone rang, and Jenny hurried to answer it. "It's for you, Mom," Jenny said. "Somebody from work."

Taking the phone from her daughter's hand, Joanna returned

to the relative privacy of the far end of the living room before she answered. An excited Debbie Howell was on the phone, calling from Sierra Vista.

"What's up?" Joanna asked.

"I'm looking at the photos," Debbie Howell said breathlessly. "You're not going to believe this."

"What?"

"Bradley Evans was stalking someone."

"Stalking?" Joanna repeated. "Who? And how can you be sure?"

"A woman," Debbie returned. "A dark-haired Anglo woman, a brunette. Looks to be in her late twenties. She's wearing what looks like a wedding ring. There are several pictures of her walking in a mall and several others of her pushing a shopping cart through a parking lot. Two more show her getting into a vehicle—a blue sedan. I can't be sure of the make or model."

"Does the woman know she's being photographed?"

"I doubt it," Debbie returned. "It doesn't look like she does. In fact, I'd say she's totally oblivious."

"Is there any way to identify who she is?" Joanna asked.

"Not that I can tell. There's no visible license plate, if that's what you mean."

"Can you tell where the pictures are taken? I mean, are they from Sierra Vista or maybe somewhere else you recognize? And what about the Double Cs? Have they seen the photos?"

"Not yet. They're coming here to meet me right now to take a look. Ernie wanted me to let you know what's going on."

"Thanks, Debbie," Joanna said. "I appreciate being kept in the loop. So how's your first day been?"

"Terrific, Sheriff Brady. I don't know how much of a help I've been so far, but it's what I've wanted to do for a long time. Thanks for giving me a chance."

Joanna hung up the phone feeling guilty that it had been Ernie Carpenter rather than Sheriff Joanna Brady who had opened the door on Debbie Howell's new opportunity.

And then she thought about Bradley Evans. Was it true that he had been a stalker? That idea certainly didn't square with what Ted Chapman had told her about the man. But now Joanna wondered. If he had been following an unsuspecting young woman around and snapping pictures of her without her knowledge or consent, then perhaps he had been on his way to reverting to the behavior that had put him in prison in the first place.

When Joanna returned to the dining room, the table had been cleared and Jenny was serving dessert—rhubarb pie topped with generous scoops of vanilla ice cream.

Joanna resumed her place, and Margaret looked at her questioningly. Clearly she was dying of curiosity about the phone call, but she couldn't bring herself to come straight out and ask. In that moment, Joanna understood Margaret Dixon perfectly. She was every bit as nosy as Butch had said she was, but a lifetime's worth of dealing with Eleanor—of constantly battling and frustrating her own mother—had left Joanna Brady uniquely prepared to deal with the Margaret Dixons of the world.

"No biggie," Joanna said, sending a casual smile in her mother-in-law's direction. "You know how it is—same old, same old."

CHAPTER 7

When Joanna arrived at the conference room the next morning, her homicide team was already assembled. They were studying a collection of color snapshots scattered across the conference-room table.

"I've already mentioned that Ernie will be taking a few days off at the end of this week and maybe the beginning of the next," Frank told Joanna as people came to order. "I've let everyone know that Debbie's going to be working as a detective for the next little while."

Joanna was relieved that the announcement about Ernie's upcoming absence had already been handled. Nodding, Joanna went straight to the task at hand. "What about the pictures?" she asked.

"I think we'll need several copies of each of these," Frank said. "Enough to go around, and enlargements, too. Eight-by-tens at least. Then we may be able to use Photo Shop to enhance the images so we can figure out where these were taken."

"You're right," Ernie agreed. "We should all have copies, but it isn't going to take some high-tech computer program to see what we need to see." Ernie tapped one of the photos with a thick forefinger. "Look at the background on this one. If those aren't the Huachuca Mountains, I'll eat my hat."

Joanna picked up the photo and studied it herself, looking beyond the woman pushing the grocery cart to the undulating wall of mountains looming behind her.

"I think you're right, Ernie," she agreed. "If I'm not mistaken, we're going to find this was taken in the parking lot of that Fry's grocery store out on Highway 92."

"Do you want me to check on that?" Debbie asked. "I could take copies of a couple of the photos out there. If the woman is a regular customer, one of the clerks or carryout people will recognize her."

If it's not already too late, Joanna worried. *What if Bradley Evans had already done his worst before someone got to him?*

"Good thinking," Joanna said. "We need to know who she is and why Evans was following her around snapping photos."

Joanna glanced around the table, settling on the Double Cs. "Do we have a viable suspect in this case?" she asked.

Ernie shook his head. "Not yet," he said as Jaime Carbajal nodded in agreement.

"All right then," Joanna said. "That brings us back to Evans himself. What do we know about him so far?"

"Evans may have been a loner, but his landlady thought he walked on water," Jaime conceded. "That's why she was so adamant about not letting us into his place without a search warrant. The guy didn't smoke or drink; paid his rent on time; never gave her any trouble; didn't have women spending the night; and helped out occasionally with little jobs around the house. When it comes to renters, it doesn't get any better than that. So either

Evans really was a good guy or else he was really good at creating a screen so people *thought* he was a good guy."

"Which is it?" Joanna asked.

Jaime Carbajal shrugged. "The jury's still out on that," he said. "We need to see if we can track down Bradley's credit-card use and telephone records. Frank will be focusing on that. Credit-card receipts will help us track his movements in the days before he died. So will his phone calls. In the meantime, Ernie and I will spend most of today interviewing people at the prison down in Douglas. We know Ted Chapman's opinions about Bradley Evans. Personally, I'd like to see if there are any dissenting ones. If he had something going with the girl in the pictures, maybe he confided in one or more of the people he was working with at the prison."

Joanna nodded. Thumbing through her stack of paperwork, Joanna settled on one that dealt with Bradley Evans's vehicle. "All right," she said. "Let's talk about his truck for a minute. Were you able to figure out when it showed up on that vacant lot?"

"Not the exact hour and minute," Jaime responded. "But we do know that it was sometime between Friday night and Saturday morning. We talked to the two guys who are selling the vehicles that were parked on either side of Evans's Ford. According to them, the truck definitely wasn't there on Friday. One of them, Rick Gomez, remembers seeing it for the first time around ten on Saturday morning, when he came by to meet up with someone who was interested in buying his Toyota."

"There's a lot more presence technology out there nowadays than there used to be," Joanna said. "We should probably check out traffic security videos from neighboring businesses. One of those might have caught the pickup and / or driver on tape."

"We can try," Jaime said, "but I wouldn't count on it. People use that particular lot for a reason. It's not in the center of town, it's been vacant for years, and it belongs to an absentee landowner. The lot itself has no security cameras at all."

"What about neighbors?" Joanna asked.

Jaime shrugged. "There are a couple of gas stations, but not much else. We can ask to see their tapes, and who knows? Maybe we'll get lucky."

Joanna turned her attention to Casey Ledford. "What's going on with fingerprints?"

"Not much," Casey replied. "All the prints I found inside the truck appear to belong to the victim and nobody else. The big difference is that the prints on the gearshift, steering wheel, and door handle have all been smudged or even obliterated."

"So the last person to drive the vehicle was wearing gloves?" Joanna asked.

Casey nodded. "That would be my guess."

"What about the prints you lifted from the exterior?"

"I didn't find any prints at all inside the camper shell or the bed of the pickup," Casey said. "There were signs that the bed of the pickup had been scrubbed out pretty thoroughly. The total absence of prints there would mean whoever cleaned it was wearing gloves—and probably not because he or she was worried about chapped hands. As for the unidentified prints on the exterior? The ones I found were mostly on the doors and side windows as well as on the liftgate on the camper shell and on the back of the pickup. All of those would be consistent with someone trying to catch a glimpse of the vehicle's interior to see what kind of condition it was in."

"In other words, innocent shoppers," Joanna said.

Casey nodded.

"What about the primer?" Joanna asked. "Do we know if

Bradley Evans himself was in the process of rehabbing the truck?"

"No," Jaime said. "I asked about that, and his landlady said no way. She claims the pickup was still a dingy red when she saw it sometime last week. She couldn't swear exactly when that was, but she says she saw it almost every day. And that makes sense. Evans's apartment is a converted garage out behind the land-lady's house. The carport next to it is carved out of her backyard and is fully visible from her kitchen window."

"So it's possible the primer was added in an effort to keep us from finding it," Joanna concluded.

"Make that *delay* our finding it," Ernie said. "Whoever did it must have known we'd find it eventually."

"How much primer would it take to cover a pickup like that?" Joanna asked.

"To cover it properly, it would have taken several cans more than our guy used," Jaime said. "If you ask me, this was a crappy, half-assed job."

"Because whoever did it was in a hurry?"

"Either that or because they had no idea what they were do-ing," Ernie Carpenter said.

He turned to Debbie. "While you're out in Sierra Vista talk-ing to the Fry's clerks, maybe you should also check with auto-parts stores in the area to find out if anyone purchased a supply of primer this past weekend."

Joanna was gratified that Ernie was making sure Debbie had something useful to do—that she was being treated like a mem-ber of the team. As Debbie jotted a reminder to herself into a small spiral notebook, Joanna turned to her crime scene investi-gator, Dave Hollicker.

"What about the blood samples you found in the bed of the pickup?" she asked. "Any word on those?"

"They're blood, all right," Dave answered. "But we don't know whose. Doc Winfield has already forwarded Evans's blood and tissue samples to the Department of Public Safety Crime Lab in Tucson. They're the ones who can give us a comparison in the shortest amount of time. I can take the new samples up there myself or I can send them. Which do you prefer?"

"By all means take them," Joanna said. "And do it today. Let's get this case moving."

Frank shot a questioning look in her direction. He didn't say anything aloud, but she knew what he was thinking. *Why? What's the big rush? And how much more is it going to add to this year's expenditures?*

With budgetary constraints always in mind, those were entirely legitimate questions, and Joanna didn't have any ready answers—at least not the kind of reasonable answers that her chief deputy wanted or would understand.

In the days before Jenny was born, Joanna remembered throwing herself into a frenzy of housecleaning and nest-building—scrubbing the refrigerator and cleaning and rearranging all her kitchen cupboards. In light of her current position, wanting Bradley Evans's homicide solved prior to the baby's birth was probably a variation on that same theme. Solving a case amounted to a sworn law enforcement officer's equivalence of nest building. From Joanna's point of view, it was infinitely preferable to cleaning a refrigerator.

"Has anyone talked to Ted Chapman since we found out about this latest development?" Joanna asked, nodding toward the photographs still spread across the table. "Maybe he'll know something about this and the photos will turn out to be totally harmless."

"I doubt that will be the case," Ernie said.

To be honest, Joanna doubted it, too.

Jaime glanced at his watch. "Sorry to rush this," he said. "Ernie and I are due to meet up with the second in command at the Douglas prison in about forty-five. Since Ted's usually around the jail here somewhere, we can probably catch up with him once we finish the Douglas interviews."

With little additional discussion, the homicide team packed up their collection of photos and left the conference room. As soon as they were gone, a grim-faced Frank reached into a file and brought out a single paper which he slid across the table to Joanna. "Take a look at this," he said.

"What is it?" she asked.

"Read it," Frank urged. "It came off the fax machine as I was on my way into the briefing. It's about one of those UDAs they picked up east of Douglas the other night."

The words TOP SECRET and CONFIDENTIAL were written in huge black letters across the cover sheet. Inside was what appeared to be a routine incident report, but as Joanna read it, she felt a sudden chill. One of the illegal crossers, a young unidentified male of Middle Eastern origin, had been apprehended by Border Patrol agents. While searching the surrounding area, the officers had discovered a backpack stuffed with fifteen thousand dollars in American currency, a collection of fake IDs and phony passports, a laptop computer, and three working cell phones.

"Yikes!" Joanna exclaimed.

Frank nodded. "That's what I say."

"If they picked him up the night before last, how come we're only just now hearing about it?" she asked.

"The way the feds operate, I'm surprised we're hearing about it at all," Frank returned. "And I don't think we would be, if they didn't need our help. Border Patrol is asking us to beef up patrols all along the southern sector."

Over the months since 9/11, there had been rumors of the Border Patrol apprehending illegal crossers who didn't fit the usual profile of UDAs simply looking for work. It was thought that some of the arrests had included possible terrorist operatives, but all the rumors in the world hadn't been enough for the federal government to bring to bear the kind of focused attention border issues clearly merited. Evidently this latest bust was one that might finally succeed in attracting Washington's attention, but until that happened, it would be up to the severely understaffed Border Patrol and outmanned local law enforcement agencies to fill in the gap.

"And we will give them help," Joanna declared. "As much as we can spare and maybe even some we can't. Is any of this being made public?"

Frank shook his head. "Homeland Security wants to see how much information they can glean from the cell phones and the computer before anyone knows the bad guy has been picked up. So, yes, they want our help, but they also want us to keep it quiet."

"Okay," Joanna said with a nod. "It makes sense. That way we do the work and they get the credit."

Frank nodded. "You've got that right," he said.

When the briefing was over, Frank started toward the door. He paused in the doorway. "I assume this means Billy and Clarence O'Dwyer are still off our surveillance list for the time being?" he asked.

"Absolutely," Joanna said.

"Jeannine Phillips isn't going to like it," Frank cautioned.

"Don't worry," Joanna said. "I told her yesterday that we wouldn't be able to divert any more patrol officers to San Simon."

"How'd she take it?" Frank asked.

"Medium," Joanna said. "Which is to say she wasn't thrilled."

Frank looked relieved. "I'm glad you told her," he said. "I don't think Jeannine likes me very much."

"She likes you well enough," Joanna observed. "You're just not her type."

Returning to her office, Joanna had barely picked up the first piece of mail when a shaken Ted Chapman appeared in her doorway.

"I ran into Jaime Carbajal and Ernie Carpenter out in the parking lot," Ted said. "The very idea of Brad stalking someone is utterly ridiculous. I can't believe it!"

"Ernie showed you the photos?"

"Yes, but this makes no sense at all."

"The photos were taken from a disposable camera that had Mr. Evans's fingerprints all over it," Joanna pointed out. "According to Casey Ledford, his were the *only* prints on the camera, so he would most likely be the one who took the pictures."

Ted shook his head and rubbed his eyes. "Even so," he said wearily, "Brad simply wouldn't do such a thing."

"Did you recognize the young woman?" Joanna asked. "Do you have any idea who she might be?"

"None whatsoever!"

"Someone he might have dated in the past?" Joanna suggested.

"No," Ted answered. "If Brad had been dating someone, I'm sure he would have mentioned it to me. Besides, the young woman in the picture looks to be in her twenties. She would have been far too young for him."

"Older men and younger women do happen," Joanna said.

"In the movies, maybe," Ted said. "Or if the old guy has bundles of money, but that's not the case with Brad. He may have had a job and a paycheck, but I can tell you from personal experience that the pay scale for members of jail ministries is only one click above flipping burgers. If I didn't have my military retirement, Ginny and I wouldn't be able to make it. Someone who looks like that girl did wouldn't throw herself at an ex-con who's just barely getting by."

"Maybe she corresponded with him while he was in prison," Joanna offered. "Suppose once Brad was released from prison, he found out his pen pal had moved on. Maybe she was dating someone else or had even gotten married. What if he wasn't ready to accept that?"

"No," Ted said. "You've got to believe me. Brad wasn't like that, but that's not why I came to talk to you just now."

"Why did you?"

"I understand Dr. Winfield is ready to release Brad's body, but so far no one has come forward to claim it."

Joanna thought back to Anna Marie Crystal's profoundly negative reaction upon learning that Bradley Evans, her former son-in-law, had listed her as his sole next of kin. It didn't seem likely that she'd be rushing to the morgue to take charge of his body.

"That's not too surprising," Joanna said.

"No," Ted agreed. "I suppose not. But since no one else is going to claim the body, I'd like to. I've talked to people at the prison down in Douglas. The warden there is willing to let me officiate at a memorial service inside the Papago Unit. That way some of the inmates Brad was working with will be able to attend. Of course, if there's any need or interest, I suppose I could do a second service outside the prison as well, although, since the unit is a minimum security facility, the warden might allow a few members of the public to attend the prison service as well."

"You'd do that?" Joanna asked.

"He was a friend of mine," Ted said. "Yes, I would. That's what friends are for."

"All right," Joanna said. "I'll call the ME and see what he says."

Moments later Joanna was on the phone explaining the situation to her stepfather. "Since we haven't been able to locate any other relatives," George Winfield said, "I suppose that would be fine. What mortuary?"

"Cochise Mortuary and Funeral Home," Ted replied in answer to George's relayed question. "They're in Douglas. On G Avenue."

"I know where they are," George said. "Have Mr. Chapman stop by. Once he signs the necessary paperwork, I'll call the funeral home and get things under way."

"Thank you," Ted said to Joanna once she was off the phone. "This means a lot to me. I really appreciate it."

"You're welcome," she returned. "But are you all right?"

Ted sighed. "I'm disappointed," he admitted. "If this stalking thing turns out to be true, I can't help feeling that Brad betrayed the trust I put in him. I pride myself on being a good judge of character. Maybe I'm losing my touch."

"I doubt that," Joanna said. "Maybe Brad Evans was really good at pulling the wool over people's eyes."

But Ted Chapman was in no mood to give himself a break. "Even so," he said, getting up to leave, "I should have seen through it."

Joanna's phone was ringing again before Ted Chapman was all the way out the door. "I forgot," George Winfield said. "I meant to apologize for dumping all that stuff on you the other day without so much as a by-your-leave, but with Don and Margaret there, I didn't want to go into it."

"It's all right, George," she said. "Better late than never. Don't worry about it."

"You know how your mother is," George continued. "Once she gets the bit in her teeth, there's no stopping her. We've been talking about cleaning out the garage ever since we got married. This weekend we finally went to work on it, and now Ellie wants it all done yesterday. I'm sure some of the stuff has been lying around collecting dust for decades. But not anymore, and now that we've started the process . . ." He paused. "Now she wants it all done immediately, if not sooner."

"Sounds pretty familiar," Joanna said with a sympathetic laugh.

"Some of the boxes she had set aside for you and Jenny are filled with knickknacks. If you don't want them, I wouldn't blame you at all, but when it comes to the diaries . . ."

"What diaries?" Joanna asked.

"Your father's diaries," George answered. "Several boxes were full of books. They were up in the rafters of the garage. When I started bringing them down, your mother knew what was inside without even having to look. She claimed they were just a bunch of worthless old books and that I should take them out to the dump and get rid of them. She was so adamant about it that it piqued my curiosity. When she went into the house, I unsealed one of the boxes and what did I find? Your father's diaries."

"My father kept diaries?" Joanna asked.

"Volumes of them, Joanna," George returned. "As soon as I saw them, it occurred to me that maybe you or your brother or Jenny might want to take a look at them. If you want to get rid of them yourself later, fine. But bearing all that in mind, I loaded those boxes into the back of the van along with everything else. Instead of taking them to the dump, I dropped them off at your place on Sunday along with the things Ellie actually wanted you to have. The problem is . . ."

He paused uneasily.

"You don't want me to let on to Mother that I have them," Joanna said.

"Exactly," George Winfield breathed. "Ellie would be terribly upset if she found out that I had gone against her express wishes."

"Don't worry," Joanna said with a laugh. "Your secret's safe with me. I've lived with Eleanor long enough to know when to keep my mouth shut. I didn't even know my father kept diaries. It will be wonderful for me to have a chance to look at them. So thanks. Sometimes I think you know me better than my mother does."

Once Joanna got off the phone, she sat at her desk marveling and reliving the stab of memory that had assailed her when she had glimpsed her father's handwriting on the evidence log in Lisa Marie Evans's file.

D. H. Lathrop had been gone for a very long time. Sometimes Joanna wondered if what she remembered about him was real or if it had been filtered and changed somehow through the hero-worshiping eyes of his unsophisticated daughter. For instance, when she had recalled that fragmentary memory of him sitting hunched with pen and paper at the kitchen table, she had assumed he'd been laboring over some mundane piece of job-required paperwork. Now, though, it seemed possible—likely, even—that he'd been writing in a diary.

Had Joanna's father grappled with his natural adversary, the written word, in order to leave pieces of himself behind for those who followed? Had he wanted or expected whatever he had written there to survive him? Had he imagined that someday a grown-up Joanna might read his words and somehow come to understand her father's hopes and dreams and aspirations? Had D. H. Lathrop ever, in his wildest dreams, thought that the son he and Eleanor had given up for adoption might someday come back into their lives and be able to study the diaries, thus learning about the biological father who would otherwise forever be a stranger? And what about Jenny and this as-yet-unborn grandchild? Could the diaries shed light on the existence of a man they had never met? Now, through George Winfield's kindness, all those things were possible.

For a moment Joanna considered picking up her cell phone and sharing this amazing news with Bob Brundage, her long-lost brother whose out-of-wedlock birth had predated their parents subsequent marriage by a number of years. Given up for adoption as a newborn, he had come looking for his birth parents years later, and only after the deaths of both his biological father as well as his adoptive parents. Eleanor had welcomed him and his wife, Marcie, with open arms.

Joanna scrolled through the stored numbers in her cell phone until she located Bob Brundage's name and number, but she paused before pressing the "talk" button. Joanna had told George Winfield that she wouldn't betray his secret in preserving the diaries, but what about her brother? Bob hadn't grown up at odds with Eleanor Lathrop. Joanna knew all about keeping things from her mother. For her it had been a matter of survival—as necessary as breathing. What if Joanna told Bob, and he somehow let slip to their mother what George had done?

No, Joanna told herself firmly, putting the phone back down. *Let sleeping dogs lie.*

She picked it back up a moment later, however, and called home. "Did anyone ever tell you you're a very smart man?" she asked Butch when he answered.

"Not recently," he said.

Hurriedly she explained what George had done. "So it's a very good thing you didn't let your mother get her hands on any of those boxes."

"George was acting funny," Butch said. "It made me think something was up. But I'm glad the boxes are safe and sound."

"And how are things on the home front?" Joanna asked.

"Quiet. Mom and Dad unhitched their Tracker and went out sightseeing this morning. They told me not to plan on cooking dinner. They want to take us out."

"Where to?"

"Someplace nice was what I was told, so I've made reservations at the restaurant at Rob Roy Links."

"Sounds good," Joanna said. "I'm looking forward to it."

With that she went back to work. She stayed glued to her desk until almost two o'clock dealing with a slew of end-of-the-month reports.

Finally Kristin showed up in her doorway. "I thought you had a doctor's appointment," she said, pointing at her watch.

With a dismayed glance at the clock on her office wall, Joanna bounded out of her chair. "Thanks," she said. "I was so engrossed that I would have missed it."

While sitting in Dr. Tommy Lee's waiting room, Joanna found her head lolling back. The next thing she knew, Sugie Richards, Dr. Lee's receptionist, was shaking her awake.

"Sheriff Brady. Sheriff Brady. Are you all right?"

Embarrassed, Joanna looked around the room to see if anyone else had noticed. Obviously several people had.

"I'm fine," she said impatiently. "It's nothing a good night's sleep wouldn't fix."

"Well, it's time for you to come in now," Sugie said. "The doctor's ready to see you. Come on in and put on a gown."

With people still staring at her, Joanna got up and waddled into the examination room. "How are things?" Dr. Lee asked when he appeared in the doorway several minutes later.

"I'm tired," she said. "I'm tired and cranky and ready to be done carrying this baby. Other than that, I'm fine."

"I'm sure you are," Dr. Lee agreed.

His examination was perfunctory. "A few more days," Dr. Lee said at last. "It won't be long now."

That's easy for you to say, Joanna thought. *Your mother-in-law isn't parked in your driveway waiting for this damned kid to put in an appearance.*

"You can get dressed now," the doctor added. "Then we'll talk."

Stuffed back inside the confines of her maternity uniform, Joanna went into Dr. Lee's office and took a seat beside his desk.

"You seem a little stressed," he said. "Are you all right?"

"Butch's parents are here," she said.

Dr. Lee studied her face. "Is that all?"

She remembered her panicked call to Marianne. "You'd tell me, wouldn't you?" she asked.

"Tell you what?"

"If something was wrong with the baby," Joanna said in a rush. "I mean, if there were pieces missing or if something wasn't working right."

"Of course I would," he assured her with a smile. "I would

have told you long before this. Whatever would have made you think I wouldn't?"

"I don't know," Joanna answered wanly. "I guess I just needed something to worry about."

"We doctors call it third-trimester paranoia," he said with a smile. "Believe me. That kind of thinking is completely normal."

CHAPTER 8

Joanna had barely returned to her office when an almost giddy Debbie Howell bounded into the room. "Look," she said, waving a fistful of papers in the air. "The woman in Brad Evans's pictures. I finally talked to a Fry's checkout clerk who was able to look at the pictures and give me the woman's name—Leslie Markham. I came back to the office, Googled the name, and found her! Here she is. She and her husband, Rory Markham, own a real estate company out in Sierra Vista. I downloaded this from their website."

Joanna took the proffered pieces of paper. While she read through them, Debbie, too excited to sit, paced the floor. Rory Markham, Real Estate Group, LLC, was a brokerage specializing in "fine homes and ranches." Rory, who was evidently both owner and broker of the firm, was a tanned, silver-haired gentleman who looked to be in his late fifties. Just under the company name was a color photo of Mr. Markham with a radiantly smiling Leslie standing at his side. Leslie's photo turned up a second time among the head shots of salespeople working for the company. In the associates section her caption read: "Leslie Tazewell Markham."

"Looks like she started out as an associate and ended up marrying the boss," Joanna said.

Debbie nodded. "I believe it's called marrying up."

"In every sense of the word," Joanna added. "She looks like she's barely mid-twenties and he's what, early fifties?"

"At least," Debbie agreed. "He could be even older than that."

Joanna remembered what Ted Chapman had said—something to the effect that younger women only threw themselves at older men if money was involved. From the looks of the man in the picture it appeared that there couldn't be more than a couple of years of difference in age between Rory Markham and Bradley Evans. So maybe Leslie Markham had a thing for older men.

"Do Jaime and Ernie know about this?" Joanna asked.

"Not yet," Debbie said. "I came straight here to tell you."

"I'm glad to know about it, but they're your partners on this," Joanna reminded her. "Whatever you know, they need to know."

"Right," Debbie said. "I'll see if I can locate them."

She left Joanna's office, taking the website information on Rory Markham Real Estate with her when she went. Within minutes Debbie was back, bringing the Double Cs with her.

"Look who I found," she said. "They were just pulling into the parking lot."

Ernie was scanning the Leslie Markham info as he followed Debbie into Joanna's office. "Well," he said, tossing the papers on the small conference table in one corner of the room, "this is all very interesting. Now that we know who she is, the question has to be: Is she a victim here or is she the perpetrator?"

"Maybe she's both," Joanna suggested.

"What do you mean?" Ernie asked.

"First, tell me. What did you find out down in Douglas?"

"Nothing bad," Jaime admitted. "All the guys at the prison, the ones Brad Evans was working with on a regular basis, thought he was a great guy. For one thing, he evidently learned to speak Spanish—fluent Spanish—while he was in prison. So when he was counseling the guys, he could do it in English or Spanish, which isn't nearly as common as you'd think. And he's evidently stayed in touch with a couple of the guys who were local after they were released. They told us that they saw him at AA meetings, in Douglas and in Agua Prieta. But none of them mentioned Brad having a girlfriend. Nobody hinted that he might be gay or anything like that. It's just that if he had relationships with women, he never told anyone."

"Did anyone mention a pen-pal situation?" Joanna asked.

"Nope."

"So here we are then," Joanna said. "What we know is that, for whatever reason, Brad Evans was definitely interested in Leslie Markham—a happily and possibly recently married woman. Let's suppose for a minute that she and Brad did have a relationship of some kind, one that none of his friends happen to know anything about. Maybe it was over as far as she was concerned, but Brad was still hanging on."

"I see where you're going with this," Ernie said. "Somehow she gets wind that Brad Evans is still sniffing around. Leslie doesn't want to rock the boat with her husband, this Markham guy, so she takes Evans out of the picture permanently."

"Which makes her a possible stalking victim and a possible homicide suspect," Joanna returned. "Like I said earlier—maybe she's both."

"For right now, we'd better take the victim option," Jaime said. "If we even acknowledge that she could be a suspect—"

"Exactly," Joanna said. "First let's try to find out everything we can about the woman. Then tomorrow, maybe you can go talk to her."

"Did you have any luck tracking down whoever bought primer over the weekend?" Ernie asked Debbie.

She shook her head. "I spent all day on this."

"That's all right," Ernie said. "Tomorrow will be plenty of time to do that."

For a change Joanna left the office right at five. Dinner at the Rob Roy was good—at least the food was. Margaret was off on another tirade, but Joanna, taking Butch's advice, simply tuned her mother-in-law out. Instead, Joanna found herself thinking about Bradley Evans—a convicted murderer and a murder victim as well, a man whose life in prison and out of it seemed to be a complete contradiction. The people who knew him best—like Ted Chapman, for instance—seemed to have thought very highly of him. On the surface it appeared that he had lived an almost monastic life.

But somewhere along the line Brad Evans had met up with someone who hadn't liked him nearly as well as other people did. This unknown person had disliked Evans enough not just to kill him but to mutilate his body as well.

How much do you have to hate someone, Joanna wondered, *to systematically remove their fingers?*

"Well," Margaret Dixon asked impatiently, "what do you think?"

Joanna's attention returned to the dinner table in time to find the other four people seated there staring at her and waiting for an answer. Butch, seeing what must have been a totally blank look on her face, came to her rescue.

"Dessert," he said quickly. "What do you think about dessert?"

Joanna actually didn't want dessert. Caught off guard, though, she ordered some anyway. "I'll have the crème brûlée," she answered at once. Which was why, when midnight rolled around, she was wide awake, tossing and turning and suffering from a terrible case of indigestion.

Not wanting to disturb Butch, she and Lady abandoned the bedroom. For a while, Joanna and the dog sat on the couch in the living room. Finally, though, recognizing that this was a time when she'd have a bit of privacy, Joanna headed for her office. Butch had carried through on his promise to lock the door, but the key was hidden beneath one of his prized O-gauge model train engines displayed on a nearby shelf.

Joanna let herself into the office, where she found Butch's laptop in the middle of her desk. No doubt he had used the office as a refuge from his parents during the course of the previous day.

Putting the computer aside, Joanna focused on the boxes stacked along the wall. One by one, she lifted them. It wasn't necessary to open them in order to discern which ones held knickknacks. Those were all fairly light. The boxes at the bottom of the stack were too heavy to lift. Slicing open the top one, she found that the box was chock-full of books.

Some of them were old history texts. D. H. Lathrop had been a self-taught history buff. She remembered him regaling her with stories of the Old West, and it didn't surprise Joanna in the least to find a collection of history books among her father's treasured possessions. And there were several outdated law enforcement manuals as well. D. H. Lathrop had left off formal schooling without completing high school. When he had wanted to switch from mining to law enforcement, signing up for a college degree in criminal justice hadn't been an option. Instead, he had pored over the textbooks and manuals on his own, using what he learned there to bootstrap himself out of a dead-end job as a miner into the Cochise County Sheriff's Department.

He may have started out there as a deputy, but he had worked his way up through the ranks until eventually he had been elected sheriff. Just seeing the books he had used to accomplish that transformation gave Joanna a whole new sense of her father's single-minded struggle to better himself.

Joanna found the diaries in the second of the two heavy boxes. When she picked up the first of the leather-bound volumes, she did so almost reverently. Two dates—March 26, 1964, to June 8, 1969—were inscribed in indelible black ink on the front cover of the book and repeated again, in the same hand, on the spine. It took Joanna's breath away to think that the small volume in her hand contained five years of her father's life—five years she knew nothing about. At the time D. H. Lathrop had been writing in this diary, his daughter, Joanna, hadn't been born.

She opened the first page. It was yellow and brittle to the touch, but her father's distinctive handwriting leaped out at her.

"Work," the entry dated March 1964 read. "I hate it. I hate working in the mine. I hate being dirty. I hate the dust and the dark. Fell in a stope today. It's a wonder I didn't break my neck. I don't know how long I can keep this up, but I promised Ellie . . ."

Joanna stopped cold, allowing the word to sink into her consciousness. Ellie! Her father had called her mother that. So did George Winfield. Two very different men with the same wife who used the same affectionate nickname.

". . . that I would support her until death do us part. And I will. A promise is a promise."

And there it was. Joanna had always known that much about her parents' relationship—that her mother had married someone who had been considered beneath her and that Eleanor had never, not for one day, allowed her husband to forget that fact. Regardless, though, Eleanor hadn't bolted. She had married D. H. Lathrop for better or for worse. She may have been disappointed. There may have been far more "worse" days than "better," and her husband may not have measured up to Eleanor's lofty expectations, but she had stuck with him, too.

For the very first time, it occurred to Joanna that in reading her father's version of his life, she might be doing her mother a disservice—that if she read the diaries she might come away with too much information about both of them.

Eleanor isn't perfect, Joanna thought. *But maybe neither was he.*

Closing the book, Joanna threw it down. Then she took out the others—fifteen of them in all—and arranged them in chronological order across her desk. At volume eight, the format suddenly changed. The handsome leather-bound volumes were replaced with reddish cloth-bound books, with only the word "Journal" stamped on the front, with a blank space provided where her father had dutifully inked in the dates.

Joanna was lost in thought when Butch appeared in the doorway. "What are you doing?" he asked.

She jumped. "You startled me," she said. "I couldn't sleep. I didn't want to disturb you, so Lady and I came in here."

"Your father's books?" Butch asked.

Joanna nodded. "His diaries and some other books as well."

"What are you going to do with them?"

"Keep them," Joanna answered.

"I know that. I guess, I meant, *where* are you going to keep them? My mother isn't the only one who might pay your office an unauthorized visit. Your mother wouldn't be above doing some snooping, either."

In the end, they stowed all of the books in the bottom drawer of Joanna's file cabinet. And because bending over was too cumbersome for Joanna, Butch was the one who actually put them away.

"This is silly, you know," she said. "After all, it's our house."

Butch straightened up and looked at her. "How much luck have you had changing your mother's behavior?" he asked.

"None."

"Same thing with my mother," he said. "So let's just deal with it—and keep the door locked. Now come to bed. It's going to be another long day tomorrow."

Joanna had just stepped out of the shower a little past seven the next morning when Butch tapped on the bathroom door, reached in, and handed her the telephone.

"It's Jeannine Phillips," Tica Romero said when Joanna answered.

"What about her?"

"Her damaged truck was found abandoned in the westbound rest area at Texas Canyon," Tica said.

There was a terrible sinking feeling in the pit of Joanna's stomach. Texas Canyon was only a matter of miles away from

San Simon and from Billy and Clarence O'Dwyer's Rooster-comb Ranch.

"What do you mean, damaged?" Joanna demanded. "Is it wrecked?"

"Somebody put a rock through the passenger window. Officer Phillips is nowhere to be found."

"When's the last time someone heard from her?"

"She radioed in to Dispatch at midnight to say that everything was fine and she was going off shift."

"Did she give her location at that time?"

"No."

"Has someone secured the vehicle?" Joanna asked.

"Yes. Deputy Raymond is on the scene."

"Tell him to hold the fort. Then call everyone else—Dave Hollicker, Casey Ledford, and Chief Montoya. Tell them to meet me at the scene."

"What about Homicide?" Tica asked tentatively. "Should I call them?"

Tica's question confirmed Joanna's own worst fears—that Jeannine Phillips wasn't just missing; that she could already be dead. "Yes, them, too," she said at last. "The Double Cs along with Debbie Howell."

Butch came into the bedroom while Joanna was getting dressed. "What's going on?" he asked. "It sounded serious."

"It is," Joanna said. "I'm on my way to Texas Canyon." When she finished explaining the situation, Butch headed for the kitchen. "You can't afford to go through a day like this on an empty stomach," he said. "I'll fix you a traveler."

Don and Margaret Dixon were at the table eating bacon and eggs when Joanna stepped into the kitchen, briefcase in one hand and car keys in the other.

"Aren't you going to have some breakfast?" Margaret asked Joanna on her way past. "After Butch went to all this trouble . . ."

"She is having breakfast, Mom," Butch corrected. "I made her order to go."

He followed Joanna out to the garage. Once she was settled into the Crown Victoria with her seat belt buckled, Butch reached in through the open car door. He handed her an open Ziploc container with two peanut-buttered English muffins inside it and an insulated thermos cup filled with freshly brewed tea.

"Be careful," he said, kissing her good-bye. "Be really, really careful."

"I will," she said.

She downed the muffins before she even reached Highway 80. Once there, she turned on her lights and siren and drove like hell, fuming as she went. After all, Joanna had called off the dogfighting-ring surveillance, and she had ordered—*ordered!*—Jeannine Phillips to stay away from San Simon and the O'Dwyers. Now Joanna's department, shorthanded and strained to the breaking point, would have to turn away from an ongoing murder investigation and from the Border Patrol's request for additional assistance to deal with Billy and Clarence O'Dwyer.

The first order of business, though, was to find Jeannine Phillips. Joanna reached for her radio and was patched through to Frank Montoya.

"Where are you?" she asked.

"On the far side of the Divide." Frank's home in Old Bisbee put him a good seven or eight miles ahead of her.

"Have you put out an APB on Jeannine?" she asked.

"Tica is handling that," he said. "I'm sure it's been issued by now, but I doubt it'll do much good. We have no idea what kind of vehicle she might be traveling in or even if she's in a vehicle.

And if she was dumped out in the desert somewhere, it could be months before we find the body."

"Or years," Joanna added.

"Do you think she was still working the O'Dwyer angle?" Frank asked.

"Probably," Joanna said. "I told her to drop it, but it's pretty clear she didn't."

Joanna's cell phone chirped the distinctive cockadoodle rooster crow that amounted to a ring. "Gotta go," Joanna told him.

"Sheriff Brady?" someone said.

"Yes."

"It's Millicent Ross. I hope you don't mind my calling you on your cell phone. I had the number in my files."

"No," Joanna said. "I don't mind. What's up?"

"Well . . ." Dr. Ross hesitated before saying in a rush, "Jeannine didn't come home last night."

Joanna heard the words and grappled with what they might mean. Were Jeannine and the vet living together? Why hadn't Joanna known that?

"I'm up so early every day that when she comes in off night shift, I don't even hear her," Millicent continued. "But when she wasn't home this morning when I woke up, I wasn't sure what to do. I didn't know if I should call in and report her missing or what. And then I decided I'd call you and ask your advice. I mean, if anyone would know what to do, it would be the sheriff, right?"

"You and Jeannine are roommates?" Joanna asked.

Millicent Ross hesitated. "We're actually a little more than roommates," she admitted. "In fact, we're a lot more than roommates, but we haven't exactly advertised it. Bisbee's such a small place and all. Once gossip gets going, it can be vicious."

Joanna took a deep breath. "I'm sorry to have to tell you this, Millicent. Jeannine is missing."

"Missing," Millicent Ross echoed. "What do you mean, missing?"

"I mean her truck was found over in Texas Canyon, but she's not in it. The last time anyone heard from her was when she radioed in to the department at the end of her shift. Did you hear from her last night?"

But Millicent didn't seem capable of hearing or acknowledging the question. "How can she be missing?" she demanded. "Where would she go?"

"That's what we're trying to find out," Joanna said patiently. "Did she say anything to you about where she was going or what she might be doing?"

"She was still upset about the dogfights," Millicent answered after a pause. "She traded shifts with Manny so she could go up to San Simon and keep an eye on the O'Dwyers. That's what she said to me—that she was going to keep an eye on them."

She must have done more than that, Joanna thought.

"Do you really think they'd hurt her?" Millicent asked.

Joanna heard the growing concern in the woman's voice.

"We don't know," Joanna answered. "All we know for certain is that she's missing."

"Do you think she's dead?"

Probably, Joanna thought.

"She *may* be," Joanna said. "It's possible."

There was a long pause after that. Joanna heard Millicent draw a long breath. "I don't suppose there's any point in my coming there," she said finally. "I'd probably just be in the way."

"You're right," Joanna said. "There'll be a whole crew of people on the scene, and you would be in the way. But I'll call you the moment we learn anything."

"All right then," Millicent agreed. "I have animals that need to be attended to and appointments that are due in. But please call me. Please."

"I will," Joanna promised, ending the call.

When she came through the tunnel at the top of the Divide, she saw the great expanse of bright blue sky spread out in front of her. That spot on Highway 80 was a particular favorite of hers. It was a place where the slightly upward elevation of the road, combined with the abrupt drop of the Mule Mountains, gave Joanna the sensation of being able to fly off the edge of the earth. Today, though, with Jeannine's possible fate weighing heavily on her heart, Joanna felt instead as though she were falling into an abyss.

A few miles later, she had another thought. Once again she radioed in and asked to be put through to Animal Control. Manny Ruiz took the call.

"You've heard?" she asked.

"Tica called me," he said. "Any news?"

"Not yet."

"What are we going to do about the workload?" Manny asked. "With Jeannine and me splitting the burden, it's still not easy. Our part-time clerk is fine, but she can't run the office and look after the animals, too. And if I'm taking care of the animals, who's going to be out in the field? I can't handle this place all by myself."

"No, you can't," Joanna agreed. "Let me see what I can do to get you some temporary help until we know how things stand."

Her next call was to her former in-laws. Jim Bob Brady answered the phone. "I need a favor," Joanna said.

"Name it," Jim Bob returned.

When she finished explaining the situation, Jim Bob was all business. "I'll be glad to do what I can," he said. "And Eva Lou will, too. She's great with animals. We'll go out to the pound right now and find out what's needed."

"How is Eva Lou with snakes?" Joanna asked.

"Did you say snakes?" Jim Bob asked.

"Yes, one of the impounded animals happens to be an abandoned python."

"Well," Jim Bob said thoughtfully, "I may have to take care of that one. But don't worry about it. I'm sure Manny Ruiz will be able to tell us whatever it is he needs us to do."

Joanna hung up the phone thankful that Jim Bob and Eva Lou Brady continued to be far more supportive and helpful than Margaret and Don Dixon would ever be.

When she finally got out of her car, the rest area was already teeming with activity. In fact, she was the last person from her department to arrive on the scene.

Stamping his feet against the frosty morning chill, Frank Montoya hurried over to meet her. "What have we got?" she asked.

Frank shook his head grimly. "Come take a look," he said.

Jeannine's Animal Control truck was parked at the far end of the parking area. Approaching it from the driver's side, nothing seemed amiss. But the passenger-side window, out of view from passing vehicles, was completely missing. Joanna had to stand on tiptoe to peer inside. A bloodied rock the size of a basketball lay on the passenger seat. The police radio had been pulled from its console. It lay, its wire dangling loose, on the floorboard along with a clipboard, a single shoe, and other debris.

"What's that?" Joanna asked, pointing. "A nightscope?"

"That's right," Frank said. "She must have been using that inside the vehicle when her attacker surprised her, probably by heaving that rock through the window. She never had time to call for help, but from the looks of things, she put up a hell of a fight."

Everything around Joanna—Jeannine's shoe in the footwell, the bloodied rock on the seat, the bare mesquite branches beyond the truck, and the looming, bubble-shaped rocks of Texas Canyon—stood out in a kind of stark relief that reminded Joanna of photos observed through her old View-Master. The idea that one of her officers had been attacked and perhaps murdered left Joanna sick at heart but furious and utterly focused.

"Did it happen here?" she asked.

"No," Frank said. "Whoever did it drove the truck here after the attack."

"Because they didn't want us to identify a crime scene?" Joanna asked.

"That would be my guess," Frank said. "They also took off and left the engine running. It's out of gas."

"So whoever abandoned it did so in a hell of a hurry," Joanna said.

Frank nodded. "Being in a hurry breeds mistakes. With any luck, maybe we'll find that they left a little something behind—something we can use to find them. Once Jaime finishes taking his photos, Casey will start dusting for prints."

"Any witnesses?"

"It was called in at six forty-five A.M. by a maintenance guy who stops by early to service the rest rooms. He saw the truck and thought it was unusual for the vehicle to be here with no sign of an officer present. Ernie Carpenter is interviewing him right now. Some of the long-haul drivers may have been parked here overnight. Debbie is checking with them to see if any of them noticed something out of line."

With nothing much else to do, Joanna stood on the sidelines while her people worked. It was only half an hour later when the first of the Tucson-based television news vans, its top bristling with antennas, arrived on the scene. Most of the time Frank handled the media types. Since he was conferring with the crime scene investigators, Joanna stepped forward to head off a swift-footed female news reporter who was followed by a cameraman.

"Sorry," Joanna said. "No unauthorized personnel beyond this point."

The woman stopped and then held up her ID. Isabel Duarte was with KGUN-9 News, but Joanna recognized her on sight without having to check her identification. She was young—barely out of college—and the newest member on the news team, but Joanna had seen her before out on the campaign trail as well as on the air.

"Sheriff Brady?" Isabel asked. "We heard that one of your deputies is missing. Is that true?"

The lens of the video cam was already focused on Joanna with its red light showing. "Not a deputy," she corrected. "One of my ACOs."

Isabel looked puzzled. "ACO?"

"Animal control officer," Joanna explained. "Her vehicle was found abandoned here a little over an hour ago, and yes, she is missing. Chief Deputy Montoya, my media relations officer, won't be making any further statements until later. Now, if you'll excuse me . . ."

Joanna started back toward her team of investigators, but Isabel didn't take the hint. Instead, she followed right on

Joanna's heels. "Did you say a female officer? How old is she? Anglo? Hispanic?"

Shaking her head and trying to keep her temper in check, Joanna turned back to the pushy reporter. She was gratified to see that the cameraman had stayed behind.

"Look, Ms. Duarte," Joanna said. "I appreciate that you have a job to do, but so do we. As I just told you, my department won't have any further comment until later in the day. We're all very busy right now."

"Please, Sheriff Brady," Isabel insisted. "Tell me how old she is."

"How old? Early thirties."

"Anglo?"

"Yes, but I'm not releasing the name, if that's what you're looking for."

"I just came from University Medical Center," Isabel Duarte replied. "About three o'clock this morning, an unconscious Anglo female—badly beaten—was dropped off at the entrance to the Trauma Unit. Two men in a pickup truck went running into the hospital, screaming for help. Neither of them spoke any English. The clerk I talked to said she was sure they were illegals. They claimed that they didn't know the woman; that they had found her lying naked along the side of the road and brought her to the hospital because they were afraid she was going to die. They had transported her, wrapped in blankets, in a camper shell on the back of a pickup. A third man was in the camper with her. When the attendants took the woman inside, the three guys in the pickup took off."

Was it possible that the unidentified woman was actually Jeannine Phillips? "Early thirties?" Joanna asked. "Anglo?"

Isabel nodded. "Stocky build. She was in surgery when I

left. The hospital was giving out information in hopes of identifying her."

"Do you have the phone number?" Joanna asked.

In answer, Isabel simply opened her cell phone, punched it a couple of times, and then handed it over. Moments later, Joanna was speaking to UMC's information officer. "This is Cochise County Sheriff Joanna Brady. One of my female officers has gone missing, and I'm wondering if the woman who was dropped off there earlier . . ."

In the course of the next minute and a half, with Isabel Duarte looking on, Joanna was passed from one staff member to another. Finally she found herself speaking to Dr. Grant Waller.

"I'm given to understand you may be acquainted with our unidentified patient?" he asked.

"That's right," Joanna said. "One of my ACOs disappeared after the close of her shift last night. I was wondering if . . ."

"The woman who was brought here early this morning has come through surgery," Dr. Waller replied. "She's currently in grave but stable condition."

"Is she going to be all right?" Joanna asked.

The doctor's tone shifted and became more distant. "Due to privacy constraints," he said, "I'm unable to tell you any more about the severity of the patient's injuries, but I will say that if she had arrived at our emergency room even twenty minutes later than she did, you and I wouldn't be having this conversation."

Joanna had been holding her breath. Now she let it out.

"It would be helpful, however," Dr. Waller continued, "if we knew who she is. The emergency surgery had to go forward when it did, signed authorization or no, in order to save her life. But in order to treat her other injuries . . . Would it be possible for you to stop by to see if you can identify her?"

Joanna was already striding in the direction of her team of investigators, with Isabel Duarte hurrying along behind her. "I'm on the far side of Benson right now," she said. "With any luck, I can be at the hospital in a little more than half an hour."

"Good," Dr. Waller said. "Just check in at the desk in the lobby. I'll send someone right down to bring you to ICU."

Joanna closed the phone and handed it back to Isabel. For the first time in her life, she felt like hugging a member of the media. "Thank you," she said. "Give me your card. I'll see that you get an exclusive on this."

"You won't have to worry about finding us," Isabel Duarte declared. "Larry and I will be right on your heels."

CHAPTER 9

Joanna paused long enough to pull Frank away from the group of investigators gathered around the abandoned truck. "I'm on my way to Tucson," she said.

"How come?"

"A badly injured unidentified female was dropped off at UMC earlier this morning."

"Jeannine?" Frank asked.

"Maybe," Joanna said. "I'm going to go check it out, but let's not say anything to the others until we know for sure. I don't want to get people's hopes up. I'll be back as soon as I can."

"Good luck," Frank said. "It sounds like we need it."

Driving through Benson westbound on I-10, Joanna called Kristin. "I'd like you to check Jeannine Phillips's employment records," Joanna said. "I need to know her next of kin."

"This sounds bad," Kristin said. "Is it?"

"We don't know," Joanna replied. "At least not yet. Regardless, though, I'm going to need to notify someone about what's happened."

"I'll get right back to you," Kristin said. When she called back a few minutes later, she sounded dismayed. "The next-of-kin section is blank," she said.

"What about the beneficiary of her group life insurance policy?" Joanna asked.

"All that's listed here is the Humane Society of Southern Arizona," Kristin returned. "What does this mean?"

"I don't know," Joanna said, "but thanks for the help."

The troubling lack of next of kin made Jeannine's situation eerily similar to that of Bradley Evans, who had lived such an isolated life that he had been forced to choose his former mother-in-law as his beneficiary.

Mulling this new revelation as she drove, Joanna suddenly remembered something Jeannine had mentioned to her in passing months earlier—something that had hinted at a troubled family life when she was growing up.

Forty minutes after leaving Texas Canyon, Joanna pulled into the parking garage at University Medical Center and walked across the chill but sunny breezeway to the front entrance. The hospital may have been given over to the healing arts, but it happened to be the place where Andy Brady's life had come to an end. It was also where Marianne and Jeff's beloved Esther had died in the aftermath of a heart transplant. Years of constant construction and reconstruction had completely changed the lobby from what Joanna remembered from previous visits, but the physical changes did nothing to dispel the sense of impending doom that flooded over her the moment she stepped through the glass sliding doors.

Dr. Waller was good as his word. Once Joanna gave her name to the receptionist, the doctor himself came downstairs to retrieve her. His voice on the phone had led Joanna to expect someone much older and larger. Grant Waller, however, turned out to be a relatively small man and only a few years older than Joanna.

"Thank you for coming, Sheriff Brady. You made very good time."

"There wasn't much traffic," she said, which was nothing less than an out-and-out lie.

"Let's go upstairs and see if you can identify our patient for us," he said, leading the way.

Upstairs in the surgical ICU waiting room, she was escorted past a group of anxious people gathered there. Once inside the unit, she was motioned into a rest room and directed to wash her hands before donning a gown, mask, hair covering, booties, and latex gloves.

"The patients in this unit are very ill," Dr. Waller explained. "We don't take any unnecessary chances. We're working to prevent secondary hospital-based infections."

When Joanna was properly attired, she was led down the hallway and into a dimly lit room where the only sound was the gentle beeping of a monitor. A sleeping figure lay on the bed. Stepping closer, Joanna saw that the patient's head was almost entirely swathed in bandages. One eye and one badly bruised cheek was all that was visible, but it was enough.

"It's Jeannine," Joanna managed as her legs turned to jelly beneath her. "Jeannine Phillips."

Supported by Dr. Waller's steadying arm, Joanna was led out into the hallway and lowered onto a chair at the nurses' station. "Are you all right?" he asked.

"Just a little woozy," Joanna answered. "It hit me harder than I expected. She looks awful."

Waller nodded. "I suspect she's going to lose the sight in that one eye, and she'll probably require reconstructive facial surgery, but what you saw in there was only the tip of the iceberg. She had severe internal injuries. We had to remove her spleen and one kidney. With all that and the amount of blood she had lost, it's a miracle she made it to the hospital alive."

"Will she live?" Joanna asked.

Waller shook his head. "Too soon to tell," he said. "What I need now, though, is information—her name and the name of her next of kin. It would also help if you could provide any insurance information, although of course we'll continue treating her in any case, regardless of whether or not she's insured."

While speaking, Waller had removed a PDA from a coat pocket. He paused with the stylus poised at the ready. "Did you say her name is Jeannie?" he asked.

"Jeannine," Joanna corrected, "Jeannine Phillips," spelling out both names, one letter at a time.

"Next of kin?"

"I don't have that information right now," she said. "Once I have it, I'll get it to you right away."

"The sooner the better," Dr. Waller said, returning the PDA to his pocket. "I'll be going then," he added. "You can leave the gown and booties in a receptacle in the rest room."

But Joanna wasn't ready to be dismissed quite that easily. "What do you think happened to her?" she asked.

Waller turned back to her. "Sheriff Brady," he said, "with all due respect, I really can't give you any additional information. Considering the new federally mandated patient confidentiality rules, I've probably said too much already. Since you're not a parent or spouse or on a list to receive her private medical information . . ."

Joanna bridled at his patronizing tone. "With all due respect," she returned curtly, "at the very least my agency is conducting an aggravated assault investigation, one that could well turn into a homicide if Jeannine dies. In that case, I'm sure the autopsy will tell me everything I need to know about her private medical information. In the meantime, you're all I've got."

They were still at the nurses' station. Dr. Waller glanced around as if concerned someone might overhear what was said. When he spoke, he did so in an undertone. "She was stripped naked, kicked, and stomped, and left to die," he said at length. "And when I say kicked, I mean kicked within an inch of her life. She has severe internal injuries, several broken ribs, and compound fractures of both arms and legs. You already saw what they did to her face."

"They?" Joanna asked. "You mean there was more than one?"

Waller nodded. "Some of the bruises show actual shoe prints," he said. "There was more than one pattern."

"Will we be able to have photos of the shoe patterns?" Joanna asked.

Dr. Waller nodded grimly. "Eventually, I suppose," he said.

"Was she raped?"

"That I don't know," Dr. Waller said. "We've been a little too busy saving her life to spend any time processing a rape kit."

"If DNA evidence is available, I want it," Joanna said. "It may be the only way to nail these bastards."

But Waller, having given a little, retreated back into the world of rules and procedures. "We'd need a signed consent form for that."

"Jeannine is in no position to sign anything," Joanna pointed out.

Waller shrugged. "That's why we need to speak to her next of kin," he said. "One of her relatives could probably give consent."

"What if I speak to them first?" Joanna asked. "What should I tell them?"

Dr. Waller sighed again. "I don't really recommend that. Next-of-kin notifications are best left to the professionals."

"I am a professional," she reminded him. "A law enforcement professional. It turns out I, too, have had some experience with next-of-kin notifications."

"Yes," he agreed. "Of course."

"So what can I tell them?" Joanna persisted. "How would you characterize her condition?"

"Grave," Waller said at last. "Her condition is grave but stable."

With that, Dr. Waller walked away. Joanna went into the rest room and removed her hospital garb. When she walked out through the waiting room, she was aware that the people there were watching her. She knew that, even caught up in their own pain, they all were wondering which patient this very pregnant law enforcement officer had been allowed to visit and why.

On her way down in the elevator, Joanna puzzled about her next move. Jeannine may not have disclosed information about next of kin on her employment records, but there was someone who might have access to information that wasn't in the written record—someone who was waiting and worrying and wondering what was going on—Millicent Ross.

When the elevator door opened, Joanna had her phone in her hand and was preparing to use it when, on a bench near the front door, she caught sight of Isabel Duarte. As the reporter sprang to her feet and hurried to meet her, Joanna returned her phone to her pocket.

"Is it her?" the reporter asked.

"Yes." The answer was out before Joanna had time to think about whether or not replying was the right thing to do.

"Is she going to be all right?"

Joanna was struck by the expression on Isabel's face and the way she asked the question. She seemed less focused on getting the story than she was about voicing concern for a fellow human being. Even so, in answering, Joanna took her cue from the way Dr. Waller had danced around the issue.

"We're not making any comment about her condition at this time."

Nodding, Isabel looked slightly disappointed. "But you did promise me an exclusive," she objected. "If we hurry, we can just make the deadline for the *Noon News*."

So the story was part of it after all. Joanna had lots of other things that urgently needed doing, but Isabel was right. Joanna had promised, and without the reporter's timely intervention, it was likely Jeannine Phillips's whereabouts would still be a mystery.

"You're right," Joanna agreed. "That is what I said. Is your camera guy around here somewhere?"

"He's outside smoking a cigarette."

"Let's go do it then," Joanna said.

When summoned from his cigarette break, the cameraman grimaced, ground out the stub, and then grudgingly hefted the camera to his shoulder. Standing posed before the UMC logo, Joanna held a microphone in her hand and spoke into the lens. "This morning a Cochise County Animal Control officer was attacked and severely beaten in northeastern Cochise County. We're currently withholding the victim's name, pending notification of next of kin, but I can assure you, my department will leave no stone unturned until we have brought all those responsible to justice."

"Thank you," Isabel said, when she came to retrieve her microphone.

"It wasn't much," Joanna said. "I'm sorry I couldn't say more."

Isabel smiled. "It's more than anyone expects me to get," she said. "The news director didn't send me to the hospital in the middle of the night because he thought I'd actually come away with a story."

"You think this will help show him what you can do?"

"Something like that."

"But whatever made you think that there might be a connection between the woman here and the incident at Texas Canyon?"

The reporter shook her head. "I'm not sure," she said. "I heard the police scanner reporting that the missing officer was a woman, and I just put two and two together. I guess you could say it was gut instinct or maybe even woman's intuition."

"Good gut instinct," Joanna said, shaking the reporter's hand. "Thank you."

Once Isabel and her cameraman had left, Joanna settled onto a concrete bench next to a reeking outdoor ashtray and dialed Frank Montoya's number. "It's her," Joanna said when he answered. "It's Jeannine."

"How bad is it?" he asked.

"Very bad."

"Is she going to live?" Frank asked after a pause.

"Too soon to tell."

"Want me to contact her next of kin?" he asked.

"No," Joanna returned. "I'll do it. There's evidently some

kind of discrepancy with the office records. Notifying them isn't going to be the kind of slam dunk you'd think it would be."

"Okay," Frank said. "Once it's done, I'll talk to the press. There's a swarm of reporters out here, all of them clamoring for information."

"Not all the reporters are there," Joanna corrected. "One of them, Isabel Duarte from KGUN, ended up following me here to the hospital. I gave her a brief statement, but I didn't ID the victim."

"The others are going to be bent out of shape," Frank said.

"Too bad. She was on the ball, and they weren't."

"But you don't usually talk to the press." Frank sounded puzzled.

"I made an exception this time," Joanna said. "I'll get back to you later." She ended the call, then located Millicent Ross's number in her incoming-calls list and punched the button.

"Hello?" Millicent said anxiously when she picked up. "Joanna?"

"Yes."

"Have you found her?" Millicent demanded. "Is she all right?"

Joanna took a steadying breath before she answered. "I have found her," she said. "But she's not all right. Jeannine's at University Medical Center in Tucson—in grave but stable condition."

There was a long pause before Millicent Ross spoke again. "Oh my God! What happened?"

"Someone attacked her while she was sitting in her truck, pulled her out of the vehicle, and beat her up," Joanna said. "And we're not talking your everyday, run-of-the-mill beating here, Millicent. They damn near killed her. I was just talking to her doctor—Dr. Waller," she continued. "He needs the name of her next of kin. I don't seem to have any record of that. For some reason the information appears to have been either omitted or obliterated from her records."

"It's not strange at all," Millicent returned. "She doesn't want to have anything to do with those people, and I don't blame her."

"So she does have relatives?"

"Yes, of course she does."

"Do you know who and where they are?" Joanna pressed. "Do you know how we can reach them?"

Joanna wanted that rape-kit consent form signed. If contacting Jeannine's parents was the only way to accomplish that goal, then that's what she would do.

"She was born in Truth or Consequences, New Mexico," Millicent said.

"Good," Joanna said. "Are her parents still there? Do you have a name and address?"

"You mustn't contact them," Millicent said.

"Don't be silly," Joanna said. "Their daughter has been injured and is in the hospital. Of course I have to contact them. Why wouldn't I?"

Millicent took a deep breath. "Do you know anything about how Jeannine was raised or why she left home?"

"A little, I suppose," Joanna conceded. "She told me once that she'd had a troubled childhood."

"Troubled?" Millicent snorted derisively. "I'll say it was troubled. Her father sexually abused her regularly from the time she was little. It's her first conscious memory. When she finally got up nerve enough to tell her mother about what was going on, her mother called her a liar and threw her out of the house. Those people are monsters. The way they treated Jeannine is absolutely criminal, but to have them called in when she's lying helpless in a hospital bed and has no say in the matter . . . No. You just can't do that."

"Millicent," Joanna said. "Someone needs to be here with her."

"And I will be," Millicent said at once. "It'll take me a little while to cancel my appointments and make arrangements to close the clinic for the day, but I'll be there as soon as I can. You say she's at UMC? What's her doctor's name again? I'll need to talk to him."

"Waller. Dr. Grant Waller."

"All right," Millicent Ross said. "I'm on my way."

After Millicent hung up, Joanna paced in the breezeway. Dr. Waller had already alluded to the new patient privacy rules on more than one occasion. And the sign posted on the door into the ICU had been plainly marked: Authorized Visitors Only.

In the narrowly observed rules of medical treatment, Joanna guessed that the relationship between Millicent Ross and Jeannine Phillips wasn't going to qualify Millicent as authorized. For more than ten minutes, Joanna walked back and forth, wrestling with what was the right thing to do in a wrong situation. Finally she redialed Millicent Ross's number.

"Has something happened?" Millicent demanded as soon as she heard Joanna's voice. "Has her condition gotten worse?"

"No," Joanna said. "Nothing has changed. But I was thinking. How much older are you than Jeannine?"

"Love is love," Millicent snapped back, her voice suddenly cold. "Age has nothing to do with it."

"How much older?" Joanna persisted.

"Several years," Millicent conceded reluctantly. "My daughter's a year older than Jeannine is and my son's a year younger. But still, I don't see how the difference in our ages has anything to do with—"

"Actually it does," Joanna said. "In fact, it's the whole point. Dr. Waller is a stickler for the rules. He expects me to contact Jeannine's mother, so presumably he's expecting her to show up even though he has no idea where she lives or what her name is."

Suddenly Millicent grasped where this was going. "If I were to show up claiming to be her mother, how would he know the difference?"

"Exactly," Joanna said, "but you never heard it from me."

"No," Millicent Ross agreed. "I certainly didn't. Thank you, Joanna. I owe you one."

Joanna thought about Jenny, who wanted to be a veterinarian. Even though Jenny wasn't yet in high school, Millicent Ross had been unfailingly encouraging about the chances of Jenny's achieving that somewhat lofty dream.

"No, you don't," Joanna said. "You don't owe me a thing."

"I'm coming as soon as I can," Millicent said. "Will you still be at the hospital when I get there?"

"Maybe," Joanna said. "But it might be best if we didn't cross paths."

"I understand," Millicent returned.

"But there is one other thing we need," Joanna added. "Dr. Waller didn't do a rape kit."

Joanna heard Millicent's sharp intake of breath. "You think she was raped?"

"I don't know for sure, but performing the exam is the only way to confirm whether or not she was. And it's also the only way to gather possible DNA evidence and photograph her wounds for the legal record. Without a signed consent form, that isn't going to happen."

"Believe me," Millicent said determinedly. "There will be a signed consent form."

"And insist they photograph whatever bruising there is and also that they do scrapings from under her fingernails," Joanna added. "If she fought them—and from the way the truck looks, I think she did fight—there may be usable DNA material under her nails as well. The problem is," she added, "there's always a chance that, if word gets back to them, Jeannine's parents will show up at the hospital after all. What you do then, I don't know."

"I'll be able to handle it," Millicent Ross returned.

Relieved that she had done as much as she could, both for Jeannine and for Millicent, Joanna put her phone away and headed back to the emergency room, where she corralled the first available clerk.

"I'm investigating that beating victim who was brought in early this morning," she said, showing the clerk her ID. "I need the names of all the attendants who were on duty at the time she was admitted."

"I can get you a list if you like," the clerk said with a shrug. "But you see that guy over there—the tall skinny one?"

"Yes."

"His name's Horatio. Horatio Gonzales. He's pulling a double shift right now. I'm pretty sure he was here overnight."

Horatio Gonzales was indeed tall—six-four at least. And he wasn't exactly skinny. Well-defined muscles showed under his hospital scrubs. "What can I do for you?" he asked when Joanna approached him with her ID in hand.

"Were you here this morning when that beating victim was dropped off?"

His dark eyes went even darker. "I was here," he said. "She was hurt real bad."

"What about the three men who brought her in. You saw them?"

"I guess," he said.

"What can you tell me about them?"

Horatio shrugged. "Not much," he said.

"Do you think they were the ones who did it?"

This time there was a spark of real anger when he spoke. "No way!" he declared.

"But if they weren't responsible, why didn't they stay around after they dropped her off?"

"Why do you think?" he said. "They didn't speak much English. Maybe they were illegal or something. Or maybe they didn't have the right kind of insurance for their vehicle or the right kind of license. I'm sure they were scared. If they'd talked to a cop, even a little lady cop like you, they might have gotten in some kind of trouble."

On most occasions a "little lady" comment like that would have sent Joanna into a fury, but somehow, coming from Horatio Gonzales, she understood it was due to their very real disparity in size rather than a patronizing put-down. Joanna Brady was tiny compared with him.

"They wouldn't have gotten in trouble with me," she said. "That woman is a member of my department. They saved her life. All I want to do is thank them."

That wasn't entirely true, of course. Joanna *did* want to thank them. And they wouldn't be in any trouble as far as she was concerned, but she desperately needed to know where they had found Jeannine. Locating the crime scene was most likely her investigators' only chance of finding any real evidence. The attack had begun inside the truck. The rest of it had been carried out elsewhere—in the desert someplace. Whatever evidence remained would be there, too, waiting to be discovered.

Despite ten more minutes of questioning, Hector Gonzales

was unable to recall anything of use. Looking at the list of names the clerk had given her left Joanna feeling even more discouraged. The other ER attendants probably wouldn't be any more interested in answering Joanna's questions than Hector had been. She was standing near the entrance, thinking, when an ambulance rolled up to the door. Watching the action unfold, Joanna noticed, for the first time, the security cameras discreetly set in the supporting columns on either side of the driveway.

She turned and went straight back to the desk. "Who monitors the security tapes?" Joanna asked.

"The campus cops do that," the clerk said. "We have nothing to do with it."

Frank called her while she was driving from UMC to the University of Arizona campus proper. "Any luck finding the next of kin?" he asked. "The natives are restless. If I don't give the reporters some info pretty soon, they're going to go berserk."

Joanna felt uneasy. Telling Millicent Ross wasn't exactly abiding by the rules, but she had done it, and the chips would have to fall where they may. "It's handled as well as it's going to be," Joanna told him. "Talk away."

Ten minutes later she was on the U of A campus in the cubbyhole office of Captain George Winters, the man in charge of the University Police Department. "We usually have an officer stationed at the ER entrance," he said. "Last night Dick went home sick around midnight, and we weren't able to locate a sub on such short notice. The best I can do for you is to let you view the security tapes."

Seated at a console, Joanna scrolled through a series of security camera videos. The time readout read 03.33.46 when a 1980s vintage Chevy LUV pickup with a camper shell over the bed pulled into view. Two people leaped out of the truck and went running inside. Moments later, in a flurry of activity, attendants—one of them clearly Horatio Gonzales—appeared pushing a gurney. It took some time for them to maneuver a blanket-swathed figure out of the pickup, load her onto the gurney, and then roll her inside.

Once the patient disappeared into the building, the three men from the pickup conferred briefly, then they all piled back into the pickup and drove away. Try as she might, Joanna was unable to make out the letters and numbers of the license plate. The image simply wasn't clear enough. Captain Winters had given her two different tapes to review, taken via two different cameras. When she examined the second one, taken from a slightly different angle and from closer to the vehicle, she was able to read the last three numbers on the license—464—and the saguaro cactus that identified it as an Arizona plate, but the preceding part of the license wasn't visible at all.

Captain Winters came into the room as she finished rewinding the second tape. "Did you find what you needed?" he asked.

"Some, but not all," she answered. "Is it possible to make copies of these?"

"I don't see why not," he said. "It'll take a few minutes. Maybe you'd like to come back for them later."

"That's all right," she said. "I'll wait."

While waiting, she redialed Frank Montoya. "I've got a security video of the vehicle that dropped Jeannine off at the hospital, but I can't read the whole license number—the image is too grainy. Where would you suggest I go to have the images enhanced? Should I take the tapes to the Arizona State Crime Lab here in Tucson?"

"No way," Frank said. "Those guys are a bunch of amateurs. Go to Pima Community College, the one out on Anklam

Road. One of my cousins, Alberto Amado, teaches computer science there. He does photo imaging on the side. I'll call and see if he's in."

"Please do that," Joanna said.

By one o'clock that afternoon, with Alberto's help, Joanna was armed with the complete license number from the Chevy LUV as well as the name and address of the registered owner. She felt guilty as she called the Department of Public Safety to put out an APB on a man named Ephrain Trujillo, who listed a Douglas, Arizona, home address, but there wasn't any choice. No doubt, Mr. Trujillo was one of the good Samaritans who had rescued Jeannine Phillips from certain death and brought her to the hospital. That meant he and his friends were the only witnesses who would be able to take Joanna and her investigators to the spot where the attack had occurred.

Regardless of any adverse consequences for Mr. Trujillo, Joanna understood that locating the crime scene was the next essential piece of the puzzle.

Joanna felt guilty about making the call, but she did it anyway. She had to. It was her job—her job and her duty.

CHAPTER 10

Joanna could have left Tucson for Bisbee immediately after
issuing the APB, but she didn't. The people in the LUV may
have been Mexican nationals, but they were familiar enough
with Tucson to have brought Jeannine to the only working
trauma unit in the city. It was possible that they knew their way
around Tucson because they lived and / or worked there. Joanna
wanted to wait around to see if the APB would bear fruit.

What she really craved for lunch was a hot dog from one of
the vendors parked along the side of the road, but those didn't
come equipped with readily available rest rooms, and at that
point in her pregnancy, rest rooms were a moment-by-moment
necessity. She stopped instead at Las Cazuelitas, a Mexican food
joint on South Sixth near the freeway. It was one of the mysteries
of the universe that even a hint of crème brûlée could give her
indigestion while she could down tacos and refritos with complete impunity.

Frank called while she was stowing away the last of her lunch.

"We're getting ready to haul Jeannine's truck back to the Justice Center," he said. "It'll be easier for Dave and Casey to work on it if it's inside the garage instead of sitting out in the open."

"Any word on the APB?" Joanna asked.

"Not so far."

"What's everyone doing?"

"Until we can get some kind of break on Jeannine's case, there's not much more for the detectives to do here. The Double Cs and Debbie are on their way to Sierra Vista. Debbie's going to be checking on primer paint purchases, and Ernie and Jaime are going to try to check out that Markham woman. We figured we should keep working on that while we can. You do know that Ernie will be out tomorrow—for his procedure?"

"I thought that was scheduled for Friday," Joanna said.

"There was some kind of change in plans, and they moved it up. I think Ernie is anxious to get it over with," Frank continued. "But we've got two major cases hanging fire. Having him out right now is going to put us in a hell of a bind."

"We'll get through it," Joanna assured him. "We always do."

She had paid for her food and was making one last trip to the rest room when her phone rang again. "A patrol officer from Tucson PD just spotted that LUV," Frank reported. "It's parked near a construction project on the far north side of town, on the northeast corner of the intersection at Campbell and Sunrise. Tucson Dispatch wants to know what you want them to do about it."

"Have them keep the vehicle under observation until I get there," Joanna said. "If the guy leaves, have them follow but don't stop. I already told you that the driver is a potential witness—a person of interest rather than a suspect."

"I'll remind them," Frank said.

"And since we're dealing with people whose ability to speak English is limited, how soon can you meet me there?" Joanna asked. "I'm going to need backup as well as a translator."

"Fortunately I was just getting ready to head back to Bisbee from Texas Canyon," Frank said. "I'll be there ASAP."

After being patched through to Tucson PD, Joanna stayed in touch via radio while she drove from one end of Tucson to the other. Not wanting to attract any kind of notice, she traveled without benefit of lights or siren. When she arrived at Sunrise and Campbell, she found a Tucson PD patrol car waiting for her in a restaurant parking lot on the northwest corner of the intersection. Across the street, parked in among a dozen or so equally dilapidated vehicles, was the battered LUV she had seen in the UMC security video.

As she pulled in next to the patrol car, a uniformed officer stepped out of the waiting vehicle and hurried toward her. "I just got another call," he said. "Do you need me to stay here or . . . ?"

"No," Joanna said, "it's fine. One of my officers is on his way and will be here soon. You go ahead."

The officer left, and Joanna settled in to wait. Across the street a crew of about a dozen men were at work constructing a concrete block wall. It was hard physical labor, and they worked at a steady but unhurried pace. Two men were using wheelbarrows to drag stacks of block from a nearby flatbed trailer over to where other workers were laying the blocks. Another two maintained a steady supply of cement from a mixer. One of the men manhandling a wheelbarrow looked a lot like the guy who had scrambled out of the camper shell in Alberto Amado's digitally enhanced security video. Joanna recognized one of the guys at the cement mixer as the passenger from the front of the pickup. The driver, however, wasn't visible.

At the stroke of three, all work stopped. As block layers began gathering and cleaning tools and equipment and putting them away, Joanna reached for her phone. "Where are you, Frank?" she asked, trying to keep the panic out of her voice. "It looks like they're closing up shop."

"I just turned off I-10 onto Kino," he said. "It'll take me another fifteen minutes to reach your location."

"Hurry," she urged. "Otherwise they'll all be gone by the time you get here."

"I understood from Dispatch that someone from Tucson PD was there with you."

"He was here, but he had to leave," Joanna said. "He had another call."

"Just follow them, then," Frank advised. "Let me know where they end up, and I'll go there."

Unwilling to risk losing track of the pickup in afternoon traffic, Joanna was already putting her Crown Victoria in gear. It seemed unlikely that Ephrain Trujillo commuted more than a hundred miles one way from his home in Douglas to a job in Tucson. That meant he was probably staying somewhere in the Tucson area. Joanna didn't want to delay speaking to him until the following day, when he might not reappear at the job site.

"I'm going to go talk to him," Joanna said into the phone. "Get here as soon as you can."

"Wait a minute, Joanna," Frank said. "For God's sake. Are you even wearing a vest?"

"What do you think?" she returned, and then she hung up.

The truth was, she wasn't wearing a vest—hadn't worn one in weeks because the one she owned no longer fastened around her bulging belly. But these were the guys who had saved Jeannine's life, right? Surely they wouldn't hurt her.

A middle-aged Hispanic man was approaching the pickup with his car key extended when Joanna pulled in behind the LUV, effectively blocking its exit.

"Mr. Trujillo," she called. "Could I speak to you for a minute?"

He turned to look at her. Two younger men, presumably his passengers, had been walking in the direction of the LUV as well. They stopped and melted back into the construction site. Joanna made no effort to stop them. The driver was the one she wanted. His face, hair, and worn work clothes were all covered with a thin layer of grimy gray dust that made him resemble a ghost. The man's hardened gaze left Joanna wishing that she weren't alone.

"What do you want?" he asked.

Hearing his heavily accented but perfect English, Joanna was relieved. While waiting in the car she had struggled to imagine how, without Frank Montoya there to translate, she'd be able to communicate with this man.

"The woman you took to the hospital this morning works for me," Joanna said hurriedly. "I wanted to say thank you."

The man's expression softened slightly. "She is still alive then?" he asked.

"Yes."

"And she will live?"

"The doctors don't know, but she wouldn't have even a chance at living if it hadn't been for you."

"I'm glad," he said, inserting his key in the lock. "I'll be going then."

"No," Joanna objected. "Please. We need to find the people who did this. Did you and your friends see what happened?"

Ephrain Trujillo looked at her and didn't answer, but his silence spoke volumes. He didn't trust her, and Joanna understood why. There was a gulf of antipathy between Joanna Brady with her uniform and badge and this hardworking laborer and his most likely illegal friends. For immigrants without green cards, Joanna represented the enemy. People like her were the ones who stood in the way of UDAs coming to the United States, doing work American citizens had no desire to do, earning a living wage, and supporting their families back home in Mexico or Nicaragua or El Salvador. But in order to learn the truth about what had happened to Jeannine Phillips, Joanna had to find a way to bridge that gap.

"I don't work for the Border Patrol or INS," Joanna explained. "It makes no difference to me whether or not you and your friends have green cards. I simply need to know what you saw and where it happened."

"Are you placing me under arrest?"

"No," Joanna returned. "You're not under arrest and you won't be. Neither will your friends, but I do need your help. Please, Mr. Trujillo. Jeannine's arms and legs are broken. Her face has been smashed. She will most likely lose the sight in one eye. The doctors removed one kidney and her spleen. The people who did this must be caught. You helped her once by saving her life. Please help her again."

Ephrain sighed. "What do you wish to know?"

"Where did you find her?" Joanna asked. "How did you find her?"

Shaking his head, Ephrain walked to a stack of unused blocks and sat down on it. Joanna followed, taking out a notebook as she went. When she reached the stack of bricks, he took off his bandanna and used it to whack some of the dust off the bricks beside him, cleaning a place for her to sit.

"Thank you," she said.

He nodded and went on. "My wife's nephew and two of his friends came across the border near Naco the night before last and made it to our home in Douglas. My wife was worried about them being there. She called and asked me to go down and get them. Her nephew had a job that was promised to him on a farm up near San Simon, and I thought that, with this big job to do here in Tucson, my boss would maybe hire his friends. So I went down to Douglas after work yesterday afternoon to pick them up."

"You're saying there were three of them, not just two?"

"That's right. It was already late when we left Douglas, and the trip here took a long time. We had to come up the back way, through McNeal, because there's a big Border Patrol checkpoint between Douglas and Elfrida. The place where my nephew was going is a long way north of San Simon on a dirt road. As we were driving there, I came around a curve and saw a truck parked along the road. I saw the light rack on top and was sure it was Border Patrol and that we would be stopped. But then, when we got closer, I saw all the little dog doors on the side. So I knew it wasn't Border Patrol after all."

"The truck was just parked along the road? Where?"

"A couple of miles north of San Simon."

"Did you see anyone in it or around it?"

"The engine was running—most likely because it was so cold—and someone was inside," Ephrain acknowledged.

"What time was that?" Joanna asked.

"One o'clock or so. Maybe later."

"And then?"

"We drove on up the road and dropped my nephew off. Then we turned around and came back. It's a long way and the road is very rough, so it took an hour or so. But when we got close enough to see where the truck had been parked, there were lights there—lots of them."

"What kind of lights?"

"Car lights. Headlights. I wanted to know what was going on, but I didn't want them to see us. I shut off my headlights and drove for a while by moonlight. Then, when I was afraid they might hear the engine, I got out of the truck and walked closer."

"By yourself, or did the others walk with you?"

"I have my green card," Ephrain answered. "The others don't. I told them to wait in the truck. I walked close enough until I could hear her. She was screaming, begging for them to stop. They were laughing and shouting. 'Kick her again,' one of them said. 'Kick her again.' And they did," he added. "Once you have heard that sound—the sound of someone being kicked in the belly or the ribs—or once you've felt it, you don't forget."

He paused and wiped his face with the soiled bandanna. When he took the cloth away, some telltale dampness lingered on his cheek. Joanna couldn't help but wonder where it was that Ephrain Trujillo had come to know so much about how it felt and sounded for one human being to kick another.

"And then what happened?" Joanna asked.

"They were too busy having a good time to notice me."

"How many were there?"

"I don't know. Half a dozen, maybe."

"Men?" Joanna asked. "And could you see them?"

"Not very well. They were behind their cars."

"Behind them?"

"They were all in a circle. The cars, four of them at least, had their lights on and were shining on the circle. That way they could all see what was going on. Animals!" Ephrain spat disgustedly into the dust beside him. "They wanted light so they could see what they were doing to her."

Had she been able to, Joanna might have spat, too, but her mouth was too dry. "What happened then?" she asked.

Ephrain shrugged. "I made them stop," he said.

"You did?" Joanna asked. "By yourself? I thought you said your friends stayed in your truck. But still, even with three of you, you were still outnumbered."

"I made them stop," Ephrain repeated, emphasizing the first word so there could be no mistake about it. "By myself," he added. He turned and looked at her. "The world is a dangerous place," he said softly. "If you are raised in a certain way or in a certain place, you have to learn to take care of yourself. If you don't, you die."

"How did you stop them?" Joanna asked.

Ephrain shrugged. "The coyotes and the drug smugglers—they are always on the roads, always looking for trouble or making trouble. They beat people up and steal their cars. And there are lots of people in this country who can't call someone like you to come help them."

Finally Joanna caught the gist of what he was saying. "You have a gun?" she said.

When he looked at her again, he nodded. "In my truck," he said at last. "I keep it under the seat. For protection."

So this man—this hardworking man who had saved Jeannine Phillips's life—was also driving around southern Arizona with a loaded weapon concealed under the seat of his pickup truck. Ephrain Trujillo was right, the world truly was a dangerous place.

"What happened then?" she asked.

"I went back to my truck, got the gun, and came back. I didn't try to shoot them. I shot over their heads, but they took off like a bunch of scared rabbits. One of them tripped over a rock. He fell down. He must have twisted his ankle because he couldn't get up right away. He was calling for his friends to come help him; to wait for him. But they didn't. They took off and left him there alone. When he did get up, he hobbled over to the truck—the woman's truck. He got in that and drove off. They all drove off and left her there to die."

"But you didn't," Joanna said.

"No," Ephrain agreed. "I did not. At first I thought she was dead. But when I realized she wasn't, I ran back to my truck. My nephew and his friends had all been riding in the camper. We had blankets there because it was cold, but that way it looked like I was driving alone. We wrapped her in the blankets and came here to Tucson, to the hospital."

Frank arrived just then. Jamming on his brakes, he brought his Crown Victoria to a stop next to Joanna's and leaped out of the driver's seat. As Frank ran toward them, Ephrain rose to his feet as if to defend himself. Joanna leveled a warning look in Frank's direction, then she reached out and took Ephrain by the hand.

"This is my chief deputy, Mr. Trujillo," she said. "His name is Frank Montoya. Frank, this is Mr. Ephrain Trujillo. He and his friends are the ones who saved Jeannine's life last night. He's just been telling me all about it."

The two men stood there for an electric moment, regarding each other warily, then Frank held out his hand. "Gracias, Señor Trujillo," he said. "We can't thank you enough." It was enough to break the tension, but instead of resuming his seat, Ephrain started back toward his truck.

"It's getting late," he said. "I should be going now."

"Please, Mr. Trujillo," Joanna said. "There's one more thing. We need you to show us where all this happened."

"It's on Doubtful Canyon Road," he said. "North of San Simon. I'm sure you'll be able to find it."

"But we'll be able to find it much faster if you show us where it is," she said. "And the sooner we process the crime scene the better. Other vehicles may drive through the area and disturb tracks. Evidence can blow away in the wind . . ."

When it had been just the two of them—Ephrain and Joanna—the man had seemed at ease. Now that Frank had been added to the mix, however, Ephrain was outnumbered. Joanna didn't want to lose him.

"You lead the way in your vehicle," she said. "Frank and I can follow in ours."

"So I am not under arrest? I can take my truck?"

"You are not under arrest," Joanna confirmed. "And yes, you can take your vehicle. My detectives will need to interview you, but once they've done that—"

"But I already told you what I saw and what I did."

"Yes," Joanna said. "But I'm the sheriff, not a detective. They're the ones who take the official statements. I'll have them meet us in San Simon and do it there. That way you won't have to miss any work."

"But if there are detectives . . ." he objected. "What if they . . ."

"The detectives work for me," Joanna declared. "And they do what I say. You will not be placed under arrest by them or by me. Once you show us where all this happened and give my investigators an official statement, you will be free to go."

"What about my two friends?" he asked. "They rode here with me. They have no way to get back to where they are staying."

"They were there with you?" Joanna asked. "They were the ones who helped you bring Jeannine to the hospital?"

Ephrain nodded.

"It would be helpful to have them go along as well," Joanna said. "They may have noticed something you didn't. And, if you're hungry, we can stop off in Benson and have some food along the way."

"But you will not turn them over to INS?"

"No, Mr. Trujillo," she said. "I promise."

It took a few minutes for Ephrain to find his lurking compatriots. Shortly after that, an odd-looking caravan headed south on Campbell through afternoon-rush-hour traffic, headed for the freeway. The faded red Chevy LUV led the way, followed by the two Crown Victorias. Joanna took the opportunity to grab for her radio. Her lead dispatcher, Larry Kendrick, took the call.

"Time to roust out the troops," she said. "Dave Hollicker, and the homicide guys, Jaime Carbajal, and Debbie Howell," she said. "And if you happen to have an extra deputy hanging loose in the northeast sector, you might send him along as well. We'll meet everyone at the near end of Doubtful Canyon Road in San Simon. Since we don't know exactly where we're going, we'll lead them from there."

By the time they reached the little Mexican food dive in Benson, Joanna's flattened bladder was in a world of hurt. She went inside and used the facilities. When she returned from the rest room, Frank was busy ordering food for Ephrain and the others.

"I'm going outside to call Butch," she told Frank when he finished with the waitress. "I need to let him know that most likely I'll be late for dinner."

Frank nodded absently and Joanna hurried outside. But not to telephone—at least, not right away. The first thing she did was open the Crown Victoria's trunk and take out her Kevlar vest. She finally had to lie down flat on the passenger side of the front seat before she could fasten the damned thing, and once it was on, she could barely breathe. But Ephrain Trujillo's casual admission that he routinely carried a gun—a telling reminder that lots of people, good and bad people—carried guns, had gotten Joanna's undivided attention. In opting not to wear the bulky vest—in choosing temporary comfort over safety—she had put both herself and her baby at risk.

What's the matter with you? she lectured herself. *I thought you were all about leading by example.*

Feeling like a little kid stuffed into last year's snowsuit, she managed to stand up. Only then did she call Butch.

"When are you going to have this baby?" he asked.

"I hope it'll be any day now. Why?"

"Because my parents are driving me crazy," he said. "Mom saw you on the *Noon News*. She wanted to know why a sheriff's office would be in charge of the dogcatchers."

"So you know about Jeannine Phillips then?" Joanna asked.

"I do," he said. "Heard about it from Jim Bob. We were supposed to go there for dinner tonight, but he and Eva Lou have spent the whole day filling in at the pound, so he called a little while ago to beg off. We're going out for pizza instead, much to Jenny's delight. What about you?"

"We've located someone who witnessed part of the attack on Jeannine," Joanna said. "We're on our way to the crime scene right now. I don't know when I'll be home. Probably not in time for dinner."

"Right," he said. "You're probably hiding out in your office and only pretending to be on your way to a crime scene. I know the real story. You don't want to have anything to do with my parents. The truth is, neither do I."

"You'll just have to buck up," Joanna said. "They won't be here forever."

"Oh, yeah?" Butch returned. "That's easy for you to say. You're not stuck here at the house with them. I may call Dr. Lee and ask what it would take to convince him to induce labor."

"From the way I'm feeling right now," Joanna said, "that doesn't sound like such a bad idea."

When she went back into the restaurant, the two younger men were greedily and silently mowing their way through individual platters of tacos. No doubt they were hungry after a hard day of physical labor, but they ate as though their hunger went deeper than that—as though it had been a long time since they'd been able to eat their fill.

Frank Montoya and Ephrain Trujillo had been speaking in Spanish. When Joanna finally managed to maneuver her bulky self onto a chair at the table, the two men politely switched to English. "Mr. Trujillo tells me that he came here from Nicaragua twenty years ago," Frank said. "He was granted political asylum."

Nicaragua. A country, yes, but also a word from the history books. Joanna recalled what had happened earlier, how just talking about the sound of someone being kicked had been enough to cause Ephrain's tears to flow. No wonder he carried a gun. And knew how to use it. And what about the two young men with him? Where did they come from? What had they seen? Whatever their origins, they trusted Ephrain enough to come here with him, to sit quietly in this restaurant with two police officers and to believe that, whatever was coming, Ephrain Trujillo would see them safely through it.

"Are you all right?" Frank asked.

"I'm fine," she said. "Why?"

"You look . . . I don't know . . . sort of uncomfortable. I was afraid . . ."

I am uncomfortable, she wanted to say. *I'm wearing this god-awful vest and I can hardly breathe.* "I'm fine," she said.

"Would you like something to eat?" Frank asked.

I couldn't squeeze in a bite without popping the Velcro, she thought. What she said was "No, thanks. I just had lunch."

Forty-five minutes later, they pulled into San Simon, where two more sheriff's department vehicles joined the caravan for the drive out to Doubtful Canyon Road. Half a mile beyond the locked and gated turnoff to Roostercomb Ranch, Ephrain Trujillo stopped the LUV just short of a low rise. He and his friends as well as Joanna's team of investigators exited their various vehicles and hiked up the hill behind Ephrain. Once at the top, Ephrain stood in the middle of the dirt roadway and pointed to a small, rock-strewn clearing off to one side.

"There," he said, pointing. "That's where it happened."

While Dave Hollicker and Casey Ledford began their painstaking examination of the crime scene, Jaime Carbajal and Debbie Howell began interviewing Ephrain Trujillo and his two so far nameless passengers. Debbie's Spanish wasn't fluent enough to do the questioning, so Jaime took the lead. With no definite jobs to do, Joanna and Frank stood off to one side while she briefed him on everything Ephrain had told her. They were standing there speculating about what Jeannine had been watching through her night-vision goggles when they heard a vehicle churning up the hill behind them.

They barely had time to scramble out of the way before an

old open-air jeep, spewing smoke and raising a cloud of dust, charged over the top of the rise.

"What the hell do you think you're doing?" the driver demanded as he stood on the brakes and brought the speeding vehicle to a skidding stop a few feet shy of where Joanna and Frank had been standing.

Joanna recognized Clarence O'Dwyer at once from the jagged scar that ran down one side of his face, a remnant of a barroom brawl in which younger brother Billy had attacked his older sibling with the business end of a broken Budweiser bottle. Both brothers had been hauled into the county jail. The sutures to stitch Clarence's face back together—all fifteen of them—had been done at sheriff's department expense. She also noted the wooden butt of a rifle sticking out of a scabbard next to the man's knee.

I wonder if this vest would stop a 30-06 slug at close range? she thought as she stepped forward to answer his question.

"Good afternoon, Mr. O'Dwyer," she said. "We're here investigating the attempted homicide of one of my officers around midnight last night. She was here investigating a complaint about a possible dogfighting ring. You wouldn't happen to know anything about that, would you?"

"Screw you!" Clarence said.

Somebody already did that, she felt like saying, but this was no time for tasteless jokes. "Do you know anything about it?" Joanna persisted.

"I don't know nothin'," Clarence growled. "Now get off my land!"

"We're well outside the fence line, which means we're all in the public right-of-way," she said. "It also means that we won't be leaving until we're good and ready or until we're done, whichever comes first."

In reply, Clarence flashed her a one-finger salute. Then he ground his gearshift into reverse and tore off back down the hill.

"Same to you, buddy," Joanna whispered under her breath. "Have a nice day."

CHAPTER 11

Joanna was still at the crime scene when Dr. Waller reached her. "Sheriff Brady," he began. "I can't imagine what you were thinking. You put me and the hospital in a terrible position!"

"Me?" Joanna asked innocently, but of course she knew exactly what was coming.

"When a woman claiming to be Jeannine Phillips's mother showed up late this morning and when she asked that we process a rape kit, I assumed she was legitimate—that you or one of your officers had actually made a next-of-kin notification. Imagine my surprise this afternoon, during rounds, when there was a near brawl in the ICU waiting room between two women, both of whom said Ms. Phillips was her daughter. The one had come all the way from Truth or Consequences, New Mexico. She only found out her daughter was hospitalized because a friend from Tucson called to check on her after seeing Ms. Phillips's name on the local news."

"How do you suppose such a thing happened?" Joanna re-turned. As she said the words, though, she was thinking about how the raised voices of two very angry women would have sounded in the hushed gloom of the ICU waiting room. And had the battle escalated to more than voices, Joanna suspected Milli-cent Ross would have been quite capable of physically defending herself.

"Right," Dr. Waller said sarcastically. "I'm sure you can't. And since the rape kit was illegally obtained, I'm not at all sure the re-sults will stand up in court."

Joanna felt a sudden chill. "So she was raped then?"

"Your name isn't on the approved notification list." Dr. Waller's reply was crisp. "Privacy rules preclude me from giving you any information concerning her condition. Once I realized that we were dealing with an impostor, I would have thrown the woman out altogether, but it happened that Jeannine had re-gained consciousness enough by then to make her wishes known. So the fake mother is now on the official visitors and notification list. As for the real mother? She bitched me out three ways to Sun-day. I finally had to have security escort her out of the building."

Dr. Waller was pissed, and he was calling to do his own bitching-out. If he expected Joanna to repent her actions, his words failed to have their intended effect. Jeannine Phillips had been raped by her assailants. Knowing that left Joanna sick at heart, but at least Millicent Ross was now cleared to be there with Jeannine rather than the parents who had betrayed her time and again. In the face of Jeannine's otherwise dire circumstances, at least that one small thing had gone right, but Joanna could hardly blame Dr. Waller for his entirely righteous anger.

"I'm sorry for all the confusion," Joanna said. It was all the apology she could muster.

"No, you're not," Waller returned and slammed the phone down in her ear. Joanna didn't blame him for needing to have the last word. She deserved it.

Frank had been standing there hanging on every word of the conversation. "She was raped?" he asked when Joanna flipped her cell phone shut.

Joanna nodded grimly.

"If they did a rape kit, we'll have DNA evidence," Frank said.

Joanna didn't respond to that. She didn't want to acknowledge that evidence from the rape kit might not be admissible, but it would still give them information they could use in the investigation to verify possible evidence they might collect in some other fashion.

"But is she going to make it?" Frank continued.

"No word on that," Joanna returned. "At least not from the doctor."

In the course of the next hour or so, she tried to reach Millicent Ross several times but never got through. Joanna finally left the crime scene and dragged her weary butt into the house at 10 P.M. Everyone else seemed to be in bed. Two pieces of somewhat bedraggled pepperoni pizza had been left out for her on the kitchen counter. She downed them gratefully. If indigestion visited her again tonight, so be it.

In the bedroom, Butch was asleep with the light on and with a book plastered to his nose. Once she was undressed, she removed the book, put it on the nightstand, and doused the light. When she got into bed, Butch stirred.

"You're home," he said. "Are things okay?"

"Not really," she said. "We still don't know if Jeannine's going to make it, and it turns out she was raped."

"I'm sorry," Butch mumbled sleepily. "What about you? Are you all right?"

"I'm fine," she said, although she didn't feel fine. "All I need is a decent night's sleep."

But a good night's sleep wasn't in the cards. She had to get up three different times overnight, and each time she came back to bed she lay awake for an hour or so agonizing over what was going on at work. When she finally awoke the next morning, she could tell it was late by the way the sun was shining into the bedroom. When she looked at the clock, she was astonished to see it was already after eight.

After showering and dressing, she went looking for Butch and found him in the kitchen at his computer. "Why did you let me oversleep?" she demanded.

"Because you obviously needed it," he returned. "You were snoring up a storm when I got out of bed. I called Frank and told him you'd be late. He said not to rush, so sit down and have your tea. I can have your breakfast ready in five."

Glad for the temporary respite, Joanna did as she was told. "Where are your parents?" she asked.

"I asked Jenny for some help, and she sweet-talked them into taking her to school," Butch answered. "That way I have a few minutes to work, and you can make it through the morning without any of my mother's dogcatcher comments."

Joanna tasted her apricot-flavored tea. It was heavenly. Butch pushed his computer aside and then went over to the stove. "What would you like?"

The question made Joanna smile. "You still sound like a short-order cook," she said.

"I am a short-order cook," he returned. "Eggs, bacon, toast?"

"Sounds wonderful," Joanna said, and took another sip of tea. "So your mother was still off on her dogcatcher tangent this morning?"

"In spades," Butch said. "Especially after Jim Bob called."

"What did he have to say?"

"He wanted me to tell you that he and Eva Lou would be back at the pound today and for as long as you need them. He also said you shouldn't worry, that Eva Lou and the python are getting along just fine." Butch paused long enough to crack a pair of eggs into a skillet. "Which causes me to ask," he added, "what python? I don't remember anyone mentioning that Animal Control had picked up a stray python. I thought they mostly did dogs and cats."

"They mostly do," Joanna answered. "Jeannine picked the snake up out in Sierra Vista the other day. Some guy left town and abandoned his pet python in his old apartment. The landlady was evidently quite upset."

"Well," said Butch, "apparently the python is trying to become the next Houdini. He had made it out of his kennel or cage or whatever you call it and was on his way to find himself a tasty morsel of kitty-cat when Jim Bob and Eva Lou showed up. According to him, the clerk was a complete basket case, and Eva Lou spent most of the day taking care of her."

"I so do not need a python right now," Joanna said.

Butch grinned. "But you should have seen the effect hearing about it had on my mother. Gave a whole new meaning to her idea of what a 'dogcatcher's life' is all about. Of course, if you like, we could always trade. I'll go into the office for you or go help out around the pound, and you can stay here with my parents."

"No deal," Joanna returned.

"I didn't think so."

Joanna arrived at the office at nine-thirty. She hadn't come in all day yesterday, so her desk was buried under one day's worth of paperwork, and Kristin was already hard at work sorting out the latest batch. Instead of starting to play catch-up, Joanna picked up her phone and dialed University Medical Center. When she asked to be put through to Jeannine Phillips's room, Millicent Ross answered.

"How's she doing?" Joanna asked.

"It was a rough night," Millicent replied. "But they finally upped her pain meds. She's sleeping now. The phone didn't even wake her."

"And how are you?" Joanna asked.

"Tired but okay," Millicent said, although she didn't sound okay.

"I know about the rape," Joanna said.

"The lousy bastards!" Millicent breathed. "I always thought Jeannine was strong as an ox. How did they . . . ?"

"The guy who chased them away said there were at least six of them. She didn't stand a chance."

"Did the O'Dwyers do it?" Millicent asked. "Are they the ones responsible?"

"We don't know one way or the other," Joanna said. "We're investigating, of course. And that's going to take time. How is she? The doctor wouldn't give me any information."

"I'm not surprised. I thought Waller was going to have a heart attack when he realized I wasn't Jeannine's mother. Thank you for that, by the way," Millicent added. "It meant a lot to both of us. At least I'm able to be here for her. As for her long-term prospects? They're not very good. The broken bones will mend. A decent plastic surgeon may be able to do something with her face, but her internal injuries are still life-threatening. As for her right eye? It's gone."

"Gone?" Joanna repeated.

"She'll be totally blind in that eye."

"I'm so sorry," Joanna murmured.

"Don't be sorry," Millicent said. "Just get the bastards."

"We're doing our best," Joanna said. "But how are you managing? Is everything under control at your clinic?"

"Yes. I dropped off all the animals from my clinic—including the little pit bull Jeannine found—with Dr. Tompkins out in Sierra Vista. If I have any emergencies, they'll be directed to him as well."

"You're going to stay there then?" Joanna asked.

"Yes," Millicent said. "For as long as it takes."

Kristin came to the door and mimed that Joanna had another call. "Sorry to cut you off," Joanna said, "but I have to go." She hung up. "Who is it?" she asked Kristin.

"Tom Hadlock," Kristin replied.

Tom was Joanna's jail commander. "We've had a little incident," he said when Joanna came on the line.

Fresh from the disturbing news about Jeannine's injuries, the idea of any kind of jail incident—little or otherwise—made Joanna's blood run cold. "What kind of incident?" she asked.

"There was a dustup with some cell-made weapons out in the exercise yard."

"Was anyone hurt?"

"Not badly enough for stitches. The guards broke it up right away. The two guys involved are in solitary, and the whole jail is under lockdown while we search for additional weapons. In other words, it's all under control, but I wanted you to know what's going on."

"Thanks, Tom," she said. "I appreciate it."

For a few minutes after the second phone call she sat staring into space. Then she picked up the notebook she took to the briefings and wrote: "Discuss with Frank. Need new ACO."

Moments later, the man himself appeared in her doorway. "Time for the briefing," he said.

"You heard about the problem at the jail?"

Frank nodded. "It's a good thing the guards stopped it when they did. It could have been a lot worse, but there is some good news."

"What's that?"

"Casey Ledford rides again," he said with a grin.

"Are you saying she got a hit on AFIS?" Joanna asked. "What kind?"

"She didn't give me the details," Frank returned. "She said she'd meet us in the conference room to go over what she's found."

Casey, Jaime Carbajal, and Debbie Howell were already assembled by the time Joanna and Frank got there. Dave Hollicker came rushing in a few minutes later as Joanna was giving the group an update on Jeannine's condition, including the disturbing news that the animal control officer had been raped.

"In other words," Frank said when Joanna finished, "we've got to nail these guys!"

"Exactly," Joanna said. "Not only the ones who actually did the dirty work, but the ones who are behind it."

"The O'Dwyers?" Frank asked.

"That would be my guess." She turned to Casey. "Now, then, I understand you may have found something?"

"I found lots of somethings," Casey said. "For one thing, I lifted prints from the boulder that was used to smash the window on Jeannine's truck. AFIS says those prints belong to a guy named Antonio Zavala, a nineteen-year-old gangbanger from Tucson. He's got a string of moving violations, including driving while suspended. Pima County has a warrant out on him for suspicion of grand theft auto. And the guy who got left behind and drove away in Jeannine's vehicle? His name is Juan Mendoza. He was released from Fort Grant just two months ago on the occasion of his twenty-first birthday. He was sixteen when he got locked up in juvie for vehicular manslaughter, which probably should have been Murder One. The guy who got run over just happened to be dating Juan's ex-girlfriend."

"Do we have addresses on those two guys?" Joanna asked.

"Possibly," Casey said. "But not for sure. Pima County is in the process of forwarding whatever they have."

"Back to the prints. Are those the only ones you have?" Joanna asked.

"No," Casey replied. "There are lots more that I haven't been able to process yet. Dave collected a whole bunch of rocks where Luminol located blood spatter. Once he gets what he needs from those, I'll process them to see if I can lift any prints from them as well."

Joanna turned to Detective Carbajal. "You and Debbie will head up to Tucson?" she asked.

"Yes, ma'am," he said. "As soon as we get the info from Tucson, we're on our way. Should we go by the hospital while we're there?" he added. "Is Jeannine in any shape to be interviewed?"

"I doubt it," Joanna returned. "But since you're going to be in Tucson anyway, you could just as well check and see. Millicent will be able to say whether or not Jeannine can handle visitors or questions."

"Millicent?" Jaime said. "Millicent who?"

"Millicent Ross, the vet. She and Jeannine are together."

Jaime raised an eyebrow. "As in partners?"

"As in," Joanna returned.

Jaime made a note. "What about the Bradley Evans investigation?" he asked. "Are we dropping it for the time being, or what?"

"Something has to give," Joanna said. "With Ernie gone, we're way too shorthanded to do everything. As far as I can tell, no one other than Ted Chapman is particularly upset over Evans's death, which means no one is going to be pressuring us to solve that case. Jeannine Phillips, on the other hand, is one of our own. She was in the process of investigating possible criminal activity when she was attacked."

"In other words," Jaime said, "we're pulling out all the stops."

Joanna nodded. "That's right," she said.

Around the table Joanna's grim-faced team of investigators nodded in solemn agreement.

"Is there anything else?" she asked. When no one volunteered anything, Joanna nodded. "All right then, you guys," she told them. "Go get 'em."

The investigators hustled out of the conference room, leaving Joanna and Frank alone. "What are we going to do about Jeannine's position?" Frank asked.

"Fill it," Joanna said.

"A temporary fix or a permanent one?"

"Temporary for now," Joanna said. "Check with the part-timers. Maybe one of them will be able to work full-time for the next little while, but if Jeannine's injuries are as severe as Millicent said, she may never be able to come back."

"That's tragic!" Frank exclaimed.

Joanna nodded. "I couldn't agree more. I know you're working on checking phones and credit-card charges on Bradley Evans, but if you have any spare time, see what you can find out about the O'Dwyers. I have a general idea of what they've been up to the past few years, but we need specifics. If they sicced that gang of thugs on Jeannine because she was too close to something, I want to find out what that something is."

"Will do, boss," Frank told her.

The remainder of their morning briefing took the better part of an hour. After that, Joanna went into her office and dived into the paperwork. It was close to one when the phone rang. "Are you ready for lunch?" Butch asked. "Dad heard it's pasty day at Daisy's Café. I called and they still have a few left. I put three of them on hold. One each for Mom and Dad and another for the two of us to split."

"Sounds great," Joanna said. "I'll be right there."

Cornish pasties—meat pies filled with cooked beef, rutabagas, and other vegetables—had migrated from Cornwall, England, to Bisbee, Arizona, along with the miners who had hailed from there. Because pasties were readily portable, miners had taken them underground in lunch pails. Most mining operations in and around Bisbee had been shut down for decades, but the foods the miners had brought with them from all over the world remained part of Bisbee's traditional fare. Don Dixon had been astonished to find pasties available in southeastern Arizona on a previous visit and had been thrilled to find that the ones served at Daisy's compared very favorably with the ones he remembered finding in Upper Michigan.

Junior Dowdle met Joanna at the door. "I want to see the baby," he said with his customary grin.

"So do I," Joanna said.

"When?"

"Soon now," she said. "I hope."

Junior led her to the table where Butch and his parents were already seated.

"Is he always here?" Margaret asked with a frown and a nod in Junior's direction as he walked away from the table. "He's so weird."

"He's not weird, Mom," Butch explained. "Junior may be developmentally disabled, but he's far less weird than a lot of so-called normal people around here."

"Still," Margaret insisted. "It seems to me that having someone like him hanging around all the time would be bad for business."

"He isn't hanging around," Butch said. "He actually *works* here—as in making a contribution."

Seeing Butch's temper fraying, Joanna tried to smooth things over. "He's really very nice."

Junior returned with a glass of water, which he placed in front of Joanna. "Yes," he said, thumping his chest while looking directly at Margaret Dixon. "Nice, not deaf." And then he stalked off.

As Junior walked away that time, Joanna was gratified to see Margaret blush to the roots of her peroxided hair. Junior Dowdle had nailed her. It was about time someone did.

"Are you ready to order?" Daisy Maxwell asked.

They ordered and ate, but lunch wasn't a complete success. Joanna, Butch, and Don downed their pasties with gusto. Margaret picked at hers.

"I doubt Mom will be eager to come back here anytime soon," Butch said to Joanna as he walked her to her car.

"You're right," Joanna agreed. "But I wouldn't have missed it for the world."

Butch grinned. "Me either."

B ack at the Justice Center, Joanna was disappointed not to hear anything from Debbie Howell and Jaime Carbajal. While waiting for word, she returned to the drudgery of paperwork. She was lost in concentration when Ted Chapman showed up an hour later.

"Any progress?" he asked.

He was asking for progress in the Bradley Evans case. Joanna was reluctant to tell him that the Jeannine Phillips assault case had knocked his friend's down a notch as far as priority was concerned.

"Not much," she answered.

"What does that mean?"

"It means we've located the person he was stalking," Joanna said. "That is, we know who she is, but no one's had a chance to interview her yet."

"Why not?"

"Because we're shorthanded, Ted," Joanna returned. "Ernie's off for the next several days. We've got another important case that we're working on up near San Simon. But believe me, she will be interviewed."

"Oh," Ted said. "All right. I just wanted to let you know that Brad's funeral is tomorrow at one o'clock in the afternoon. It'll be held at the Papago Unit at the prison down in Douglas. People who want to attend need to be on the guest list for security reasons. Do you think any of the detectives on the case will want to go?"

Joanna knew Ernie was out and Debbie and Jaime would be busy with the Phillips case. Frank would have his hands full all morning with the board of supervisors meeting. That left only one person available.

"Put me on the list," she said. "I'll be there."

"Thanks," Ted said. He started to leave. As he turned, Joanna noticed the name badge clipped to his shirt pocket—a name badge that came complete with a photo ID.

"Do the jail ministry guys down in Douglas wear the same kind of name badge?" she asked.

Ted looked down at his. "Sure," he said. "Why?"

"Do you think you could get someone from there to fax me a copy of Bradley Evans's ID photo?"

"Probably," he said. "I'll see what I can do."

He left. Joanna went back to work, but her mind wandered. She kept going back to what she had said to Ted. Yes, Debbie had located Leslie Markham, the woman who had been Bradley Evans's stalking target. That had happened day before yesterday. More than twenty-four hours had passed without anyone interviewing the woman. Regardless of what else was going on in Joanna's department, it was inexcusable to allow an important lead to lie fallow for that long this early in an investigation.

A few minutes later, when Kristin came into her office carrying a faxed copy of Bradley Evans's ID photo, Joanna made up her mind. She rummaged through the mess on her desk until she located an interoffice envelope containing her copies of the prints from the camera found in Bradley Evans's vehicle. The same envelope also contained a mug shot of Bradley Evans that dated from his original arrest back in 1978. There was some resemblance between the young man in the mug shot and the guy in the ID photo, but clearly the years spent in prison hadn't been kind to him.

With all the photos now collected in the same envelope, Joanna stuffed it into her briefcase. Then she jotted down the address of Rory Markham Real Estate Group, told Kristin she was on her way to Sierra Vista, and left the office. As she drove, she was honest enough to realize that the main reason she was going was to get away from the paper jungle on her desk, even though she knew that leaving it for another day would only make matters worse.

Something's got to give, she told herself sternly. And then, as if she had heard it yesterday, she remembered the advice her boss, Milo Davis, had given her years ago when she was working in his insurance agency. "You've got to stop majoring in the minors," he had told her. "Don't get sidetracked by the little stuff. Do the important stuff first."

That was good advice then, and it's good advice now, she told herself. *Tomorrow's the day you start running the paperwork instead of letting the paperwork run you.*

When Joanna had first arrived at the department as its duly elected sheriff, Kristin had been more than a little hostile. She had also been very young. Joanna had been accustomed to managing an insurance office. In the beginning it had been easier for her simply to do the work herself than to give Kristin more responsibility while, at the same time, making sure things were done right. But now she was on a much better footing with Kristin, and it was time to teach her the difference between what really needed to land on Joanna's desk and what didn't.

When it comes time to sort tomorrow morning's mail, Joanna vowed, *Kristin and I will do it together. We'll sort the new stuff as well as what's already on my desk. Once we finish . . .*

Her reverie was interrupted by the baby suddenly launching a drop kick into her lowest rib hard enough to make her Kevlar vest rise and fall. The kicks came along sporadically when she was in the office or out in public, where she mostly managed to ignore them. This time, though, she was alone in a vehicle, and the baby's movements made her feel incredibly happy. He or she was alive and kicking in the middle of the afternoon. Maybe that meant the child would arrive with an inborn knowledge of the difference between day and night. Having a baby that slept through the night from the beginning would be an incredible blessing. Of course, the opposite was always possible.

Joanna was still thinking about the baby when she arrived at Rory Markham Real Estate Group on Fry Boulevard just west of Highway 92. The building had once housed a local fast-food establishment before it succumbed to the competition from too many nationally owned franchises. Someone had spent time and money trying to take away the distinctive Tacos to Go aura, but somehow the lowbrow image still lingered. The website had made the place sound far more upscale than the company's physical presence warranted.

Trying to brush off this negative first impression, Joanna went inside. "I'd like to see Mrs. Markham," Joanna said, handing her card to the receptionist.

The receptionist studied the card for a long moment. "Can I tell her what this is about?" she asked.

Joanna smiled. "It's personal," she said.

The clerk went away and returned a few moments followed by Leslie Markham. Joanna's first impression was that she was familiar; that Joanna had met her somewhere before—perhaps at one of the many campaign functions she had attended prior to the election.

The photos Joanna had seen of Leslie Tazewell Markham—Bradley Evans's stealthily captured images or the promotional ones downloaded from the Internet—had not done the woman justice. Leslie was an attractive brunette with lush wavy hair that surrounded a fine-boned face. Her complexion was flawless, and the blue eyes she turned on Joanna were disarmingly direct. Still, there was an air of sadness about her, something that her upscale business attitude and attire didn't quite conceal.

"Sheriff Brady?" she asked, holding out her hand. "You wanted to see me?"

"Yes, I did," Joanna said. "Is there somewhere we could talk privately?"

Leslie turned back to the receptionist. "Is anyone in the conference room, Fran?"

"No, it's free," Fran said, casting a suspicious glance in Joanna's direction.

Leslie led the way into a small conference room. "What's this all about?" she asked. "Is there a problem?"

Joanna reached into her briefcase, pulled out Bradley Evans's ID photo, and slid it across the table. "Does this man look familiar?"

Leslie picked up the picture, studied it closely, and then handed it back. "No," she said. "I don't think I've ever seen him before. Who is he?"

"Maybe he came through your office here looking to buy a house," Joanna suggested.

"Then he must have spoken to someone besides me," Leslie replied. "I remember all my clients. I don't recognize him."

Listening as Leslie spoke and watching her reactions, Joanna believed she was telling the truth.

"What about these?" Joanna asked. She held the envelope over the table and let the photos spill out.

Leslie studied several of them. When she looked back at Joanna there could be no doubt about her dismay. "Where did you get these?" she demanded. "Who took them? Am I under surveillance for something?"

"These aren't police photos," Joanna said. "We believe you were being stalked."

"Stalked," Leslie echoed faintly.

"Do you have any idea when they were taken?" Joanna asked.

Leslie studied the photos more closely. "It must have been sometime last week," she said. "I bought that outfit on my last trip to Tucson two weeks ago. Last week was the first time I wore it to work."

"Do you know what day that was?" Joanna asked.

"Wednesday or Thursday. I guess it must have been Wednesday, but tell me, who took these pictures?" Leslie demanded. "And how were they taken without my knowledge? Whoever did it must have followed me for hours—from the post office to the mall to the grocery store. This is too creepy." She paused and then shivered slightly as a look of understanding crossed her face. "Wait a minute. It's him, isn't it," she said. "The guy whose picture you just showed me is the one who was following me around. Who is he? What does he want?"

"His name is Bradley Evans," Joanna said. "I was hoping you could tell me what he wanted."

"How can I? I've never met the man or even heard his name."

"Is it possible you might have met him somewhere? Maybe he went by another name."

"No. I already told you. I've never seen him before."

"And you have no idea why this complete stranger would have wanted to take your photograph?" Joanna asked.

"None whatsoever," Leslie said defiantly. "Here's an idea. Why don't you ask him?"

"We can't because he's dead," Joanna answered. "Because somebody murdered him. We found the camera with the photos still in it hidden in his vehicle."

Leslie Markham's eyes widened. Then she stood up. "If you'll excuse me," she said, "I think I need to go get my husband."

CHAPTER 12

L eslie Markham returned to the conference room a few
minutes later with her husband on her heels. Rory
Markham was tall, tanned, fit, good looking, and notice-
ably older than his wife. Seeing him, Joanna couldn't help
remembering her conversation with Debbie about how it looked
as though Leslie Tazewell had managed to marry up. At first
glance that still seemed to be the case.

"So some maniac is going around taking pictures of my
wife," Rory Markham said. "Isn't that against some law or another? Isn't it an invasion of privacy?"

"It may be disconcerting," Joanna said, "but it's not against
the law."

"Well, it should be," Rory returned. "And it's a good thing
the son of a bitch is already dead. If he weren't, I'd track him
down myself and tear him a new asshole."

"Rory!" Leslie admonished. "You shouldn't talk that way."

He leveled a look in Leslie's direction, and she subsided into silence. This bullying exchange wasn't lost on Joanna. Was this man understandably concerned for his wife's well-being, she wondered, or was there something else at work here? Jealousy, perhaps? That was always a powerful motivator, and Rory didn't look like the type who would appreciate or tolerate having an interloper poaching on his turf. Not only that, it was clear that underneath Markham's suave exterior of perfect clothing, perfect hair, and perfect teeth lurked something far rougher. Like the refurbished building that held Rory Markham's business, the man's lowbrow Tacos to Go roots lingered despite an extensive makeover.

"You wouldn't happen to have any idea about how that might have happened, would you?"

Rory drew himself up and glared down at Joanna with total disdain. "Certainly not!" he exclaimed. "Are you accusing me of having something to do with the man's murder?"

"I'm simply asking questions," Joanna said. "That's what we do in the aftermath of a homicide—ask questions, particularly if someone seems to have issues with the victim."

"Show him the man's picture," Leslie urged. "Maybe he'll recognize him."

Joanna produced the faxed copy of Bradley's jail ministry ID photo and handed it to him. Rory looked at it for a moment and then gave it back. "I've never seen this jerk before in my life. Who the hell was he?"

"His name was Bradley Evans."

"What was he, one of those papa-whatevers?"

"Paparazzi?" Joanna supplied.

"Right," Rory said. "That's what I meant. One of those . . . paparazzi. Maybe that's why he was taking pictures of Leslie. Maybe he worked for one of those scumbag kinds of newspapers. You know what I mean—the ones they sell in grocery stores—the *National Enquirer* or something like that."

"Why would they be interested in your wife?" Joanna asked.

"I suppose it's possible," Leslie mused. "With my father up for that federal appointment . . ."

"Your father?" Joanna repeated. "Who's he?"

"Justice Lawrence Tazewell. He's on the Arizona Supreme Court, but now he's up for a possible federal judgeship."

For the first time it occurred to Joanna that she had been wrong. Leslie wasn't the one who had married up. Her husband had. And as far as that went, it meant Leslie was following a long-standing family script—one that remained a lingering part of Cochise County's social fabric. Joanna simply hadn't connected Leslie to that particular family of Tazewells.

Local lore had it that, in the late sixties, while an impoverished law school student at the University of Arizona, Lawrence Tazewell had won the heart of Aileen Houlihan, a fellow student who sprang from some of southeastern Arizona's finest pioneer stock. Aileen's paternal great-grandparents had settled in the northeastern corner of the San Pedro Valley while marauding Apaches, annoyed at being barred from their traditional hunting lands, were still a very real danger. The Triple H Ranch, in the foothills of the Whetstones, had been named for the family patriarch, Henry Hieronymus Houlihan. The Triple H had started out as a cattle ranch, raising Herefords, but now it was primarily known for its prizewinning quarter horses.

"My parents divorced a long time ago," Leslie continued. "But now that my father's being considered as a possible nominee for one of the open federal judgeships, everything about his life is back in the news, including my mother and me. This could be related to that."

"I doubt it," Joanna said. "Bradley Evans was working as a drug and alcohol counselor at the Arizona State Prison Complex down in Douglas. He went to prison in 1978 for murdering his wife. After his release two years ago, he started working for a jail ministry organization. He was still working for them at the time he died."

"That doesn't come close to explaining why he was taking pictures of Leslie," Rory Markham put in.

"No," Joanna agreed. "It doesn't. Are there any other possibilities that come to mind?"

Rory turned to his wife. "Well?" he asked.

The one-word question wasn't asked in a polite way. His tone of voice underscored the decades of difference in their ages. Rory sounded less like a husband and more like an irate father who had caught his teenage daughter smoking forbidden cigarettes out in the backyard.

"Maybe he's someone from before," Rory suggested. "Maybe he's someone you dated before I came along."

Leslie looked stricken. "You know better than that," she said, blushing furiously. "You're the only man I've ever dated. And, as I already told her, I have no idea who this person is."

Rory picked up one of the photos and examined it before tossing it back down on the table. "If he was close enough to take a picture like this, how can you claim you never saw him?"

"As you can see, I was busy," Leslie said. "I was pushing the grocery cart. I was opening the car door. I was walking. He may have seen me, but I didn't see him. Besides," she added, turning to Joanna, "don't these guys have telephoto lenses?"

"Not this one," Joanna answered. "He used a throwaway."

"See there?" Rory demanded. "What did I just tell you?"

Without answering, Leslie rose and fled the conference

room. She wasn't in tears, but she was close to it. Rory stayed where he was for a moment longer after the door slammed shut, then he turned to Joanna and shrugged. "I guess we can't help you," he said.

"I guess not," Joanna agreed. "Thank you anyway."

"Can you find your own way out?"

"No problem." Joanna gathered up the photos and put them back into the envelope and then returned to her Crown Victoria. No wonder Rory Markham Real Estate Group boasted such a humble physical presence. Rory had started out by making a bad impression, and it had been all downhill from there. In a service industry based on interpersonal relationships, it was a miracle he was able to stay in business at all.

I wouldn't buy a used car from that turkey, Joanna thought to herself as she headed back to Bisbee. *What in the world does Leslie see in him?*

But as far as what Rory might see in Leslie, that was much clearer. Leslie Tazewell was bound to turn into an heiress the moment her mother died. That explained why, in addition to her youth and good looks, Rory might be interested in her, but nothing Joanna had learned came close to explaining Bradley Evans's interest in the woman. That was still very much a mystery.

By the time Joanna made it back to the Justice Center, it was already after five. She was tired. *If something urgent happens,* she told herself, *they can call me at home.* And home she went.

Along the road the scrawny trunks and tangled bare branches of mesquite trees gleamed black in the late-afternoon sun. Ready to be home and warm, Joanna was surprised to find Jenny out on High Lonesome Road riding Kiddo at a full gallop, with all three dogs trailing along behind. When Joanna pulled up beside her and rolled down her window, Jenny reined in the horse.

"Out having fun?" Joanna asked.

"Not exactly," Jenny said with a scowl. "I had to get away. Butch's mother follows me everywhere I go, even into my room, asking me all kinds of stupid questions—things that are none of her business. When are they ever going to leave, Mom? It feels like they've been here forever. Why did Butch let them come?"

"He didn't," Joanna said. "Having them show up was as much a surprise to him as it was to us."

"But that's rude. I mean, shouldn't they have waited for an invitation?"

"Yes," Joanna agreed. "It is rude, but Margaret and Don are Butch's parents. We have to put up with them."

"Why?"

"Because we have to. They're excited about the baby, and they want to be part of it."

"I want you to have this baby right now!" Jenny urged.

"Believe me," Joanna said, "that makes two of us. If there were something I could do to speed things along, I would. Come on now. It's cold. Let's go home."

"Do I have to?"

"Yes, you do. I'm sure it's almost time for dinner."

"All right."

When Joanna drove into the yard, she could see the glow of the Dixons' flat-screen TV inside their motor home, which meant they were probably there watching the news. Hoping for a few moments of privacy, she hurried into the house looking for Butch. She found him in the kitchen fixing dinner, but he was in no better spirits than Jenny had been.

"What's wrong?" Joanna asked.

"The same thing that's been wrong around here for days," he grumbled. "I'm glad I got to see Junior put my mother in her place at lunchtime, but she's been on a tear ever since. I came within two seconds of asking them to leave."

"You can't do that, Butch," Joanna said. "I know they're annoying as hell, but they are your parents. They're here because of the baby."

"The baby," Butch said ominously, "needs to get a move on."

"Jenny said pretty much the same thing," Joanna said with a smile. "And if the way my back hurts is any indication . . ."

"Your back hurts?" Butch said. "Maybe you should go lie down for a while—at least until dinner is ready."

Joanna did as she was told, and dinner turned out to be surprisingly uneventful. At first Joanna thought Margaret was merely subdued. About the time they finished their salads, Joanna realized that her mother-in-law wasn't speaking to anyone, which turned out to be a blessing. Jenny and Joanna were in the kitchen putting away leftovers and loading the dishwasher when the phone rang.

"Jaime Carbajal," Butch said, handing Joanna the phone.

"How'd you do?" Joanna asked.

"Not that well. We never located Antonio Zavala, but Tucson PD was able to give us the names of a couple of his associates. One is an eighteen-year-old girl named Lupe Melendez. She was cited two months ago for letting her pit bull loose in an off-leash area of a city park, where it mauled three other dogs. We couldn't find her today, either, but Debbie and I will take another crack at that tomorrow."

"Did you hear anything from Ernie?"

"I heard from Rose. He's home and resting and seems to be doing all right, but Rose said the only way he's coming to work tomorrow is over her dead body."

"I'm glad to hear it went well," Joanna said.

She went on to tell Jaime about her trip to Sierra Vista. "Doesn't sound as though talking to the Markhams helped much," he said when she finished.

"It didn't," Joanna agreed. "But I'd like to know more about Rory Markham. He pretty much accused his wife of having had a previous relationship with Bradley Evans and then lying about it."

"You'd say Rory Markham is the jealous type?" Jaime asked.

"Enough that I think we should check him out," Joanna said. "But Frank and I can work on some of that background information. And tomorrow I'll attend Bradley Evans's funeral. In the meantime, though, I want you and Debbie to keep working on Jeannine's case. How's Debbie working out, by the way?"

"She'll be fine once she gets a little experience under her belt. She's still unsure of herself. And speaking of Jeannine, Debbie and I stopped by UMC to check on her before we left Tucson," Jaime added. "Jeannine's still in the ICU, but her condition has been upgraded to serious. We didn't see her, of course, but we talked to Dr. Ross. By the way, thanks for warning me in advance about the deal between her and Jeannine. Otherwise I might have said something stupid. How long has this been going on?"

"Beats me," Joanna said. "I only just now found out about it myself."

When she got off the phone with Jaime, Joanna dialed Ernie Carpenter's number. Rose answered.

"How's he doing?" Joanna asked.

"Okay," Rose answered. "But he's lying down right now. Want me to get him?"

"No," Joanna said. "Just give him a message. Tell him Sheriff Brady says if he gets past you tomorrow and tries to come to work, he'll have to deal with me."

Rose Carpenter laughed. "I'll tell him, all right," she said.

With Margaret still not speaking to anyone, she and Don retreated to their motor home early. The rest of the house, emotion-
ally drained from dealing with their disruptive guests, went to bed
shortly thereafter. Butch was still watching the *Nine O'Clock News*
on Fox when Joanna rolled over on her side and went to sleep. But
going to sleep that early had its disadvantages. By three o'clock in
the morning she and her lead-footed baby were both wide awake.

She lay there for a long time thinking about Bradley Evans
and about Leslie and Rory Markham. After murdering his wife,
Bradley had gone off to prison where he had paid his debt to society and become what seemed to be an exemplary citizen—
right up until a week earlier, when he had suddenly gone off the
rails and started taking stealth photographs of a woman who
claimed to know nothing about him. Joanna knew there had to
be some connection.

What is it? she wondered. *What am I missing?*

After an hour's worth of restless tossing and turning, Joanna
finally bailed out of bed and padded into her office with Lady at
her heels. She had read her father's official version of Bradley
Evans's arrest in the case log, but she wondered if D. H. Lathrop
might have written something more about the case in the privacy
of his daily journal—something that might shed some additional
light on Bradley's present circumstances all these years later.

Grunting with the awkward position and effort, Joanna managed to rummage through the bottom file drawer until she located the volume in question, one that covered most of 1978 and
the beginning months of 1979. She found what she was looking
for on Monday, October 30, 1978. The entry read:

Picked up a drunk yesterday morning up on top of the Divide.
Blood all over him and everywhere in his truck. His pregnant

wife's missing and most likely dead. The guy must have killed her, but he doesn't remember a thing. Why do people drink?

That passage was what she had been looking for, and reading something that was related to the case she was working on seemed justified—it didn't feel like prying. Originally that was all she had intended to do, but of course she didn't stop reading after that one entry. She kept right on. Not only had D. H. Lathrop faithfully entered notations about his life as a Cochise County deputy sheriff, he had also set down his views of what was going on at home.

Ellie just can't get used to the fact that I make a lot less money working for the sheriff's department than I did working underground for P.D. She likes nice stuff, and she got used to being able to go to the P.D. Store and getting whatever she wanted by just signing for it. I keep telling her we can't live this way. We won't be able to keep our heads above water. I'm trying to see if they'll let me put in some overtime.

A few pages later she came across the entry for December 17, 1978.

The Christmas Pageant was tonight. J. sang "Silent Night" and "Away in a Manger" with the Junior Choir. She was wearing a beautiful green velvet dress. When I asked Ellie where it came from, she just shrugged. I asked her how much it cost. She said it only cost $40.00!!! Only!!! For a dress J. probably won't wear more than once or twice. E. and I had a big fight about it, but J. looked so pretty in that dress, I probably should have kept my big mouth shut. We'll pay for it somehow.

Joanna remembered that dress like no other. It had been a deep, rich green with rhinestone-studded buttons. She had thought it the most beautiful dress she had ever seen, and she remembered her mother telling her to go in the dressing room and try it on. They had been upstairs in Phelps Dodge Mercantile, in the children's clothing department. When she came out of the dressing room wearing it, she had felt like a princess, and she had been amazed when Eleanor had said to the saleslady, "We'll take it."

On the way home she had added, "Now you mustn't tell your father about this. It'll be a surprise."

It had been a surprise, all right, and not a particularly welcome one. But it was one of the few times in Joanna's life when she remembered her mother going to the mat for her.

Joanna had thought that reading her father's diaries would be all one-sided, and yet here she was remembering something nice about her mother that she had forgotten completely. She was almost idly skimming through pages when she came across the entry for Friday, February 2, 1979.

Drove Bradley Evans up to the state prison in Florence today and dropped him off. Got eighteen to twenty-five for pleading guilty to killing his wife. I was the one who arrested him the morning after it happened. The problem is, I think the legal system's got this whole thing dead wrong. Even though he said he did it, I don't think Bradley Evans killed anybody, and I can't say why. Call it gut instinct. The judge believed him, and the county attorney believed him. I don't. Somebody missed something, and I don't know what it is. As Mama used to say: "Stand alone. Eventually the crowd may fall." So I'll just keep on thinking what I'm thinking and wait to see what happens.

Joanna sat for a long time staring at the entry. Stand alone . . .
Those familiar words were ones her father had said to her often,
and she had never known they came from her grandmother, a
woman who had died long before Joanna was born. And how did
those words apply now. Had Bradley Evans willingly spent more
than twenty years in prison for a crime he hadn't committed?
Was that possible? And, if so, didn't that mean that Lisa Evans's
real killer had gone free all this time?

From what anyone had been able to learn, as long as Bradley
Evans had stayed put in Douglas, everything had been fine. But
once he ventured as far afield as Sierra Vista—once he started
stalking Leslie Markham and snapping her picture—things had
changed. Before he finished shooting that one camera's worth of
film, Bradley Evans was dead.

After talking to Rory Markham that afternoon, Joanna had
come away thinking that the real estate broker was a plausible
suspect in the Bradley Evans homicide. Jealous husbands were always a good possibility, and no doubt Rory Markham deserved
further investigation. But D. H. Lathrop's journal entry opened
the door to other avenues of investigation as well. He claimed
something had been missed in the original investigation. What?
And how? And by whom? Had it simply been overlooked or had
it been deliberately overlooked? And was it possible for a new set
of eyes to spot that missing ingredient all these years later?

Joanna felt energized, but she was realistic enough to know
her limits. Tomorrow was another long day. She needed her rest.
Closing the book, she returned it to the file cabinet drawer. Then
she stood up and switched off the lamp. "Come on, girl," she said
to Lady. "Time to go back to bed."

She managed to get back into bed without disturbing Butch.
After that it took time for her to find a comfortable position and

time to turn off her brain, which had suddenly slipped into overdrive.

She was in the bathroom the next morning putting on her makeup when Butch came into the room, bringing her a cup of apricot tea and grinning from ear to ear.

"You're not going to believe it," he said.

"Believe what?" Joanna asked.

"They left."

"Who left? You're not making any sense."

"My parents. Overnight, they folded up their awning and took off."

"For where?"

"Home. For Arkansas. They left a note on the kitchen table. Here it is."

Taking the note, Joanna read: "Thanks for the hospitality. Obviously we've worn out our welcome. Mom."

"Worn out their welcome? How can she say that? We all bent over backwards."

"And walked on eggshells," Butch added. "But that's the way she is."

Joanna was incredulous. "After driving all this way they're going to miss out on the birth of their grandchild because of what happened at lunch, because Junior called her on being rude?"

"I guess," Butch said. "I suppose that's what started it, but now that she and Dad aren't speaking, they could go on like that indefinitely. Believe me, we're better off with them giving each other the silent treatment as far away from here as possible. I had a bellyful of that nonsense growing up, of passing messages back and forth between them for days and weeks at a time. I sure as hell don't need it now. Actually, though, this is a real stroke of luck for Dad. Mom's an inveterate backseat driver. With her not speaking to him, it'll probably be the most enjoyable cross-country drive he's made in years."

Joanna shook her head. "That doesn't sound like a nice way to travel or to live," she observed.

Butch shrugged. "They're used to it," he said. "They've been doing it for years—for as long as I can remember. Now come on. Breakfast is almost ready. I'm making omelets to celebrate. And with them gone, you don't have to rush things with the baby anymore. He can arrive whenever he wants."

"That's easy for you to say," Joanna said. "You're not the one who's nine and a half months pregnant." Then she paused. "Wait a minute. Did you say he?"

Butch heaved a sigh, then he nodded. "Yes, I did," he said.

"Was that just a figure of speech, or . . ."

"Mom opened the envelope," he said. "The one on the refrigerator with the ultrasound results in it. I didn't know what she'd done until she asked me what we're going to name him. I wasn't going to tell you, but I let it slip. Sorry."

Joanna could barely contain herself. "Your mother actually opened the envelope—the envelope we've left sealed all this time? You let her do that?"

"Joey," Butch said, "I didn't *let* her do anything. I told you she's a snoop. I should have realized she couldn't leave well enough alone. I should have locked the envelope away in the office along with everything else. I just didn't think about it. And when I found out what she'd done, I climbed all over her about it. I'm sure that's the real reason they left. I doubt Junior Dowdle's comment had a thing to do with it."

Just then Jenny and the three dogs bounded into the master

bedroom behind them. "Hey," she said, flopping onto their unmade bed. "I was out feeding Kiddo and I just noticed. The motor home is gone. What happened? Where'd they go?"

"They went home," Butch said.

"Home?" Jenny asked. "But I thought they were going to stay until the baby got here. Why would they leave now? I mean, it can't be that much longer."

"It's a long story," Butch said.

He looked so disheartened that Joanna couldn't help feeling sorry for him. Whatever Margaret Dixon had done, it wasn't her son's fault.

"It doesn't matter why they left," Joanna said quickly. "The whole point is, they did. Now let's have some breakfast. We need to figure out a name for this little brother of yours."

"Little brother?" Jenny repeated wonderingly. "You mean we know it's going to be a boy?"

"Yes," Joanna said. "Thanks to Margaret Dixon, we do now."

CHAPTER 13

Joanna left the house after breakfast feeling very pregnant but incredibly lighthearted. It was wonderful to have their lives back again. By now the in-laws from hell should be past the New Mexico border and well into Texas. As she walked out to the garage, Butch was happily hauling his laptop out of its in-office exile and back onto the kitchen table, where he preferred to work.

And, without much fuss and a minimum of discussion, the three of them had settled on an acceptable boy's name: Dennis Lee Dixon. No Frederick Junior. No lurking grandfathers' names. No traditional family names. Just a solid boy's name with a good ring to it. No doubt Eleanor wouldn't approve, and neither would Margaret, probably for entirely different reasons, but that didn't matter. It was the name Joanna and Butch and Jenny had chosen together, and that's what counted.

When Joanna stepped out of her Crown Victoria in the Justice Center parking lot, the chill March wind blowing off the flanks of the Mule Mountains did nothing to dampen her spirits or take the spring out of her step. Maybe Joanna's initial reaction to Margaret's snoopiness had been negative, but now she felt as though a cloud of indecision—one she hadn't known was there—had been lifted off her shoulders.

And Butch was thrilled as well. As he had said at breakfast, he had been worried about living in a family where girls outnumbered boys three to one. And Eleanor, regardless of her likely disapproval of the baby's name, had been lobbying for a boy all along. So she would be thrilled as well.

Frank was already on his way to the board of supervisors meeting. With Debbie and Jaime headed back to Tucson, the morning briefing had been shifted to later in the day. That left Joanna free to spend the morning working with Kristin on sorting the mail and figuring out how best to handle routine correspondence issues on a day-to-day basis, both for now and for when Joanna went on maternity leave. As they worked to create a workable system, Joanna saw how her own almost irrational insistence on "Little Red Henning" it had been a bad idea. In the process, she had done a grave disservice to Kristin and had made her own job far more complicated than it needed to be. No wonder she had always been buried under an avalanche of paperwork.

"It's going to mean more responsibility," she told Kristin.

"Good," Kristin said. And that was that.

Late in the morning, Joanna found herself sitting in front of an improbably clean desk. While she'd been working with Kristin, she hadn't given her father's journal entry a thought. Now, though, remembering, she picked up her phone and called the evidence room, where Buddy Richards answered.

"Do you still have that evidence box we brought down from the old courthouse the other day?" she asked.

"Lisa Evans?" Buddy answered. "Sure do. I was gonna ship it back up to storage today, but I hadn't quite gotten around to it. Want me to bring it over?"

"Thanks," she said. "I'd appreciate it."

Buddy limped into her office a few minutes later, lugging the box. Buddy had started out as a deputy, but a badly broken leg from a rodeo bull-riding mishap had left him unfit for patrol duty. In lieu of disability, he had taken over as the department's chief evidence clerk.

"This was long before my time," he said, setting it on Joanna's desk.

"Before mine, too," Joanna said. "My father was the arresting officer."

"Must've done a good job of it. I was curious, so I read through the case file. The prosecuting attorney got a conviction even though they never found a body."

"The victim's husband copped a plea," Joanna said. "That's not exactly the same thing as getting a conviction."

"Right," Buddy said. "I suppose not."

Once Joanna was left alone, she carefully lifted the lid off the box. After that initial report, D. H. Lathrop was no longer part of the official investigative process. There was no further evidence of his being involved and no clue to tell Joanna why, despite the way court proceedings had turned out, her father had felt Bradley Evans was innocent.

It was getting on toward noon and almost time to head to Douglas to attend Bradley's funeral service when Joanna picked up the next item in the box—Lisa Evans's wallet. She was absently thumbing through the brittle plastic holders when she came to the one containing Lisa's driver's license. What she saw in the photo stunned her and made the hair on the back of

Joanna's neck stand on end. The name on the license said Lisa Marie Crystal, but the photo could have been Leslie Markham's—except for one inarguable fact: Leslie Tazewell Markham hadn't been born when the photo was taken. She flipped through the plastic folders until she found the graduation photo. The resemblance in that one was even more striking.

For a long time, all Joanna could do was flip back and forth between the two photos and stare. Finally she reached down, opened her briefcase, and rummaged through it until she found the envelope that contained the photos Bradley Evans had taken of Leslie Markham. The hair, the shape of the forehead, mouth, and chin, the set of the eyes. The two women were eerily similar. Looking at them, Joanna could draw only one conclusion: they had to be mother and daughter.

Bradley Evans had gone to jail for the murder of his pregnant wife, Lisa, and her unborn baby, but from where Joanna was sitting, it looked like that baby was very much alive more than two decades later. What if D. H. Lathrop was right? What if Bradley Evans really had gone to prison after confessing to a crime he hadn't committed? Had anyone ever examined the blood evidence that had been found in the vehicle or on Lisa Evans's purse? Was it possible that it hadn't even been hers?

In the late seventies, DNA identification had been rudimentary at best. It wouldn't be used as evidence in legal proceedings until years later. But times had changed. Now even minute traces of blood evidence and sperm were routinely used to solve long-unsolvable crimes. Nothing in the case file had indicated that the bloodied purse had ever been subjected to any kind of forensic examination. That alone indicated that the Lisa Evans investigation had been something less than thorough.

Fired with a new sense of purpose, Joanna put all the items

back in the box and then carried it through the building to the evidence room. "Can you scan a copy of these?" she asked, handing Lisa's driver's license and yearbook photo to Buddy. "And I'll need you to bag up the purse for me."

Buddy gave her a questioning look but then shrugged. "I can scan them if you want me to, Sheriff Brady, but are you sure? Chief Deputy Montoya's equipment does a better job than mine."

"Frank isn't here," Joanna said. "I need this now."

While she waited, she tracked down Dave Hollicker and handed him the bagged purse.

"What's this?" he asked.

"Lisa Marie Evans's bloodstained purse," she said. "I want you to run it up to the DPS crime lab in Tucson."

"Today?" Dave asked. "Casey and I have been working on evidence we gathered from Jeannine's crime scenes—"

Joanna cut him off. "Yes, today," she said. "And I want results ASAP. Ask if they can extract a DNA sample from the old bloodstains. I also want them to check for fingerprints. I don't know if they'll be able to spot any old ones. I know for sure that mine are on it from handling it recently, so they'll need to run mine for elimination purposes."

"But why the big rush?" Dave objected. "This homicide is decades old."

"That's just it," Joanna said. "I have some new information that suggests maybe that 'decades old' homicide never happened."

Ten minutes later she was on her way to Douglas with the newly scanned copy of Lisa's license in the same envelope with her collection of Leslie Markham's photos. It took a while for Joanna to clear security to get into the prison unit. By the time she was admitted to the chapel, the service was already under way. Ted Chapman, officiating, nodded to her as she slipped into the last row of folding chairs.

Bradley's memorial service wasn't particularly well attended. There were a dozen or so prisoners and three suit-and-tie-clad men Joanna assumed to be some of Brad Evans's colleagues or supervisors from the jail ministry. The other attendee was an elderly white-haired Anglo woman who sat apart from the others and sobbed inconsolably into a lace-edged handkerchief. Listening to the grieving woman, Joanna decided she must be some heretofore unidentified relative of Bradley Evans who had managed to show up in time for his funeral.

Joanna tried to pay attention to what was being said, but her mind was going at breakneck speed. The striking resemblance between the long-presumed-dead Lisa Marie Evans and Leslie Markham presented Joanna with a startlingly new possible scenario. What if Lisa had somehow faked her own murder and allowed her husband to go to prison for it? Did that mean Lisa herself still was alive? And how was it that her daughter had been raised as Leslie Tazewell?

And if Bradley Evans had spent the better part of a quarter of a century believing that both his wife and daughter were dead, what would have been his reaction when he suddenly encountered living breathing proof to the contrary?

Joanna remembered all too well her own sense of shock, amazement, and disbelief when, a few years earlier while she had been sitting in a hotel lobby in Peoria, Arizona, a man who looked exactly like the ghost of her long-deceased father walked toward her. The spooky resemblance had been easily explained once she learned that the man was actually her brother, Bob Brundage, the baby her parents had given up for adoption years before their marriage and long before Joanna's birth.

Joanna now knew that the similarities between D. H. Lathrop and his son went well beyond mere looks. Bob sounded like his father both when he spoke and when he laughed. He walked and carried himself in the same fashion. Bob Brundage now was an exact replica of D. H. Lathrop at the time of his death.

Joanna could easily empathize with everything Bradley Evans must have felt upon first encountering Leslie Markham, either in person or in a photograph. It seemed likely that he might well have questioned what he had seen, and doubted his own perceptions. In order to quiet those doubts he might have decided to photograph Leslie so he could examine the pictures at leisure. Perhaps he was searching for proof one way or the other. Either Leslie Markham was his daughter or she wasn't.

But Joanna knew that there were other tools available that would be far more reliable than a few surreptitiously taken photos. And even if an examination of the bloodstained purse failed to yield a usable sample, there were other available avenues of investigation. Mitochondrial DNA, passed from mother to daughter, could prove definitively whether or not Leslie Tazewell Markham really was Lisa Marie Evans's daughter. The only difficulty was figuring out a way to make that testing possible.

". . . he was someone who knew he had done wrong and who took full responsibility for his actions," Ted Chapman was saying. "He had repented and believed the Lord God Almighty heard his prayers and granted him forgiveness. It was in that state of God-given grace that he was able to turn his life around and start helping others. If Bradley were here and able to speak for himself, I know he would be the first to forgive those who trespassed against him. And I hope that we can, too. Let us pray . . ."

But who were those trespassers? Joanna wondered. Obviously, first on the list would be the person who had murdered the poor man. But if Lisa Marie hadn't died at her husband's hand, what about the person or persons who had conspired to rob Bradley Evans of twenty-plus years of his life by letting him rot in prison? Yes, Joanna's department needed to find out who had murdered the man, but if he had been wrongfully convicted, then they needed to do more than simply identify and punish his killer. There was the moral obligation of clearing an innocent man's good name.

"Warden Howard has kindly granted us the use of the rec room next door," Ted Chapman announced. "Anyone who wishes to do so may gather there for a time of fellowship and recollection. Punch, coffee, and cookies will be provided by the jail ministry."

Joanna paused at the door of the chapel long enough for Ted to introduce her to the men in suits who were, just as she suspected, jail ministry people. When she went into the rec room, the elderly woman was standing at the refreshment table trying to juggle a styrofoam cup of coffee and a paper plate of cookies along with her walker.

"Here," Joanna said, "let me help carry something."

Gratefully, the woman passed her the coffee and cookies, then made her way to a nearby cafeteria-style table and dropped onto the bench seat. "Thank you so much," she said. "The basket holds my purse, but the cookies and the coffee would have dropped right through."

"Do you mind if I join you?" Joanna asked.

"Help yourself."

Joanna went back to the refreshment table and snagged a cup of punch and a single cookie. "Are you a relative?" she asked as she returned to the table.

"Oh, heavens no," the woman said. "No relation at all. I'm

Marcelle Womack, Brad's landlady for the past three-plus years. He was far more of a son to me than my own son is. Always helping me around the house. Always fixing things. Always so polite and understanding and never too busy to take the time to listen to an old lady flapping her jaw. I'm going to miss him so very much. So very, very much. You look familiar," the woman added. "Who are you, one of Brad's friends?"

Joanna reached into her pocket and produced one of her business cards. "I'm Sheriff Joanna Brady," she explained as the woman held the card at arm's length and squinted at it.

"Yes, I suppose you are," Marcelle agreed. "That's why you look familiar. I must have seen your picture in the paper or on TV. Why are you here?"

"My department is investigating Mr. Evans's murder."

"That's right," Marcelle said. "I've seen how that works in the crime shows on television—the detectives always come to the victim's funeral looking for suspects."

"More likely looking for information," Joanna said.

"I already talked to one of your detectives," Marcelle said. "The big one with the bushy eyebrows."

"That would be Ernie Carpenter."

"Right. Carpenter was his name. I told him everything I knew, but he wasn't very happy with me."

"Why not?"

"Because I made him go get a search warrant before I'd let him into Brad's apartment. I wasn't about to let him in without one. You know how those things work. Police treat ex-cons like dirt even though they've paid their debt to society."

"Ernie did mention something about that," Joanna said. "And you're right to be cautious about letting anyone into a tenant's apartment. But do you mind if I ask you to repeat what you told

Ernie? I'm sure it's all in his report, but things have been so hectic the last few days that I haven't had a chance to read it."

"I told the detective that Brad was a very nice man, but a very lonely one. All alone in the world."

"When's the last time you saw him?"

"I saw him leave home on Wednesday morning. I could see his carport from my kitchen window. I often saw him drive off in his pickup truck on his way to work when I was sitting at my kitchen table having my morning coffee. But the last time I talked to him would have been Tuesday night."

"And why was that?"

"I took him some soup—navy-bean soup. The back wall of my kitchen is also the back wall of his apartment. So whenever I cooked something that smelled good—like soup or stew—I always took him some. It didn't seem fair for him to come home from work and have to smell the food without being able to eat any of it."

"So you took him soup?"

Marcelle nodded. "In one of those new Ziploc containers."

"And was there anything out of the ordinary about your visit? How did he seem?"

"He was just the regular Brad, sitting there reading his Bible. If I hadn't brought him the soup, he might not have remembered to eat. He was like that sometimes. He'd just get all caught up in his Bible study and forget about eating. He asked me if I wanted to sit with him and share some of his soup. I knew he would, you see, so I brought plenty for both of us. Wait until you get to be my age. You'll see that it's no fun eating alone."

"You ate dinner with him?"

"Yes, and we talked about Revelations," Marcelle said. "He liked one passage in particular. Revelations 21:4. I looked it up when I got back home. It didn't make much of an impression on me then, but after I knew he was dead, I looked it up again. I even memorized it in Brad's honor—at least I tried to. It goes something like this: *God shall wipe away all their tears; there shall be no more death or sorrow or crying or pain because the former things are passed away.*

"Do you think he knew he was going to die, Sheriff Brady? Do you think he had some kind of premonition?"

"Maybe," Joanna said.

But right then it seemed far more likely to her that Brad Evans wasn't seeing his own death in those words. He was, instead, seeing his supposedly murdered daughter inexplicably alive. Still, if he had made such an earth-shattering discovery, wouldn't he have been shouting it from the rooftops rather than making oblique Bible-based comments about it to his landlady? Whom else would he have told? Or perhaps he himself wasn't yet fully convinced and he hadn't confided in anyone while he waited to make some kind of confirmation. That might be where the camera and the stealth photos came in.

"Did he seem sad or unhappy?" Joanna asked.

"Not at all," Marcelle replied. "In fact, I'd say he was the exact opposite of sad. When he said grace before we ate, I remember him thanking God for the many blessings in his life—including me. I took that as a compliment."

"I'm sure you were a blessing in his life," Joanna said.

Marcelle nodded and dabbed at teary eyes with her already sodden hanky. "I hope I was," she murmured and then frowned. "And he said something else—that he was grateful for second chances."

"What kind of second chances?" Joanna asked.

"He didn't say, not specifically, but I hoped it meant he had met a woman—a woman who was as nice as he was. It's hard living alone, you know. I miss my Roger so much, and I had been praying for Brad to find someone who would make his life less lonely."

"So you're pretty sure the last time you saw him was Tuesday?" Joanna asked.

Marcelle nodded. "Wednesday was his day off. On Thursday I had an early-morning appointment with my dentist, so he might have been there and he might not, but not seeing him for a day or two at a time wasn't all that unusual, either—not unusual enough for me to think about reporting him as missing. Brad often went out at night—to meetings and such. He was very involved in AA, you know. He must have been quite a drinker at one time, but I never saw any sign of liquor once he moved into my apartment. As I said, he was a very nice man, and I'm going to miss him."

Ted Chapman appeared at Joanna's elbow. "Sorry to interrupt," he said, "but Mrs. Womack's ride is here. So anytime you're ready to go . . ."

"I'm ready to go right now," Marcelle said, getting to her feet. "I've monopolized Sheriff Brady for far too long. Very nice meeting you," she added. "I hope you find out who did this."

"So do I," Joanna replied.

As Marcelle tottered away with Ted Chapman at her side, Joanna turned to survey the rest of the room. Most of the inmates were gone by then. The two that remained were gathering up paper plates and plastic glasses and clearing off the refreshment table under the watchful eyes of two of the suit-clad jail ministry honchos.

Joanna walked up and introduced herself. One of the men was Rich Higgins, the human resources guy Ted Chapman had called. The other was Dave Enright, who identified himself as the executive director.

"Are you making any progress?" Dave asked, once he realized who Joanna was.

"Some," she said. "But not much. We're checking his phone and credit-card records to see if we can track what he was doing or who was in contact with him in the days before his death."

"That would include his cell-phone records?" Rich Higgins asked.

"I'm not sure we knew he had a cell phone," Joanna said. "I know we're checking his home number. If my investigators had discovered a billing for a cell phone, I'm sure they would have included that in their request for phone company records."

"There wouldn't be a billing in his name," Rich told her. "Our company cell phones are an in-kind contribution from one of the cell-phone-service providers. They provide the phones and the service both, so there is no individual billing as such."

"Do you happen to have that number?" Joanna asked.

"Sure do." Rich Higgins unsnapped a cell-phone case from his belt and scrolled through a list of numbers. "Here it is," he said.

As Rich read off the number, Joanna jotted it down. Once she was out of the prison and back in her vehicle, she called Frank Montoya.

"How was the funeral?" he asked.

"About what I expected. Got to talk to Bradley's landlady and to a couple of his jail ministry colleagues, which is why I'm calling. Have you had a chance to check Bradley Evans's phone and credit-card records?"

"The phone was easy," Frank said. "I don't know why he even bothered to have one. From what I could see, he hardly used the damned thing."

"I know why," Joanna said. "He had a cell phone somebody else was paying for." She gave Frank the number. "What about credit-card usage?"

"Nothing after he disappeared," Frank answered. "The last time it was used was on Wednesday. He had lunch at Denny's in Sierra Vista on Tuesday. From the size of the bill, I'd say he ate alone. On Wednesday he bought a camera from a Walgreen's on Fry Boulevard."

"Maybe he spotted her somewhere in Sierra Vista," Joanna mused, more to herself than to Frank.

"Spotted who?" Frank asked. "What are we talking about?"

Joanna had forgotten that Frank had been stuck at the board of supervisors meeting when she had made her latest discovery. "I think Bradley Evans must have run into Leslie Markham, realized she had to be his dead wife's daughter, and decided to take the pictures as a form of verification."

"Are you serious?"

"Go to the evidence room and check the box on the Lisa Evans homicide," Joanna told him. "Take a look at the picture of Lisa Evans on her driver's license and compare it with Leslie Markham's photos from the website. Call me back and tell me what you think."

Joanna was halfway back to the Justice Center when the phone rang.

"Whoa!" Frank exclaimed. "These two women could be twins. So what's going on? Are you saying Lisa Marie Evans handed her baby off to someone else and then faked her own

murder? Are you thinking maybe the wife's alive and well somewhere while her husband spent twenty-plus years of his life in
the slammer for killing her?"

"It's a possibility," Joanna said. "Meanwhile, the baby's adoptive father happens to be Judge Lawrence Tazewell."

Frank whistled. "As in the Arizona Supreme Court Justice?"

"One and the same. Not only that, according to Leslie
Markham, he's currently being considered as a nominee for a
federal judgeship."

"Which might explain why, once Bradley Evans got too close
to the truth, someone felt obliged to knock him off."

"Yes, it might," Joanna agreed. "Especially considering how
the FBI seems to be very good at turning up all that old dirty
laundry. Dave Hollicker is taking Lisa's bloodstained purse to
the crime lab in Tucson so they can try running DNA tests on it.
If someone was faking a murder, who knows where the blood
came from?"

"Is DNA testing possible on a sample that old?" Frank asked.

"We'll see," Joanna agreed. "But we can also go at this from
the other direction. I want to collect DNA samples from Leslie
Markham and from Lisa's mother as well. We should be able to
tell from that whether or not those two women are related. A
DNA match won't tell us if Lisa Evans is still alive, but it'll be a
step in the right direction."

"How do you plan on obtaining those other samples?"
Frank asked.

"I'm not sure," Joanna said. "I'm thinking. Once I figure it
out, I'll let you know. And one more thing. If you have time, see
what you can find out about Rory Markham."

"How come?"

"I don't know. I didn't like the way he treated Leslie, for one thing. But there's something about him that doesn't ring quite true. It gave me a funny feeling."

"Okay," Frank said. "I'll see what I can do."

By the time Joanna reached the Justice Center, she had made up her mind on the DNA samples. She stopped off in the rest room long enough for a very necessary pit stop before she went looking for her detectives. "Where are Debbie and Jaime?" Joanna asked Kristin.

"Still in Tucson, as far as I know. How come?"

Joanna didn't answer. She was already on her way to Frank's office. She found him with his face glued to his computer screen while a nearby printer shot out page after page of material.

"Ready to take a run out to Sierra Vista?" she asked.

"In a minute," he said. "We need to wait for the end of this print job. When you see it, you're not going to believe it."

"Why? What's going on?"

"Once I got off the phone with you, I decided to do some research into Judge Lawrence Tazewell's background. What do you suppose he was doing in February of 1979?"

"I have no idea."

"He was serving as a Cochise County Superior Court judge."

"You don't mean . . . ?"

"Yes," Frank said, picking up the sheaf of computer printouts and handing them to Joanna. "That's exactly what I mean. Judge Lawrence Tazewell is the judge who accepted Bradley Evans's guilty plea and sent him off to the slammer."

"And now he's an Arizona Supreme Court justice who's a possible presidential nominee for a seat on the federal bench. I didn't think things could get any worse."

"Guess again, boss," Frank said. "They just did."

CHAPTER 14

"W here are we going?" Frank asked once they were in his Crown Victoria.

"Anna Marie Crystal's place on Short Street in Sierra Vista."

"Lisa's mother?"

"Right," Joanna said. "Do you know how to get there?"

"No," Frank said. "But I can find it." While he adjusted his portable Garmin GPS, Joanna shuffled through the stack of papers he had handed her. Most of the material consisted of archived articles from various Arizona newspapers—many of them dealing with Arizona Supreme Court decisions in which Lawrence Tazewell was mentioned briefly as part of either the majority or dissenting opinion. After skipping over most of those, Joanna settled in to read a long feature article from the *Arizona Reporter*.

It was a mostly laudatory piece with several color photographs of Judge Tazewell and his wife, Sharon. One showed them posing arm in arm on the patio of their home, with Camelback Mountain looming in the background. Another showed them standing in a living room next to a white grand piano with a huge oil painting of the Grand Canyon covering the wall behind them. There were mentions of the Tazewells both as participants and movers and shakers in various social and charitable events. Clearly they were members in good standing of the Paradise Valley and greater Phoenix social scene.

Lawrence Tazewell, a man who had come from humble beginnings in the copper-mining town of Morenci, Arizona, had obviously done all right for himself. No doubt hard work accounted for what he had achieved and acquired along the way, but Joanna suspected that a couple of fortuitous marriages—one of them to Aileen Houlihan of Triple H Ranch—had benefited Judge Tazewell's plentiful bottom line, but the only reference to that long-ago marriage came at the very end of the article in a sentence that read:

Judge Tazewell's only child, a daughter from a previous marriage, still resides in Sierra Vista.

"So," Joanna said when she finished reading. "Aileen and Lawrence Tazewell convince Lisa Marie Evans to hand her baby over to them, she disappears into thin air, and then Judge Tazewell makes sure Bradley goes away for a very long time. Neat. Ties up all the loose ends."

Frank nodded. "Everything goes swimmingly until Bradley comes back, runs into Leslie Markham by accident, and then there's trouble. If any of the old stuff comes out, then it's bye-bye to Larry Tazewell's next judicial appointment."

Joanna's telephone rang.

"Hi, Sheriff Brady," Debbie Howell said. "Wanted to let you

know what's going on. Jaime and I are still in Tucson. We're still not having much luck tracking Tony Zavala and his friends. They all seem to have gone to ground. The media coverage probably has them scared."

"So keep looking," Joanna said.

"We will," Debbie agreed. "We're particularly interested in talking to Tony's girlfriend, the one with the city of Tucson dog-fighting citation. From everything we're hearing on the street, she's a ringleader. We did spend some time over at the Humane Society. According to the guy we spoke to there, Roostercomb pit bulls are legendary in dogfighting circles for being killers. They go for top dollar."

"The O'Dwyers sell them?" Joanna asked.

"That's right."

"If all this is happening in my jurisdiction, why don't I know about it?"

"It turns out there's a lot we don't know about the O'Dwyers," Debbie answered. "Not only do they breed and sell the dogs, they also offer a venue for the fights and run a lucrative betting operation on the side."

"Sounds like they're a regular pair of entrepreneurs. I'm surprised someone hasn't signed them up for the local chamber of commerce."

"Right," Debbie said. "The only question is figuring out which chamber of commerce applies."

"What do you mean?"

"They're pretending to operate out of New Mexico," Debbie explained. "People who come to see the fights evidently use a road off I-10 that runs through New Mexico in order to gain access to Roostercomb Ranch through a back entrance. That way they don't have to drive through San Simon, where extra traffic would be more noticeable."

"Which also explains why the surveillance we set up in San Simon over the weekend came up empty," Joanna said.

"Exactly. As far as sales are concerned, the kennel's official address is actually a post office box in Road Forks," Debbie added. "By operating in another state, they've managed to stay under everybody's radar."

"Until Jeannine started finding dead and dying dogs along I-10."

"Right," Debbie agreed. "So is it time someone went over to Roostercomb Ranch and had a chat with them?"

"No," Joanna said. "Absolutely not. Let's see what we can do to get the goods on them before we make contact. That means, if and when you do find one of the gang of thugs who beat up Jeannine, let them know that we're willing to deal. Tell them that the first guy who gives us enough evidence to convict Clarence and Billy O'Dwyer of conspiracy to commit murder can plan on getting special treatment."

"A bargaining chip?"

"You bet," Joanna said. "And if they're taking bets, once we wrap them up I'm sure the feds will be interested in little things like income-tax evasion. It should turn into quite a nice package."

"We'll keep plugging," Debbie said. "We're motivated."

"I know you are," Joanna said. "But the hours . . ."

"Don't worry about Bennie," Debbie returned. "He's having a great time with his cousins. Believe me, the extra hours are not a problem."

Frank waited until she ended the call. "Sounds like you could be venturing into the unauthorized-plea-bargain business," he said. "Shouldn't you clear that offer with the county attorney before you make it?"

"I'll call Arlee Jones first thing in the morning and bring him into the loop, but I'm not particularly worried about it. He's so lazy he'd rather do a plea bargain any day. Actually trying a case would require his getting off his dead rear end."

"Don't hold back," Frank said with a grin. "Why don't you say how you really feel?"

"But there is someone else I need to call," she added. "Sheriff Randy Trotter."

Through the years Joanna had had enough dealings with Hidalgo County Sheriff Randy Trotter in New Mexico that his numbers were programmed into her cell phone. Minutes later she had the man on the phone.

"Are you still working?" he asked once he knew who was calling. "I thought you'd be off having your baby by now. What can I do for you?"

"What would you think if I said the names Billy and Clarence O'Dwyer?" Joanna asked.

"I'd think I was glad Roostercomb Ranch is mostly on your side of the state line," Randy Trotter answered. "Those two guys are mean as snakes, and the less my officers and I have to do with them the better. Why?"

"Because it looks like they're operating a criminal enterprise that straddles the state line the same way their ranch used to."

"I don't think I want to hear this," Randy said, "but I guess you'd better tell me."

It was ten after four and Joanna had just gotten off the phone with Sheriff Trotter when Frank pulled up in front of Anna Marie Crystal's modest home on Short Street.

"You never did say how we're going to play this," Frank observed as they walked up the sidewalk. "Are you going to tell her about Leslie Markham's resemblance to her dead daughter?"

"Not if we don't have to," Joanna returned. "For one thing, until we know whether or not her daughter is dead or alive, I don't want to get the poor woman's hopes up."

Fritz, the silky terrier mix, began barking the moment they stepped onto the porch. Through the door they could hear Anna Marie muttering to herself while she shut off the blaring television set, confined the dog to the kitchen, and then came to the door. When she opened it, a thick cloud of stale cigarette smoke wafted outside.

"Oh," Anna Marie said, looking at Joanna and shaking her head in apparent disgust. "It's you again. What do you want this time?"

"This is my chief deputy, Frank Montoya," Joanna said. "We'd like to talk to you for a few minutes if you don't mind."

"I've already told you everything I know about Bradley Evans," Anna Marie said. "Personally, I don't give a damn if you ever find out who killed him."

"This is about your daughter," Joanna said.

"About Lisa?" Anna Marie gave Joanna a shrewdly appraising look, but finally she stepped back into the room, allowing Frank and Joanna to enter. "What about her?"

"Do you mind if we sit?" Joanna asked.

"It's okay, I suppose," Anna Marie answered.

Joanna immediately chose a spot at the far end of the couch and seated herself next to an end table that contained a reeking ashtray. One of the stubs was still smoldering.

"What do you want to know?" Anna Marie asked brusquely.

"What can you tell us about your daughter's marriage to Bradley Evans?" Joanna asked.

"I don't see that it matters. I thought they were too young to be married. And I thought he was on the wild side and not ready to settle down. I thought he drank too much. Why? Why does any of this matter now?"

"Was Lisa unhappy with him?" Joanna persisted.

"Are you kidding? She was head over heels in love with the guy. And she told us—Kenny and me—that she was sure he'd straighten up once she had the baby."

"Did she ever threaten to leave him?"

"Never."

"You don't think it's possible she tried to run away from him?"

"If she did, he stopped her, didn't he. Murdering her would be one way to keep her from leaving."

"Yes," Joanna said, "I suppose it would." She eyed the ashtray where the smoldering cigarette stub had finally extinguished itself. "I'm sorry," she said. "I seem to be thirsting to death. Could I trouble you for a glass of water?"

"All right," Anna Marie said grudgingly. She stood up with a sigh and headed for the kitchen. Before the door had swung shut behind her, Joanna had collected the cigarette stub, stuffed it into an evidence bag, and shoved the bag into her pocket. Grinning, Frank gave her a quick thumbs-up.

Anna Marie returned to the living room with a glass of water in one hand and her yapping dog in the other. "I don't know what any of this has to do with the price of tea in China," she said.

"We're trying to find out if it's possible that Bradley Evans's murder now has something to do with what happened to your daughter all those years ago."

Anna Marie put down the dog. Then she collected the ashtray, her cigarettes, and her lighter and took them to the opposite end of the couch. She lit a cigarette and then blew a new puff of smoke into the already saturated air. By the time she looked back at Joanna, her countenance had changed.

"I certainly hope so," she said fiercely. "I always thought the son of a bitch got off way too easy. I prayed every night for years that he'd die in prison. You see how much good that did. But he's dead now, so why are you still asking questions?"

"Since Bradley Evans confessed to the crime and also went to prison for it, it's possible that the investigation into your daughter's death was something less than thorough," Joanna explained. "We're exploring the possibility that someone else may have been involved."

"You're saying Bradley had an accomplice?"

That wasn't at all what Joanna meant, but since that idea seemed to satisfy some of Anna Marie's objections, she let it slide. Joanna knew from reading the casebook that the Lisa Evans homicide had been closed so quickly and so definitively that few of the victim's friends and associates had ever been interviewed.

"Possibly," Joanna said.

"Was it a woman?" Anna Marie asked. "I always wondered about that—if he had a girlfriend or someone on the side—and that's why he got rid of Lisa."

"Did your daughter say something that led you to think that might be the case?"

"No. According to what she told me, everything was hunky-dory, except for Bradley's drinking, that is. She was worried about it. That was the only thing she ever complained about."

"It may be the one thing she mentioned to you, but she might have said something more to someone else," Joanna said. "You see, Mrs. Crystal, although I love my mother very much, there are issues in my marriage that I would never discuss with her. Is it possible that Lisa had friends other than you, people her age, that she might have told her troubles to?"

Anna Marie considered for a moment before she answered. "Lisa's best friend would have been the Tanner girl—Barbara Tanner. Lisa might have said something to her."

"Who was Barbara Tanner?"

"Her parents owned the dry cleaner's where Lisa worked. In fact, Barbara was the one who got Lisa the job in the first place. She worked part-time there while she was still in high school and then full-time after she got out. Barbara worked there, too, some of the time, but after she went off to college, she only worked on winter breaks and during the summers to help her parents."

"What about Lisa?" Joanna asked. "Why didn't she go to college?"

Anna Marie shrugged. "She wasn't interested, mostly. Kenny would have found a way to pay for it if she had really wanted to go, but her grades weren't all that good, and she never really liked school."

"Do the Tanners still live around here?" Joanna asked.

Anna Marie shook her head. "They sold out a long time ago, and they're both gone now. Barbara was a change-of-life baby, so her parents were a lot older than Kenny and me."

"What about Barbara?"

"I have no idea," Anna Marie said. "The last time I saw her was at Lisa's funeral. She was there with her fiancé. I know she introduced me to him, but I don't remember his name or anything about him. I don't think he was from around here."

"Did Lisa have any other friends?"

"Not really. She wasn't a very outgoing person; she was pretty but shy. I thought working in the dry cleaner's would help bring her out of herself. Instead, she ended up meeting Bradley. He asked her out and that was it. He was the only person she ever dated, and for some reason she didn't think she deserved anyone better."

Joanna thought about what Leslie Markham had said—that Rory was the only person she had ever dated. It sounded as though Lisa Marie Crystal's history had repeated itself in Leslie. Both of them had settled for someone who probably wasn't the very best specimen of manhood. And what about Lisa's father, Anna Marie's beloved Kenny? Maybe he wasn't any better than the men his daughter and granddaughter had chosen. Was the propensity for choosing men badly also to be found on mitochondrial DNA?

Joanna closed her notebook and rose to her feet. "We'll see what we can do to track down Barbara Tanner."

Anna Marie rose, too, and followed Frank and Joanna to the door. "You will tell me, won't you?"

"Tell you what?" Joanna asked.

"Tell me if you find out someone else was involved," Anna Marie said. "It wouldn't change anything, but at least then I'd know why Lisa died—that there was an actual reason for it. That's what I really wanted Bradley to tell me—why he did it. If he'd given me at least that much, maybe I could have forgiven him, but without knowing . . ." Anna Marie shook her head and didn't finish.

"If we find out," Joanna said, "I promise we'll let you know. But tell me one more thing, Mrs. Crystal. Do you happen to remember when your daughter's baby was due?"

"Oh, yes," Anna Marie said. "I remember that perfectly. Her due date was November the fifteenth. That's my birthday, too, so of course I remember. When Lisa told me she was pregnant, I remember telling Kenny, 'Oh, boy! By Thanksgiving we'll be grandparents.' But that wasn't to be," she added sadly.

"The families never do get over it, do they," Frank observed, once they were back in his Crown Victoria. "But I admit, the family resemblance from Anna Marie to Lisa and from Lisa to Leslie is downright spooky. Where to now?"

But Joanna already had her phone out and was dialing Markham Realty. "Since Leslie and her husband own the place, let's hope she doesn't go home at the stroke of five."

"Ms. Markham is in with a client writing up an offer," Fran, the receptionist, told her. "It may be some time before she's available, and I'm not allowed to interrupt."

"That's all right," Joanna said. "We'll stop by the office and wait for her to finish."

"What's the plan?" Frank asked.

"Leslie presumably knows the least about what went on in 1978, but she still may be able to tell us things that will help. She may be aware that she's adopted. Then again . . ."

"You're going to tell her?"

"I'm not sure," Joanna said. "Maybe. If not, our fallback position will be DNA."

"Which could take weeks or months to give us an answer." Frank sighed. "I suppose it would be asking too much to hope that Leslie Markham smokes, too."

"No," Joanna said, "I'm sure she doesn't. We're going to stop by the Starbucks on our way and pick up a latte for her. When it's time for us to leave, I'm going to count on you to bus the table—and to keep the cups straight."

"I should be able to manage that much. By the way, Leslie is number four."

"Number four what?"

"Mrs. Rory Markham the fourth," Frank returned. "He married Leslie two weeks to the day after his divorce from number three was final."

"No wonder I didn't like the guy," Joanna said. "He gave me the heebie-jeebies."

"More of your good ol' woman's intuition?" Frank asked.

"More like woman's radar," Joanna replied.

They waited in the lobby of Markham Realty until a quarter past six. When Leslie finally emerged from the conference room and escorted her client to the front door, she frowned at Frank and Joanna as she walked past. Only when the client was safely out of earshot did she whirl on them.

"What are you doing here?" she demanded. "I already told you everything I know. I've never met the man who took those pictures, and Rory's still mad at me about it. He thinks I had some kind of relationship—"

"Actually," Joanna said, "I'm quite certain you never had a romantic relationship of any kind with the man in question. In fact, our investigation will be able to lay your husband's concerns to rest on that score. But could we please go somewhere a little more private to discuss this? And we brought you a drink. It's probably cool by now, but . . ."

She was relieved when Leslie accepted the proffered cup without a murmur and then led them into the conference room.

"Tell me about your parents," Joanna said once they were all seated.

"My parents?" Leslie repeated. "I thought I already did that." She paused and, to Joanna's relief, took a tentative sip of the latte. "My father is Lawrence Tazewell—Judge Lawrence Tazewell of the Arizona Supreme Court. He lives in Phoenix with his second wife, Sharon. My mother's last name is Houlihan," she continued. "She took her maiden name back after the divorce, and she's never remarried. Rory and I live with my mother on the ranch that originally belonged to her family over at the base of the Whetstones. We live in one house and Mother lives in another. She used to raise quarter horses, but she doesn't do that anymore."

"Used to?" Joanna asked.

Leslie nodded. "She hasn't been well for several years now— one of those degenerative things. When it got to be too much for her, we sold off most of the livestock."

"What's your date of birth?" Joanna asked.

"Why?" Leslie returned.

"Humor me," Joanna said.

Leslie sighed. "All right. October twenty-eighth, 1978. Actually, it's a fun story."

Joanna felt a quickening of excitement. Leslie's birth date fit. October 28 was the day before Bradley Evans had been arrested. Anna Marie had told them Lisa Evans had been due on November 15, but if the baby had been born two weeks early, no one might have noticed.

"What kind of story?" Joanna asked.

"More like a family legend," Leslie conceded. "And, of course, everything I'm telling you is secondhand. The first time I heard it, I was just a kid and I thought it was incredibly embarrassing. Now it seems pretty amazing. Anyway, my father was away the week my mother was due to give birth. He was somewhere out of state at a conference for judges, and my mother was out on the ranch. My grandfather had remodeled the old bunkhouse for them to live in. As a matter of fact, that's the same house where Rory and I live now.

"Anyway, Mother went into labor so hard and fast that there wasn't time enough to get her to the hospital. Fortunately, Grandma Ruth was there to help. She always said it was a real pioneering experience. They boiled water and everything. She used a kitchen shears to cut the umbilical cord. After I was born, they packed Mother and me off to the hospital in Sierra Vista to be checked out. By the time my father came home from his conference, we were both back home safe and sound."

Of course, Joanna thought. *It's much more difficult to pull a baby switcheroo if you're in a hospital setting.*

Joanna had come to the office with every intention of pulling out the damning photographs and trying to get some straight answers, but clearly Leslie was an innocent bystander here. She didn't deserve to be asked the tough questions. Aileen Houlihan was another matter.

"Did your mother ever mention a friend or acquaintance named Lisa?" Joanna asked. "Lisa Marie Evans?"

Leslie shook her head. "Not that I remember. Who's she?"

"She was married to Bradley Evans, the man who took the photographs of you."

"I remember now," Leslie said. "You told us about her yesterday. You said Evans went to prison for murdering her—for murdering his wife."

Joanna nodded. "Lisa was pregnant at the time she disappeared in late October of 1978," she said. "Recently my investigators uncovered new evidence that suggests perhaps she wasn't murdered after all."

"And you think Lisa Evans and my mother may have been friends?"

"Possibly. I'd like to ask her about it."

"I don't think so," Leslie said.

"Why not?"

"I already told you. Mother's ill. She's not up to having visitors."

Rather than arguing about it, Joanna simply moved on. "What about your father?" she asked. "We'll want to talk to him as well. I'm sure we can reach him through his office next week, but can you tell us how to get in touch with him over the weekend?"

Leslie shook her head and a shadow of sadness clouded her face. "Sorry. His home number is unlisted, and I don't have it to give. He and my mother divorced years ago. He and I have never been close."

Not having her father's home phone number was about as "not close" as Joanna could imagine, but that small admission made Rory Markham's presence in Leslie's life far more understandable. Estranged from her father, Leslie had gone looking for a father figure—and had found one. It wasn't all that surprising, then, that she had settled on a man who was probably only a few years younger than her biological father.

"That's all right," Joanna said reassuringly. "I'm sure we'll be able to locate him even without your help."

Leslie glanced at her watch and her eyes widened. "I didn't know it was so late!" she exclaimed, dropping her paper cup in the trash. "Rory and I are supposed to meet someone for dinner ten minutes from now. I really must go."

"Of course," Joanna said. "Sorry to have kept you so long."

"Is there anything else you need?"

"Not at the moment."

Frank paused at the doorway, motioning for the women to leave first. Once they were out in the hall, Joanna caught sight of him ducking back to retrieve Leslie's cup.

Neither of them said anything more until they were back in the car.

"She doesn't even have her father's unlisted phone number?" Frank commented. "What kind of family is that?"

"A broken one," Joanna said. "As sad as she was, I just couldn't bring myself to blow her out of the water," she added once the car doors closed.

"I couldn't have done it either," Frank said. "So it's on to plan B, which means we're back to getting the DNA tested?"

"That's about it," Joanna said. "The testing itself can be done in a matter of hours. The big problem will be pushing this to the top of the list. Once we have the samples there, I'll see what I can do to get things moving."

"What about me?" Frank asked.

"See what you can do about locating Lawrence Tazewell's address as well as his unlisted phone number. With a federal judgeship hanging in the balance, I'm wondering about him."

"As in, Bradley shows up with a handful of pictures that pretty well proves Lawrence Tazewell knowingly sent an innocent man up the river. The next thing that happens is his federal bench nomination is in the toilet."

"Exactly," Joanna agreed. "Sounds like possible motive to me."

"But if he's a suspect, what makes you think the man will talk to us?" Frank asked.

"We'll just have to try," Joanna said. "And if he doesn't, maybe Aileen will."

"But Leslie said . . ."

"I know she said her mother wasn't up to having visitors," Joanna returned. "But this is a homicide investigation. One way or the other, we're going to talk to the woman."

"Tonight?" Frank asked.

Joanna looked at the clock on the dash. It was almost seven, and she had yet to call Butch to let him know she'd be late for dinner.

"No, not tonight," she said. "If Aileen really is ill, it's probably too late to drop by to see her. Tomorrow will be plenty of time."

"But tomorrow's Saturday," Frank objected. "Are you sure you want to work on Saturday?"

"Working on a Saturday before the baby is born will be easier than working any day of the week afterward. Yes, I'm working tomorrow. What about you?"

Frank Montoya shook his head. "You're hopeless," he said.

"What do you mean?" Joanna asked.

"If you can't figure out how to take even so much as a weekend off, I doubt you're going to be any good at maternity leave."

Joanna should have been able to object, but she couldn't because it occurred to her as soon as Frank said it that he was probably right.

CHAPTER 15

B y the time Joanna got back to High Lonesome Ranch, Butch and Jenny were watching a movie in the family room with all three dogs scattered around them. Lady came into the kitchen to keep Joanna company while she reheated her dinner in the microwave. She was finishing eating when the program ended and Butch joined her.

"That's the great thing about green chili casserole," he said. "The older it gets, the better it tastes."

"You're right," Joanna agreed. "It was great."

"So how's it going?" he asked. "You look upset."

"I am upset," she said. "Sometimes being a cop sucks."

Sitting down at the table, Butch took her hand. "What's wrong?"

Joanna shrugged. "In the process of investigating a homicide, I'm about to blow someone's life wide open."

"Presumably not the killer's," Butch said, "or you wouldn't be concerned about it."

It was gratifying that Butch knew her so well.

"That's right," she agreed. "Not the killer's. We're about to tell a totally innocent twenty-five-year-old real estate agent out in Sierra Vista that she isn't who she thinks she is, that the people who claim to be her biological parents aren't even related to her."

"Lots of people don't find out they're adopted until they're grown," Butch suggested. "It's not fatal."

"In this case the biological mother evidently pulled a phony disappearing act. She handed her baby off to someone else to raise and then left the child's father to go to prison for the alleged 'murder' of his wife and child. The biological father did his time and was finally released a couple of years ago. The trouble started when he accidentally ran into the daughter, who looks spookily like her mother. As soon as he tumbled to the fact that the baby probably didn't die, he did. Someone murdered him. To make matters worse, the faux father, who may turn into a likely homicide suspect, happens to be a much respected member of the Arizona Supreme Court—Justice Lawrence Tazewell."

"Not good," Butch said. "What are you going to do about it?"

"I have no idea. In fact, that's what I'm sitting here trying to noodle out. Someone needs to go up to Phoenix to interview him, but Ernie is off on medical leave, and Jaime and Debbie are busy tracking down the people who beat up Jeannine Phillips. With the department so shorthanded—"

"No," Butch interrupted.

"What do you mean, no?" she asked.

"I mean the baby's due within the week. I don't want you traipsing all the way to Phoenix to talk to a homicide suspect. Get Frank to do it or one of the other deputies."

"But the man is a state supreme court justice," Joanna objected. "I can't very well send one of my deputies to talk to him."

"Yes, you can," Butch declared. "You're pregnant. Who would end up interviewing the guy if the baby were already here and you were off on maternity leave?"

"I don't know," Joanna said gloomily.

"Well," Butch returned, "get used to it. You're going to have to let go sometime."

"That's what Frank said."

"That you're going to have to let go?"

"That I'm going to flunk maternity leave."

"He's right," Butch observed. "That's a distinct possibility, but in the meantime, what are you going to do about this?"

"Keep on thinking, I guess," Joanna said. "Maybe even sleep on it."

Butch collected her plate and silverware and took it over to the sink. "That's right," he said. "I almost forgot. I have a message for you from Eva Lou and Jim Bob. They said to tell you that you're not allowed to have the baby until after they get home tomorrow night."

"Where did they go?" Joanna asked. "I didn't know they were planning a trip."

"Neither did they," Butch said. "They took Monty to Albuquerque."

"Monty?" Joanna asked. "Who's Monty?"

Butch shook his head and rolled his eyes. "Monty the python. That's what Jim Bob says you called him, Monty Python."

"The snake!" Joanna exclaimed. "I've been so busy I'd forgotten all about him. What happened?"

"It turns out there's a python rescue guy over in Albuquerque who's willing to take on the one from here, and Manny Ruiz was very eager to unload the snake and get him out of the kennel. He said the python was driving the other animals nuts and the receptionist as well." Butch paused and then added, "Speaking of Animal Control, what do you hear about Jeannine Phillips?"

"Not much," Joanna said. "As far as I know, she's still in the ICU. Jaime Carbajal and Debbie Howell are working full-time to track down whoever did it. So far they don't seem to be making a lot of progress."

"What you need more than anything," Butch said, "is a decent night's sleep."

"You might tell that to that son of yours," Joanna replied. "He seems to spend half of every night kicking the daylights out of me."

"Speaking of baby Dennis," Butch said with a grin, "before they left, I told Jim Bob and Eva Lou that we now know we're having a boy. And I told your mother and George as well. I knew there'd be hell to pay if one set of grandparents found out far in advance of any other set of grandparents. Did your mother call you?"

"Not yet," Joanna said. "That means she's probably pissed because she didn't hear the news directly from me. No matter what we do, there's no way to win with that woman."

"You shouldn't be so hard on her," Butch said.

He had finished loading the last of the dishes into the dishwasher when Jenny came into the kitchen carrying the phone with her hand held firmly over the mouthpiece. "It's your office," she said with a frown. "Cassie and I were right in the middle of a conversation. Could you please hurry?"

Cassie Parks was Jenny's best friend. Joanna had noticed that the older the two girls grew, the harder it was to pry the telephone receiver out of Jenny's hand.

"I've got Justice Tazewell's unlisted number," Frank Montoya announced as soon as Joanna answered. "Do you want to call him or should I?"

"I will," Joanna said. "Give it to me."

Minutes later she was dialing Lawrence Tazewell's number in Paradise Valley. The woman who answered the phone sounded Hispanic. "Justice Tazewell isn't here," she told Joanna.

"Could I speak to Mrs. Tazewell then," Joanna asked. "This is Sheriff Joanna Brady from Cochise County."

"Mrs. Tazewell isn't here, either. Would you like to leave a message?"

Joanna was reluctant to leave a message, but there didn't seem to be any other option. "Yes," she said finally. "Please ask him to call me. It's not an emergency, but it is about his daughter."

After relaying her numbers, Joanna returned the phone to her daughter. Five minutes later, a frowning Jenny was back in the kitchen, once again handing her mother the phone.

"Sheriff Brady?" a man's voice asked. "This is Justice Lawrence Tazewell. You called? What's this about my daughter? Is she all right?"

Joanna had expected Tazewell to be a distant and indifferent father, but there was nothing indifferent in his tone of voice.

"Your daughter's fine," Joanna said.

"Oh," Tazewell uttered with obvious relief. "Thank God for that. What's this all about then?"

In the background Joanna heard a buzz of voices. Tazewell was returning her call from a relatively public place—not the best kind of environment to pose the kinds of questions she needed to ask.

"We've learned that someone's been stalking her," Joanna said, hedging her bet. "Taking Leslie's picture without her knowledge. Her husband suggested to my investigators and me that the stalking might have something to do with your possible nomination to the federal bench."

"I doubt it," Tazewell answered. "And for the record, I wouldn't believe anything Rory Markham has to say."

Not an indifferent father at all, Joanna thought.

"Look," Tazewell said. "I'm sure you and I need to discuss all of this, but I can't do it right now. What about tomorrow?"

"Where would you like to meet?" Joanna asked.

"I'm in Tucson at a meeting, but I have my own plane. Why don't I just fly into Bisbee sometime in the morning. We can talk there."

"In the municipal airport?"

"Sure," Tazewell said. "When I was a superior court judge in Bisbee and living out on the ranch, I used to do it all the time. Saved myself all kinds of commuting time and wear and tear on my car. I'll show up, we can have our little chat, and I'll fly right back out again. What time would you like me there, and can someone meet me?"

"Nine will be fine," Joanna said at once. "And I'll pick you up myself."

"Good," Tazewell said. "See you then."

Joanna was still looking at the phone in amazement when Cassie Parks's voice said, "Jenny, are you there?" Once again Joanna handed the phone back to her daughter.

"So he's coming here?" Butch asked.

Joanna nodded.

"Well," Butch said, "that's better than your having to go there."

They went to bed relatively early. As usual, Joanna didn't sleep well. Her back hurt. She couldn't get comfortable. As predicted, little Dennis kicked up a storm. In the quiet between kicks, Joanna spent the waking hours trying to imagine what questions she would pose to Justice Lawrence Tazewell, who might or might not be a suspect in the Bradley Evans homicide.

The fact that Tazewell had offered to come to Bisbee for the interview should have made her less nervous, but it didn't. Joanna was enough of a poker player to realize that Tazewell's willing cooperation might be nothing more than a cagey defensive gambit. By feigning a willingness to help, he might actually be deliberately trying to throw her off track.

She was still nervous about the upcoming interview at nine the next morning as she watched a blue-and-white Cessna 180 circle for a landing on the single runway of Bisbee's municipal airport. She felt inexplicably better, however, when the door opened and a man wearing jeans, alligator-skin cowboy boots, and an enormous Stetson stepped off the plane. She might be worried about talking to a state supreme court justice, but a supreme court justice who also happened to be a cowboy might be somewhat easier to handle.

Emerging from her Crown Victoria, Joanna walked forward to meet him. Once he finished setting the chocks, he stood up and wiped his hands on the back of his jeans.

"Justice Tazewell?" Joanna asked. "I'm Sheriff Brady."

"And you're also very pregnant," Tazewell observed.

Accustomed to people's veiled glances and behind-the-back comments, Joanna found Lawrence Tazewell's directness surprisingly disarming.

"Yes," she agreed with a laugh, "I am."

"When are you due?" he asked.

"Sometime this week," Joanna replied.

Tazewell nodded. "I know a little about babies," he observed as he followed Joanna back to the Crown Victoria. In order to accommodate her short legs, Joanna kept the bench seat as far forward as possible. That meant that Lawrence Tazewell's knees were crammed up against the glove compartment. He seemed oblivious, however.

"My stepdaughter had her little girl just a week ago today," he continued as he shifted in search of a more comfortable position. "Seven pounds six ounces, born screeching her lungs out at ten o'clock last Thursday morning. Suzanne named her Destry Annette. Funny name for a girl if you ask me, but no one did— ask me, that is. My only contribution to the process was to be on hand to wield the digital camera once the nurse had her wrapped and put her in Suzanne's arms. We loaded the photos into a computer and e-mailed them to her daddy within an hour of her birth. My son-in-law's in the military, you see. He's a pilot in the air force and doing a tour of duty in the Middle East right now. That's why Sharon and I were called in as reinforcements."

By then they had settled into the vehicle, and Joanna was headed back to the Justice Center. "Where?" she asked.

"Where's he stationed?" Tazewell returned.

"No," Joanna said. "Where does your stepdaughter live?"

"Denver," Tazewell answered. "Ron is from there. His parents own a bunch of apartment buildings, and they're letting Suzanne and the kids stay in one of them rent-free while Ron is overseas. Destry's brother, Johnny, is three years old and a real pistol. The other grandparents looked after him while Sharon and I were at the hospital."

As Tazewell spoke, Joanna was doing some calculating of her own. Bradley Evans had died sometime the previous Wednesday or Thursday. If, as Lawrence Tazewell claimed, he had been off in Colorado doing grandfather duty, it seemed likely that he had no connection to the Evans homicide.

"Did you fly your own plane up there?" she asked.

"Of course," he said. "Commercial flying is such a pain these days that I avoid it whenever possible. We left right after I got off work on Wednesday and were there in time for dinner. It could have taken us the same amount of time just to clear security at Sky Harbor."

As they came up over the hill south of the ballpark, Tazewell looked around and sighed. "Looks like nothing's changed," he said. "When I first got elected to the superior court, I thought Aileen and I would move over here. I'd even made an offer on a nice place over on the Vista, but she refused to leave her folks' ranch. Her mother was starting to have some health issues about then. And she stayed on even after both her parents passed away. As far as I know, she's still there. I'm the one who moved on."

There was a clear hint of regret in his voice. "You don't sound particularly happy about it," Joanna said.

"Being here brings it all back, I guess," he said. "My colossal failure in life. The funny thing is, I didn't see it coming even though one of my fraternity brothers from the U of A tried to warn me. Dudley told me he thought I was getting in over my head, only I didn't believe him. Old Dud was of the opinion that marrying a rich man's daughter was a bad idea. Turns out he was right. Which brings us, I suppose, to Leslie. What's going on with her? What's this about stalking? I'm willing to bet it has a lot more to do with that slime bucket named Rory Markham than it does with me."

"I take it you don't approve of your son-in-law?" Joanna asked casually.

"Look," Lawrence Tazewell said. "Aileen wrote me out of my daughter's life a long time ago. I've had no contact with Leslie at all since she was little, but I still care, and I try to keep track of what's going on with her. When I found out she had married Rory Markham, I assumed it was Rory's son. I knew he had at least one. I didn't find out until much later that wasn't the case. When I learned she had married the father instead, the Rory I knew, I couldn't believe it. Why would someone like Leslie, a girl in her twenties, want to hook up with an old goat almost as old as her father?"

Joanna had her own ideas about why Leslie had married Rory Markham. "So you and he knew each other?" she asked.

"I knew him slightly, but Rory and my ex have been pals forever," Tazewell answered finally. "Maybe even more than pals on occasion. I suspect Aileen is the one who engineered the whole thing."

Joanna was thunderstruck. "You're saying your wife allowed your daughter to marry one of her ex-boyfriends?"

"Encouraged probably more than allowed," Tazewell replied. "In fact, she probably manipulated the whole transaction and poor Leslie probably still hasn't figured it out. Aileen's like that, you see—someone who always gets her way. That's one of the reasons I divorced her."

"But—" Joanna began. Lawrence Tazewell stopped her mid-objection.

"Look," he said. "Just because someone gives birth doesn't make her a decent mother—present company excepted, of course. Now tell me about this stalking business. You say the guy was taking pictures. Do you have any idea who it is?"

Joanna hadn't expected the interview to progress this far without being back at the department and having someone else to witness and record exactly what was said, but she was into it now, and there was no turning back.

"His name is Evans," Joanna answered. "Bradley Evans."

She glanced in Tazewell's direction to see if there was any visible reaction to this revelation, but there was nothing—no sign of recognition or even interest.

"And he is?"

"An ex-con," Joanna said. "And he's dead. Someone murdered him last week."

"A friend of Rory's?" Tazewell asked.

"No," Joanna said. "Not as far as we've been able to determine. You may know him, though."

"Me?" Tazewell asked. "How would I know the man?"

"You're the one who sent him to prison."

"What's the man's name again?"

"Bradley Evans. He went to prison in 1978 for the murder of his pregnant wife. You were the judge who accepted his plea agreement and imposed the prison sentence."

"Wait a minute. I think I do remember now. The guy was an ex-soldier from Fort Huachuca, right? He copped a plea even though no one ever found his wife's body."

Joanna nodded.

"And you're right. I'm the one who imposed his sentence. It wasn't a good time for me, though. I barely remember the proceedings. But what would he have against Leslie?"

By then Joanna was pulling into the Justice Center complex. "Let's talk about it when we get inside," she said.

"All this is new?" Tazewell asked.

Joanna nodded. "Relatively," she said.

"When I was here everything was still located in the courthouse up in Old Bisbee—the jail, the sheriff's department, the courts."

"Times change," Joanna said. "Come on in." She ushered him into her office through her private entrance and offered him a chair. "Would you mind excusing me?" she asked. "Nature calls—urgently."

Tazewell smiled. "I understand," he said. "Take your time."

Leaving him alone in her office, Joanna hurried to the rest room and then back to Frank's office. "Got him?" Frank asked.

"He's in my office. Do you have anything for me?"

"Not yet," Frank answered. "Nothing on the blood work, if that's what you mean. Trying to get the crime lab moving on this is like pulling teeth."

"Having a supreme court justice sitting in my office may be our secret weapon on that score," Joanna said. "Care to join us?"

Nodding, Frank followed Joanna from his office to hers. After introductions, the three of them settled into chairs around the small conference table in the corner of the room. "What can you tell me about your former wife's friends?" Joanna asked.

"What friends?" Lawrence Tazewell asked with a snort of derision. "Rory was the only one I knew of, and he was a chum of hers from grade school on. Rory earned money by working on the Triple H during the summers and on weekends. Aileen was totally preoccupied with her parents and her horses. In that order. Her father came first, her mother second, the horses third."

"What about Leslie?"

"A distant fourth. They hired the wife of one of the Triple H ranch hands to look after her."

"Did you sue for custody?" Joanna asked. "If you knew your ex-wife wasn't much of a mother and that your daughter was being raised by a paid caregiver, I should think you would have tried to gain custody."

Lawrence Tazewell said nothing for a very long time. Instead of answering, he stared out the window at the gray limestone cliffs rising in the distance. "No," he said finally. "I wasn't tough enough. I took the easy way out. Aileen said she wanted a divorce, so I gave it to her. And Max made it worth my while to get out and not to rock the boat."

"Max?" Frank Montoya asked.

"Maxfield Houlihan," Tazewell answered. "Aileen's father. Once she made it clear she wanted to be rid of me, Max did whatever he could to make it happen. And I have to hand it to the man. Max Houlihan may have looked like a rube, but he was surprisingly well connected. With the clear understanding that I would go away and stay away, Max pulled a few choice strings. I ended up being offered a great position with a law firm up in Phoenix, one that was far too lucrative to turn down. And that position inevitably resulted in where I am today."

"You're saying that it's because of your ex-father-in-law's string pulling that you're a supreme court justice?"

"He didn't get me the appointment," Tazewell said. "I got that on my own, but that first job he obtained for me was certainly a springboard to bigger and better things. It put me on a fast track in a way being a superior court judge in Cochise County never would have. But, yes, that is what happened. I've felt guilty about it for years. I paid my child support every month, but other than that, I stayed out of Aileen's and Leslie's lives. I didn't want to be involved. I had already lost them once, and I didn't want to face losing them again. Over the years I've tried to make up for my shortcomings with Leslie by doing my level best to be a good father to my present wife Sharon's two daughters."

There was something in Tazewell's demeanor that made Joanna think he was leaving something out. "What do you mean, lose them again?" she asked.

"HD," he said.

"What's that?"

"Huntington's disease," Tazewell answered.

"I've never heard of it," Joanna said. "What is it?"

"It's a degenerative disease," he said. "It's hereditary and incurable. They used to call it Huntington's chorea because it causes chorea—violent, uncontrollable spasms. It progresses over a period of time—ten to fifteen years, rendering its victims more and more helpless. Ruth, Aileen's mother, had it, and so did two of her brothers. HD would have killed Ruth eventually, but she committed suicide before things progressed that far. Since Aileen's mother had HD, there's a fifty-fifty chance that she'll develop it too. The same goes for Leslie. God forgive me, but I wasn't tough enough to stay around and watch it happen."

"Leslie told us last night that her mother was ill with some kind of degenerative disorder. She didn't say what kind."

Lawrence Tazewell's eyes blinked with tears. "Sorry to hear it," he said gruffly. "I always hoped she'd dodge that bullet. I think they do genetic testing now. I hope Leslie has it done before she has kids. If she doesn't have the HD gene, she can't pass it along to her children."

"Genetic testing may not be necessary," Joanna said.

She struggled up out of the chair, went over to her desk, opened her briefcase, and removed the envelope containing the photos of Leslie Markham and Lisa Marie Evans.

Ignoring Frank's warning look, Joanna returned to the conference table with the envelope in hand. "How long has it been since you've seen your daughter?" she asked.

"Eighteen years or so," Tazewell answered. "The last time I saw her was at her grandmother's funeral. She must have been seven then. I haven't contacted her since. Why?"

Wordlessly Joanna shuffled through the photos and removed

one that Bradley Evans had shot of Leslie pushing a grocery cart across a parking lot. She handed it over to Lawrence Tazewell. He fumbled a pair of reading glasses out of his pocket, put them on, and then studied the photo for several seconds. "This is her?" he asked at last.

Joanna nodded. "You haven't even seen pictures of her?"

"No," Tazewell said at last. "Not since she was in grade school. She's beautiful, but she doesn't look like anybody—not her mother's side of the family or mine."

"There could be a reason for that," Joanna told him as she extracted Lisa Marie Evans's senior picture from the envelope and handed it over.

Lawrence Tazewell studied the photo for a long time. Then he picked it up and held it next to Leslie's picture. When he spoke, his voice was a hoarse whisper. "Who the hell is this?" he demanded. "The women in these two pictures could be twins."

"Not twins but close," Joanna said. "The one woman's maiden name was Lisa Marie Crystal. Her married name was Evans. She was Bradley Evans's wife, our murder victim's supposed murder victim. We have reason to believe Lisa Marie Evans may have been Leslie's biological mother."

Tazewell looked stunned. "Not Aileen?" he asked. "How could such a thing be possible?"

"That's what we're trying to find out. We've collected some DNA samples that should confirm Leslie's real parentage. It'll take time to have them processed, of course. In the meantime, Leslie told us a few things about the unusual circumstances surrounding her birth, including the fact that you were out of town at the time it happened."

Tazewell nodded. "I was in Dallas at a conference. Leslie was delivered at home with her grandmother's help and then taken to the hospital later." He paused and then added, "But if Leslie is someone else's baby, what happened to Aileen's?"

"Are you certain she was pregnant at the time?"

"That's what I thought," Tazewell said. "It's what Aileen told me. So did her doctor."

"Do you remember the doctor's name?"

"Carstairs, Carston, Carmmody," Tazewell answered. "I don't remember exactly, but I think his name started with a C."

"Maybe something happened to that baby," Joanna suggested. "Some kind of late-term miscarriage. And if she and Lisa Evans were friends, maybe they arranged for Aileen to supposedly give birth at home so they could pass Lisa's baby off as your wife's. Doing that would have cleared the way for Lisa to leave her husband and simply disappear."

"The murdered man, Bradley Evans," Tazewell said. "He would have been the husband, the same man I personally sentenced to prison."

Joanna nodded. "That's right," she agreed.

"But he pleaded guilty, didn't he?"

"Yes."

"If he wasn't responsible for his wife's death, why would he do a thing like that?"

"Who knows? If he was drunk, maybe he was operating in a blackout and felt ultimately responsible for whatever had happened to her regardless of who actually did it," Joanna offered. "Now tell me. Did your wife ever mention having a friend named Lisa?"

"No, not that I remember," Tazewell responded. "But our marriage was what one could charitably call troubled. With the notable exception of Rory Markham, I wasn't really privy to

Aileen's circle of acquaintances. Still, are you saying that she knowingly participated in some kind of conspiracy that resulted in my sending an innocent man to jail for murder?"

"At this point," Joanna said, "all I'm suggesting is that's a possibility."

"And Evans was innocent the whole time?"

Joanna nodded. "Also possible."

"If I'd had any idea—if I'd had even the slightest hint that Aileen knew the woman—I would have recused myself immediately. I never would have agreed to preside over the Evans case. You do believe me, don't you?"

Joanna nodded. "Yes, I do," she said.

"But supposing Evans didn't kill his wife. Where the hell did she go? Is she still alive and well somewhere, living under an assumed name? And what if that other baby—my baby—didn't die either? Where is that child?"

"I don't know the answer to any of those questions," Joanna told him. "That's what we're trying to find out. The idea that Lisa is alive and well is certainly one possible scenario. The other is that she's been dead all along. The fact that Bradley Evans is dead, too, tends to suggest he ended up spooking someone who had something to hide."

"How did that all come about?" Tazewell asked.

"Pure bad luck," Joanna replied. "We've learned that Bradley Evans and Leslie Markham both happened to have lunch in the same Sierra Vista restaurant on Tuesday a week ago. Evans must have noticed the striking resemblance between Leslie and his presumably dead wife. He spent most of the next day following her around Sierra Vista taking pictures with a disposable camera.

"Maybe he wanted to confirm for himself what he thought he was seeing. Or maybe he planned on showing the photos to

someone else. But he never got a chance to show them to anyone. Before he finished shooting that roll of film, he was dead—
stabbed to death. When his vehicle was impounded after his
death, we found the camera hidden under the front seat of his
vehicle."

"Am I a suspect?" Tazewell asked.

The man's direct question caught Joanna off guard. He certainly had been a suspect initially, but the longer she talked to
him, the less she thought Lawrence Tazewell was directly involved in Bradley Evans's murder. Still, without substantiating
his alibi, there was no way to be sure.

"Possibly," Joanna admitted. "Although not much of one. Is
there any way to confirm that you were in Denver last week?"

Nodding, Tazewell removed a PDA from his pocket and
reeled off a telephone number. "That's the FBO—Fixed Base
Operator—at the general aviation airport north of Denver
where we landed and where the plane was parked from Wednesday until Monday morning. Sharon and I spent a lot of time at
the hospital, but we were at our daughter's in-laws' apartment a
good deal of the time as well, and we met some of her friends
and neighbors. Do you want their names and phone numbers?"

"Wherever possible," Joanna said.

It took several minutes for Joanna to collect the information.
While she took notes, Frank Montoya did the same. When
Tazewell finally returned his PalmPilot to his pocket, his face was
grave. "So everything was fine until Evans stumbled on to the
fact that maybe his dead daughter really wasn't dead."

Joanna nodded. "That's how it looks."

"Has Leslie been informed about any of this?" Tazewell asked.

"Not yet," Joanna said. "And until we have some kind of solid
confirmation . . ."

"Right," Tazewell said. "Of course. It would be irresponsible to mention any of this to her while it's still a matter of supposition, but when the time comes, are you going to tell her or should I?"

"I'd prefer to have that handled by a family member—either you or her mother."

Tazewell nodded. "That may not be possible," he said.

"Why not?"

"Depending on how far Aileen's HD has progressed, she may not be able to talk."

"I'd like to hear Aileen's side of the story," Joanna said. "But in case that's not possible, what can you tell us about her?"

Lawrence Tazewell shook his head. "I really don't have any idea where to start," he said.

Frank Montoya caught Joanna's eye and then stood up. "If you'll excuse me, there are a couple of things I need to attend to."

"Fine," Joanna said, then she turned back to Lawrence Tazewell, who was holding the pictures of Lisa Evans and Leslie Markham and gazing back and forth between them. "I guess you'd best start at the beginning."

CHAPTER 16

B ut Lawrence Tazewell was still mulling over what he'd just heard. "I'm surprised she hasn't done herself in the same way her mother did. I wouldn't blame her, but this does go a long way to explaining the Rory thing."

"What do you mean?"

"He saw what happened to Ruth. And I'm sure he knows that, one way or the other, Aileen is a short-timer. By marrying Leslie, Rory puts himself in a position to be half owner of a very valuable parcel of Cochise County real estate."

"Are there any other children?"

Tazewell shook his head. "Max and his first wife, Margie, had a little boy who died of leukemia when he was twelve. Margie suffered a debilitating stroke while she was still in her forties. Ruth was the nurse Max hired to take care of Margie. Max and Ruth married within months of Margie's death. The only child the two of them had together was Aileen. Max was delighted beyond bearing when Aileen showed up, and he and Ruth spoiled her rotten."

"You said Ruth's brothers died of Huntington's?" Joanna asked.

Tazewell nodded. "But they were younger than she was. The brothers were only in their twenties when they started going downhill. Ruth was in her thirties when Aileen was born. Because she still wasn't sick, I think she must have thought it wasn't going to happen to her."

"But it did," Joanna offered.

"Yes. Ruth was just beginning to show symptoms of HD when Aileen and I married. And when she found out Aileen was pregnant, Ruth went nuts. She wanted Aileen to have an abortion, but neither Max nor Aileen would hear of it. Aileen because she really wanted to have the baby, and Max because he wanted to keep the Triple H in the family."

Tazewell paused. "Damn!" he exclaimed. "I had forgotten all about that."

"About what?"

"Sometime early in October of that year, Ruth and Aileen flew to Albuquerque to see her brothers. By then both of them were confined to a nursing home. I offered to fly Ruth and Aileen there, but Ruth wasn't having any of that. She insisted on flying commercial. At that stage of her pregnancy, Aileen had to have written permission from her doctor to fly at all. I remember she was really offended that she had to have a permission slip. But when she came back from that trip, Aileen was a completely different person."

"How so?" Joanna asked.

But Lawrence Tazewell, lost in his own thoughts, didn't seem to hear her. "Do you think that's what happened?" he asked. "Do you think that, after seeing Ruth's brothers, Aileen decided she couldn't risk having a child of her own, so she got rid of her own baby and took someone else's?"

"Tell me about Aileen Houlihan," Joanna said.

"As in do I think she's capable of doing such a thing? No," he said after a pause. "I don't."

"What was she like then?"

The faraway look returned to Tazewell's eyes. "When I first met Aileen Houlihan, she was a pistol," he said at last. "Head-strong, stubborn, and spoiled rotten. She came to the University of Arizona with a whole catalog of parental rules and a single-minded determination to break 'em all. I was a case in point."

"How so?"

"Aileen's daddy wanted his daughter to graduate from the University of Arizona with honors, go on to law school, and then come home to do her parents proud—maybe end up going into politics. She carefully deconstructed that whole program. Her freshman year she did three things that sent her old man round the bend—she flunked out of school, married me, and brought me home to live on her parents' ranch. Max was in his late seventies when Aileen came dragging home with me and told him that she didn't need a college degree to raise cattle and horses."

"You're saying she married you out of spite?"

"Pretty much. Did you ever meet Max and Ruth Houlihan?"

Joanna shook her head. "Never. It sounds like they were a lit-tle before my time."

"I suppose," Tazewell agreed. "They were quite a pair. Ruth was beautiful. Fortunately for her, Aileen took after her mother in the looks department. Old Maxfield was ugly as a stump—a crotchety old bowlegged cowboy who never got over his incredible good luck at finding himself such a gorgeous young woman to be his second wife. He didn't know about the Huntington's, at least not before they got married, and I don't think it would have made any difference if he had. I'm sure he would have married Ruth anyway. Max was stubborn as hell. Aileen takes after her father in that regard."

"So you and Aileen got married. What happened then?"

"Max was disappointed, but he decided to make the best of a bad bargain. He was the one who bankrolled my first election here in Cochise County. And, as I told you earlier, after Aileen dumped me, Max used his contacts to help me get a foothold up in Maricopa County. I suspect he was grateful that I left the marriage without making a fuss over custody arrangements or demanding a property settlement."

"And you left the marriage because . . . ?" Joanna asked.

"Because Aileen told me to get out. She made it perfectly clear that I'd never measure up to her father. She said she was bored with me. She said that she wasn't ready to settle down— that she needed to live a little. When she hinted around that I probably wasn't Leslie's father, I finally decided she was right. Having a wild woman for a girlfriend is one thing, but having a wild woman for a wife is something else. I hung around for a while after Leslie was born, but when it came time for the next election, I didn't bother to run. Instead, I took the job offer Max had found for me, moved to Phoenix, got a divorce, and went on with my life."

"And Aileen?" Joanna asked. "According to Leslie, she never married again."

"How long has she been sick?" Tazewell asked.

"Leslie didn't say."

"Once her HD symptoms started coming on, I can see why

she would have stayed out of another relationship." He paused and looked past Joanna to the ocotillo-and-bear-grass-dotted landscape outside her window. "I wonder . . ." he said thoughtfully.

"What?"

"Maybe Ruth convinced her to have a late-term abortion after all. And Aileen made arrangements to pass this other child off as her own so no one would know. Not even me, but I do have a right to know. I have half a mind to fly straight out to the ranch right now and ask Aileen about it face-to-face."

"No," Joanna said at once. "Please don't. Interference like that could very well jeopardize our investigation into the Evans homicide. I'm convinced Bradley Evans died because he stumbled on a long-buried truth someone didn't want exposed to the light of day."

"Are you going to talk to her about this?"

"I'm going to try."

"You'll let me know what you find out?"

Joanna nodded.

"I loved her once, you know," Tazewell added with a bleak smile.

"I know you did."

With a light tap on the door, Frank Montoya reentered the room and placed a stack of papers in front of Joanna. At the bottom of the top sheet was a discreetly handwritten note: "T's alibi checks out."

"Is there anything else, then?" Tazewell asked. "Anything more you need from me?"

"Not that I can think of," Joanna said. "Only your contact numbers so we can be in touch with you when we need to."

Tazewell nodded and handed Joanne a business card.

Joanna stood and extended her hand. "Thanks for coming,"

she said. "I know this has been hard on you. I'll have a deputy take you back to your plane."

"Thanks," Tazewell said, then he added, "I don't suppose you believe that I knew nothing about any of this—about the connection between my wife and the family of the man I sent to prison."

"Actually," Joanna returned, "I do believe you."

"Thank you," he said. "But once they get wind of it, I doubt the press will be that kind. Best case, I'll lose the federal nomination. Worst case, I'll be forced off the bench."

"I hope not," Joanna said.

Tazewell shook his head. "I'm not so sure about that. If Aileen was able to pull the wool over my eyes as thoroughly and as easily as this, I'm too damned stupid to sit on the Arizona Supreme Court!"

With that he turned and strode out of the office.

"He's upset," Frank said as the door closed.

"I'll say," Joanna responded. "He has every right to be. As soon as we can get someone to take him back to the airport, we'll go out to the Triple H and see what we can do to get to the bottom of this."

"Right now?" Frank asked.

"Does either one of us have something better to do?" Joanna asked. "Besides, if he thinks about it too long, Lawrence Tazewell may decide to have his own little chat with Aileen Houlihan. What about these?" she asked, picking up the fistful of papers.

"Bring them along," Frank said. "I'll drive. We can talk about those as we go."

Buckled into the passenger seat of Frank's Crown Victoria, Joanna scanned through the documents. The several pages dealt with the telephone numbers Lawrence Tazewell had given them. One after another, people had verified what he had said about the times he had arrived in Denver, where the plane had been tied down, as well as people he had seen while there. And, in every regard, each of the several people—from the guy in charge of the FBO to Tazewell's stepdaughter—told the same story. Frank's assessment about Tazewell's lack of involvement in the Evans homicide seemed validated. The next sheet was a printout from classmates.com with information on Barbara Tanner Petrocelli.

Joanna was amazed. "You found Lisa Evans's friend!"

"Yup," Frank agreed with a grin. "Address, phone number, and everything. Isn't that why you keep me on the payroll?"

"And she still lives in Sierra Vista," Joanna marveled. "Once we finish up with Aileen Houlihan, maybe we can see Barbara, too. After all, it'll be on our way home."

The last piece of paper was a copy of a phone message addressed to Debbie Howell. It listed the name Manfred Oxhill along with a Sierra Vista telephone number.

"Who's Manfred?" Joanna asked.

Frank grinned again. "That's the best part," he said. "I noticed a message in Debbie's box and decided to take a look at it. Turns out Mr. Oxhill manages the auto-parts section of Sierra Vista's Target store. I called him. He apologized for taking so long to respond to Debbie's inquiry about primer. He's been out sick all this week until yesterday, but it turns out they sold a whole case of primer last Friday morning. He's going back through the records to see if he can find out if it was a cash or credit transaction."

"Surely we wouldn't be lucky enough that the killer used a credit card," Joanna murmured.

"You'd be surprised," Frank replied. "Most crooks get caught because they're dumb, not because we're all that clever."

"What time does Mr. Oxhill get off work?"

"Six," Frank answered. "So maybe we can see him today as well."

"Anything on Jeannine this morning?" Joanna asked.

Frank nodded. "I called Millicent and checked with her. Jeannine's been upgraded to serious, so that's good. It sounds like she's making progress."

Glad for any sign of improvement, Joanna stuffed the papers into her briefcase and then leaned back in her seat. As the Crown Victoria motored through the morning sunlight, she closed her eyes and thought about the upcoming interview. If Aileen's Huntington's symptoms were as advanced as Joanna suspected, then there was no way the woman could have been directly involved in the murder of Bradley Evans. Indirectly involved, though, was another matter.

After nights of chronic sleep deprivation, Joanna soon fell victim to the warmth inside the vehicle and to the steady hum of tires on pavement. With the baby quiet for a change, she was lulled into a sound sleep and roused herself only when Frank slowed to turn off Highway 90 onto Triple H Ranch Road.

After crossing three separate cattle guards and opening and closing two gates, they arrived. There were two distinctly separate ranch houses on the property. What appeared to be the main one was set behind a white picket fence. It was a rambling old-fashioned, frame-style place with recently added vinyl siding and a standing-seam metal roof. A generous roof overhang created a shady front porch and allowed for covered verandas on either side of the house. A bank of brightly blooming honeysuckle grew around the base of the front porch. Halfway to the house a well-made wooden wheelchair ramp broke away from the side-walk and led up to the side of the porch, where one section of wooden rails had been removed to allow access.

Frank was turning into the yard when, on the far side of a metal barn, Joanna caught sight of a small airplane parked next to a corral.

"What the—!" she began.

"Is something wrong?"

"That's Lawrence Tazewell's blue-and-white Cessna."

"But you told him not to come here," Frank returned.

"Evidently he didn't pay any attention."

Joanna was out of the car before Frank had shifted into park. She caught the beginning of a radio transmission as she slammed the door shut, but she was so intent on Lawrence Tazewell that she didn't stay still long enough to listen. Hurrying through the gate and up the sidewalk, she heard the sound of raised voices.

"Get out! You've got no business coming here!" Leslie Markham shouted.

"I just want to see her, to talk to her," Tazewell objected.

"She doesn't want to talk to you," Leslie declared. "She doesn't want anyone to see her like this, especially you. How dare you come flying in after all these years as if you still owned the place?"

The front door was open. Joanna stood on the far side of the screen door with her hand poised to knock.

"I never 'owned the place,' as you call it," Tazewell said rea-sonably. "The Triple H always belonged to your grandparents and to your mother. I was always an interloper."

"And you still are. Now go."

"Have you asked your mother if she wants to see me?" he asked. "Does she know I'm here?"

"She doesn't, and I'm not going to tell her," Leslie responded. "She's too ill. I want you to leave. Now."

"I know all about Huntington's disease," Tazewell said. "How far has it progressed? How bad is it?"

"You don't know anything about it!" Leslie shot back. "How would you? You've been up in Phoenix the whole time. Dolores Mattias and I are the ones who've been taking care of her— Dolores and Rory and me and a couple of nurses who come in on a part-time basis. And we don't talk about it with outsiders, either. Mother didn't . . . doesn't want people to know about this Huntington's thing. It's nobody else's business what's wrong with her."

"Rory!" Tazewell exclaimed. "What the hell can you see in an old coot like him? For God's sakes, Leslie, you're a beautiful young woman. Rory Markham is almost as old as I am."

"And unlike you, Rory's always been here for me," Leslie retorted. "He's helped me take care of Mother and locate the kind of nursing help we've needed. He's looked after the business end of the ranch all the while he's been running his own business as well. Rory doesn't have anything to apologize for. You're the one who's a Johnny-come-lately."

"Of course he's looking after the ranch," Tazewell said. "What do you expect? That's what he's here for. He's always wanted the ranch. Don't you understand, Leslie? Your mother is dying. Marrying you is one sure way for Rory Markham to finally lay his greedy hands on the Triple H."

"That's not true. Now get out and leave us alone!" Leslie's final outburst was followed by the sound of breaking glass. Dodging splintering crystal, Lawrence Tazewell burst out through the screen door, almost flattening Joanna as he did so.

"I told you not to come here," a seething Joanna Brady told him once she'd righted herself.

Tazewell had the good grace to look chagrined. "Sorry," he said. "I flew over to see if the landing strip was still here and usable. It was, so I landed. I just . . ."

"I don't care why you came. Now you're leaving."

"But—"

"No buts. You're leaving now!"

"All right," Tazewell agreed reluctantly. "I didn't mean any harm."

Frank, hurrying up the sidewalk, passed by a retreating Tazewell on the way. "What's wrong?" Joanna asked. "Has something happened?"

"There's more trouble over at San Simon," Frank answered. "Evidently a dogfight was scheduled there for later on this afternoon. When the first group of attendees arrived, they found a dead woman, an apparent gunshot victim, lying in the front yard. The people who found her had come in from the New Mexico side, and they must have thought they were still on that side of the state line. They left the scene and called an anonymous 911 tip from a pay phone at Road Forks. Randy Trotter's people forwarded the call to us. Debbie and Jaime are on their way to the scene from Tucson. Dispatch says our crime scene people are also en route. You and I should probably go there, too."

Joanna stood for a moment thinking. In the background she could hear the sound of the Cessna's engine warming up for takeoff. In a matter of seconds it was once again airborne.

She was here looking for answers in the Bradley Evans homicide. It was a case she urgently wanted to solve, and she didn't want to be pulled away from it yet again. And if Aileen Houlihan was lingering close to death, the time for finding answers to those questions was in danger of slipping away right along with her.

Leslie Markham was obviously someone who kept her life carefully compartmentalized. When she put on her professional persona, she left the caregiving part locked up at home. But now, without her work face on and having just endured a fierce confrontation with her father, Joanna knew instinctively that Leslie would be vulnerable and far more susceptible to answering whatever questions Joanna threw in her direction.

"No, Frank," she said. "You go. I want to stay here for a little while and talk to Leslie."

"But we're in the same vehicle," he objected. "How will you get back?"

"I'm a big girl, Frank," Joanna said. "I'll be able to find my way. Call the substation in Sierra Vista and see if they can send someone out to pick me up. If not, I can always call Butch."

"You're sure you won't change your mind?"

"I'm sure."

"If you do, call."

Joanna nodded. "I will. Now get going."

Shaking his head, Frank left the porch and headed for the Crown Victoria, while Joanna began knocking on the screen door. For several long minutes, no one answered. At last Joanna opened it and called inside, "Leslie? It's Sheriff Brady. I need to talk to you."

Leslie came into the living room wearing a pair of scrubs and drying her hands on a paper towel. "What are you doing here?" she demanded. "My mother isn't accepting visitors, and neither am I. And why did you send my father here? He had no right to show up after all this time."

"I didn't send him," Joanna said. "In fact, I told him specifically not to come here."

"But he did anyway."

"Yes, I know. He was just leaving when I arrived."

"He wanted to see her," Leslie continued, "but Mother wouldn't want that. She was a very beautiful woman once. She doesn't want anyone to see her like this, especially not him."

"She never married again after the two of them divorced?" Joanna asked.

"Why would she?" Leslie said. "She knew what was coming. She didn't want to put him through it. That's what's good about being married to Rory. He's old enough that he doesn't want kids, and maybe he'll be long gone before it happens to me."

"Before what happens to you?" Joanna asked.

Leslie's face was a study in bleak hopelessness. Finally she shrugged. "I guess it doesn't matter anymore," she said ungraciously. "You could just as well come in and sit down. Do you want something to drink?"

Even coming from the shaded front porch, Joanna found the interior of the house dark and gloomy. Heavy curtains were pulled shut. Only a single lamp in the far corner of the room offered a semblance of light. Joanna made her way to an outsize leather couch whose massive size and old-fashioned lines spoke of another age.

"Thanks," Joanna said. "I don't need anything to drink, but I need to understand what you mean. Are you saying before HD happens to you?"

"So my father told you about that?" Leslie asked.

"Yes," Joanna said. "Some. He mentioned that Huntington's had affected your grandmother. After what you told me last night about your mother's being ill, it was easy enough for both your father and me to assume your mother was suffering from the same ailment."

"It's hereditary," Leslie said. "Since my mother has it, there's a fifty-fifty chance I'll have it, too."

Except that isn't true, Joanna thought, *not if Aileen isn't your biological mother. How can she leave you living in this kind of unnecessary hell?*

Sitting there, Joanna was well aware that the photographs of Lisa Evans and Leslie Markham were right there in her briefcase. It would have been easy enough for her to bring them out and set Leslie's mind at rest about the future, but doing so without having definitive scientific proof from the crime lab seemed irresponsible.

"Can't they check for that these days?" Joanna asked. "Isn't there some kind of genetic testing they can do now that will tell you whether or not you'll fall victim to HD?"

"My mother wanted me to be tested years ago when those tests first became available," Leslie answered, "but I refused. For me, knowing would be far worse than not knowing. I actually prefer being in the dark, and since I have no intention of ever having children, it doesn't matter. Besides, if I knew for sure that Huntington's was bearing down on me someday, I'd be holding my breath over every tweak in my body, over every mood swing, and wondering if that was the beginning of it. Maybe I'm crazy, but I'd rather walk up to the edge of the cliff and fall off it when I get there rather than anticipating the cliff every moment of my existence. I couldn't live that way."

Falling off a cliff, Joanna thought. *Ernie said the same thing about finding out he had prostate cancer.*

"If I were in your shoes, maybe I couldn't either," Joanna conceded. "So tell me about your mother. What was she like?"

"Before she got sick?"

Joanna nodded.

"She was fun," Leslie answered. "And wild. She taught me to ride almost as soon as I could walk. We'd go riding for hours. Sometimes we'd take a packhorse and ride up into the mountains to camp out under the stars, just the two of us. We'd build a campfire and cook our food over an open flame. It made me feel like I was a pioneer. That was my first clue that Mom's HD was starting—when she stopped being fun."

"How long ago was that?" Joanna asked.

"When I was eleven."

"That's a long time," Joanna said.

"It's typical," Leslie replied. "Fifteen to twenty years or so of steady decline with no way to stop it."

"And you've been taking care of her ever since?"

"Most of the time. Not by myself, mind you. Dolores has been here from the start."

"Dolores?" Joanna asked.

"Dolores Mattias," Leslie answered. "She and her husband, Joaquin, have worked here on the ranch for as long as I can remember. Since before I can remember. I wouldn't have been able to manage without them. Joaquin looks after the ranch. Dolores comes in every day to look after my mother when I'm at work and on weekends as needed. And Dolores's niece, Juanita, helps out, too. She goes to Cochise College by day and sleeps here overnight on a daybed in Mother's room so she can call me immediately in case something happens."

"Where do Dolores and Joaquin live?" Joanna asked.

"In a mobile home parked just down the road. You came past it on your way here, right after you turned onto Triple H Ranch Road."

"So you have help," Joanna said, "but it sounds as though most of the burden for looking after your mother falls to you."

Leslie nodded. "Mom wanted me to go to college. That was her dream, but by the time I graduated from high school, she was already too sick for me to leave her. Besides, since she never finished college, why should I?"

"So you got your real estate license instead?" Joanna asked.

"That was Rory's idea. He and Mom have been friends since they were kids. I think at first she was glad when I went to work for him. It made her feel like she had hung around long enough to see me launched. I think that's the only reason she didn't do the same thing her mother did."

"As in commit suicide?" Joanna asked.

Leslie nodded. "Later, when Rory and I ended up falling in love and wanted to get married, Mother approved. She was relieved to know that if something happened to me—that if I did come down with HD—there'd be someone around to take care of me. And the truth is, even though Rory is older than I am, maybe he'll outlive me. In the meantime, while Mother's gotten worse and worse, Rory's been a huge help. For the last couple of years he's handled all the Triple H's financial dealings. I don't know how I would have managed without him. The thing is, I really don't like real estate all that much. It's not in my blood the way it is with Rory. Once Mom is gone, I'll probably forget about real estate, see about getting back into the horse and cattle business and focus on running the ranch."

Listening to Leslie, Joanna tried to reconcile her description of Aileen Houlihan with what Lawrence Tazewell had said about his ex-wife. Other than the "wild" part, the two descriptions had nothing in common. They might have been discussing two entirely different people.

Leslie had been chatting amiably enough, but now she suddenly seemed to realize what she was doing and pulled back. "Why all the questions about my mother? If you're hoping she'll be able to shed some light on the stealth photographer situation, it's not going to work. As you've no doubt gathered, she's far too sick to answer any questions."

Irresponsible or not, Joanna was reaching for her briefcase to retrieve the photos when she heard a car pull up outside. A moment later Rory Markham, wearing a suit and tie, burst into the living room.

He stopped short just inside the door with his face registering a mask of disapproval. "For God's sake, Leslie, why aren't you ready? It's late. The wedding's due to start in less than an hour. You should be dressed already. We're going to be late."

At that point he must have caught sight of Joanna, because his tone changed from private bullying to one somewhat more suitable for public consumption. The look on his face moderated as well. "Sorry, Sheriff Brady. I didn't know we had visitors."

"Rory," Leslie said. "It's only a wedding. Do we really have to go? Dolores isn't here yet, and with Mother the way she is . . ."

"The bride's parents are important clients of ours," Rory returned. "We told them we'd be there. Now, come on. I'm sure Dolores will be here soon. She's more than capable of looking after your mother."

"I didn't mean to delay you," Joanna said, rising to her feet. "I was just leaving."

"How can you?" Rory asked. "On foot?"

"My initial ride was summoned to another incident," Joanna explained. "I've called for a deputy to come from Sierra Vista to pick me up. He should be here any minute."

"But why are you here to begin with?" Rory asked.

"She came to talk to Mother about the photographs," Leslie put in quickly. "Obviously, considering Mom's condition, that isn't going to work. Now, if you'll excuse me, Sheriff Brady, I guess I need to go change."

As she hurried out the front door, Joanna caught sight of a departmental SUV pulling up in front of the gate, followed by a Dodge Ram pickup truck. A gray-haired Hispanic woman emerged from the pickup and hurried into the house. "Sorry I'm late, Mr. Markham," she said.

She glanced in Joanna's direction. "This is Dolores Mattias, Sheriff Brady," Rory explained. "She's one of Aileen's caregivers. Nurses from Hospice will start next week."

With a nod in Joanna's direction, Dolores disappeared down a hallway toward a bedroom. Before the door clicked shut behind Dolores, Joanna caught the briefest glimpse of what appeared to be one end of a hospital bed.

"Hospice?" Joanna asked. "You mean Ms. Houlihan is dying?"

Rory Markham nodded. "Yes," he said. "And in her condition, I can't imagine why you'd think she'd be able to shed any light on the man who took those photos."

"It was an outside chance," Joanna admitted, "but I was really hoping to talk to her."

"That's not possible."

Rory Markham was just as adamant as Leslie had been. Short of fighting her way past them and forcing her way into Aileen Houlihan's room, there was no way Joanna was going to speak to the woman. Since that avenue seemed closed, Joanna chose to make nice instead.

"Your wife is impressive, Mr. Markham," she said. "Considering it's entirely possible that she'll suffer the same fate as her mother, it's brave of her to shoulder the burden of her mother's care the way she does. A lot of people in similar circumstances wouldn't."

Rory nodded. "You're right. Huntington's disease is a terrible scourge, and dealing with Aileen's condition is anything but easy. I'm not sure how Leslie copes sometimes, either, but for the most part, she's a very sensible girl."

Joanna bridled at Markham's condescension toward his wife's daunting endeavor. *Sensible and a long way from poverty-stricken,* Joanna thought, but when she replied, she was careful to keep her tone even and nonconfrontational. "Leslie gives you a lot of credit for helping out."

"Oh, that," Rory returned with a dismissive shrug. "I do what I can."

They stood uneasily, looking at each other across a dim expanse of room. Finally, realizing that he wasn't going to add any more, Joanna picked up her briefcase. "I'll get out of here then, so you can be on your way."

At the end of the sidewalk, a Chevrolet Yukon emblazoned with the Cochise County Sheriff's Department logo sat idling outside the gate. Deputy Rick Thomas reached over and pushed open the passenger door as she approached.

"Sorry it took a while for me to get here, Sheriff Brady," he apologized. "I was already involved in a traffic stop when the call came in."

"Don't worry," she told him. "You arrived in plenty of time."

"Where to?"

"Do you know where the Target store is in Sierra Vista?"

"Sure," Deputy Thomas said. "No problem. Why?"

"I want you to take me there," she said. "And let's hope that our bad guy was dumb enough to use a credit card."

CHAPTER 17

Once the Yukon was under way, Joanna took out her cell phone and turned it on. There were five missed calls, all of them from Frank. Rather than bothering to check voice mail, Joanna simply called him back.

"What's up?"

"You're not going to believe it," Frank returned. "Our one gunshot victim has turned into three."

"Three!" Joanna exclaimed.

"That's right. We've tentatively identified the female found in the yard at Roostercomb Ranch. She turns out to be Lupe Melendez, Tony Zavala's presumably ex-girlfriend."

"Her identification was on her?" Joanna asked.

"Not exactly," Frank returned.

"How did you identify her then?"

"She was naked. We found her ID inside the O'Dwyers' house, in a bedroom along with the second victim, who's evidently one of the O'Dwyers—the one with the scar on his neck."

"That would be Clarence," Joanna said. "He's dead, too?"

"It looks like he took a bullet in the middle of the forehead while he was sound asleep."

"So Lupe hooked up with Clarence, and Tony Zavala took exception?" Joanna asked.

"That's a likely scenario," Frank replied. "And our crime scene folks just got here to work the yard and the ranch house."

"What about Billy?"

"Unfortunately, we found him a little while ago," Frank answered. "He's dead, too, but not here at the ranch. It looks like he took off through the desert, trying to get away. Someone chased him down and shot him off his ATV just over the state line in New Mexico. We found a disabled Toyota RAV abandoned a mile or so from where we found Billy O'Dwyer's body. In chasing after the ATV, the shooter evidently broke the Toyota's front axle."

"Who's it registered to?"

"The Toyota? Amelia Zavala, Tony's mother."

"We're assuming he's the shooter and he's on foot then?" Joanna asked.

"For the moment."

"Have you called in the K-9 unit?"

"Like I said, Billy O'Dwyer's body was found just across the state line," Frank explained. "The Toyota was found a mile or so beyond that. So Sheriff Trotter is organizing the ground search. He's called for the Hidalgo County K-9 unit, although the last I heard, they had yet to arrive."

"Are there visible tracks?" Joanna asked.

"Not really," Frank answered. "It's pretty rocky terrain."

"There's no guarantee that just because Zavala started out in New Mexico he ended up staying there," Joanna said. "He could easily have retraced his steps and come back this way. I want Terry and Spike working the scene."

Terry Gregovich and his German shepherd Spike made up Joanna's K-9 unit.

"I'll call them," Frank said, "but speaking of dogs . . . We do have a problem."

"What kind of problem?"

"A potential PR disaster. The O'Dwyers were running a pit bull breeding kennel here, if you can call it a kennel. Puppy mill is more like it. But Clarence and Billy are both dead, so we can't leave the dogs here."

"How bad is it?" Joanna asked.

"Bad," Frank replied. "Bad enough to make me think it was probably a good thing someone took a gun to those two yahoos. There are at least ten dogs chained in the yard—fighting dogs so vicious that our officers can't get anywhere near them without being torn to pieces. They'll all have to be tranquilized before we can unchain them in order to move them. Then we've got a bunch of starving bitches with batches of starving puppies locked in filthy runs. Seventy-five dogs in all, by my count."

Joanna was aghast. "That many?"

"That many," Frank repeated. "What the hell are we going to do with seventy-five dogs, Joanna? Even if we had room for them at the shelter, which we don't, we don't have the manpower to care for them. Some of them are in really bad physical shape. With the owners dead, we can't leave them here, and we can't just put them down, either—not if you intend to stand for re-election anywhere in Arizona ever again."

Great! Joanna thought. *Another dog disaster!*

Ever since Animal Control had been moved into the sheriff's

department on a temporary basis, Joanna had been faced with one AC crisis after another.

"Where's Manny?" Joanna asked.

"Out at Animal Control. He's shifting animals around and doubling them up wherever possible to create more room. Once he's finished with that, he'll be coming here to start picking up dogs."

"What about Randy Trotter? Can he help us out with any of the AC issues?"

"Hidalgo County Animal Control has offered help, but only with transportation," Frank replied. "And I believe two of their AC trucks and officers are already en route, but since the dogs are all physically located on our side of the line . . ."

"I get it. I get it," Joanna said. "They'll help all right, but only up to a point because dealing with starving or abused animals is political suicide. Everybody else is going to pass the buck on this, so we're stuck with it."

"That's right," Frank said.

"Well, let me think about it," Joanna told him. "I'll see what I can do."

"Where are you right now?" Frank asked.

"Deputy Thomas just picked me up from the Triple H, where I didn't get to first base interviewing Aileen Houlihan. I did talk to Leslie, though, and to Leslie's creep of a husband. Now we're on our way to the Target in Sierra Vista. I wanted to talk to Mr. Oxhill."

"Wasted trip," Frank said. "Manfred Oxhill called me a little while ago and told me that he had tracked down the transaction. The primer was purchased on Friday afternoon and paid for in cash. We're not going to find a paper trail."

"We're having a bad week," Joanna said.

"That's what I say," Frank agreed.

"Since there's no sense going to Target, I'll have Deputy Thomas bring me there. At least that way I'll be able to see first-hand what's going on. I seem to remember there was a warrant out on Zavala. Do we have a current mug shot?"

"Yup," Frank said. "I've loaded it into the website, and I've put out an APB. You should be able to access it from the computer in Rick's Yukon."

"Great," Joanna said. "Will do."

"All right," Frank said. "We're at the Roostercomb ranch house. See you when you get here."

Joanna closed her phone and leaned back in the seat. *Seventy-five dogs! And with Jeannine still out, how are my people going to handle that many animals?*

Joanna sat up straight. Then she opened her phone and scrolled through the incoming-calls section until she found what she hoped was the one belonging to Millicent Ross. She punched talk and was relieved to hear the veterinarian answer.

"Dr. Ross."

"Sheriff Brady here," Joanna said. "How are things?"

"Better," Millicent responded, her voice sounding lighter than air. "Much better, in fact. Jeannine's been moved out of ICU. Dr. Waller says by tomorrow or the next day, depending on how she's doing, she may be ready to come home. Plastic surgery comes later. I don't know what I would have done if I'd lost her, Joanna. Thank you so much for everything you've done."

Clearly Jeannine and Millicent's relationship had turned a corner. Whatever the gossipmongers in Bisbee might have to say, Jeannine Phillips would be coming home to Millicent Ross's house in every sense of the word. Pretending to be simply room-mates wasn't going to cut it any longer.

"In fact," Dr. Ross continued, "I'm thinking of running home for a little while this afternoon to check on things and maybe pick up a change of clothing. I hadn't exactly planned to be here this long."

It was the opening Joanna had been waiting for. "Actually," she said, "I'm calling to ask a huge favor." Briefly she explained what had happened at Roostercomb Ranch.

"So those two assholes are dead?" Millicent asked. "Good riddance. As far as I'm concerned, they got what they deserved, but what do you need from me?"

"Help with their dogs," Joanna said. "From what Chief Deputy Montoya told me, some of them are too dangerous for anyone to approach, and some of the others are verging on starvation. I need someone—a trained professional—to go and assess the situation. Save the ones you think can be saved and—"

"And deal with the others," Millicent interrupted.

"Exactly," Joanna said. "I'm not sure how much the county will pay you for this . . ."

"I'm not doing this for the county," Millicent Ross declared. "I'm doing it for Jeannine. It's Saturday, so there won't be any supply houses open. I'll stop by several vets I know on the way and gather what I think I'll need."

"Thank you," Joanna said.

When she finished the phone call, Deputy Thomas was looking at her out of the corner of his eye. "So where are we going?" he asked.

"San Simon," she said. "Once we get that far, I'll direct you the rest of the way."

As they drove toward Benson and the junction with I-10, Joanna considered her dog-care options. Frank was right. Euthanizing that many animals would be a public relations nightmare, but what were the alternatives? For form's sake, she called the Humane Society in Tucson, but it didn't take long for the director to disabuse her of looking there for help.

"We're already overcrowded. We could take in five or maybe ten animals at the outside, but none of the vicious ones."

"That's about what I thought," Joanna said.

By the time they reached the junction, the urgent pressure on Joanna's bladder could no longer be ignored. "Sorry," she told Deputy Thomas. "Being pregnant is hell. I need a pit stop. While you're waiting, log on and download a copy of Antonio Zavala's mug shot. Now that we've got printers and computers in the patrol cars, we might as well use 'em."

She was washing her hands at the rest-room sink when Deputy Thomas pounded on the door. "Sheriff Brady. We've gotta go!"

"What is it?"

"Carjacking," he announced as they hurried back to the Yukon. "It just came in over the radio. It happened at the Texas Canyon Rest Area a few minutes ago. A woman was in the process of belting her child into the backseat when a man—a young Hispanic guy—appeared out of nowhere, pushed her out of the way, knocked her to the ground, grabbed her purse and keys and took off with her two kids belted in the backseat. He's headed our way with some old guy in an RV in hot pursuit."

Deputy Thomas's words and the presence of two helpless children made Joanna see red. The rashness and desperation behind a daylight carjacking done in the presence of witnesses was all too obvious. And Texas Canyon—the same place where Jeannine's abandoned vehicle had been discovered—was a natural stopping-off place for a ruthless killer fleeing San Simon and heading back to Tucson.

"The guy who did this has to be Tony Zavala," Joanna breathed as she fastened her belt. "Has to be!"

"The guy in the mug shot?" Deputy Thomas asked. "The guy suspected of shooting those three people over by San Simon?"

Joanna turned to look at him and realized with some dismay that, in this life-and-death situation, she was stuck with her most inexperienced deputy as her only asset. Thomas had the Yukon running and was putting it in gear when she demanded, "Are you wearing your vest?"

"Well, no," he replied. "I had it on for the traffic stop, but once Dispatch sent me out to the Triple H to pick you up, I took it off and put it in back."

"Stop the car and put it on," Joanna told him.

"But we're wasting time," he began. "Shouldn't we just—"

"That's an order, Deputy Thomas!" Joanna barked. "I said stop the car!"

Thomas jammed on the brakes. Mumbling under his breath, he exited the car and headed toward the tailgate while Joanna reached for the radio.

"Sheriff Brady here," she said. "Dispatch, what have you got?"

"Red Dodge Grand Caravan with Texas plates heading westbound on I-10 with two unidentified children in the back," Larry Kendrick announced. "Repeat: two children in the back."

"Where are they?"

"An RV driver took off after them. He followed them as far as the second Benson exit, but the grade's too steep for him to keep up. He's falling behind and says the guy is driving like a bat out of hell. Where are you?"

"At the third Benson exit," Joanna answered. "We'll wait at the bottom of the exit in case the guy gets off there. Even if he's slow, have the RV keep following and let us know when he passes the Sierra Vista exit."

Deputy Thomas slammed the cargo doors shut and returned to the driver's seat, fastening his Kevlar vest. "Where to?"

"Drive as far as the freeway and stop underneath," Joanna directed. "If he gets off the interstate there, we'll have him. If he goes on by, we'll have to catch up. How good are you at pursuit driving?"

Thomas shrugged. "Okay, I guess. I mean, I passed that part of my academy exam."

"What about target shooting?"

"I did all right."

A bare "all right" wasn't the answer Joanna wanted to hear. With two children in mortal danger in the back of a speeding stolen minivan, "all right" wasn't nearly good enough.

"Okay, then," she said. "Turn on your lights. You drive. I'll shoot."

By then they were parked under the freeway. "Dispatch," Joanna said into the radio. "What's the word?"

"The RVer still has a visual. According to him, the 'Van's approaching your exit right now. Nope. He's not stopping. Went right on past."

"Okay," Joanna said, nodding in Thomas's direction and motioning for him to take off. As they started up the entrance ramp, the car skidded wildly from side to side. Eventually, though, Thomas got it back under control and they sped forward. It wasn't a performance to instill much confidence, but still . . .

"We're on it," Joanna said into the radio. "Who else is in play here?"

"We've called DPS. They know of the situation. They've got

cars headed that way, but with children involved, they're not going to lay down any spike strips."

"Right," Joanna said. "What about our guys?"

"Frank's on his way, but he's a long way off."

"Okay. We'll do our best."

She watched as the speedometer rose past seventy-five miles
per hour, past eighty, past eighty-five. The interstate was chock-
full of eighteen-wheelers. As Deputy Thomas dodged between
them, Joanna remembered how, on another occasion, she had uti-
lized truck drivers to slow down and help capture a fleeing suspect.

"Hey, Larry," Joanna said into the radio. "How were you
communicating with the RV guy?"

"On his radio. Why?"

"If he's still around, see if he can send word to trucks up
ahead to keep a lookout for the Caravan. Once the drivers catch
sight of him in their mirrors, have them slow him down and keep
him trapped behind them."

"Good idea," Kendrick responded. "Hold on. I'll see what I
can do." There was a long pause before the dispatcher returned.
"A couple of J. B. Hunt drivers had him stuck in behind them, but
one of them just reported that the suspect turned off at exit 297.
He's headed northbound on Mescal Road. Got that?"

Joanna looked at Deputy Thomas, who nodded grimly. Exit
297 was coming up fast. They were in the wrong lane with a
long line of semis and oversized RVs to their right. At the last
possible moment, Thomas managed to dodge back into the right
lane. He veered onto the ramp with the rough-shoulder warning
strips whining beneath their speeding tires. By the time they hit
the stop sign at the bottom of the ramp, Joanna's heart was in
her throat. Still, as bad as Thomas's driving was, she had to take

him at his word that he was better at that than he would be wielding a gun.

"Sorry," he muttered.

"Just keep after him," she urged. And to Larry Kendrick she said, "Okay. We're on Mescal heading north, too. Does everyone else know?"

"Yes."

"And what are we looking at here?"

"The road's paved for a mile or so, then there's a Y. The left-hand fork peters out at the beginning foothills of the Rincons in about five miles or so. The right-hand one takes you along the base of the Little Rincons and dead-ends at Paige Canyon in about fifteen or so. Do you have a visual on him yet?"

"Not so far," Joanna said. "But once the pavement ends, we should be able to see his dust. I doubt there's any other traffic out this way."

When they reached the Y, Deputy Thomas stood on the brakes hard enough that the seat belt clamped tight across Joanna's thighs and her and her oversize breasts. Far ahead of them and to the right, a cloud of dust roiled into the air behind a speeding vehicle.

"Okay," Joanna said as the Yukon sped forward once more. "We don't see the vehicle, but we do see the dust. What are the chances of calling in a helicopter on this?"

"I was just talking to DPS about that. They have one on the scene of a fatality wreck near Marana. Someone from the state patrol will see if they can break away from there and get back to me on it. Frank's just now coming through Benson. So is Jaime Carbajal, but in the meantime, you and Deputy Thomas are pretty much on your own."

"I already figured that out," Joanna said. "Where's Detective Howell?"

"She stopped off at the rest stop to interview the mother."

"Great," Joanna said. "I need the names of those kids."

"Hold on." There was another long pause.

Watching the cloud of dust rising skyward ahead of them, Joanna tried to judge whether or not they were closing the distance. The speedometer in the Yukon was hovering around fifty-five miles per hour. On this washboarded gravel surface, that was far too fast.

"Slow down," she said. "If we push him too hard, he's liable to go off the road."

Shaking his head, Thomas slowed to a slightly more moderate but still dangerous fifty.

Larry Kendall came back on line. "Hannah and Abel," he said. "Hannah is four. Abel just turned two."

"Okay. Have Debbie find the mother a Kevlar vest and bring her in this direction. If this thing turns into a standoff, I want her on hand to talk to her kids."

"Will do," Larry replied.

By now Mescal Road was rising abruptly into the foothills. As it wound back and forth, the dust cloud was still visible but only intermittently. Carefully Joanna removed Thomas's standard-issue Colt .223 semiautomatic rifle out of its holder. She was more comfortable with her Glock, but with the possibility that the suspect might grab one of the children and flee, she wanted the rifle available if needed.

"Is this thing clean?" she asked.

"Yes, ma'am," Thomas replied. "How much longer?"

Looking at him, Joanna noted beads of sweat streaking down the side of his face and the back of his neck, soaking his collar.

The man was scared to death, she realized, and rightly so. She was scared, too, but she didn't dare show it, not with Deputy Thomas looking to her for confidence and direction.

"Not long," she assured him. "According to Dispatch, the road should end in another seven or eight miles. I doubt the suspect has any idea that's going to happen, and it'll be a rude awakening for him. When the road does end, one of two things will happen. He'll either abandon the kids and take off on his own, or he'll grab one or both of the kids and try using them as human shields. It'll be one or the other," she added grimly. "There won't be any middle ground."

"So what do we do?"

"We get as close as we can. If he takes off without the kids, I'll use either your rifle or my Glock to bring him down."

"And if he uses the kids?"

Joanna took a deep breath. "In that case," she said, "we play it by ear."

"Sheriff Brady," Larry Kendrick cut in. "DPS reports that their helicopter is on its way, but it's probably a good forty-five minutes out."

Too little too late, Joanna thought, but she didn't say so.

"Great," she said into the mike. "I have a feeling we're going to need them."

The Yukon rounded a sharp turn and almost smashed into the Caravan, which was now stopped and sitting perpendicular to the roadway. On the far side of the vehicle, Joanna saw someone struggling to remove a flailing child from the backseat.

"Stop!" Joanna ordered. "Now. Hit the ground and stay low. I'll try to take him out."

Joanna was out of the Yukon and onto the shoulder before the vehicle had come to a complete stop. The impact took her breath away for a moment, but not her focus. She heaved herself over on her bulging belly. Abandoning the Glock, she aimed the semiautomatic beneath the parked minivan's dusty undercarriage. From inside the van she could hear children wailing. As the struggle continued, Joanna realized one of the kids was desperately battling being forcibly removed from a car seat.

"No! No! No!" came the scream. "Let me go! Let me go! Go away!!! I want my mommy! I want my mommy!"

All Joanna could see was tennis-shoe-clad feet topped by a pair of jeans. Then a gym bag appeared beside the feet. It occurred to Joanna that the suspect had dropped the bag in order to use both hands in his attempt to grasp the struggling child. According to officially mandated procedures, Joanna should have issued a verbal warning to the suspect at that point—she should have shouted at him and warned him to freeze. But not with the child's life hanging in the balance.

Knowing that the minivan's sheet-metal body wouldn't adequately protect the children from flying bullets, Joanna nonetheless carefully sighted in on one of the moving tennis shoes, aiming slightly above the shoe itself to account for the bullet's trajectory. With a heartfelt prayer on her lips, she pulled the trigger.

There was a screech of pain as the bullet smashed into the man's ankle. The unexpected blow forced the suspect backward and sent him sprawling onto the ground, where he lay for a moment, bellowing with a combination of rage and pain. Then, with a purposeful roar, he flopped over on his belly and scrambled toward the fallen gym bag. Instinctively, Joanna knew she couldn't let him reach it.

"Stop right there," she ordered. When he didn't, she shot again. This time the bullet kicked up a cloud of dirt and gravel inches from his face. Even at that distance she knew who he was from Frank Montoya's mug shot. She had been right. The car-jacker was none other than Antonio Zavala.

Howling in pain once more, he stopped and lay still.

"Freeze," Joanna shouted, and then, over her shoulder to Deputy Thomas, "Take him." Joanna sprang to her feet with an ungainly but adrenaline-fueled agility that surprised even her. Once upright, she darted forward and around the van with the ri-fle still at the ready. As she ran, she heard a distinctive click. Mis-taking the sound for a handgun hitting on an empty chamber, she momentarily ducked for cover. But instead of a shot, the next sound Joanna heard was the low-throated rumble of the minivan's rear passenger door. Somehow, one of the resourceful children in-side the van had pushed a button and shut the door. The next click was actually the sound of the van being locked from the inside.

That's one smart kid! Joanna thought gratefully.

"You shot me, you bitch!" Zavala groaned, writhing on the ground. "I'm hurt. I'm bleeding. I'm gonna lose my foot."

"If you move again, you're going to lose your life," she told him. "Face on the ground; hands over your head." Deputy Thomas materialized at her side. "Cuff him," she added.

As Deputy Thomas complied, Joanna kept him covered, all the while edging closer to the fallen and half-open gym bag. When she saw the semiautomatic lying just inside the bag, a cold chill ran down her body. With a quick kick, she sent the bag a good fifteen feet away from Tony Zavala.

Furiously she turned on the now-cuffed prisoner. Seeing the gun had brought home the grave danger they'd all been in. It was then she knew for sure that shooting first and warning later had been the right decision—her only possible decision. It was also when she realized that for Zavala's well-being as well as her own, she needed to stay away from him.

"Here," she said, handing Deputy Thomas his rifle. "I'll go check on the kids."

Behind her the terrified children in the van were still screaming their lungs out. Oblivious to the racket, Joanna hurried to the Grand Caravan and knocked on the front passenger window. Inside the screaming stopped abruptly. The little girl, now in the driver's seat, knowledgeably switched the switch that unlocked the door, allowing Joanna to wrestle it open.

Behind her Zavala continued to screech, "My foot! My foot. You shot the hell out of my foot."

"Shut up!" Joanna snapped. "Or I'll shoot you again. Put a tourniquet on his leg, Thomas. Do what you can to stop the bleeding. If he keeps blabbing, put one on his mouth, too!"

Inside the van, the little boy, his face wet with tears, remained strapped in his car seat while his sister huddled next to the door on the driver's side. "Are you all right?" Joanna asked.

The little girl, her eyes huge, nodded slowly.

"I'm Sheriff Brady," Joanna said. "Are you Hannah?"

The girl nodded. "Who's he?"

"Don't worry," Joanna said. "We've got him. He can't hurt you now."

"Did you really shoot him?"

"Yes," Joanna agreed. "I did. He was trying to take you away. I didn't have any choice."

"Did he hurt our mommy? Where's she?"

That last question was enough to galvanize Joanna to action. Somewhere back down Mescal Road, Hannah and Abel's mother was living in a world of terrible uncertainty.

"Your mommy's on her way here right now," Joanna said. "But come on. Let's go see if we can talk to her."

The car-seat fasteners that had so baffled Antonio Zavala let go easily under Joanna's practiced hand. Moments later, she was carrying Abel and leading Hannah back to Deputy Thomas's Yukon.

"Dispatch?" Joanna said into the radio.

"Sheriff Brady! Are you all right?"

"Yes. The suspect is wounded but in custody."

"Do you need an ambulance?"

"Yes," Joanna said. "You'd better send one."

"Where do you want him taken to?"

"Maybe the Copper Queen on Bisbee, but we'll let the EMTs make that call," Joanna said. "I shot him in the foot, but it looks like he's hurt pretty bad. As soon as the ambulance crew decides where to take him, let the jail commander know. Tom Hadlock will need to post a guard wherever Zavala goes. In the meantime, please patch me through to Debbie Howell's vehicle. I have two very brave children here with me. Their names are Hannah and Abel. They want to talk to their mother."

CHAPTER 18

For the next several minutes Joanna was completely engrossed in helping the children talk to their ecstatically relieved mother over the Yukon's police radio. Busy as she was with that, she scarcely noticed Frank Montoya's arrival or the noisy DPS helicopter hovering overhead.

"Do you want me to wave off the helicopter?" Frank asked finally.

Joanna nodded. "Tell them they can go. We don't need them. I've called for an ambulance to take Zavala to the Copper Queen."

Frank walked away to do her bidding. He returned with Jaime Carbajal in tow. "I'm here, Sheriff Brady. Should I start interviewing the children?"

"Not yet," she said. "We'll wait until their mother gets here. It shouldn't be too long."

"They're both okay?" Jaime asked.

"The kids are fine."

"What about you?" he asked.

"I'm fine, too," she told him, but that wasn't entirely the case. Joanna knew that, in the aftermath of her use of force, some other outside agency would have to be called in to investigate the incident. She would need to be interviewed, and so would Deputy Thomas. Dealing with that investigation would siphon time and energy from her already staff-deprived department. There were bound to be plenty of tough questions about her not having issued a verbal warning before pulling the trigger.

She pointed Jaime toward the place where the gym bag had come to rest. "That's Zavala's bag. There's a semiautomatic weapon inside," she said. "We'll need photos."

"Understood," Jaime said.

Joanna turned to Frank Montoya. "Have you asked the Department of Public Safety to send their investigators?"

Frank nodded. "Two of them are on their way from Tucson right now."

"Good call," she said. "Thanks."

"Are you putting yourself on administrative leave?" Frank asked.

"No, I'm not," she declared. "Now where the hell is that scumbag?"

"He's in the back of Deputy Thomas's Yukon, waiting for the ambulance. Rick put a tourniquet on his leg and has his foot elevated."

"How badly is he hurt?"

"The foot took a lot of damage. Your bullet nailed him right in the ankle. I don't think he's going to be walking on it anytime soon. Good shot, by the way."

Joanna gave Frank a wan smile. "Thanks," she said. "It was the best I could do under the circumstances."

When they reached the Yukon, Deputy Thomas, with the sweat stains drying on his collar, stood to one side, keeping a wary eye on Antonio Zavala.

"Good job, Rick," Joanna said, stopping long enough to shake his hand. "And great driving."

Thomas nodded modestly, acknowledging her compliment.

"Did Frank tell you that we'll both have to be interviewed by DPS? It'll be a third-party deadly force investigation."

"What choice did you have?" Thomas objected. "What were we supposed to do, let him grab the kid and run off with her?"

"Welcome to the world of post-incident second-guessing, Deputy Thomas," she told him. "Just tell the investigators what happened. It'll be fine."

Having done her best to reassure her young deputy, Joanna went over to the Yukon and pulled open the back door. Antonio Zavala had been quiet for several minutes, but as soon as he saw her, he resumed his tirade.

"I want a lawyer!" he demanded. "You shot me with no warning, and it hurts like hell. That's police brutality."

"What kind of warning did you give the people you shot?" she asked.

Zavala quieted again. He answered her question with nothing but a hard-edged stare.

"How badly do you suppose they hurt before they died?"

Again Zavala didn't answer her question. Instead, he asked one of his own. "Why am I just sitting here? Aren't you supposed to be taking me to a hospital or something? Are you just going to leave me here to bleed to death?"

"Believe me," Joanna said, "I wouldn't be that lucky. I've called for an ambulance, and it'll get here when it gets here. But what's the matter, Tony? You can't stand a little pain or the sight of blood? When it comes to beating up women and committing murder and terrorizing little kids, you're a regular tough guy. But a little pain turns you into a crybaby? A cool macho dude like you should be ashamed of yourself. Now tell me, why'd you do it?"

"Why'd I do what?" he retorted belligerently. "I don't have to tell you nothing. I know my rights. I already asked for a lawyer."

"And you'll have a lawyer, but in the meantime, let me tell you something," Joanna said. "You beat up my officer Jeannine Phillips because you thought you could get away with it. And you murdered Lupe because she decided she could do better than hang around with a loser like you. Poor Lupe. Clarence and Billy O'Dwyer weren't much, but they must have looked like giants compared to a punk like you. And so you murdered all three of them in cold blood—Lupe and Billy and Clarence, too."

"You can't prove that."

"Oh, we'll prove it all right," Joanna returned. "I just have one problem with you, Mr. Zavala. I only shot you in the foot. I wish to hell I'd hit you someplace vital, because dirtbags like you aren't worth the time or money it's going to take to sew you back up or put you away for the rest of your useless life!"

With that, she turned away from the Yukon and slammed the door shut behind her. Frank Montoya caught up with her as she walked away. "With DPS due here any minute," he cautioned, "you might want to downplay those kinds of inflammatory comments."

"What?" Joanna demanded. "Calling a dirtbag a dirtbag?"

"No. Saying you wish you'd killed him. Zavala's already screaming police brutality and asking for a lawyer. Claims you shot him with no warning."

Joanna was outraged. "So what? He's a triple murderer who was trying to drag a screaming kid out of a car so he could use her as a hostage. I'm supposed to handle him with kid gloves and observe all the politically correct niceties? Give me a break."

"Still . . ." Frank began.

Just then Debbie Howell arrived with the children's tearful mother in tow. After gathering Hannah and Abel into a grateful hug and kissing them, Chantal Little turned to Joanna.

"Are you the one who rescued them?" she asked.

Joanna nodded. "I'm Sheriff Brady. Deputy Thomas here and I were the ones on the scene, but believe me, little Hannah was doing her very best to save herself."

Chantal put down the children. She enveloped first Deputy Thomas and then Joanna in impassioned hugs. "I don't know how to thank you," she said tearfully.

"You already did," Joanna told her. "Believe me, the look on your face is thanks enough."

The next several hours flew past in a blur of activity. By the time the ambulance arrived to transport Antonio Zavala, it had to make its way through a throng of media cams which had appeared out of nowhere and now lined both sides of Mescal Road. Joanna dealt with the EMTs, who overrode Joanna's Copper Queen Hospital call, telling her that, due to the nature of Zavala's injuries, they had no choice but to transport him to University Medical Center. Since Jeannine Phillips was in that same facility, Joanna immediately started making arrangements to post a twenty-four-hour guard on Antonio Zavala's room there.

While Frank handled multiplying media concerns, Debbie Howell and Jaime Carbajal took statements from both Chantal Little and her children. Eventually the two detectives left—Jaime to return to the crime scene at Roostercomb Ranch and Debbie to go to Tucson to make a next-of-kin notification to Lupe Melendez's family.

Through all this two DPS investigators were also on the scene. Detectives Dave Newton and Roger Unger needed to take their own statements from Chantal and the children. They also took possession of the semiautomatic rifle Joanna had used during the incident and then painstakingly searched and photographed both the Dodge Caravan and Deputy Thomas's Yukon.

By then it was mid-afternoon and quickly turning chilly. "The kids are tired and hungry," Chantal complained to Joanna. "Are those two detectives ever going to let us go? I talked to my parents in Tucson over an hour ago. My mom offered to come get us, but I told her the van isn't wrecked or anything. Couldn't I just take it and go?"

Joanna was tired and hungry, too. She sympathized, but she shook her head. "Your minivan may not be wrecked, Mrs. Little, but it'll need to be processed for evidence. Your parents live in Tucson?"

Chantal nodded. "My dad's scheduled for triple bypass surgery on Monday."

"Let me see what I can do," Joanna told her.

She went looking for the two DPS investigators and found them off to the side of the road, comparing notes. Newton, the older and clearly senior of the two, seemed annoyed by the interruption.

"Look, Sheriff Brady, these things can't be rushed. We're working as fast as we can."

"But does it all have to be done here?" Joanna asked. "Everybody's cold and hungry, especially those two little kids."

"I suppose we could finish up at the office in Tucson," Newton replied grudgingly. "But we'll need to tow both these vehicles."

"Why?" Joanna demanded.

"For evidence."

"What evidence? The Dodge? Yes, that makes sense. That's the vehicle Zavala drove, but he was never anywhere near my deputy's Yukon. There's no need to impound that."

"Sheriff Brady . . ." Newton began.

"Here's the deal," Joanna interrupted. "You're unreasonably detaining a mother and two children who have already been through hell today. They have family members in Tucson who are anxiously awaiting them. It happens that there are still plenty of reporters around who will be glad to pass on the information that you kept these people here for no good reason. I suggest you release the Yukon so Deputy Thomas here can drive Mrs. Little and her children into town. After that we can all meet up at your office so you can interview Deputy Thomas and me. How does that sound?"

Joanna doubted that Detective Newton came around due solely to her powers of persuasion. What really made the argument for her was Newton's need to avoid any adverse publicity.

Frowning, he capitulated. "I suppose that could work," he said reluctantly.

By the time Chantal Little and the children were belted into the Yukon, a DPS-dispatched tow truck had come to collect the minivan. As the Yukon drove away, picking its way between media vans and emergency vehicles, Frank came back to Joanna.

"Care for a ride?" he asked.

"Thanks," Joanna said. "It looks like we need to pay a visit to the DPS office in Tucson, but I'm going to need to eat something along the way. I'm starved."

Once back on the highway and with a reliable cell-phone signal, Joanna called home. "I'm on my way to Tucson," she told Butch. "There was a bit of an incident . . ."

Her feeble attempt at minimizing was immediately blown out of the water.

"You mean the big shoot-out west of Benson?" Butch asked. "The one with the carjacker who kidnapped those two kids? I already heard about it. It's been on the news all afternoon. Don't tell me you were involved."

"Actually, I was," Joanna admitted. For the next several minutes she gave Butch a brief overview of all that had happened.

"But are you all right?" he asked when she finished.

"Yes."

"And the kids are all right, too?"

"Yes."

"Good work, then. When will you be home?"

"After the use-of-deadly-force interviews with DPS in Tucson. Frank's driving me there. He'll bring me home when we're finished."

"Something's terribly wrong with this picture," Butch objected. "You save two kids and wing a triple murderer, but you're the one who's being investigated? It makes no sense."

"Thank you," Joanna said, smiling at his obvious outrage.

"For what?"

"For understanding."

"You're welcome. See you when you get here. I'm not holding dinner."

By then Frank was turning off the freeway at an exit on the far outskirts of Tucson. At the Triple T Truck Stop, Joanna had ordered her hot roast beef sandwich and was studying her swollen ankles when her phone rang. The caller turned out to be Dr. Millicent Ross.

"This is a very bad scene, Joanna," the vet said.

"How bad?"

"You were right. The dogs that were chained in the yard were so vicious even I couldn't get near them," Millicent said. "I had to tranquilize them first and put them down."

"How many?"

"Ten."

Joanna closed her eyes. Ten dead dogs would be a public relations disaster. No one would be the least bit interested in the fact that the Cochise County Sheriff's Department had dealt with three human murders and saved the lives of two innocent children that same day. All media attention would be focused on the poor unfortunate dogs whose lives had been lost.

"What about the puppies?"

"They're in bad shape, too," Millicent said. "So are the bitches. They're sick, filthy, covered with fleas and ticks, and practically starving. But the worst thing about it is, they're really a pack of wild animals. They've had absolutely no socialization."

"Does that mean you're going to have to put them down, too?" Joanna asked.

"Maybe not," Millicent said. "I just had an idea."

"Dr. Ross, we don't have the manpower or the facilities to take on that many—"

"Hear me out," Millicent interrupted. "I've been reading about how various prisons around the country have been using prisoners to care for abused and abandoned animals as a way of turning around the prisoners' lives and the animals' lives as well."

"What are you proposing?"

"I'm suggesting that we talk to the inmates in the Cochise County Jail. I'll be glad to do it if you want me to. We'll let them know what the problem is and that the only chance these dogs have to survive is if they can be cared for and nurtured back to health so that they can be placed in adoptive homes. I'll also be glad to help out with this," Millicent added. "I can come to the jail and show the inmates how to feed the puppies as well as how to handle, care for, and train them."

"You're suggesting turning my jail into an extension of the dog pound?" Joanna demanded.

"A temporary rehab facility," Millicent said. "After all, desperate times call for desperate measures. Temporary and entirely voluntary. Only inmates who genuinely want to be involved should be allowed to participate. Each one would be given responsibility for a single dog. If an inmate breaks any rules—any rules at all—their dog would be taken away. I can't help but think that having one person fostering each animal would be good for the individual dogs because what these animals need is personal attention. I'm guessing that being responsible for raising and training a puppy would be good for your inmates, too."

Across the table, Frank was watching Joanna with one eyebrow raised inquisitively. She held the phone away from her ear and explained to her chief deputy what was going on.

"Do it," Frank said immediately.

"Do it?" Joanna repeated. "Are you kidding?"

"No," he said. "I'm not. Think about it. Putting down even vicious dogs is political suicide. Saving poor puppies is a PR dream— everybody's best bet for a touchy-feely feature. It'll turn you into a folk hero. Look at the guy up in Maricopa County. When the health department condemned one of his jails as 'unfit for human habitation,' he stuck his inmates in tents and turned the air-conditioned ex-jail into an animal shelter. You'd be doing him one better, since both the dogs and the inmates would be inside.

"And think about the results Ted Chapman has been getting

with some of these guys," Frank continued. "Sometimes expecting inmates to do the right thing makes them do exactly that."

"But what about the mess?" Joanna objected. "These are puppies, after all. Once the health department gets wind of the—"

"Dr. Ross is right," Frank interjected. "Cleaning up the messes puppies make is part of the responsibility of taking care of them."

The waitress showed up with their food just then. "Let me think about this," she said into the phone. "Frank Montoya and I will talk it over, then I'll call you back."

"I think it'll work," Frank said.

Joanna dug into a mound of gravy-smothered mashed potatoes that accompanied her sandwich. "But how?" she asked.

"Let's get Tom Hadlock on the speakerphone," Frank suggested. "Since this would affect his operation and his people, let's see what the jail commander thinks."

To Joanna's amazement, once Frank explained it, even Tom Hadlock was amenable to the idea. "It wouldn't be permanent, of course," he said. "How long does it take to get puppies ready for adoption? Six weeks or so?"

"About that," Joanna agreed. "Maybe longer for the sick ones."

"So it's not forever. I think it's an interesting idea," Hadlock added after a moment's reflection, "especially considering the sticky situation we had here last week. Having a group of bad-boy puppies around for a while might help to resolve some of the tension that's built up in the jail. I agree, of course, that participation would have to be on a totally voluntary basis. If there are prisoners around who don't want to have anything to do with the program, we'll move them into separate units from the ones who do. What kind of equipment do you think we'll need?"

Joanna thought about Jenny's deaf black Lab puppy. Lucky

had come into the family as a demonically possessed chewer who had mangled his way through one of Jenny's cowboy boots after another—and only one boot per pair—until he'd finally grown up enough to stop being called Destructo Dog. How many inmate shoes would be chewed up in the process of socializing almost wild puppies? She thought about the messes of housebreaking and the knocked-over food and water dishes.

"Lots," Joanna said finally. "Bowls, beds, food, you name it. I can't see how we can afford to take this on."

"Why don't I talk to Dr. Ross and get back to you?" Tom Hadlock returned. "Maybe between the two of us we can get a better handle on everything that's involved."

"Go ahead," Joanna agreed at last. "It looks like I'm outvoted on this one."

After that, Joanna managed to choke down only a few more halfhearted forkfuls of food. Finally, giving up, she laid her knife and fork across her plate.

"What's the matter?" Frank asked. "Food's no good?"

Joanna shook her head. "I guess it's all starting to hit me. Three people are dead, two little kids could have been, and one man has been shot, yet here we are focused on saving a bunch of dogs. It doesn't seem right."

"The dogs are in jeopardy *because* the people were killed," Frank returned. "And we all know they weren't nice people to begin with. Our department is in charge of cleaning up a problem someone else created, so don't go around giving yourself a hard time feeling guilty about it. What you should be doing is patting yourself on the back. If it hadn't been for you and Deputy Thomas, one or both of those kids might be dead right now."

"You're going to have to keep reminding me of that," she told him.

After leaving the Triple T, Frank drove directly to the DPS office on South Tucson Boulevard. Deputy Thomas was leaving the building as Joanna entered.

"How'd it go?" she asked.

"I don't know," he said. "I did like you said, Sheriff Brady. I told them the truth."

"That's all you needed to do."

"But I'm not sure they believed me. Especially the part about you shooting him under the car."

"Maybe they'll like it better if they hear the same thing from me," Joanna said.

Newton and Unger were waiting for Joanna inside a small interview room. For the better part of an hour they shot one question after another in her direction. Most of the questions were straightforward enough: How had the incident begun? When had Deputy Thomas taken up the chase? As Thomas had warned, everything moved along smoothly until they reached the part about the shooting incident itself. When Joanna explained how that had gone down, Detective Newton's disbelief was clear.

"You and Deputy Thomas expect us to believe that you supposedly jumped out of his vehicle, threw yourself flat on the ground, and then shot the suspect by aiming under the parked Dodge Caravan?" Newton asked.

"Yes. That's what happened."

"That would have taken a hell of a good shot."

"I am a good shot," Joanna returned.

"In your condition?"

Joanna felt her temper rising. In the present situation, that wasn't a good thing. "What do you mean, 'my condition'? You mean because I'm pregnant, Detective Newton? Are you under the impression that pregnant women are incapable of shooting, or are you objecting to my being able to shoot from a prone position?"

"Well, yes," Newton admitted sheepishly. "That does seem highly unlikely."

"I'll tell you what, Detective Newton," she said quietly. "Let's you and I take a trip out to your target range. We'll both use semiautomatic rifles. I'll lie on my stomach. You lie on a soccer ball. We'll see which one of us can hit a moving target. Twice."

"I didn't mean to imply . . ." Newton began.

"Yes, you did," Joanna returned sharply. "I've been patient. I've answered all your questions. I'm assuming Deputy Thomas's story and mine jibe, because that's what happened. Now, unless you have something substantial to add, I'm done. All things considered, it's been a pretty big day—for someone in my condition."

"Sure, Sheriff Brady," Detective Unger put in quickly. "If we need anything else, we'll call."

"You do that."

"This doesn't mean our investigation is over," Detective Newton growled.

"It is for tonight," she told him. She knew she had nailed the man with her soccer-ball comment and she had not the slightest doubt that, if push came to shove, she could outshoot him.

Getting to her feet, Joanna stalked from the room. In the lobby, Frank was talking on his cell phone, pacing back and forth. "Oh, wait," he said. "Here she is. If we leave right now, we can be there in a little over an hour, Mr. Oxhill. You're sure that won't be too late? Okay. Fine."

"What's that all about?"

"He's the manager of the Target in Sierra Vista."

Still rankled by Newton's remarks, Joanna answered impatiently as they headed for Frank's car. "I remember who he is. What does he want?"

"I told you he called earlier and said the primer had been purchased with cash."

"Yes, I remember that, too."

"He evidently spent all afternoon worrying about it until he finally realized something. Even though there was no credit-card trail, he did have the product numbers. He decided to try going through cash-register records to see if he could find out exactly when the purchase was made. And he did. He wants us to come look at the store security tapes. He believes he has photos of a woman making the actual purchase."

Suddenly Joanna's annoyance with Detective Newton dissipated and she was no longer the least bit tired. "Let's go then," she said, scrambling into Frank's Crown Victoria. "Let's not just stand around jawing about it."

"Oh, I almost forgot," Frank added, as they headed back to the freeway. "I've got some other good news. Tom Hadlock and Millicent Ross have been talking. He's gone through the jail and talked to the inmates and ended up with four more volunteers than he had puppies. He and I talked it over. He's going to use four trustees as a work group to help with all the extra dogs that will be staying at the pound right now while we're so shorthanded. And Millicent has tracked down some deep-pockets pit-bull-rescue guy who's agreed to underwrite whatever equipment or additional expenses we have to run up in order to make this thing work.

"Millicent says she'll stow as many dogs and puppies as she can at her clinic tonight. Tomorrow morning she'll go to Tucson armed with the guy's credit-card number and purchase whatever equipment we need—beds, dishes, puppy food, toys, bowls, collars, leashes. We'll bring the dogs to the jail tomorrow afternoon after she gets back."

"Leashes?" Joanna asked. "Did you say leashes? We just had a major fight at the jail last week—a fight with homemade weapons. Are you telling me that now we're going to issue leashes to our inmates?"

"We can't have the dogs there without leashes," Frank said. "There wouldn't be any way to control them. And I think it's going to work. According to Tom, the inmates are so excited you'd think it was Christmas."

When Frank and Joanna arrived at the Target store in Sierra Vista, Manfred Oxhill was waiting just inside the front door. He turned out to be a tall African-American man with a ready smile and an accent that suggested a Caribbean heritage.

"I'm so glad to meet you," he said. "Right this way."

They followed him through a door marked "Employees Only," up a narrow set of stairs, past what was clearly an employee breakroom and into a warren of offices that lined one whole end of the store. Beyond a door marked "Security," they squeezed themselves into a room that included one wall lined with monitors and another lined with recording equipment. Manfred Oxhill introduced them to the lone operator in the room, then gave the man a piece of paper covered with a series of handwritten scribbles. Within a matter of minutes, Joanna was staring at a screen where customers, totally oblivious to the watching cameras panning back and forth across the scene, casually went about their business.

"There!" Manfred Oxhill said, pointing at one of the monitors. "That's register sixteen and this should be the right time— two fifty-two P.M. on 02:25:2005."

Joanna stepped closer to the monitor. At first all she could see was a back view of a woman standing in front of the cash register. Only when she turned and looked nervously from side to side did Joanna recognize her—Dolores Mattias, Aileen Houlihan's caregiver. Joanna's heartbeat quickened in her breast as she watched the cashier put one can of primer after another into a series of plastic bags and then hand them over.

"I'll be damned," Joanna exclaimed.

"Who is it?" Frank asked.

"Dolores Mattias," she said. "I met her this morning." Joanna turned to Manfred Oxhill. "Can we have a copy of this tape?"

"Of course," he said. "If you'll wait here, I'll bring a new tape from downstairs."

"What does this mean?" Frank asked.

They had been so caught up with other events and concerns all afternoon and evening that Joanna hadn't had either the time or the energy to tell Frank what she had learned during her earlier trip to the Triple H.

"Aileen Houlihan may be bedridden with Huntington's disease," Joanna said, "but I'm betting she's still calling the shots."

CHAPTER 19

With their copy of the security tape in hand, Joanna and Frank sat in his car in the Target parking lot and discussed what to do next.

"I think we should go talk to her," Joanna said.

"Do we know anything else about Dolores Mattias other than the fact that she purchased the primer?" Frank asked. "How do we know that was the primer used on Evans's vehicle?"

"According to Leslie, Dolores and her husband have been living on the Triple H since about the time Leslie was born."

"Do you think Dolores may have some knowledge about what went on between Aileen Houlihan and Lisa Marie Evans back in 1978?" Frank asked.

"Maybe," Joanna replied. "And that's probably where we should start. We'll go see her. We'll bring up the primer to begin with, then we'll switch over to what happened to Lisa. Dolores most likely won't be expecting questions on something that happened that long ago. We may surprise her into saying something she shouldn't."

"What about Leslie herself?" Frank asked. "Does she have any idea that Aileen may not be her biological mother?"

"I certainly haven't told her," Joanna returned. "And from what she told me, I don't believe she has a clue. She's fully expecting that she'll end up just like her mother, bedridden with HD."

"Are you going to tell her?" Frank asked.

Joanna shook her head. "Not until we have DNA evidence to substantiate that theory."

"You must be getting older," Frank said.

"What do you mean by that?" Joanna demanded.

"You're sure as hell getting wiser. So do we need backup to go see Dolores Mattias, or are we doing this on our own?"

"Between the two of us, I think we can probably handle Dolores Mattias," Joanna said after a moment's consideration. "Besides, at this point all we're going to do is ask her a couple of questions."

"Where to, then?" Frank asked, turning the key in the ignition.

"The Triple H. Dolores and Joaquin have a place on Triple H Ranch Road."

The Mattias place was easy enough to find. It had apparently started out as a double-wide mobile home, but with the addition of a screened front porch and a covered back patio, there was no longer anything mobile about it. The Dodge Ram Joanna had seen earlier in the day was nowhere in evidence as they drove up to the house. A dog, a shaggy black and white mutt, raced out to meet them, barking furiously. By the time Frank stopped at the front of the house, the front light had switched on and the door to the screened porch slammed open.

"What's happened?" Dolores Mattias called before Joanna

had even set foot outside the car. "Has there been an accident? Is Joaquin hurt? Where is he?"

Joanna switched gears. "Your husband is missing?" she asked.

"He was supposed to come up to the house to get me when my shift was over, but he didn't. I had to ask the night nurse to give me a ride home."

"Have you tried calling him?"

Dolores shook her head. "He doesn't have a cell phone."

"When did you see him last?"

"This morning," Dolores said. "When he dropped me off at Aileen's place."

"Did your husband have plans for the afternoon?" Joanna asked. "Have you checked with his friends?"

"He said he was going to be working around here," Dolores asserted. "At least that's what he told me at breakfast—that he wanted to finish painting the front gate. That's one of the reasons I'm worried. Nothing's been done on the gate—nothing at all. It's not like him to go off somewhere without letting me know. But if you're not here about Joaquin, why did you come?"

"To speak to you, Mrs. Mattias," Joanna said.

"Me?" Dolores asked. "Why me?"

"This is my chief deputy, Frank Montoya. We're investigating the homicide of someone named Bradley Evans. May we come in?"

Dolores Mattias gave no sign of recognition at hearing the murder victim's name. Instead, she opened the door wide enough to allow them entry to the screened porch and then escorted them into the living room.

"How can I help you?" she asked, seating herself and motioning for Joanna and Frank to do the same.

"We understand you purchased some automobile paint primer a week or so ago," Joanna ventured.

Dolores nodded. "Yes, I did." She made the admission easily, as if it were of no consequence at all. "Joaquin had agreed to help a friend paint his car that weekend. My husband was supposed to pick up the primer, but he ran out of time. Since I was going to town anyway, Joaquin asked me to pick it up, and I did."

"What friend?" Joanna asked.

"Someone who works at the restaurant in Sonoita."

"What's his name?"

"I don't know," Dolores said. "Joaquin didn't say. As moody as he's been lately, I didn't press him. He's been so upset that he's been almost impossible to live with."

Being involved in a murder is upsetting, Joanna thought. "Upset about what?" she asked.

"The survey," Dolores answered. "Ever since Joaquin found out about it, he just hasn't been himself."

"What survey?"

"He was going around the ranch in late January, checking fence lines. That's one of his jobs—making sure the fences are okay. He was down at the far western corner of the ranch when he came across a survey crew. He asked them what they were doing. They told him they were working for Mr. Markham and doing preliminary survey work in advance of subdividing the ranch—this part of the ranch," Dolores added. "The part closest to the road. It's going to be called Whetstone Ranch Estates."

Joanna sent Frank a questioning look. For the last several months, he'd been the one attending the board of supervisors meetings. Perhaps this proposal had come up in one of the Planning and Zoning reports. In answer to Joanna's unspoken question, her chief deputy shrugged his shoulders and gave a slight shake to his head.

"Joaquin was very upset to hear it," Dolores continued. "Señora Ruth promised that we'd always be able to keep our place here, no matter what. So did Aileen. Naturally, Joaquin went straight to Mr. Markham and asked him about it. He said not to worry. That he'd see to it that, no matter what happened to the Triple H, we'd be taken care of."

Joanna thought back to what Leslie had said earlier, about her planning to give up her career in real estate in order to focus her attention on running the ranch once her mother was gone. It sounded as though she and her husband were of two different minds on the subject.

"Does Leslie know anything about this?" Joanna asked.

Dolores shook her head. "I don't know. She's already dealing with so much concerning her poor mother that it didn't seem fair to ask. I told Joaquin not to worry—that we'd be fine. We've saved our money over the years, and we haven't had to pay rent. Maybe we'll be able to buy a place in town."

"How did your husband react when you told him that?" Joanna asked.

"He was fine. At least I thought he was fine, but then last week, he was all upset again. He couldn't eat. Couldn't sleep. I asked him what was bothering him, but he's a man. He told me nothing was bothering him and that I should leave him alone, so I did."

"It sounds as though you and your husband have lived and worked here on the Triple H for a very long time," Joanna ventured.

Dolores nodded. "The whole time we've been together," she

answered. "Joaquin was working here when we first got married. He wasn't the foreman then, just a hand. He wasn't even legal. When Leslie was about to be born and they wanted someone to help out, Joaquin suggested that I go to work for them. I've been working for the Houlihans ever since. I took care of the house and looked after Leslie when she was a baby. Then when first Señora Ruth and later Señora Aileen got sick, I took care of them as well, and I pray every day that the same thing won't happen to Leslie."

"You mean Huntington's disease?" Joanna asked.

"It's a terrible thing, that disease," Dolores replied. "It's something that passes from one generation to another, from parent to child. I would not want to live and die that way. Now that I've seen what's happening with Aileen, I can see why her mother did what she did."

"Have you ever noticed that Leslie doesn't look very much like her mother?" Joanna asked.

"Yes," Dolores said. "I always thought maybe she took after her father's side of the family. Mr. Tazewell left soon after Leslie was born, though. I never knew very much about him."

"What if I told you that perhaps Aileen Houlihan isn't Leslie Markham's mother?"

"It wouldn't be true," Dolores Mattias declared. "Couldn't be true. She had the baby here at the ranch. Joaquin told me all about it—how Señora Ruth took Aileen and the baby to the hospital after Leslie was born."

"You're sure Aileen Houlihan was pregnant?" Joanna asked.

"Of course I'm sure."

"How do you know that?"

"Because I came to the ranch with Joaquin one day and *saw*

her," Dolores retorted. "I knew Aileen was pregnant with Leslie the same way I know you're pregnant—just by looking."

"Didn't you think it was odd that Leslie was born at home?" Joanna asked.

"Señora Ruth said the baby came too fast, that there wasn't time enough to get to the hospital. They were up at the other house—at the house where Leslie and Mr. Markham live now. But Señora Ruth was a nurse, you know. She was able to take care of things just fine."

"Having a baby can be very messy work," Joanna said. "Who cleaned up the mess afterward? Did you ever wonder about that?"

Dolores shook her head. "No. I told you, Señora Ruth was a nurse. She took care of it all—Aileen, Leslie, and everything."

Frank Montoya's "older and wiser" comment was still fresh in Joanna's ears, so she didn't glance in her chief deputy's direction as she opened her briefcase and pulled out the envelope containing the photos. She removed the high school graduation picture of Lisa Marie Evans and passed it over to Dolores. She looked at it for a moment through squinted eyes, then she located a pair of reading glasses under the top of her dress.

Dolores Mattias examined the picture for a very long time, then handed it back. "She does look like Leslie. And I've seen that picture before," she said quietly.

Joanna felt her heart quicken. "When?" she asked.

"When that man came to the house."

"What man?" Joanna asked. "And which house are you talking about? This one?"

"No, to Señora Aileen's house. I was there. It was late in the afternoon some day the week before last, maybe Wednesday or Thursday. A man drove up to the house in a red pickup truck.

When he knocked on the door, I thought maybe he was one of those missionaries that are always coming around, but he wasn't a missionary at all. Instead, it was some crazy man who came storming up onto the porch and started pounding on the door. I was getting ready to give Aileen her bath. When I came to the door, the man told me he was there to see his wife, Lisa somebody. I don't remember the last name. He said he wanted to talk to her.

"I told him he was mistaken—that the only person living there was named Aileen Houlihan and that she was very ill, too ill to see anyone. Then he said, 'Is she Leslie Markham's mother?' I said, yes, of course she was. At that point he pulled out this picture—maybe not this exact one, but one just like it. He waved it at me and said, 'Isn't this Aileen?' And I told him no, it wasn't. Not even close. Then he just went nuts. He pounded his fist on one of the posts so hard that it made the whole porch shake. It scared me to death. I was afraid he was going to force his way into the house no matter what I said. I don't know what would have happened if Mr. Markham hadn't driven up right then. He had come to deliver a prescription he had picked up in town. He came up on the porch and asked what was going on. I told him. He said I should go inside and that he'd handle it. And he did."

"What do you mean, he handled it?" Joanna asked.

"I don't know exactly. I went back inside to take care of Aileen. When I came back out, the man was gone along with his truck. So was Mr. Markham."

Once again Joanna reached into the envelope. This time she pulled out the enlargement of Bradley Evans's ID photo. "Is this the man who came to the door?"

Using her reading glasses again, Dolores Mattias studied the photo. "Yes," she said finally. "This is the man from the porch. Who is he?"

"His name is Bradley Evans," Joanna said. "He's the man we told you about when we first got here, the man who was murdered. His body was found on Friday morning out near Paul's Spur. A few days later his pickup was found with a For Sale sign on it in a vacant lot in Huachuca City. The truck was red at one time, Mrs. Mattias, but it had been painted over with gray primer."

Dolores Mattias sucked in her breath. "And so, because I bought primer, you think I had something to do with this?" she demanded. "Or that my husband did? You tricked me into talking to you, Sheriff Brady. I think you should leave now." Then suddenly she stopped speaking. After a long pause, her face seemed to collapse on itself as she reached some appalling conclusion.

"No," she said.

"No what?" Joanna asked.

"Joaquin is involved, isn't he!"

"Why would you say that?"

"He must be. That's why he was so upset this morning when he dropped me off. When we drove up and he saw the cop car there in front of the house, he almost drove right past. When I asked him what he was doing, he said . . ."

Sobbing uncontrollably now and too overcome to continue, Dolores Mattias paused again.

"What did he say?"

"It wasn't just what he said. It was how he looked. His face went pale; his hands shook. I was afraid he might be having a heart attack or something. I asked him if he was okay and he said, 'No matter what happens, I love you.' I thought it was odd—

strange even. Joaquin isn't sentimental. My husband says he loves me sometimes—on my birthday or our anniversary or on Valentine's Day, but not out of the blue like that, for no reason. He was really telling me good-bye, wasn't he! Joaquin saw the cops were there and he was afraid because he was involved in whatever happened to that man. What if Joaquin's dead now, too?"

"Please, Mrs. Mattias," Joanna said. "You mustn't jump to conclusions. Your husband is probably fine. He's just gone off somewhere and we have to find him, that's all. But what makes you think Joaquin may be involved?"

"He was gone Thursday night," Dolores admitted softly.

"What do you mean, gone?" Joanna asked.

"I mean, he left the house. He was away for several hours—for most of the night. We turned off the TV after the news and went to bed. He waited for a long time—until after he thought I was asleep, then he got up and snuck out of the room. The next thing I heard was him driving out of the yard. He didn't come back until almost sunup. I was still awake, but I kept my eyes shut when he came in. He snuck back into bed and pretended to be asleep when I got up a little while later."

"Did you say anything to him about it?" Joanna asked. "Did you ask him where he'd been or what he'd been doing?"

Dolores shook her head. "Joaquin's a cowboy. He's always been a handsome man," she said. "Years ago he had a girlfriend. When I found out about it, he broke it off, but I was afraid it might be happening again—that he had a new girlfriend."

"And what do you think now?"

"I no longer believe he was using the primer to help a friend paint his car," she said slowly. "I think Joaquin may have done something far worse than having a girlfriend." It was a painful admission for Dolores to make. Joanna's heart went out to her.

"I'm sorry to put you through all this, Mrs. Mattias. Maybe we're all wrong. Maybe when we find Joaquin, he'll be able to give us a reasonable explanation for all this. But for right now, we should probably be going. Here's my card. Please call me if he comes home or if you hear from him. We need to talk to him."

Dolores Mattias stared blindly at the card without benefit of her reading glasses. Then she dropped it on the table beside her. "Will he go to prison?" she asked.

If Joaquin Mattias was convicted of being involved in a murder, he would certainly go to prison. It was possible Joaquin's involvement was limited to helping move the body, but these days even that was considered a felony.

"I don't know," Joanna said. "That depends on what, if anything, he's done."

"Yes," Dolores Mattias said softly. "I understand."

As they walked toward the Crown Victoria, Frank made his feelings clear. "What the hell was that all about?" he demanded. "We want to *talk* to him? It sounds to me as though Joaquin Mattias is in this up to his eyeballs."

"I didn't want to scare the poor woman any more than necessary, but what she told us was important. If we play her right, she may tell us even more."

"For instance."

"We know from her that Bradley Evans came to Aileen's house. Given Bradley Evans's frame of mind at the time, I think it's fair to assume that he and Rory Markham would have had some kind of altercation. Yet, when I showed Bradley's photo to the Markhams, Rory categorically denied ever having seen the man."

"So Rory's a liar."

"He's a liar, all right," Joanna said. "He lied to me, and I believe he's also lying to his wife. If we were to ask Leslie about it, I bet we'd learn that she's entirely in the dark about her husband's grand plan to subdivide the Triple H. Leslie is young, relatively inexperienced, and susceptible to Rory's bullying. I've seen him do it firsthand. He's under the impression that the moment Aileen dies, the coast will be clear for him to do whatever he wants."

"If Hospice is coming in on the case, it probably won't be long before that happens," Frank added. "Days or even weeks. What are the chances he's already greased the skids as far as Planning and Zoning is concerned?"

"Can you check on that?" Joanna asked.

"Will do."

"So here's Rory, about to make a killing with this real estate deal. Everything is going swimmingly, then Bradley Evans shows up. Next thing you know, Evans is dead, and Rory Markham seems to be the last person who saw the victim alive. Given the lies he told us about not knowing Evans, that turns him into our prime suspect."

"But why would Markham do it?" Frank asked. "What's his motive?"

"Somehow Bradley Evans posed a threat to Rory Markham's grand design."

"What kind of threat?"

"That's what we need to find out."

"Where to next?" Frank asked, turning his key in the ignition. "Home?"

"Sounds good to me. It's been a very long day."

Frank took her as far as the Justice Center, where she moved from his Crown Victoria to hers. By the time she got home it was after eleven and the household was asleep. Only Lady came to the door to greet her, and Butch didn't budge when she crawled into bed beside him.

She woke up late to the smell of frying bacon and waddled out to the kitchen. "I won't even ask how your day was yesterday," Butch said, kissing her good morning. "I think I already know. How'd you sleep?"

"Like a brick. I was too tired to do anything else."

"Are you going in to work today?"

"Not if I can help it."

"What about church?" Butch asked.

"I need a robe day," Joanna said. "Call me a backslider, but I just want to sit around in my nightgown for a change."

"You've certainly earned it," Butch said, "but you might want to give your mother a call before it gets much later. She phoned yesterday."

"Annoyed because she hasn't heard from me?"

"You must be psychic," Butch said with a grin.

"Are you in labor?" Eleanor Lathrop Winfield demanded as soon as she heard her daughter's voice.

"No, Mom, I'm not."

"Oh," Eleanor said. "Since you couldn't be bothered to call with the news that you're having a boy, I thought this must be really important."

"I've been busy," Joanna said. "I've been working."

"I don't know why," Eleanor sniffed. "Someone in your condition shouldn't be traipsing all over hell and gone and getting involved in shoot-outs, for Pete's sake. It was all over the news. I can't imagine what you're thinking."

Eleanor's disapproval of her daughter's continuing to work

during her pregnancy was a long-standing bone of contention between them. Forget the fact that the "shoot-out" had most likely saved a little girl's life. Detective Newton's snide references to Joanna's condition had been annoying. Eleanor's were far more hurtful.

"I was doing my job, Mother," Joanna said. "And I intend to continue doing it."

"I don't understand how DNA works," Eleanor said. "You're just like your father and nothing at all like me."

Thank God, Joanna thought.

"But now that I have you on the phone, do you and Butch want to come over for dinner? George is all hot to trot to fire up his barbecue. It's only March, but as far as he's concerned it's the beginning of summer."

"I'll check with Butch and let you know."

Butch, it turned out, was agreeable. "It'll give us a chance to do a little fence-mending," he said. "Find out what time."

After making arrangements with Eleanor for them to go to dinner at six, Joanna spent the rest of the morning at the desk in her home office. She called into the department and talked to Frank, who brought her up-to-date on the latest happenings. There was still no word of any kind from Joaquin Mattias. Dolores had now filed a formal missing-persons report. Antonio Zavala had undergone surgery at UMC to repair his damaged foot, and Jail Commander Tom Hadlock had made arrangements to hire two off-duty Tucson PD officers to stand guard duty at Zavala's hospital room. Jeannine's condition, meantime, had been upgraded once again. Frank had even managed to speak to her on the phone. Pain meds or not, Jeannine had been thrilled to hear that Millicent was moving forward with the pit-bull rescue project.

"You are coming in, aren't you?" Frank asked once he finished with his telephone briefing.

"No," Joanna said. "I hadn't planned on it. Why?"

"Millicent Ross just came back from Tucson and dropped off her truckload of pet supplies. Tom has guards unloading and distributing those right now. Millicent expects to be back here around two to start delivering puppies to inmates, but the reporters are already here."

"What reporters?"

"The pit-bull-rescue guy—the guy who paid for all the puppy goodies—evidently has media connections out the ying-yang. He issued some kind of press release. So far we've got TV camera crews and print media here from Phoenix and Tucson, but a crew from *Good Morning America* is supposed to show up as well. They're all asking when you'll be here."

Joanna sighed. "I guess you called that shot."

"What shot?"

"You said this was going to be a PR bonanza."

"Remind me to be careful what I wish for," Frank said ruefully. "This is nuts."

"All right," Joanna returned. "I'll be there about the same time the puppies are, and not a minute before."

The briefcase she had carried with her from place to place the day before was now a jumbled mess. While sorting through it, she stumbled across the classmates.com printout Frank had given her a good twenty-four hours earlier—the on-line profile for Lisa Marie Bradley's friend, Barbara Tanner Petrocelli. When Joanna picked up the phone to call the woman, she did so more for the sake of closure than out of any real expectation that the conversation would be of value to the investigation.

As soon as Joanna introduced herself on the phone, Barbara

Petrocelli was nothing short of cordial. "I read about Bradley's death in the paper last week," she said. "It made me terribly sad. I remember that time like it was yesterday. According to what my parents told me, Lisa left the cleaner's that day in mid-shift. She left the money in the till, turned off the lights, locked the door, and disappeared. The next thing I knew, Bradley was being charged with murder. It was such a horrible waste. Now he's gone, too."

"Mrs. Crystal said you and Lisa Marie were friends."

"I felt sorry for her to begin with," Barbara admitted, "but we became good friends."

"She confided in you?"

"Absolutely," Barbara returned. "The same way I confided in her."

"Did she mention anything to you about being unhappy in her marriage?" Joanna asked.

"To Bradley? Anything but," Barbara answered. "She adored him. She may have been worried about his drinking, but she was looking forward to raising a family with the man. She loved him so much. I could never understand how he could betray her like that."

"As far as you know, then, there wasn't any particular quarrel that would have provoked him to attack her?"

"Not really, but by the time the murder actually happened, I had been back at school for several weeks. I just wish I had been here. Maybe I could have done something to help Lisa the same way she helped me."

"What do you mean?"

"If things were going badly with her husband, I could have listened to her, offered her a shoulder to cry on the same way she did for me during my breakup with Rory. I mean, if he had been treating her badly and was turning violent or something, maybe I could have helped her find a place to go, a shelter or something."

At first Joanna was afraid she had been mistaken. "Did you say Rory?" she asked.

"Sure," Barbara returned. "Rory Markham, notorious snake in the grass, and one of my worst youthful transgressions. I met Claudio and started dating him while I was still on the rebound. Fortunately, it's a rebound romance that defied all the odds and is still working very well, thank you."

"Wait a minute," Joanna said. "You were dating Rory Markham?"

"Yes," Barbara returned. "And I broke up with him, too. I might not have caught on if Lisa hadn't warned me about him."

"Warned you? About what?"

"About his coming into the cleaner's and flirting with her when I wasn't around."

"You're saying he knew Lisa Marie Evans?" Joanna asked. "That they were acquainted?"

"Of course he knew her," Barbara said. "I was the one who introduced him to her when he came by to take me to lunch."

Joanna took a deep breath. No one had ever made any kind of connection between Rory Markham and the long-ago disappearance of Lisa Marie Evans. Now that had changed.

"Did Rory know that Lisa had told you what he was doing behind your back?"

"I may have told him, but it didn't really matter. I didn't break up with him because of some harmless flirting. It turned out that was just the tip of the iceberg. He actually had a thing for older women—older married women. One of those Mrs. Robinson deals. I probably shouldn't be telling you this since he's still around here and running a real estate office in town, but the woman involved has been dead for a long time."

"What married woman?" Joanna asked.

"I really shouldn't say," Barbara hedged. "Really. People could still get hurt. I mean, he's married now. Knowing about this would probably hurt her feelings."

"If it happened long before he married his current wife, why would it hurt her?" Joanna asked.

Barbara sighed. "Because the woman's name was Ruth," she said at last.

"Ruth Houlihan?" Joanna demanded. "Leslie Markham's grandmother?"

"You already know about them, then?" Barbara asked. "In that case I don't suppose my two cents' worth will make any difference. Ruth's husband was a lot older than she was, and Rory was a real hunk back in those days. Old Mr. Houlihan hired Rory to do odd jobs around the ranch, and he ended up balling the missus behind the old man's back. The two of them would ride up into the hills to an old line shack and screw their brains out. The Houlihans had a daughter named Aileen who was about the same age as Lisa and me. Ruth and Rory both pretended he was interested in the daughter, but that was just a convenient cover."

Barbara stopped talking for a moment, then added, "I do feel guilty to be gossiping like this, but even after all these years, I'm still more than a little pissed at the man for what he did to me. Thank God I didn't marry him, though. I can't imagine what that would have been like. Rory Markham is a real piece of work."

I couldn't agree more, Joanna thought.

Her cell phone rang just then. "I'm sorry, Mrs. Petrocelli. I need to take that. Can I call you back later?"

"Sure. Feel free. I'll do whatever I can to help."

When Joanna picked up her cell phone, Frank was on the line. "When are you going to be here?" he said. "The cameras are ready to roll, and so is the first batch of puppies."

"I'm afraid you and I are going to miss the puppy party," Joanna said.

"Why? What's going on?" Frank demanded.

"We need to pay a call on Rory Markham," Joanna said. "Because one of Lisa Marie Evans's friends has just connected some of our missing dots."

CHAPTER 20

Knowing there was no way she'd be able to dodge in and out of the Justice Center without being photographed, Joanna took time enough to do what she could with her hair and makeup before she left the house. And she was right. As soon as she drove into the complex, a group of reporters began following her. Rather than leading them to the relative privacy of her backdoor entrance, she stopped directly in front of the building and marched through the throng to the spot near the front entrance where Frank, holding a wiggly pit bull puppy, was doing his best to carry on a press briefing.

He looked at her gratefully. "And here's Sheriff Brady right now," he said.

As Joanna stepped to the collection of microphones, Frank took the opportunity to duck inside and divest himself of the puppy. Prepared for a grilling about the fate of the unfortunate animals Millicent Ross had found it necessary to euthanize,

Joanna was astonished to find no one was the least bit interested in those. Everyone wanted to know about the puppies. How long would they be in her jail? Who had come up with the idea? Did the inmates mind? Did the guards? Was it true that a benefactor was providing the money to pay for this so it wasn't coming out of public funds?

When Frank reemerged minus the wiggling puppy, Joanna was happy to turn the briefing back over to him. "With this mob to handle, I can see you're not going anywhere," she said. "What about Debbie or Jaime?"

"They're back up at San Simon," he said. "But Ernie's here."

"Ernie!" Joanna exclaimed. "I thought he was off on medical leave."

"So did I," Frank said. "But he turned up first thing this morning itching to go back to work."

"Where is he?"

"At his desk reading up on everything he's missed."

Joanna went inside and found Ernie in his cubicle. "Are you sure you should be working?" she asked.

"I wouldn't talk if I were you," he returned. "But yes, I need to be here. Rose said either I came to work or she was getting a divorce. Besides, Frank said you might need some help."

"It's the Bradley Evans case. As I recall, you weren't too thrilled about working it last week."

"That was before I was stuck at home for what felt like forever. I'll work whatever needs working. Where are we going and what car do we take?"

Joanna handed him her keys. "We'll take mine," she said. "It's parked out front, but there's no way I'm going back through that crowd of reporters to get it."

Minutes later, Ernie drove the Crown Victoria up to Joanna's private entrance. They left the Cochise Justice Center complex without fanfare.

"Where to?"

"It's Sunday afternoon," Joanna said, glancing at her watch. "Prime real estate time. Let's see if Mr. Markham happens to be in his office."

"I'm sorry," the receptionist told Joanna when she called. "He's not in. Some kind of family emergency. Can I take a message?"

"Never mind," Joanna said without leaving her name. "Maybe I can catch him at home."

"To the Triple H, then?" Ernie asked.

Joanna nodded. On the way she told Ernie as much as she could remember about what they had uncovered concerning Lisa Marie and Bradley Evans and about Rory and Leslie Markham as well. Ernie was appalled.

"You're telling me Rory Markham once had an affair with the grandmother of the woman who's now his wife? What is he, some kind of pervert?"

"The presumed grandmother," Joanna corrected. "And no, I don't think Rory's necessarily a pervert. He's a cagey operator who's also very dangerous. I'm almost certain that he must have had some involvement with whatever happened to Lisa Marie back in 1978. Having Bradley show up unexpectedly on his doorstep after all these years and start asking about Lisa must have thrown Markham for a loop. He couldn't afford to have his possible involvement come to light. He opted for damage control and got rid of Bradley. I'm sure he was convinced there'd be no way to link the crime back to him and that would be the end of it."

"This is all gut instinct, though," Ernie grumbled. "Gut instinct and theory. We've got no solid evidence to back any of this up."

"You're right," Joanna said. "But by the time we finish talking to him, maybe we will have."

"You take the lead, then," Ernie said. "I can't see how this is going to pull together."

Joanna wasn't sure she did either, but she spent the next part of the drive thinking about the entry in her father's diary—about how he felt that sending Bradley Evans to prison for his young wife's murder was "dead wrong." Other than Bradley, no other possible suspects had ever been named or even mentioned.

But here was Rory Markham caught up in the middle of it. And not, as Lawrence Tazewell had so readily assumed, as Aileen's sometime boyfriend, but as Ruth's. And who was Ruth? Someone cold-blooded enough to want her daughter to abort a child rather than give birth to one at risk of developing Huntington's disease.

"What if Aileen never knew about any of it?" Joanna said aloud.

"Never knew what?"

"That Ruth and Rory had somehow arranged to substitute Lisa Marie's baby for Aileen's? According to Leslie, Aileen was eager for Leslie to be married so that if and when she did develop HD, she'd have someone to take care of her. But if Aileen had known about the switch, then she'd also have known that there was no reason for her to worry about the possibility of Leslie developing Huntington's."

Ernie wasn't buying it. "Women usually know when they have babies. Rose sure as hell did. How's that possible?"

"Leslie told me she was born at home—on the ranch—the

same day Lisa Marie Evans disappeared. Aileen's mother was a nurse. Maybe she exchanged one baby for another without Aileen's knowledge. Who knows? But when Ruth arrived at the hospital later on that day with a newborn baby and with a woman who had clearly just given birth in tow, no one would have thought to question whether or not the baby was really hers."

"So when Bradley Evans turns up claiming Leslie Markham is his daughter, it's news to everybody."

"News to everybody except Rory," Joanna said. "And because he was involved with whatever went on back then, Rory couldn't afford to have Bradley waving Lisa's picture around and asking too many questions."

"You're right," Ernie agreed. "That scenario provides some motive, but I still don't think it's possible. How could Rory and the grandmother pull it off? Someone had to lure Lisa away from the dry cleaner's. Someone else had to deal with Bradley Evans. And then there's the question of being there at the ranch when Aileen gave birth. How could Ruth and Rory manage all of that by themselves?"

"Maybe they didn't," Joanna said suddenly. "Maybe they had help."

"Who?"

"What about Joaquin Mattias?"

"The guy whose wife reported him missing this morning?" Ernie asked.

Joanna nodded. "The same guy whose wife bought the paint primer that was used to camouflage Bradley Evans's truck."

"But what makes you think . . . ?"

"A hunch," Joanna said. "Based on something Dolores Mattias said to me last night."

Ernie emitted a long-suffering sigh. "I always hate it when

you go off on one of these 'woman's intuition' routines," he said. "It's not professional."

"But it sometimes gets results," Joanna countered.

A few minutes later, when they pulled into the yard at the Mattias place, Dolores hurried out to meet them as they exited the car. "He's not here," she said.

Joanna sent a meaningful glance in Ernie's direction. In a missing-persons case, that was the wrong thing for a family member to say. "Did you find him?" Yes. "Has something happened?" Yes. "Is he hurt?" Yes. "He's not here?" Definitely a no-no.

"This is Detective Ernie Carpenter," Joanna said easily. "This is Mrs. Mattias, Ernie. We'd like to ask you a few more questions."

"I'm busy right now," Dolores objected. "Couldn't we do this later?"

"It won't take long," Joanna said. "I want to go over something you told us last night—about how once, a long time ago, your husband had a girlfriend."

Dolores Mattias stood absolutely still. She seemed to be holding her breath. "Yes," she said finally. "Yes, he did."

"Who was she?" Joanna asked.

"I don't see how that can matter now," Dolores said. "It's over. She's dead."

"Was Joaquin's lover Ruth Houlihan?" Joanna asked.

Dolores's mouth dropped open, then she closed it again and said nothing.

"Was she?" Joanna demanded.

"What if she was?" Dolores said finally. "I never told anyone. Certainly not Señor Houlihan, and not Aileen either. Joaquin told me it was over, and there was no reason to carry tales. It would have been too hurtful. It would have killed Señor Houlihan to know his wife had been unfaithful, and it would have embarrassed Aileen. Why bring it up?"

"You never told anyone?"

"No. Joaquin told me it had happened, and I could see why. Señora Ruth was a very beautiful woman. But when he said it was over and begged my forgiveness, I forgave him, and we moved on."

"Did you know Ruth Houlihan was thought to be having an affair with Rory Markham at the same time?"

Dolores Mattias seemed to be astonished by that news. "No," she said. "Rory was Aileen's friend, not her mother's."

While Joanna engaged Dolores in conversation, Ernie Carpenter had edged away from the Crown Victoria. Stealthily crossing the yard, he approached the double door on an attached garage. With his Colt .45 in one hand, he wrenched open one of the two hinged doors with the other. Inside the garage was Joaquin Mattias's Dodge Ram pickup, but no Joaquin.

Ernie reholstered his gun and returned to where Joanna and Dolores were standing. "There's no one there, but the back of the truck is full of luggage, Sheriff Brady," he said.

"Where is he, Mrs. Mattias?" Joanna asked.

"I can't tell you."

"You have to tell us," Joanna insisted. "Your husband is a person of interest in at least one homicide and maybe more. We need to find him."

"He's afraid," Dolores said. "Someone is after him."

"Besides us, you mean?"

Dolores nodded.

"Then let us protect him. Where is he?"

Tipping her head, Dolores gestured toward the mountains. "Up there," she said.

"In the Whetstones?" Joanna asked. "What's he doing up there, hiding?"

"No," Dolores said. "I wanted to leave two hours ago, but he said there was something he had to do first—some kind of unfinished business."

"And where are you going?"

"Back to Mexico," Dolores said. "None of Joaquin's people are there anymore, but I thought if we once crossed the border, maybe no one would know where to look for us."

"What's Joaquin doing in the mountains?" Ernie asked.

"I already told you, I don't know," Dolores replied. "He wouldn't tell me. Just something he had to do."

"Is he armed?"

"Maybe."

"Can you tell us how to get where he is?" Ernie asked.

"No," Dolores said. "But I can take you there. I dropped him off and came back here to finish packing. I'm to pick him up at four o'clock."

Joanna heard the distinctive *pop, pop, pop* of gunfire. Echoes reverberated off one canyon wall after another as three separate gunshots bounced down the mountain.

Dolores looked stricken. She turned and started for the garage and the pickup. Ernie caught her arm and pulled her back. "No," he said.

"But I've got to go," she pleaded. "Didn't you hear that?"

"Tell us how to get there," Joanna said.

"It's too complicated. You'll never find it. Please, let me go."

"Get in the back of the Crown Victoria, Mrs. Mattias,"

Joanna said. "Ernie will drive. You can direct us until we're close enough to find the way."

"But the road's too rough," Dolores objected. "You'll never make it without four-wheel drive."

"We'll make it as far as we can and then we'll walk."

Without further objection, Dolores allowed herself to be ushered into the Crown Victoria. Once Joanna was inside, she belted herself in and grabbed for the radio.

"Shots fired," she said. "On the Triple H. We need backup."

"Whereabouts?" Tica Romero asked. "That ranch is a big place."

"We don't know exactly," Joanna said. "We'll leave roadside flares along the way wherever we turn off. That's the best we can do."

At the point where the main road continued on to the ranch house, Dolores directed them off to the left and onto a much smaller dirt track. Ernie got out and collected the Crown Victoria's supply of flares. He lit one and left it in the middle of the road they were following, then he returned to the driver's seat and turned the remaining flares over to Joanna.

"Dispatch has three cars on the way," she said. "I've given them verbal instructions as well."

Half a mile later, Dolores directed them to the right along a dry creek bed and into a narrow canyon. This time Joanna was the one who got out and lit the flare. The road ahead was rough and steep. "How much farther?" she asked once she was back in the car.

"About another quarter mile," Dolores answered. "Then there's a gate."

Joanna turned to Ernie. "Do you think you can make it?"

"We'll see."

Tica's voice came through on the radio. "It turns out Deputy Raymond is in the area. He's already turned off onto Triple H Ranch Road. The other two deputies are in Huachuca City and over near Kartchner Caverns. They should arrive soon as well."

"Good work."

Several times between there and the gate, the Crown Victoria's undercarriage scraped across loose boulders and outcroppings of rock. Twice, when the creek bed switched back and forth across the road, the Crown Victoria almost mired down in loose sand. Only by maintaining sufficient speed was Ernie able to jolt the vehicle to the far side.

"She's right, you know," Ernie grumbled. "Four-wheel drive would be a lot better."

"This is where I dropped him," Dolores announced when they reached the gate. Joanna got out to open it, but the track that led beyond the gate was even narrower and rougher than the part they'd just come through. Far below in the distance she heard the faintest sounds of at least two approaching sirens signaling that backup officers were on their way.

Joanna returned to the Crown Victoria. "It looks like we walk from here," she said to Ernie. "Are you up to it? Your doctor probably wouldn't call hiking through the desert taking it easy."

"I can if you can," he said.

Joanna turned to Dolores Mattias. "You have to stay here in the vehicle."

"But . . ."

"Not buts, Mrs. Mattias. We have Kevlar vests. You don't. It's for your own safety. You can either give me your word that you'll stay here, or we lock you in. Which is it?"

"I'll stay," Dolores agreed.

"How far is it from here?"

"I don't know. Joaquin took a shovel with him and went up that path."

"Did he have a weapon with him?" Joanna asked again.

"Maybe," Dolores answered. "I don't know for sure."

That wasn't much consolation.

Ernie had gone around to the trunk and retrieved the semi-automatic rifle and twelve-gauge shotgun Joanna kept there. As he handed her the rifle, he stopped short.

"Listen," he said.

On the far side of the creek, Joanna heard a racket that had to be a fast-moving horse scrabbling over rocks and through the surrounding scrub oak. Joanna and Ernie both ducked for cover behind the Crown Victoria, but the invisible horse kept moving, sending a scatter of rocks down toward the creek bed as it raced by without pausing.

"What if he heads for the gate?" Joanna demanded as the hoofbeats passed out of range. "What if whoever it is goes after Dolores?"

"I'll go," Ernie said and was gone.

Alone now, Joanna crept forward. Fifty yards or so beyond the gate the path took a sharp right turn. Another fifty yards beyond that, Joanna caught sight of the charred remains of a crumbling rustic cabin nestled in a small clearing. Winded, she took cover behind a nearby tree. Struggling to steady her breath, she studied the terrain and saw no sign of movement anywhere.

Then, on the far edge of the clearing, something glinting in the sun caught her attention. Sticking to the tree line, Joanna moved closer until she was able to see that sunlight was reflecting off the business end of a shovel that lay to one side of a small mound of freshly dug dirt and what looked like an earth-crusted fruit crate.

Behind Joanna, one of the sirens sputtered to silence. That meant Deputy Raymond must have reached the gate and help was near at hand.

Then she heard it—a low moan that seemed to come from somewhere near the mound of dirt.

"Who is it?" she demanded. "Where are you?"

"Help me," a weak voice replied. "I've been shot."

Joanna scurried forward. She skirted the box, the mound of dirt, and a small hole. A man lay facedown in the freshly turned dirt of a larger hole, with blood seeping across the back of his denim shirt. A few shovels of dirt had been piled on top of his legs—not enough to bury him alive, but enough to start the job.

"Mr. Mattias?" Joanna asked. "It's Sheriff Brady. I know I'm not strong enough to get you out of there by myself. I've got to go get help."

"No," he pleaded. "Don't go. Stay here with me. It's too late for help."

"But . . ."

"No," he wheezed. "Someone has to hear this so people know what happened. I was digging them up. It's the best I could do. At least now they'll have a decent burial. I'm so sorry."

Joanna looked at the small dirt-covered box. It looked much too small to be a coffin, but that's what it was. "Aileen's baby?" she asked quietly.

"She made me help her," he managed. "She said if I didn't, she'd tell her husband about us."

"Ruth, you mean?"

Joaquin tried to raise himself up out of the dirt, but the effort was too much. He fell back into the musty earth, coughing and gasping.

"Ruth," he managed. "Ruth and Rory. She wanted to get rid

of Aileen's baby. I didn't know about him until it happened and he was helping her. By then it was too late. Tell Dolores . . . Tell Dolores . . ."

"Tell Dolores what?" Joanna implored. "Stay with me, Joaquin. Stay with me."

She heard the sound of a surging engine as a vehicle made its way up the rough dirt track. She turned to see a departmental Yukon materialize on the far side of the clearing. Seconds later, Deputy Matt Raymond pounded up to Joanna, with Ernie hurrying after him.

"Sheriff Brady, what do you . . . ?"

She pointed at the injured man's prone body. "See if you can lift him out of there," she said. "Ernie, call for an ambulance."

Agilely Deputy Raymond dropped into the hole, placing his feet on either side of the injured man, but just then Joaquin Mattias exhaled a single ragged breath.

"It's too late for an ambulance, Sheriff Brady," Deputy Raymond said. "I'm pretty sure he's gone."

"Leave him then," Ernie urged. "We'll come back later. The guy on the horse made it through the gate before I ever got there. He was riding hell-bent-for-leather and didn't even see Dolores sitting in the car."

"Rory Markham?" Joanna asked.

"Probably," Ernie returned. "I diverted the other units," he added. "I sent them to the house rather than having them come here."

"All right," Joanna agreed. "Let's go."

Leaving Joaquin's body where it was, the three officers raced back across the clearing. Joanna and Deputy Raymond climbed into the front of the Yukon while Ernie clambered into the back.

Halfway to the gate, they met Dolores Mattias lurching up the path on foot. When Deputy Raymond stopped the Yukon, Joanna was the first one out.

"I'm sorry, Mrs. Mattias," she said, taking the distraught woman by the arm. "You can't go there."

Dolores shook off Joanna's hand. "My husband," she said. "Where's my husband?"

By then, Ernie, too, was at the woman's side. "Like Sheriff Brady said, Mrs. Mattias, you can't go there. It's a crime scene."

"A crime scene?" she repeated. "What kind of crime scene?"

"I hate to tell you this," Joanna said softly. "It's a homicide scene. Your husband is dead, Mrs. Mattias. You must come with us. We need to catch the man who did this."

"Joaquin is dead?" Dolores Mattias said uncomprehendingly.

"Please come with us," Joanna begged. "It may be too late to help your husband, but it's not too late to keep his killer from getting away."

Wordlessly, as her body convulsed into heaving sobs, Dolores Mattias allowed herself to be helped into the Yukon and buckled into her seat.

Tica Romero's voice, distorted by static, hissed through the radio. "We have two units within sight of the ranch house now. They report there's a horse tethered to a post on the front porch. Please advise how many people, besides the suspect, are likely to be inside and what you want our guys to do."

"In addition to the suspect three people are most likely inside," Joanna answered. "Aileen Houlihan, who's bedridden; a nurse; and the suspect's wife, Leslie Markham. Tell our officers to wait," she added. "We're coming there as fast as we can."

At the gate, Ernie Carpenter bailed from the Yukon in order

to drive Joanna's Crown Victoria back down to the scene of the action. In the backseat, Dolores's sobs had quieted.

"Why?" she asked finally. "Why would Mr. Markham shoot my husband?"

"It's a very long story, Mrs. Mattias," Joanna said gently. "But I believe it's because your husband knew too much."

CHAPTER 21

O nce they arrived within sight of the ranch house, for what seemed an interminable length of time no one came or went. The house remained dead still. The only visible movement was the occasional switch of the tethered horse's tail. As Joanna's deputies took up defensive positions, she called in to Dispatch.

"Tica," she said. "See if you can find a listed phone number for Aileen Houlihan."

"I have an A. Houlihan," Tica replied. "On Triple H Ranch Road."

"That's the one," Joanna replied. "Give me the number."

When Joanna dialed it, Leslie Markham answered the phone. She sounded unhurried and completely calm.

"This is Sheriff Brady," Joanna said. "Is your husband there with you?"

"Yes, he is."

"Who else is there?"

"Just the three of us—Rory, my mother, and me. Fortunately, I sent the daytime nurse home. The nighttime one hasn't come on duty yet."

"Are you all right?" Joanna asked.

"I'm fine," Leslie returned with amazing coolness. "Rory has a gun, though, and he's threatening to use it. I told him to go ahead. As far as I'm concerned, dying of a bullet wound is infinitely preferable to dying of HD."

But you aren't going to die of Huntington's, Joanna wanted to shout.

"Put him on the phone," she said.

"He won't touch it," Leslie said half a minute or so later. "He doesn't want to talk to you."

"But I want to talk to him. Does your phone have a speaker option? If so, turn it on."

"It's on," Leslie said. "He can hear you now."

"Put down your weapon and come out of the house, Rory," Joanna said. "It's over. An ambulance is on its way to pick up Mr. Mattias and take him to the hospital, but he told us everything. We know all about you and Ruth and about Lisa Evans and Aileen's dead baby. He even told us about Bradley Evans."

That was all a calculated lie. Joaquin Mattias was dead. He hadn't come close to telling them everything. But D. H. Lathrop had taught his daughter the fine art of bluffing at the same time he was teaching her how to play poker. Joanna Brady was definitely her father's daughter in that regard.

At first the only thing coming through the phone was silence. Finally Leslie Markham spoke. "What baby?" she asked.

Joanna didn't allow herself to be diverted into that conversation any more than she could allow herself to look at Dolores.

The discussion of Aileen Houlihan's murdered baby would have to wait until Leslie's life was no longer in danger.

"Let your wife go," Joanna said without responding to Leslie's question. "If you harm her in any way, Arizona state law will never allow you to inherit, Mr. Markham. You're already looking at three separate homicide charges. Don't make it worse."

Another period of tense silence followed. Again, Leslie was the one who spoke.

"I'm going then," she announced. "I'm going to walk out."

"You can't," Rory said. "Don't do it."

"Why not? Because you're going to shoot me? Don't make me laugh. You can't hurt me any worse than you already have."

A moment later the screen door opened. As Joanna and the assembled deputies held their collective breaths, Leslie Markham walked to the edge of the porch, where she leaped off, past the startled horse, and then sprinted away from the house. She didn't stop until she reached Deputy Raymond's Yukon parked at the far end of the driveway. As she neared the vehicle, Raymond reached around and opened the door behind him, allowing her to dive inside.

"All right, Mr. Markham," Joanna continued into the phone. "Leslie is here now. She's safe. Toss down your weapon and come out with your hands up."

Rory Markham's wordless reply consisted of a single small click as he disconnected the speakerphone, followed by the chilling sound of a solitary gunshot. They all knew he was dead long before the deputy who had let himself in through the back door sounded out the all clear. When Joanna finally gave herself permission to turn around and look at the women in the backseat,

Leslie Markham, sobbing, was being comforted by Dolores Mattias. Seeing them together, Joanna wanted to gather both women into her arms and tell them what she knew—to explain how this series of calamities had befallen them, but there wasn't time. Not then.

Joanna got out of the Yukon and caught up with Ernie. "We'll need to curtain off whatever part of the room Markham used to blow his brains out," she told him. "I know it's a crime scene, but Leslie and the nurses will have to have access to Aileen."

Ernie nodded. "All right," he said. "I'll see what we can do."

As he walked away, Joanna reached back inside and plucked the radio out of its holder. She needed to call Dispatch and let them know what had happened—that they'd need crime scene people and Dr. Winfield and search warrants and all those other necessary things. But as she pushed the button down to speak, she felt the sudden gush of water running down her legs.

"Is everyone all right?" Tica was saying. "Do you need an ambulance?"

"No," Joanna began. Just then the first contraction hit and hit her hard, taking her breath away. "On second thought," she said when it ended, "maybe an ambulance is a good idea."

"I thought the two gunshot victims were both dead," Tica responded.

"They are dead," Joanna said. "But I believe I'm going to have this baby, and it could be soon."

"Ambulance is on its way, Sheriff Brady," Tica reported back a moment later. "Do you want me to call your husband and have him meet you at the hospital?"

"No," Joanna replied, "that won't be necessary. Calling him will give me something to do while I wait."

CHAPTER 22

While Dennis Lee Dixon lay sleeping in his bassinet, Joanna plucked the clicker off her bedside table and searched through the channels until she located *Good Morning America*. The last thing Butch had said before he left the hospital at midnight was that Frank Montoya had told them *GMA* was going to run a feature about what had happened the next morning and that Joanna should be sure to watch.

The orderly came in bringing her breakfast—ghastly oatmeal, cold toast, and something that was supposed to pass for coffee. It made Joanna long for one of Butch's perfectly cooked over-easy eggs and a side of his crisp bacon. But Dr. Lee had said his policy was that new mothers needed to rest and that he wanted her in the hospital for a full twenty-four hours, so twenty-four hours it would be.

Joanna ate what she could tolerate of her breakfast and

waited through the news (bad) and the weather (also bad) and the sports (marginal).

"And now," Diane Sawyer was saying, "from the southeastern corner of Arizona we have the heartwarming story of how, when faced with the potentially tragic aftermath of a triple homicide at a puppy mill, Cochise County Sheriff Joanna Brady took the law into her own hands in something our on-scene reporter is calling 'The Pit Bull Penal Project.'"

Joanna's bedside table rang. "Are you watching?" Butch demanded. "It's on right now, but I'm TIVOing it, just in case."

"Yes," Joanna said. "I'm watching. At least I'm trying to."

As she put down the phone, Joanna caught a fleeting image of herself standing in front of the door to the department with a bank of microphones in front of her. She didn't hear and didn't remember what had been said. The only thing that registered was how incredibly pregnant she looked.

The phone rang again as the cameras switched over to a scene of Millicent Ross handing out puppies while the reporter was saying, ". . . only inmates expected to be in custody for at least the next six weeks are allowed to participate."

"I can't believe it!" Eleanor Lathrop Winfield exclaimed. "You're actually on *Good Morning America*. Are you watching?"

"Sort of," Joanna said. "Can I call you back?"

Joanna expected some kind of comment about her missing dinner the night before, but no such diatribe was forthcoming.

"Is the baby all right?" Eleanor went on. "Butch called and told us that everything was fine, but I want to hear it from you so I can stop worrying."

"The baby's fine, Mom," Joanna said. "And so am I, but I'm busy right now. Let me call you back."

By then the camera was focused on Axel Turnbull. Axel was

one of the regular habitués of the Cochise County Jail. He came in several times a year for sentences of longer or shorter duration depending on how drunk and disorderly he'd been and how much property damage he'd caused in the course of his most recent bender.

There he was, sitting in his distinctive red-and-white-striped jail uniform in the exercise yard with a black-and-white pit bull puppy snuggled, sound asleep, under the man's grizzled chin. "I think I'll call him Tucker," Turnbull was saying, "'cause, as you can see, the little guy's all tuckered out."

The camera switched back to Diane Sawyer, who was beaming. "We wanted to interview Sheriff Brady for this piece, but we understand she's in the hospital in Bisbee, where, a few hours after we filmed this piece, she gave birth to a seven-pound, eight-ounce boy. We are told both mother and baby are doing well."

The phone rang again. This time it was Jenny. "Mom, did you see it? Were those puppies cute, or what? Oh, and Butch is going to bring me by on my way to school so I can see you and the baby. Does he really have red hair?"

Joanna glanced toward the bassinet. "Definitely," she answered. "An amazing amount of bright red hair."

"He takes after you then?"

"We'll see," Joanna said.

This time she didn't even bother to hang up the phone, she just depressed the receiver button with her finger. Sure enough, it rang immediately.

"I told you it would be great publicity," Frank Montoya told her. "What did you think?"

"I looked very pregnant," Joanna replied.

"It's not even eight o'clock in the morning, and I've already had four requests for interviews with you. *People* magazine, *USA Today,* the *Arizona Sun,* and *Newsweek.* What do you think?"

"I think I'm on maternity leave, Frank. Besides, you and Millicent Ross were the ones who came up with the idea. You should do the interviews."

"I'll tell them I'll get back to them later," Frank said.

"You mean you think you'll be able to talk me into changing my mind. Tell me what happened after I left the Triple H yesterday."

"I thought you were on maternity leave."

"Frank . . ."

"Doc Winfield opened the boxes Joaquin Mattias dug up. His recommendation is that we ship them, boxes and all, to the University of Arizona, where the bones that were inside can be properly examined by a forensic anthropologist. Autopsies for Joaquin Mattias and Rory Markham will be later today. As far as evidence, what we turned up is pretty damning."

"What's that?"

"Fingers," Frank said.

Joanna felt her stomach lurch. "Bradley Evans's fingers?"

"Presumably. We found ten of them preserved in a half-gallon jar of formaldehyde on a shelf in Rory Markham's garage. I can't imagine what possessed him to keep them, and now we'll never be able to ask him, either. There is a walk-in refrigerator in one of the outbuildings. We're checking but it looks as though Evans's body was stored there until they transported it to the dump site. Oops. Another call," Frank added. "Gotta go."

When Joanna put down the phone that time, the Reverend Marianne Maculyea was standing in the doorway. "Congratulations," she said. "I know it's not visiting hours, but there are times when being a member of the clergy has its advantages. How are you?"

"A little overwhelmed. I've just been on national TV."

"I know." Marianne grinned. "Jeff taped it, but then everybody in town probably taped it as well."

"It's all about the dogs, Mari," Joanna said. "What about the people who died? There was hardly a word about them."

"What happened to the guy who did it?" Marianne asked.

"You mean Antonio Zavala, the one I shot? He's at UMC, where the doctors are patching his foot back together. I didn't want them to take him there because that's where Jeannine Phillips is. I actually wanted them to bring him here so it would be easier to keep a guard on him. Now I'm glad that didn't happen. I have guards looking out for Jeannine Phillips. I guess someone else was watching over us."

Marianne smiled. "Yes," she said. "I think He was." She came over to the bed and gave Joanna a hug. "You get some rest now. You're going to need it."

But resting was out of the question. By the time Butch took Jenny off to school, the first load of flower arrangements showed up. And they continued to show up. A few came from people Joanna knew, but most came from people she didn't know—one vase after another.

Once Joanna's room was overflowing, she started sending the flowers down the hall to other rooms. And still the flowers kept on arriving, except now, with local flower inventories exhausted, the arrangements were coming from shops in Sierra Vista and Benson and even as far away as Tucson.

About two o'clock in the afternoon—after a lunch that was almost as bad as breakfast—Joanna tried nursing Dennis. It wasn't entirely successful, but Joanna remembered how it had been with Jenny. There had been a learning curve for both Joanna and the baby, and she was sure this was more of the same thing.

Dennis, fed at last and newly diapered, was back in his bassinet. Joanna was drifting into a much-needed nap when the door to her room swished open. She expected to see either Butch or else yet another flower delivery. Instead, Leslie Markham walked into the room.

She was wearing jeans, cowboy boots, a worn leather jacket, and an enormous pair of sunglasses. Her face, utterly devoid of makeup, was dreadfully pale. She stopped uncertainly just inside the door. Then, after a moment, she turned and started to leave.

"It's all right," Joanna said. "I'm not asleep."

Leslie removed the glasses. Dark shadows surrounded her eyes—eyes that had wept too much and slept too little. "I'm so sorry, Sheriff Brady. I shouldn't have disturbed you . . ."

"You're not disturbing me," Joanna returned. "I'm sorry, too, about everything that happened. If you'll get in touch with my chief deputy, Frank Montoya, I'm sure he'll do everything he can to assist you."

"He already has," Leslie said. "I came to Bisbee to talk to Dr. Winfield. I wanted to have some idea of when he'll be able to release the body—bodies, actually; Joaquin Mattias's, too. Dolores and I need to know so we can decide on services, that kind of thing. He said it'll probably be several days."

"That's how these things go," Joanna said. "It usually takes longer than you would expect."

"Everyone in your department has been very kind," Leslie continued. "Mr. Carpenter, your detective, told me about . . ." She paused and bit her lip. "He told me about what they found up by the old cabin," she added. "About the two boxes and what was in them and what he thinks happened. He showed me the picture, too, the picture of Lisa Marie Evans. When I looked at it, I couldn't tell if I was looking in a mirror or if I was seeing a ghost. A little bit of both, I guess."

She paused again. This time it was more than a minute before she gathered herself enough to go on. Joanna wanted to hug the poor woman and comfort her, but Leslie Markham was too far out of reach. She remained just inside the doorway, as if what she really wanted to do was bolt out of the room and back down the corridor.

"I came to ask a favor," she said at last.

"I'm sure Chief Deputy Montoya would be happy—"

"No, I need to ask you, Sheriff Brady," Leslie said determinedly. "I need to ask you woman-to-woman. I want you to keep your people from trying to question my mother."

"Mrs. Markham," Joanna began. "We're talking about several different homicides and a suicide here. My investigators need to get to the bottom of what happened and what caused it."

"My mother used to take me to that cabin!" Leslie Markham broke in forcefully. "That's where we'd go on horseback sometimes, just the two of us. Do you think she would have taken me there if she'd had any idea that her own dead baby was buried in that exact spot? She was terrified for me every minute, terrified that someday I'd come down with HD just the way she did and the way her mother did, too. Do you think she would have been so petrified if she'd had any idea at all that I wasn't her own?"

"But how could she not know?" Joanna asked.

"Ruth Houlihan didn't want her daughter giving birth to a baby at risk of developing HD," Leslie answered. "She was also a nurse. I have no doubt she gave Aileen drugs of some kind, probably something that induced labor. I've done some checking on the Internet. Those kinds of drugs were available back then.

"Once Aileen's baby was born, Ruth made the switch and then took Aileen and me to the hospital, leaving Rory and Joaquin to clean up the mess and take care of pinning the blame on Bradley Evans.

"Please, Sheriff Brady," Leslie begged. "Aileen Houlihan is the only mother I've ever known. She won't be around much longer. Let her die in peace. She doesn't watch the news or listen to the radio. What's going on outside her room—the things the news reporters are saying—stays outside her room, but if your detectives go there questioning her . . ."

"They won't," Joanna said. "I'll see that they don't."

"Thank you," Leslie said. "Thank you so much.

"And then there's one more thing," Leslie said. "One more favor."

"What's that?"

"I'm not ready to do it now," Leslie said. "Not until the DNA reports confirm it and probably not until after my mother is gone, but when it's time, I'd like someone from your office—Mr. Montoya or Mr. Carpenter or someone—to take me to meet Lisa Marie Evans's mother. Is that possible? I could go on my own, I suppose, but I think it would be better if there were someone there to introduce me—someone official."

Joanna thought about her father, who had somehow felt that the wheels of justice had been spinning out of control when Bradley Evans went to prison for murder. And she thought about Butch and Frank telling her she would flunk maternity leave. And she thought about doing what needed to be done.

"Whenever you're ready," Joanna said, "let me know. I'll be happy to go with you. In fact, I'd be honored."